Norman Daniels

Wyndward Fury

WARNER BOOKS

A Warner Communications Company

WARNER BOOKS EDITION

Copyright © 1979 by Norman Daniels
All rights reserved

ISBN 0-446-82991-9

Cover Art by Gary Lang

Warner Books, Inc., 75 Rockefeller Plaza, New York, N.Y. 10019

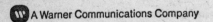 A Warner Communications Company

Printed in the United States of America

Not associated with Warner Press, Inc., of Anderson, Indiana

First Printing: March, 1979

10 9 8 7 6 5 4 3 2 1

Wyndward Fury

"I sing and dance," she said. "I'm an actress."

"Nevah met an actress befo'," he said.

"I work on a riverboat," Daisy continued. "I was on the stage in New York a couple of times. I wasn't bad either, but the man who owned the show thought he owned me and I didn't like him."

"Tell me his name and nex' time I'm in N'Yawk I'll kill him," Jonathan promised.

Daisy laughed and snuggled closer to him. "I'm really not a bad girl, Jonathan. I went to bed with you tonight because I liked you very much. You're good-looking, you're clean, even though you're only a farm boy. I was lonely and you were lonely."

"Wish we could be lonely eve'y night," he said as he held her to him and fell asleep. The last thing he remembered was her warm, lovely kiss.

But the next morning Daisy found out more about Jonathan, and she stormed at him. *"So you're just a farm boy, huh! With two thousand slaves! And your father the richest man in the county! I never want to see you again as long as I live!"*

Also by Norman Daniels

Wyndward Passion

PUBLISHED BY WARNER BOOKS

IT WAS SUMMER, PLEASANTLY HOT BUT VERY DUSTY, for the road was dry. It hadn't rained in this part of Virginia in a month, which was unusual. Still, beneath its rusty blanket the countryside was lush.

Along this lonely road, somewhere between Lynchburg and Richmond, a slow procession made its way into the late afternoon. Heading it was a carriage in which two men, remarkably alike in some respects, held back the horses to their slowest and easiest pace. Back of the carriage were strung out one hundred and thirty slaves. The women were directly behind the carriage so they wouldn't have to swallow so much dust. They were barefoot, they wore simple cotton dresses that clung to their slim figures—for they were all young—and made some of the male slaves directly behind them think of something far more pleasant than being marched these miles. Despite their weariness, their hopelessness, their sweating bodies, those near the women displayed some tumescence. For they, too, were young and prime.

In a few more days they would be standing on an auction block while an auctioneer bellowed their fine state of health, the size of their sex organs and their ability to procreate.

Behind them one black man rode a large, heavily built horse. A freed slave named Hong Kong, he was a giant of a man, bare to the waist, showing his fine body. He carried a short whip in one hand, mostly for show. There was no necessity for it; there would be no escapes from this group. The women were tied together by one long rope, fastened like a halter around their necks. Each man wore a thick iron collar padlocked around his neck. A long chain ran through the hasps of each padlock, and the men were also handcuffed in pairs. Both men and women carried gunny sacks containing their meager belongings.

There were two men in the carriage. The older was Fitzjohn Turner, the only son of Jonathan Turner, of an old Virginia family of plantation owners. His mother had been born and bred in Boston. She, like his father, had died under tragic circumstances. Fitz, as he insisted on being called, now ran one of the largest plantations in the South and was considered a millionaire several times over, and a highly successful grower of key cash crops: tobacco, horses, and slaves.

Beside him sat his nineteen-year-old son,

named after his grandfather, whom he resembled to such a degree that often Fitz, seeing him in the distance, would have been willing to swear it was his father.

Fitz was a tall man, heavy set with light brown hair, blue-gray eyes, and a mouth far more generous than that of his son, who had his grandfather's thin, uncompromising mouth. The son also had his grandfather's long arms, wide shoulders, and square, aggressive chin.

Thoroughly at ease, neither man paid the slightest attention to the coffle painfully plodding behind the carriage. To Fitz, it was like shipping some of his thoroughbreds to racing stables, or sending his casks and bales of fine tobacco to market. They were all commodities, the only difference being that the slaves, unlike the tobacco, could walk to market.

To young Jonathan it was an expedition filled with excitement and rare pleasure. He'd seldom been taken to the large cities, and for the first time he would have the responsibility for seeing that the coffle was locked up in the slave pens until the auction. That meant the men had to be outfitted with new shirts and pants, the women with more colorful dresses and pretty hair ribbons. The better a slave looked on the auction block, the higher the price.

Lately these prices had not been too high. The economy had not yet recovered from the panic and bank closing of 1837. In an era when bankruptcies had been abnormally high among planters all over the South, the Turner farm, known as Wyndward Plantation, had prospered. Fitz Turner had not only been wealthy enough to withstand the panic and depression, he had been able to profit highly by it.

"Papa," Jonathan said, fanning himself with his broad-brimmed straw hat, "I ain't never been to the Coldwell place befo' fo' overnight. Met the Colonel, o' co'se. 'Members las' time too well. The Colonel's wife gave me many a feel under the table when we was eatin'."

"Nex' time," Fitz declared matter-of-factly, "Min' yo' manners better'n that, son."

"Papa, I was mindin' mine, but she was horny as hell. Mayhap the Colonel's too goddamn ol' to take keer o' her. Leastwise, I was thinkin' that way, but o' co'se I ain't old 'nuff to know 'bout them things."

" 'Bout time you learned," Fitz said. "We gets to the city an' I'll see you gets a few lessons."

Jonathan grinned. "Lookin' fo' that, Papa. Real well, I am. Figger I'm 'bout as much a man I ever goin' to be."

"Maybe," Fitz said with a smile. "You still got lots to learn, son. An', min' you now, whut we does in town ain't no business o' yo' mama's. She kinda straightlaced. Sometimes," he added wistfully, thinking back over the years when Benay, not so straightlaced, was the bane of Fitz's existence before he married her.

"Whut I do we gets to the Colonel's place an' his wife gets horny, Papa?"

"You stay far enough away she cain't lay hands on yo', son. It ain't polite fo' a guest to flatback his host's wife. Ain't right nohow, so min' yo' manners."

"Tries, Papa, but I ain't makin' no promises."

"She old 'nuff to be your grandmammy, son.

She an old, busted-down whore of a woman. Co'se the Colonel ain't been any good fo' years an' only natural his wife gets roused up some she sees a young buck. But like I said, we guests in the Colonel's house an' we acts like gentlemen. Min' that now, Jonathan, or I takes it outa yo' hide."

"Yo' an' who else, Papa?" Jonathan asked with a mischievous grin.

Fitz didn't become angry. "Thinks yo' kin whup me, son'? Mayhap in four o' fi' mo' years, but not now. Don't try it, 'cause if yo' do, I'll fo'get yo' my son an' whale the hell outa yo'."

"Maybe I'll try someday," Jonathan said. "Jes' fo' the exercise."

"Any time," Fitz said casually. "But not where the slaves kin see us fightin'. They thinks we mad at one 'nother, they looks fo' us to maybe not watch them too close. You know, well as I do, that since the Nat Turner uprisin', things ain't quite the same all over Virginia."

"Reckon I was too young to know 'bout that, Papa. Heard tell plenty."

"Nat Turner busted loose with 'bout two-three hundred slaves. I never did know how many they was, but they butchered fifty-seven white folks 'fore the planters got a posse big 'nuff to run 'em down. When they did, they killed 'bout a hundred of the slaves. Took some prisoners an' later on, they hung twenty of 'em. Served 'em right, it did, tryin' a fool stunt like that."

"We ever have trouble like that, Papa?"

"We had trouble, sho' 'nuff. Plenty, but no rebellion. We treats our slaves better'n most. We wuks 'em hard, but they get 'nuff to fill they bellies an' we pleasures the bucks with as many gals as they crave. Gets us a good crop o' suckers that way. An' they raised real good. So they healthy, they good-lookin', an' they broke well. We gets the highest prices any plantation gets."

"They ridin' after we leave Colonel Coldwell's farm, Papa?"

" 'Co'se they ride. We hires 'nuff wagons to carry 'em all. An' we feeds 'em good too. When they get to market, they ain't tired an' droopin'. You sees they gets washed good too, so they looks like prime stock. Which they are. You got responsibilities this trip, son."

"Whut you aimin' to do, Papa, while I takes keer o' the coffle?"

"I'll be 'roun', talkin' business, makin' trades."

"Mayhap you whorin' some too, Papa?"

"Ain't none o' yo' goddamn business, Jonathan, an' you keep yo' mouth shut we gets back. Or I'll give you a chance to fight me an' I whups you good 'fore we done. Min' now."

Jonathan took absolutely no offense at the threat. He chuckled softly and accepted the reins from his father's tired hands. The rest of the trip to Colonel Coldwell's plantation was filled with casual talk, no threats or promises. Jonathan knew he was getting an education in the operation of a plantation and he was eager to absorb everything his agile brain would retain. Fitz had long ago realized that when it came time to turn the plantation over to his son, it would be in fine hands.

Fitz doted on this boy, but the fondness he had for him was not nearly as great as the adoration and love he had for his only other child. Melanie was sixteen, a beautiful, composed, rational girl, raised by her mother to appreciate the finer things and so doted upon by her father that all these better things were hers for the mere asking.

It had been months since Fitz had seen her. It seemed like years, but he'd not objected when Benay insisted Melanie be sent to a finishing school. In the North, which was strange for a southern-bred mother to do. Fitz, of course, had consented readily, for he had spent his youth in Boston and he'd never forgotten that part of his upbringing. He'd gone to fine schools, known his mother's people and loved them, despite their austerity. It would be nice to see Melanie again, at her graduation next spring.

Both men relaxed and sighed with relief as the procession came within sight of the Colonel's place. It consisted of a large two-story frame house, six pillars in front, a coach entrance at the side. Once white, it was now rendered a dull gray by time and lack of funds. The green blinds were so faded, they looked washed out. The farm itself was in better condition, mildly prospering. The Colonel was a heavy drinker, lazy as a sloth, and none too particular about his appearance, but he could handle slaves and he knew cotton. Fields of it stretched into the distance, the white bolls glistening in the late sunlight.

"It's goin' to feel mighty nice to sleep in a bed tonight, Papa," Jonathan said.

"See to it yo' alone in that bed, son. Remember yo' manners. Yo' takes the Colonel's wife an' I swear I whups yo' good."

"Papa, I only nineteen. I wouldn't know whut to do anyways."

Fitz gave his son a sidelong glance of disbelief, but let it go. They were already passing through the wooden gate and the Colonel was waiting on the ample veranda. He was a stout man, almost gross, and he invariably wore ancient, baggy suits that he had been white when he first purchased them twenty years ago. Now they were tinged with yellow and wrinkled as a turkey's neck.

Fitz brought the carriage to a halt. The slaves promptly dropped to the cool grasses before the plantation house, grateful for a chance to rest their sore feet and weary muscles.

"Mighty nice to see yo' agin." The Colonel shook Fitz's hand warmly. "Don't see many folks no mo, 'roun' heah. Seems like ev'ybody too busted to even ride over. How's things with you, Fitz? As if I had to ask. Heard tell in Norfolk, other day, you got more'n a million dollahs in the bank there an' more'n two million in no'thern banks, like in Boston."

"Yo' been listenin' to fairy tales, Colonel. Ain't got that kinda money. Yo' knows Jonathan, o' co'se."

The Colonel took Jonathan's hand in his flabby one. "Grown some, ain't yo', son?"

"Reckon," Jonathan said casually. "Seein' I'm the age when growin' happens."

"So you are." Jonathan's mild sarcasm was lost on the Colonel. "Fitz, yo' ol' dog, got some fine bourbon waitin'. Yo' wants to have one on the po'ch or yo' wants to clean up some first?"

"Clean up later," Fitz said. "Throat's gone mighty dry, it has."

The Colonel yelled, bringing a lanky slave running from the house.

"Get us some bourbon an' watah," he ordered the slave. "An' you' gets it heah fas' or yo' goes back to the fields. Yo' ain't much good bein' houseboy anyways, so yo' bettah move yo' ass, heah me?"

"Yas suh, mastah. I runs fast."

"Yo' takes them boys into the house, Fitz, an' they gets so lazy sometimes yo' thinks they's daid. Ain't nevah had me a houseboy who could run fas' 'nuff to suit me. 'Specially when I'm cravin' a drink like now. Jonathan, yo' goin' to join us?"

"Jonathan's goin' to see the coffle gets unspanceled an' washed in the creek an' then fed an' rested. Yo' still got all them big wagons, Colonel, we kin rent?"

"Sho' has. They's fine propetty. Got to charge you extra this time, Fitz. Things ain't good 'roun' heah since the panic. Gets all I kin whenever I kin."

"Yo' names the price an' I pays it," Fitz said. "We doin' fine at Wyndward."

"How's Benay?"

"Real fine, Colonel. Pretty as ever."

"An' the little gal?"

"She up No'th to some fancy school. Benay says she gots to go there an' learn to be a real lady. Yo' sees her agin, Colonel, yo' bows low an' yo' kisses her hand."

"All I'm good at's kissin' any mo'," the Colonel sighed. "Reckon the years ain't done me no good."

"The years'll do it," Fitz admitted. "But reckon all that bourbon you drunk an' all them gals yo' screwed ain't done much to keepin' yo' young. Though my papa always said the more gals yo' get, the younger yo' stay."

"Don't believe it," the Colonel said. He raised his voice in a shout to hurry up the drinks. They came, sloshed over the side of the glass during the slave's dash from the kitchen, but that didn't matter to the Colonel.

He raised his glass. "To yo' an' the kind o' frien' we been since yo' was born, Fitz."

"I was born in Boston an' you wasn't theah, Colonel, but to the years I been heah an' you knowed me."

They emptied the glasses quickly and the slave was sent running for more. Before they were delivered, the Colonel's wife moved her vast bulk through the door and greeted Fitz with a moist, whiskey-flavored kiss.

"Yo' lookin' real fine, Fitz. Wheah that good-lookin' son o' yours?"

"He beddin' the slaves, ma'am. Keep him busy 'till late, fo' sure. He been askin' 'bout yo', an' he'll see you-all fo' sho' in the mo'nin 'fore we leaves."

"Reckon," she said, but the light in her eyes was an indication she meant to see him before then.

"Fitz," the Colonel demanded, "whut's goin' to happen now, ev'ythin' runnin' like wild? Evah since President Jackson tol' South Ca'lina she leaves the union, she commits treason. Reckon South Ca'lina leaves like she says, soldiers be sent in?"

"Cain't say fo' sure," Fitz told him. "But if I

was President Jackson an' South Ca'lina says she leaves the union, I sends in soldiers real fast."

"Nothin' but trouble. Thinks them crazy Abolitionists up No'th to blame fo' most of it. Hangin's too good fo' them."

"Sho' ain't helpin' us none," Fitz agreed. "Colonel, yo' fixin' to sell me a batch o' slaves when I comes back from the city?"

"Tol' you las' time yo' came through, I'd have maybe fifty-sixty. They ain't prime, they ain't so young, but good workers. Needs money real bad, else I wouldn't sell 'em to anybody."

Fitz nodded. "Takes 'em off yo' hands soon's I come through. Have 'em ready, an' I pays yo' well. Won't bargain none. Yo' were papa's friend fo' yeahs an' now yo' mine. Ain't aimin' to take advantage o' yo' bad luck, suh. Pays highest prices. Find out whut they are when I sells my coffle."

"Call for 'nother drink," the Colonel said, well satisfied with the deal. He yelled and the slave went running.

Jonathan, standing beside Hong Kong, the massive overseer of Wyndward Plantation, looked almost diminutive in comparison. Hong Kong was no slave. Fitz had manumitted him years ago, only a few hours after Jonathan had been born.

"They's prime," Hong Kong said. "Nevah seen a better-lookin' coffle."

"Bring good prices," Jonathan observed. "They's one wench—kinda young an' kinda yella 'stead o' black. Mayhap got some human blood. Think she busted yit?"

"Knows the one, suh. Nice-lookin' wench. Yo'

wants her I sees she gits extra washed an' she be alone, back behind the necessary house."

"Yo' ain't been tellin' my papa 'bout this?"

"No, suh. You foolin' 'roun' them wenches ain't none o' my business an' ain't none o' his, reckon. 'Minds me o' yore grandpappy," Hong Kong added reflectively. "Yo' the randiest buck I seen since. Declare yo' is, suh."

"What else was he like?" Jonathan demanded.

"I was a slave when he alive," Hong Kong said. "Treated me fair an' square. I needed whuppin' I got whupped, but never when I didn't need it. Took me to the city lots o' times an' always gave me two silver dollahs to spend way I wanted. Liked him, I did. I was telling my boy——"

"You got *chillun*, Hong Kong?" Jonathan interrupted.

Hong Kong's eyes shifted away from Jonathan. "Yas, suh, I got me a son. He same age as yo', suh. Borned the same night yo' was."

"He manumitted too?"

"Reckon I don' know that, suh. Better git the coffle set fo' the night, suh. Yas, suh, sho' do make me think o' yo're grandpappy."

"Don't fo'git 'bout that high yella, Hong Kong. Got me some juices gots to get outen me."

Hong Kong shook his head. "Yo' talks like him too. Says the same words, yo' does, suh. Like he ain't nevah died, only got younger. Won't fo'git the wench, suh."

Jonathan did report to the plantation house in time for supper. Accustomed to the fine cooking of their own slave cook, he found the food unpalatable. The Colonel's wife set a poor table, not being half as much interested in food as she was in drink. Jonathan made certain he was not seated next to her so that she could not her use hand on his genitals under the table. She revolted him now, but he recalled times when she'd looked good because he was inexperienced, and she was not. He'd been fourteen the first time.

He'd stopped by with his papa for a few hours. Jonathan was told to amuse himself while the two men reminisced and talked about business matters. He was soaked with perspiration from the journey and was looking for a spot to cool off when he spotted the gazebo. It was tree-shaded and vine-covered, affording both coolness and privacy.

Jonathan went up the three steps, opened the door, and closed it softly behind him. A wicker chaise longue looked mighty inviting and he dropped on it. One leg slipped off it onto the floor and he let it lay there, too exhausted to raise it. That was all he remembered until he wakened, conscious of a tightness in his groin and the fragrance of a floral cologne.

He opened his eyes and would have got to his feet immediately, but he was held down by a pair of hands that gripped his shoulders. One of his legs was still mostly off the chaise longue. It was Mrs. Coldwell who leaned over him. Her voice was a coo when she spoke. "Don' be frightened, Jonathan. Yo' looked so lonely when yo' 'rived, my pore heart jes' ached fo' you. Don't be frightened, son. I'm jes' heah to console yo'."

And mighty good consoling she was, Jonathan thought, his mind going back. Her fichu was already opened and the bodice of her dress unlaced, freeing her ample bosom. She was seated on the chaise, bent over him, her hard nipples touching his chest.

"Yo're not frightened o' me, are yuh, son?"

"No, ma'am," he replied promptly, though he was fearful either his papa or the Colonel might seek the coolness of the gazebo. She must have read his mind, for she said, "Doan worry 'bout them two coots. They're fulla rum awready."

Her hands had loosened his trousers and were caressing his genitals. "Yo' respondin' real good, Jonathan. Shore yo' musta been pleasured before, ain't yo' now?"

"Ma'am, I on'y fourteen." He liked what she was doing to him.

"Yo' like my bosom?"

"Yes ma'am. They beautiful."

"They ain't gonna bite. Take a holda them."

Jonathan obeyed and her moist mouth came down on his. He forgot his fear of discovery and began to enjoy the favors extended to him. He had expected her to lie beside him. Instead, she slipped lower and placed his tool between her heavy breasts and squeezed gently. If his passion hadn't been so intense, he'd have been shocked. He wondered if she was scared he'd put a sucker in her, or if that was what she liked.

Afterward, she used her fichu to dry herself, then handed it to him. He cleaned up as best he could with the already sodden piece of lace. She slipped a hand into her skirt pocket, took out a fresh fichu, and put it on after she had laced up her bodice. She took the other from Jonathan and dropped it in her skirt pocket.

She smiled down at him, gave his genitals a

final pat, and left. Jonathan was so stunned, he could only lie there until he regained his senses. Not until he went to get up did he realize his trousers were still open.

Now, five years later, sitting sedately at her dinner table, he stole a glance at the Colonel's wife and wondered how she had ever been able to arouse him. Her silk gown was spotted and dirty. The curls that touched her shoulders on either side were uneven, revealing it was a wig beneath her lace cap. She caught him looking at her and raised her hand to adjust the fichu, which barely covered her breasts. Now they were almost completely revealed. He looked away and turned his attention to the conversation between his father and the Colonel.

"Yo' 'members Fisbee?" the Colonel asked. "Got his plantation 'long the way to yo' place."

"Sho' 'members him," Fitz said. "'Members the night there was an uprisin' an' them crazy black devils sliced his haid clean off. Butchered his family too. Cousin o' his been runnin' the place since, way I hears it."

"Runnin' it ain't 'xactly the word," the Colonel said. "Lessen you calls it runnin' the place to the ground. Fixin' to sell off all his slaves an' there ain't one of 'em don' want to go. Way he treats 'em ain't right, even if they ain't human."

"They ain't 'xactly animals either," Jonathan observed.

"Reckon' yo' could get some to say yo're daid wrong," the Colonel said.

"Show me an animal that kin talk," Jonathan said. "They kin' talk, they's human. Sort of."

"Yo're talkin' too damn much fo' the size o' yo

britches," Fitz said. "You got the coffle all set fo' the night?"

"Reckon, Papa."

"Well, you get yo' ass down theah an' make sure."

Which was precisely what Jonathan wanted him to say. He stood up and bowed ironically to the Colonel's wife. To the Colonel he said, "My respects, suh," and then he walked briskly out of the house. It was already dark. He made his way to the old stables where the coffle was now quartered, all of them sound asleep after their long walk in the hot sunlight. Hong Kong, his massive form stretched out on the ground in front of the stable doors, opened one eye, raised a hand, and pointed in the direction of the small stream that flowed quietly across the Colonel's property.

Jonathan reached the stream and peered about in the gloom. "Where the hell yo' at, you black wench? Cain't see yo' nohow in the dark."

"I's heah, massa, suh." The girl's voice was soft, almost reproachful.

"Keep talkin' so's I kin fin' yo'," Jonathan ordered.

She was standing beside a clump of tall bushes and he saw her dimly in the gloom. When he reached her and took her in his arms, he discovered she was naked.

"All shucked down," he said happily. "Way I likes 'em, willin' an' ready. You been busted yit?"

"No, massa, suh. I ain't been busted."

"Then yo' sho' is 'bout to be."

He tripped her neatly, without letting go of her, and when she sagged in his arms, he bore her to the ground. He shucked his pants promptly, lay on her, and entered her. She cried out briefly and then her arms went around him and she clung to him until he was breathless, and all his desire sapped from him.

He sat up, still holding the naked girl. "How come I ain't nevah had yo' befo'?" he asked.

"Don' know, massa, suh. I sho' been lookin' at yo', but yo' ain't nevah looked at me, massa, suh."

"How old yo'?"

"Don' rightly know, suh."

Jonathan nodded. No records were kept of the birthdays of slaves. "Reckon you be 'bout sixteen."

"Massa, suh, I don' want to be sold."

"Ain't nuthin' yo' kin do 'bout that. Whut yo' name?"

"Domingo, suh."

"Domingo?" Jonathan frowned, then nodded. "Must be a ship got that name."

His grandfather had named all male slaves after ports of call and all females after ships whose names had been on record. This had never changed. The new slaves brought back would be renamed according to the rules laid down by a man dead these nineteen years, but whose influence was still felt on his plantation.

"Likes to be called Domingo, suh. Likes it, I do."

"Reckon you ain't so bad-lookin'. Knows you is damn good for screwin'. Whut yo' do I asks my papa not to sell yo'?"

"Loves yo, suh. Ev'ytime yo' wants."

"Reckon yo' bettah do some mo' o' that lovin' right now. Talkin' 'bout it makes me horny. 'Sides,

[23]

yo' fingers sho' know the right places to pleasure a man. Them bucks on the plantation been fingerin' yo'?"

"No suh, massa, suh. They tries, but I says I pleasures yo' an' no one else."

"They b'lieve I busted yo' a'ready?" Jonathan found the thought amusing.

"They don' rightly know, but don' dare take chances o' coverin' me in case I tellin' the truf." Her hands and her body moved in unison with her words.

"Yo' mighty uppity fo' a slave," he said. He had already turned her on her back. Her legs were spread, her body arched, ready to receive him. His hands were stroking her buttocks. She moaned softly.

"Don' mean to be, massa, suh. Don' mean to be. Jes' wants to pleasure yo'. Give my life to pleasure yo'. Gives yo' a sucker, I will."

"Yo' sho' is uppity. That's fo' me to say."

"Fo' the Lawd, massa, suh."

"Maybe fo' the Lawd to say, but fo' me to plant the seed. Now quit talkin'."

He seized her in a savage embrace, thrust his organ into her, and satisfied himself, all the time marveling at her skill. No part of her body was still until after the orgasm and he lay on top of her, pinning her down. He rolled off, satisfied and exhausted. He then drew her to him and promptly fell asleep. The naked girl wriggled as close to him as she could, but the ground was cold. She finally pushed out a leg and with her foot, hooked his trousers lying nearby. She brought these to her, wrapped them about her body as best she could, and fell asleep too.

{ 2 }

JONATHAN HAD NOT VISITED THE CITY IN MORE THAN a year and a half, when he had come to see Melanie off to the North. At that time his mother was ailing and Jonathan had precious little time to galavant.

This time his father placed him on his own. He was supplied with money and instructed to visit the bank if he ran out. But it would not be all pleasure. First, he had to deliver the coffle to the slave-jail. This was a long, low building with iron bars across the windows and a stout door reinforced with heavy hinges and strips of metal. No slave had ever broken free from it. Inside, the walls were lined with chains bolted to the walls. Jonathan watched his coffle unshackled of the handcuffs and iron collars. They were then chained to the walls, but with enough slack to move fairly well.

Jonathan ordered food for them, in large quantities, and of a type they enjoyed—fatback, greens, and yams hot from the boiling pots. They could eat all they liked for at least two days, in which time they would regain any weight they'd lost on the trek. The grease in the food would make their skins glisten.

In the morning, Jonathan would visit one of the clothing stores that dealt in slave garments. There he would purchase colorful dresses and ribbons for the women. For the men, he would provide new trousers and shirts. On the day of the auction they must look their best.

Jonathan's duties for the day well attended to, he began looking about. Fitz would be at the hotel, where he'd talk business with his cronies and find himself a whore for the night. In the morning, Fitz would then proceed to the bank, where he had to attend to a multitude of financial transactions.

Sometime during the next day, Jonathan might run across his father, so Jonathan accepted the freedom of this night and made the most of it.

His first stop was at the hotel bar, where he walked boldly to the mahogany bar and ordered a good pouring of Barbados rum.

"Go play somewhere else," the barkeep said roughly. "We ain't got no rum an' if we did, I wouldn't sell it to you."

"You wanta bet?" Jonathan asked quietly.

"Co 'way, boy, you ain't doin' my day no good a'tall."

"Well now," Jonathan declared, "I could bust up this here place real good I'd a mind to. But I ain't lookin' fo' trouble. You ain't got rum, you give me bourbon. An' see to it next time I come in here you got Barbados rum. That's whut my granddaddy used to drink an' if it was good 'nuff fo' him, it's jes' fine with me, suh. I'll have a little cold watah with the whiskey, suh. Not too much."

The barkeep turned his back on Jonathan. One of the men at the bar said, "Bes' yo' gives him what he wants. This heah is Fitz Turner's boy an' his grandpappy was Cap'n Jonathan Turner. Don' pay to fool 'roun' with that family."

The barkeep turned back, reached for the bourbon, and poured a healthy amount, adding water from a pitcher which contained bits of ice.

"Reckon any Turner kin have whut he wants in this place," he said. "I'm glad to 'pologize, suh, an' I hopes you come back often."

Jonathan felt as if he'd added ten years. He lifted the glass, set his back against the bar, and toasted the entire barroom. "Drinks on me, gentlemen. Anythin' yo' craves."

There was a dash to the bar. Jonathan peeled a bill from the roll of money Fitz had given him, placed it on the bar somewhat grandly, finished his drink, and walked out. On the street he felt like a grown man for the first time.

That night Jonathan slept hard and long, not rising until well after seven. He discovered that his father had already left his room at the hotel. By crumpled sheets and covers of the double bed, Jonathan knew his father had not occupied it alone. He anticipated nights like that for himself, but reckoned he'd done quite well, considering his age.

. He made his purchases, talked to Hong Kong about getting the coffle ready, and spent the rest of the day prowling about. That evening he met his father in the hotel restaurant. He was alone, waiting for Jonathan to join him.

"Whar in hell you been?" Fitz asked. "Heard tell yo' near got into a mess at one of the saloons. Who said yo' was old 'nuff to go to one o' them places an' drink?"

"Seems like I did, Papa," Jonathan said easily. "Wasn't the first drink I evah had. An' I only drank one."

"That's to yo' credit, reckon. Let's have our supper now an' yo' kin tell me whut yo' done to git the coffle ready. You ain't seen one o' them auctions since yo' was too small to know whut was goin' on. Tomorrow yo'll find out."

"Didn't like whut I saw las' time," Jonathan admitted.

"Now yo' listen to me, son. We raises high-bred horses. We raises tobacco, good Virginny bright. An' we raises slaves. They's a money crop too. Maybe the best one we got. We breed slaves an' we wuks 'em, but not too hard. We don't whup 'em lessen they earns it bad. Not one o' them that goes on the block tomorrow has got a whup mark on him. Not one! We treats 'em good—fo' slaves. Cain't treat 'em too good, but ours are handled better'n mos'. Yo' knows whut I'm talkin' 'bout?"

"Sure, Papa, I knows. Ain't blamin' you. Jes' didn' like how families busted up."

"Yo' got to learn they ain't families. They's

slaves. Yo' starts thinkin' they's human, yo' ain't goin' to control 'em right."

"Yes, Papa, I knows. I ain't 'bout to bust into tears come tomorruh when they's sold."

"See you don't. Have 'em ready fo' the auctioneer by nine, y'heah me? By afternoon we wants to be on our way back."

"Yes, Papa. Tonight I'll make sure ever'thin' is goin' fine."

"I'll be busy agin, son. These heah money matters ain't easy to settle an' they takes time. Get packed in the mornin' an' we leaves right after the auction. Gots to stop at the Colonel's on the way back an' pick up a coffle I bought from him. An' then we stops agin at the old Fisbee farm. We kin buy more slaves 'thout spendin' much. Farm's 'bout ready to be auctioned anyway, so we gets 'em cheap."

"Papa, how many that make we own?"

"Ain't sure. Ain't rightly sure, but anywheres from fifteen hundred up."

"Whut yo' buyin' mo' fo' then, Papa?"

"They's breedin' kin'. Mo' yo' get, mo' suckers they gives yo'. Needs mo' hands in the field too, an' with the horses."

Jonathan nodded and arose. "Got to see the coffle gets bedded down right. I hopes these bankers don' fret yo' too much, Papa."

Fitz looked up at him with a jaundiced eye. Then he shrugged. There was no fooling this boy, not any longer. Perhaps it was just as well. Fitz ordered another drink. It was good to get into condition for another bout with the whore he'd paid for and who had serviced him so well already.

It was also time to acquaint Jonathan with certain ways of men and women. Not that Jonathan didn't know how a sucker was seeded. He'd seen enough of that. Any slave buck who wanted to favor a woman, even in the fields, was welcome to do so. Jonathan couldn't have helped but witness some of those struggles. However, there were certain niceties to be observed and Jonathan must be told about them. Fitz determined to bring up the subject during the long ride back to Wyndward.

Next morning, Jonathan was up at daybreak. He ate a hasty breakfast and then walked swiftly to the slave pens just off the auction grounds. The slaves were already up. Hong Kong had sorted out the best-looking females and bucks for early presentation, when interest was at its highest peak and prices would be best. They were already bathed and dressed in their new clothes.

Fitz joined him just before the auction began. There were about two hundred men in attendance, with a sprinkling of women enticed there by the display of nudity which was essential to any such auction.

It went well. There were other coffles for sale too. Perhaps five hundred Negroes would be bid on, bought, and marched to some farm they'd never heard of, the property of men who might be kind and gentle, or fiendishly cruel.

Jonathan was still affected when he saw brothers and sisters bid on separately and torn apart. He saw a few mothers whose children were still back at Wyndward and whom they would never again see. It was a cruel but necessary business, he thought.

Fitz, chewing on a slim black cheroot thought nothing of it. "Jonathan," he said toward the end of the auction, "figgered we brought a hundred an' fifty-six slaves, but on'y a hundred an' fifty-five been sold."

"Yes, Papa. One of 'em I lef' behind at the Colonel's place."

"Which one?"

"Gal 'bout sixteen, maybe. Kinda light."

"'Members her. She bring a fine price. Whut yo' throwin' away money like that fo', son?"

Jonathan smiled slyly. "Ain't throwin' it away, Papa. Swears I ain't."

Fitz took a long breath. "Reckon I'm a little behin' yo', son. Been thinkin' yo' not much more'n a boy. Yo' sleeps with her yet?"

"Yes, suh. Sleeps with her at the Colonel's. Likes her, Papa. I wants her fo' a pet."

Fitz nodded. "We'll talk 'bout that on the way home."

"Wants her, Papa. Don' yo' try to take her away."

"Didn' say I would," Fitz answered sharply. "All I said is, we'll talk."

"Yes suh, Papa. We talks." Jonathan was studying an aged, wrinkled woman on the vendue table. "Papa, ain't that ol' Royal George, used to be on Wyndward?"

Fitz studied the woman. "Reckon. Sold her five, maybe six years ago. Whut of it?"

"Yo' heah who's biddin' on her, Papa?"

Fitz looked around. "I be damned," he said. "Major Apperson! Whut's he want with an old woman like that?"

"Look to the foot of the table, Papa. See that

young gal, nice-lookin', with mighty fine legs? She Royal George's daughter. Major Apperson wants her an' if he buys the ol' lady too, that gal goin' to like the Major real fine. Heard the Major is a regular ol' whoremaster. Likes to bust the gals an' use 'em plenty."

The bid on the old woman was fifty dollars. She wasn't good for a thing on any plantation except perhaps to help in the kitchen or the birthing house.

"Five hundred dollahs," Fitz shouted.

All heads turned in his direction. They looked, and they saw, and they understood, especially Major Apperson.

"Six hundred," the Major called out.

"Thousand," Fitz said.

Major Apperson didn't reply to that bid. The old lady on the vendue table was helped off it. She made her way through the crowd to reach Fitz and fell on her knees before him.

"Massa, suh, I dies fo' yo'. They's goin' to take my baby 'way from me. Yo' buy her, please, suh. She goin' on the table nex', suh. She a hard-wukkin' gal. She a good gal. That ol' man wants to bust her, suh, an' wear her down to nuthin' with his pesterin'. I knows him."

Fitz reached down and helped her up. "Knows him too," he said.

The girl was on the table and the auctioneer promptly whisked up her dress to her breasts to reveal her nakedness. The Major climbed onto the table. He forced open the girl's mouth and examined her teeth. He fondled her breasts and nodded approval. He was about to investigate her legs and between them when Jonathan shouted a warning.

"Yo' ain't bought her yit, yo mizzable ol' bastahd. Bids two thousand."

Major Apperson, dressed in the height of fashion, as usual, turned to identify this new voice. He saw Fitz beside the old slave he'd just bought and on the other side of him, this tall, brawny young man. The Major knew who he was.

"Yo' means to buy this gal fo' yo' own pleasure, boy? Yo' gets her, yo' pays a mighty high price. I'll see to that."

"Ten thousand," Jonathan shouted. There were gasps. This was one of the highest bids ever offered anywhere.

The Major considered. He was tempted to keep the bidding going until even Fitz would wince at the offer, but the Major was also wary. He'd dealt with Fitz before.

"Reckon I had 'nuff," he said. "She ain't worth that much to me. Got me a better eye fo' female flesh than yo' has, boy."

"Then yo' step away from that gal," Jonathan called out. "Yo' lays a hand on my proppity, I'll bust you up some, suh. Means it."

The Major promptly climbed off the table. Jonathan called out again, with even more authority in his voice.

"Wants the auctioneer to pull that gal's dress down. Ain't fittin' she be standin' there fo' the pleasures o' the ladies an' gents lookin' at her."

The old woman stemmed a flow of tears. "Thanks yo', massa, suh. She was goin' to cut her throat ear to ear, that man buys her."

"No need now," Fitz said. "Yo' gets her ready. We leaves in two hours."

"Yes suh, massa, suh. Be mighty glad to be back on yo' plantation, suh."

"Jonathan," Fitz said, "yo' takes keer o' the auctioneer. Yo' tells him the bank will take the money we bid on this gal an' this ol' woman out of whut we gets from sellin' our coffle. Then you gets 'em dressed some bettah an' yo' sees they's well fed fo' yo' puts 'em in the carriage."

"They rides with us?" Jonathan asked with a frown.

"We walks 'em, the old woman's daid 'fore she gets to Wyndward, and sho' ain't much sense makin' the young one walk."

"Sees to it, Papa. Yo' ain't mad I buys the gal?"

"Son, my papa used to outbid that ol' whoremaster ev'y time he could. Neveh liked him. He's got a son named Horace who takes his pleasure from young bucks he buys. He likes 'em better'n he does his wife. Cain't blame him fo' that. Clarissa gets the hots for any likely man she sees."

"She evah had the hots for you, Papa?"

Fitz gave him a stern look. "That whuppin' I promised yo' is comin' faster'n yo' think, son. Now yo' takes keer o' the business I said an' no mo' crazy talkin'."

Jonathan was more practical than his father had imagined. The two newly purchased slaves did not ride in the carriage. It was necessary to hire slaves to drive Colonel Coldwell's big wagons back to his farm, and Jonathan arranged that the girl drive one, with her old mother on the seat beside her. After the wagons were delivered, then they could ride in the freight wagon.

This wagon was loaded with supplies—silks and cottons Benay had ordered by mail, a score of hats direct from Paris, shoes from Italy and France. There were also certain types of food unobtainable on the farm and several cases of good whiskey and a dozen of fine rum. One bottle of it rode in the carriage nestled between Fitz and Jonathan. Fitz nipped at it, as the journey progressed. Finally Jonathan nonchalantly took a long pull at the bottle while his startled father watched.

"Reckon' yo're old 'nuff," Fitz said. "I was drinkin' 'bout yo' age. Don' want yo' gettin' drunk. Ain't no way to handle good liquor, son. An' while we's at it, might as well talk some 'bout that mustee waitin' at the Colonel's place."

"Whut's we got to talk 'bout her, Papa?"

"Yo' likes her, else yo' wouldn't have taken her out o' the coffle. That's fine, son. Some o' them gals pesters yo' real fine. Better'n a white gal sometimes. Had one myself once. Name of Nina. An' I'm tellin' you, son, I loved her like I'd love anybody, an' she loved me. Leastwise, she did mos' o' her life."

"She pestered yo' even after yo' married Mama?"

"Why not? Days yo' mama couldn't sleep with me. All women get times like that. So Nina she comes to me, knowin' all the while I needed her. Wasn't no nigger either, son. I was told from my papa, who brought her here on his slave ship, that her papa was an Ayrab o' some kind. Maybe a king. She was real light an' we loved one 'nother."

[35]

"Where she now?"

"Buried, 'side yo' grandpappy."

"*White* folks' cemetery?" Jonathan asked in disbelief.

"That's whar. My mama loved her too, so did my papa, but she was mine. Don' mind tellin' yo' my papa busted her on the ship bringin' her here. Didn't matter none to me. When I got her, she was skeered an' kinda helpless, but she caught on fast. Talked good as yo' an' me. Sometimes."

"She daid 'fore I was borned?"

"She died the night you was born. She had a baby that night too."

"Yours, Papa?"

"Way I figgered, it shoulda been, but it was black as coal. Found out Nina been beddin' down with Themba, a nigger I bought 'cause he so good with hosses. Nevah trusted him, but I nevah knew Nina had gone to his baid."

"Whar's Themba now?"

"I killed him. I pushed him into a stall with a killer hoss an' let that hoss trample him to death. I hated him. An' I hated Nina after I found out whut she done."

"Too bad, Papa. I reckon they's all alike."

"That's whut I wants to warn you 'bout. You got this gal an' she pleasures yo' real good, but there'll come a day when she'll go back to her own kind."

"Whut if I knocks her up, Papa?"

"You'll have a good sucker we kin raise an' sell someday."

"You'd sell a chile I seeded, Papa?"

"Chile got one drop o' nigger blood an' that chile ain't human. One drop is all it takes. You kin make all the suckers yo wants, but don' trust any nigger. Yo' loves her, that's fine, but yo' 'members someday she turns against yo'."

"Papa, I pleasures myself with this gal, she gets all big in the belly?"

"Sho' 'nuff."

"White gals, they get big too?"

"Co'se, son. They's all built the same."

"Worries me some," Jonathan admitted slowly. "White gals get all swole up too, reckon I got me a sucker goin'."

"White gal? Who you been pesterin', Jonathan? Goddamn it, yo' ain't ol' 'nuff fo' that."

"Sure am, Papa," Jonathan declared. "Las' time I saw her, she gittin' swole up. That was two months ago."

"Who?" Fitz asked. "Who this gal, Jonathan?"

"Belle. She lives with her folks on the Fisbee place. We stopped there las' fall, 'member? An' she gits me into the barn. Reckon I didn't know whut to do, but she did."

"Oh, hell," Fitz said in mild anger. "Yo' gets Belle knocked up, whut yo' aimin' to do 'bout it?"

"Nuthin'. Why should I, Papa? She come to me. I nevah went to her. 'Fore I meets her, I nevah had a gal."

"Yo' ain't aimin' to marry her?"

"God damn, Papa, I don' even like her!"

"They's mean people, them Fisbees. Whut's left of 'em after that uprisin' years ago. Real mean people, but they's broke flat an' they got nuthin' to say to me. Yo' don' mean to marry that gal, yo' tells her so. Ain't right, lets her think yo' will."

"I tells her, Papa."

"When we came through las' time, she pester yo' again?"

"Sure did, an' she says she got my sucker in her belly."

"Means trouble, mayhap. Sees whut we kin do. So keep yo' mouth shut we gets there."

"Sho' will."

"An' we gets home, yo' keeps yo' mouth shut tighter'n that. Yo' mama hear tell whut you did an' she'll say yo' marries this gal, yo' loves her or not."

"Reckon Mama be mad as hell."

"Not if she don' know 'bout it." Fitz shook his head. "Been takin' you with me 'cause wants yo' to learn whut it's like 'way from the plantation. Reckon yo' sho' found out an' no he'p from me."

"Reckon," Jonathan said happily. "Kinda likes it too."

"Jesus Christ, mo' like yo' granddaddy ev'ry day. Now shut up!"

Jonathan took the advice and went to sleep, sometimes lolling against his father's shoulder.

They reached Colonel Coldwell's place in mid-afternoon. Jonathan hurried down to the stables, where he found Domingo, freshly washed, dressed, and waiting for him with open arms. A condition he was unable to take advantage of because his father was in a hurry to get to Wyndward.

Fitz wrote passes for all the slaves who had driven the wagons back. He gave each one a silver dollar and sent them walking back to their masters in the city.

Finally they were ready to leave. Hong Kong

was already astride his horse, following the heels of the small coffle which the Colonel had sold. Domingo rode in the back seat of the carriage, at Jonathan's insistence.

Fitz had looked her over with apparent appreciation. "She goin' to pester yo' real fine," he judged. Reckon she got white blood, some. Now we goes to see Belle an' that's whar yo' gonna get hell, I reckon."

"Reckon," Jonathan said glumly, but when he turned around and saw Domingo's mouth widen in a soft smile which he returned, he felt good again.

It was another overnight trip to the Fisbee farm and they spent the night in the woods alongside the trail. The slaves slept wherever they dropped. Fitz slept on the front seat of the carriage while Jonathan and Domingo were snuggled close together in back. There wasn't much room for real activity and Jonathan was too tired anyway.

They rode onto the Fisbee place at midday. Fitz was surprised at its rundown appearance. The entrance gate sagged on one hinge, the once beautiful lawns were full of weeds. The plantation house, while not big, had been very attractive, and the original Fisbee family had been rightly proud of it. Now everything seemed decayed, forlorn, and slowly falling apart. The slave row out back was especially dilapidated. Fitz wondered how the slaves had survived the winter. The windows had no panes of glass; the doors he could see were flimsy enough to be worthless and probably the makeshift work of the slaves, using whatever material they could find. The stables were in poor condition and a few horses, grazing in the fields, looked scrawny and uncared for.

As they pulled up, a girl came running, somewhat clumsily, from the house. She was not bad-looking, though she may have been inclined toward plumpness. It was hard to tell now that she was so plainly pregnant. She had dark hair and an impish face which changed to that of an unholy devil when she saw Jonathan's new slave in the back seat of the carriage.

Belle pointed a chubby arm at the girl. "Whut she doin' here, Jonathan? That slut pleasurin' yo'?"

"Sure is," Jonathan said casually. "Yo' seems kinda fat."

Belle whacked the flat of her hand against her swollen belly. "This heah yo' chile, Jonathan. Yo' gots to marry me now. Been waitin' fo' yo' to come back."

"Well," Jonathan said, "I'm back, but I be damned if I marry yo', Belle. My papa an' me stopped to buy the slaves fo' sale heah, an' we didn't stop to talk 'bout gettin' married. So stop yo' crazy talk an' see to it yo' folks get out heah an' tend to business."

She stepped back, bristling with rage. Fitz got down from the carriage.

"We ain't got all day. Yo' folks runnin' this place now, yo' sends 'em out real fast or we ain't spendin' any time."

She shouted, a wild whoop, and two men and a stout woman emerged from the house. Apparently they'd waited until Belle had shocked the visitors and thus softened them up for the proposition they had in mind.

The older of the two men said, "I be Frank Fisbee. Cousin Will, he run this heah farm 'till them black bastahds chop he haid off. Yo' 'members that, Mistah Turner?"

"That was near twenty yeahs ago," Fitz said. "Nuthin' to do with today. Come to buy yo' slaves. March 'em out heah so I kin have a look."

Frank raised his voice in a shout. "Mama, you go fetch the slaves."

"Whut's wrong with him fetchin' 'em?" Fitz indicated the lean, long-haired man who still remained in the background.

"Him?" Frank shrugged. "He jes' a slave-breaker I hired some time back."

"Slave-breaker?" Fitz's voice rose in disgust. "Whut yo' hire a bastahd like him fo'?"

"Thinks he mayhap he'p me git mo' wuk outen them blacks. On'y way to save this farm, suh."

"No slave-breaker evah got a black to wuk harder'n meant fo' him to wuk. Nevah min', bring yo' slaves out heah."

"First, whut yo' goin' to do 'bout my little gal Belle? Yo' son got her knocked up. Yo' figger'n on makin' him marry my little gal an' take her back to Wyndward?"

"I'm figgerin' on buyin' yo' slaves an' nothin' else," Fitz declared.

"My little gal Belle, she——"

"Yo' little gal Belle, she got a eighteen-yeah-ol' boy in the hay an' he didn' even know whut

[41]

to do. So yo' takes yo' little gal Belle an' go wheah-evah yo' is goin' an' it can be to hell fo' all I cares. Wants to sell yo' slaves, fetch 'em out heah or we jes' go 'way."

The woman trotted around the house and very quickly the coffle was produced. There were about thirty males and ten females, all of them in sorry condition—emaciated, weak, dressed in rags and, at first glance, worthless.

"By God," Fitz declared, "yo' sho' ain't got much sense, Mistah Fisbee. Ain't no wunda yo' plantation gone all to hell. I gives yo' fo' thousan' dollahs fo' the lot of 'em."

"Figger yo' gives me ten, on account o' my little gal Belle."

"I offers yo' fo' thousan' now an' they ain't wuth it. In two minutes I offers three thousan', two minutes after that yo' gets two thousan'."

"I takes four!" Frank said hastily. "But it ain't right yo' don't do somethin' fo' my little gal Belle."

"Whut I do fo' yo' little gal Belle is kick her fancy little ass." Fitz saw Jonathan about to jump out of the carriage in anger. He shoved him back. "Yo' stays outa this," he said sharply. He yelled for Hong Kong to line up this new coffle and have them join the first one. Hong Kong promptly went to work. A rope was enough to contain this group of male slaves, he decided. They weren't strong enough to break free and gain a hundred feet before they'd collapse. He succeeded in tying the rope around their necks and then he walked up to the carriage.

"Mastah, suh, reckon these heah so poorly they ain't 'bout to get to Wyndward alive lessen yo' feeds 'em. They's weak an' sick, way I sees 'em."

"Feed 'em," Fitz ordered. "The women rides in the wagon. Get food. We got 'nuff for all?"

"No, suh, mastah, suh. We sho' ain't."

"Take two o' the strongest an' have 'em show yo' whar they keeps the food. Don' make no mind it ain't nigger food long as it's somethin' to eat."

"Now see heah," Frank Fisbee shouted angrily. "Yo' ain't jes' takin' our food, suh. Ain't inclined to let yo' do that, suh."

Fitz dug into the small valise tucked over the carriage seat. From it he took a checkbook and wrote a check for four thousand, one hundred dollars. He handed the check to Fisbee.

"They's a hundred dollahs extra fo' food. Ain't that much food on yo' plantation, suh, so don' yo' give me no sass 'bout it. Or I cancels the whole thing."

Belle stepped up to the carriage and shook it with both hands. "Whut yo' aimin' to do 'bout me?" she demanded of Jonathan. "Yo' sonabitch got me knocked up an' yo' bettah do somethin'."

"Yo' wants money," Jonathan said, "I gives yo' fo' bits. That's whut I pays any whore."

Belle stepped back. This time she was in a cold rage and no longer pleading with him.

"When this chile borned," she said, "fust thing I do is say yo' name. I say it ev'y day 'till this chile knows whut it means an' soon's this chile able to know whut I say, I tells him on'y thing he gots to do in his life, is fix you. Maybe this chile kills yo', maybe this chile makes yo' life so mizzable yo' wish yo' was daid. This chile——"

Jonathan addressed her father. "Get her 'way from me or I'll get down off this carriage an' beat yo' up. Yo' her papa, an' yo' handle her or I handle yo'."

Fitz said, "Bes' thing yo' kin do, Mistah Fisbee, is take yo' wife an' yo' chile into the house an' stay theah till we leaves. Sick o' lookin' at yo', I am."

Fisbee bristled, but he knew if he made trouble, the check in his hand would be a worthless piece of paper before he could get it to the bank. He seized Belle's arm and hauled her back into the house, struggling and hurling curses at both her father and Jonathan. Her mother had already preceded them.

The slave-breaker came forward, hat in hand. "Suh, I he'ps yo' get yo' coffle ready yo' wants me to."

"All right," Fitz said, anxious to get away from this farm. "Bring the women. Whut yo' name?"

"Ollie, suh. Ollie Ferwell."

"Bring 'em," Fitz ordered. He twisted around to face Jonathan. "That gal real spitfire. Reckon she means whut she says?"

"Don' give a goddamn whut she means or says," Jonathan said. "She nuthin' but a slut."

"Kin' see that fo' she opens her mouth. Whut in hell keeps that slave-breaker from bringin' the women? We ain't got all day."

The women came into view from the back of the house, scrawnier and weaker looking than the men. One crone, wrinkled, stooped, and barely able to walk, clutched a month-old baby to her breast as she stumbled along. She lagged behind and the slave-breaker cursed her and kicked at her skinny legs.

The old woman's knees gave way. She fell to kneel in the dirt, still holding the baby tightly. The slave-breaker kicked her three or four times and she fell to her side. She hadn't uttered a sound. Not a single moan or a plea for mercy.

"Goddam wuthless bastahds like yo'," the slave-breaker shouted. "Ain't wuth nothin'."

He stepped back and drew a pistol from under his soiled white coat.

"Hol' on!" Fitz yelled. "Yo' jes' hol' on, suh."

"She ain't no good. Bes' I kills her heah."

"Yo' shoots her an' I string yo' up by yo' feet an' let the crows eat yo' eyeballs out fore they gets to yo' othah balls—if yo' got any."

The slave-breaker backed off hastily. Fitz said, "Jonathan, yo' sends that wench 'side yo' to he'p this po' ol' gal."

Domingo scrambled out of the carriage and ran to the woman, who was trying valiantly to get to her feet. Domingo drew an arm about her, raised her, and then gently took the baby from her, meanwhile speaking softly, consoling and reassuring her.

Fitz walked up to the slave-breaker. "Yo' an' that po' excuse fo' a man in the house ain't fit to own a slave. Now yo' reach fo' that gun yo' packin' so's I kin kill yo' legal."

"I ain't 'bout to harm yo', suh. No suh, sho' ain't."

"An' yo' a stinkin' coward to boot," Fitz said. He wound up a punch and struck the man squarely in the face. Blood spurted from his nose and lips as he staggered back. Fitz watched him, but he didn't reach for the gun. Fitz approached him again and the man covered his face with his arms. Fitz tripped him, then bent over him and removed the pistol from his back pocket. He threw it as far as he could before he returned to the carriage and took up the reins.

From inside the house, Belle was screaming. Fitz glanced over his shoulder at his son. "Yo' bring a li'l gal like po' li'l Belle into my house by the front do' an' yo' leaves by the back do' while I kicks yo' ass black an' blue."

"I ain't takin' her," Jonathan said hastily. "Yo' saw whut she like."

"Nex' time po' li'l gal like Belle gets yo' in the hay, yo' crawl out. She carryin' yo' sucker an' mayhap one day that sucker makes trouble fo' yo'. Don' fo'get whut she said. Means it, she does."

"Aw, she dumb as an' ol' goat, Papa."

"Mayhap yo' sucker ain't." Fitz looked down at Domingo, who held the baby, and also supported the old woman. "Yo' takes yo'self an' the ol' lady to the wagon. Yo' rides with her an' if she gets sick, yo' runs an' tells me. An' see that sucker taken care o'."

"Yas suh, massa, suh. I do like yo' say. She say that man yo' busted up, he kill her chile, suh, by pesterin' her 'till she die. This sucker, suh, her gran'chile, reckon."

Fitz rubbed his chin. "The sonabitch evah whup this ol' lady?"

Domingo turned the old slave around and pulled up her dress, revealing raw wounds from some sort of weighted lash.

Fitz said, "Jonathan, yo' sees that?"

"Yes, Papa, I sees it."

"Whut yo' goin' to do 'bout it, son?"

[46]

Jonathan climbed down and walked casually toward the slave-breaker, who was raising himself to a sitting position. He saw Jonathan's approach and scrambled to his feet. He backed away, his face contorted with terror. Jonathan turned around and raised a hand in the direction of his father. Fitz tossed him the whip. Jonathan sent the thin lash across the slave-breaker's face, drawing blood. Then he ripped off his coat, tore his shirt half off, and proceeded to use the whip until the man's screams died away and he toppled forward, unconscious. His chest and back were raised in welts. Some of them bled, though the whip used on him was a toy compared to the sort of instrument he must have used on the old woman.

Jonathan walked away, handed up the whip, and got aboard the carriage, and the journey home began. From inside the house, Belle's screams had faded to whimpers.

A DIRT ROAD LED DIRECTLY PAST WYNDWARD Plantation and the mansion itself stood half a mile off the road, atop a plateau which was reached by means of a driveway lined with ancient oaks. The carefully tended lawns stretched almost as far as the eye could see.

Behind the mansion were long slave rows, where small, weathertight, individual slave houses had been erected in symmetrical lines, laid out with precision, for Captain Jonathan Turner had built this house and these grounds with the authority of a sea captain who liked everything shipshape, on land or on sea. In these cabins, no slave shivered in the winter or sweltered in the summer. In the field it was different, but at least when they rested, it was in comparative comfort.

There were other buildings, many of them —kitchens, a bakery, a large dairy, curing sheds for tobacco—long lines of them, partially open to the air. There was a springhouse built around an ice-cold spring. Vegetables were kept there as well. Smokehouses, hung with great supplies of meat from the slaughtering season, emitted a tantalizing odor.

The buildings were quite elaborate, miniature houses with overhanging roofs, and chimneys to accommodate the potbellied stoves with which each was equipped. A stone walk led from them to the mansion, tree-shaded so that there was ample protection from the elements. Still, Benay had never been known to make this brief journey, in winter or summer, dry or wet weather, without something to shield her. In dry weather, a parasol; in wet, an umbrella.

The mansion itself was large, but uncompromisingly plain, a huge square structure with many chimneys above a slanted roof. Captain Jonathan Turner had been at sea in regions where cold weather predominated, and he had resolved never to be cold in his own home.

Inside were two ballrooms and a dining room where fifty people could be easily accommodated. There was a library where the plantation records were kept. Upstairs were ample bedrooms for a reasonable number of guests. It was a mansion Captain Turner had created in his dreams, during the long months when he was at sea, either with a cargo to be traded for slaves, or with the holds packed with human bodies on their way to a life of slavery, in a land they'd never even heard of.

Well behind the mansion was an oval race-track, laid out long ago for training the best horse-flesh raised on the plantation. Here a horse's wind and stamina could be tested as well as his speed. Captain Turner had won some important races before he died and Fitzjohn was not averse to learning more in that exciting way.

The wide verandah that ran around two sides of the mansion was lined with cane rockers and plain chairs. In one of the rockers Benay Turner sat fanning herself and waiting patiently. From time to time, Fitz sent back runners to apprise her of his location so she could gauge about when he'd be back. Seated on the porch steps was a lanky Negro, trying to keep from falling asleep.

Benay, at thirty-seven, was a tall, slim woman. Her outer beauty was evident, and after meeting her one became fully aware of her inner beauty, for she radiated charm. Before she met Fitz, she'd been carefree and not averse to getting into bed with her cousins. Fitz had put a quick end to that and when she married him, Benay became the ideal housewife. More than that, for she was quite capable of running this vast acreage and managing the almost two thousand slaves working here.

She heard the sound of a horse being ridden fast. Presently a young slave brought up the horse sharply and, in great excitement, began to shout his message.

"They comin', missy ma'am! They comin'— they comin'—"

"Hold on now," Benay said sternly. "Catch yo' breath an' talk sense. How far are they from heah?"

"Comin', missy. Comin' real fas'. They two miles from heah. Massa sends me to ride."

"All right. Go to the stables an' cool that horse. Water him good an' rub him down. Git!"

He turned the horse and let it amble to the stables. Benay kicked the half-asleep Negro in the ribs.

"Calcutta, yo' gettin' mo' no-account than evah. Yo' hears what he said. They comin' an' yo' bettah have drinks waitin', or yo' gets yo' black hide whupped. An' be sure the watah is cold, an' don't yo' dare do any nippin' on the way back, heah?"

"Yes, missy. Yes, ma'am. I runs now. Massa comes, I bring rum an' col' watah real fas'. I runs, missy."

His run was a shamble of loose footwork by overlong legs. He'd indulged an overly indolent nature since he was a boy, but Fitz was used to him and let him remain as a general handyman and runner for liquor. In the fields, he would have been worthless.

Benay hurried into the house and called for her personal maid, a middle-aged woman who'd served her for years. She was a slave with special privileges, and in return she took fine care of her mistress.

Benay changed into a fresh dress. The maid combed her hair and put it up expertly. Benay used a faint touch of rouge on her cheeks and more on her lips.

"How do I look, Alameda?"

The maid stepped back and surveyed her critically. "Jes' fine, ma'am. Jes' fine. Reckon yo' gits no sleep tuhnight." She giggled and covered her mouth with one hand.

"If he falls asleep on me, Alameda," Benay said quietly, "I know how to wake him up. I want to look my best."

"Sho' do, ma'am. Blue is bes' fo' yo' skin. Looks fine on yo', it does."

"I think so too," Benay said candidly. "There should be ten new gowns in the shipment my husband is bringing back today. An' hats—I'm ashamed of myself for ordering so many. Shoes too—an' perfume." She picked up a bottle with traces of scent still in it. "You kin have this, Alameda."

"They's heah! They's heah!" Calcutta was shouting from the first floor. "Ma'am, they's heah —almos'. They's comin'— Sees 'em, I do."

Benay ran to a window overlooking the front of the mansion. On the road she saw the procession, led by the carriage and trailed by two big wagons and, finally, a long line of slaves.

"Oh, God," Benay said, "he's bought mo' slaves. Cain't keep track whut we got. So he buys mo'."

She ran downstairs. When the carriage was halfway along the drive, she ran out to meet it. Without stopping the carriage, she gave a flying leap, to be caught up by Fitz and hauled onto the seat. She went to him eagerly, happily, and kissed him until they were both breathless. Then she turned to the back seat.

"Jonathan! Oh, Jonathan, whut yo' papa do? Yo' grown up."

"It's the clothes, Benay," Fitz said. "An' yo'

right. He sho' grown up. Got him a good-lookin' wench."

"Name's Domingo," Jonathan said.

Benay studied the girl. "She looks pretty. She got good manners, Jonathan?"

"Yes, ma'am, an' she good at pesterin' too."

Benay drew herself up and looked at her husband. "Whut yo' do to this boy, Fitz? Yo' took him to a whorehouse, he speakin' that way."

"Benay, he grown up plenty. Bettah he's got a pet to fool 'roun' with than gettin' hisself pesterin' all the young gals we got."

"I ain't so sure o' that, Fitz. He only nineteen."

"Shucks," Fitz said, "at eighteen I was——"

Benay clapped a hand over his mouth. "Don't brag none. It ain't fitten. An' whut yo' doin' with all these slaves?"

"Bought some from Colonel Coldwell. He's gettin' on, Benay. An' his wife nuthin' but trash. Reckon he ain't got much juice left to take keer o' her. But I'm tellin' yo' I do."

"Speakin' that way, no wonder Jonathan wants pesterin'. Pay much fo' them?"

"Reckon I nevah paid much, specially fo' the coffle I got from the Fisbee place. Now there's a hellhole I evah saw one. Reckon I may buy the whole place one o' these days. Gets it fo' little. Nobody else got cash to buy it."

"How many acres do we have now?" she asked. "It must be nearly two thousand. That's enough, Fitz. We cain't handle any mo' than that."

"We gets 'nuff slaves we kin handle it."

He pulled up and a dozen slaves came running from behind the mansion to help unload the carriage and the wagons. Domingo, meanwhile, had gone to help the old woman and the baby out of the first wagon. She brought them to where Benay waited.

Fitz said, "This heah ol' lady sho' ain't much good fo' wuk, but she been beaten by a slave-breaker that sonabitch Fisbee hired. He was goin' to shoot her, like we shoots a sick hoss. Reckon you kin' fin' somethin' fo' her to do?"

"That baby ain't hers, that's sho'."

"Her daughter's," Fitz said. "Slave-breaker killed her, I reckon,"

"I sees to the ol' woman. She kin he'p in the birthin' house. Domingo, you take her to the birthin' house an' make sho' she got plenty to eat and see the baby gets a good gal to suckle it."

"Yes, ma'am. I goes fast."

They disappeared around the side of the house. Jonathan walked on ahead. His parents followed slowly, their arms around one another.

Fitz said, "He got a gal on the Fisbee place knocked up."

"Whut kind o' gal, Fitz?" Benay showed no surprise.

"Slut."

"Don' like him gettin' in that kin' o' trouble."

"Says the gal jes' got in the hay with him last yeah when we passed through. Fust time an' he makes a sucker. Ev'y day goes by he act mo' like my pappy. Nobody evah busted mo' gals than Pappy."

"Do yo' lets him have a wench?"

"Bettah'n he go whorin' 'roun' an' makin' white suckers."

Benay nodded. "Yes, yo're right. But watch

him, Fitz. Don't let him get in too much trouble. Jonathan is jes' a boy, a chile. We ain't got the right to let him go yet."

Fitz sat down wearily in one of the porch chairs. "Whar's that lazy Calcutta an' our drinks?" he shouted. "I'll whup him good this time, he ain't got 'em waitin'."

Calcutta, waiting in the hallway just inside the door, held a tray with three tall glasses, brimful. He was shaking so much, the drinks were spilling over.

"Comin', Massa suh. Comin'—I runs——"

While he spoke, he removed each glass from the tray, wiped it somewhat dry with a big black hand, set the glasses on a table. Before he put them back he tilted the tray so the spilled liquor flowed down to one corner. He raised the tray expertly, tilted it further, and let the liquor flow into his mouth.

He was cuffed severely across the back of the neck by a very black, very fat woman in a white apron.

"Yo' goin' to the whuppin' shed sho'," she said. "Git yo'se'f out theah with them drinks. Nex' time I busts you one."

Calcutta pushed open the door and trotted out to the porch. He proffered the tray to Benay, then to Fritz, and finally to Jonathan, who lounged carelessly in a chair next to his father.

The big woman had followed Calcutta to the porch and she emitted a whoop of joy as Fitz arose and embraced her as best he could.

"Yo' gettin' fatter'n one o' them big swamp trees, Elegant. Yo' eatin' us into bankruptcy."

"Massa, suh, yo' knows I eats on'y whut I scrapes off yo' plates."

"Like hell yo' do," he said good-naturedly.

"Gots ham, redeye gravy an' got raisins in it. Got yams an' white taters an' I got pie an' cake."

"Yo' sho' is fo'given," Fitz said. "Yo' got biscuits too?"

"Yas, suh, massa, suh. Got more'n yo' kin eat."

"Reckon yo' sees to that. How 'bout him?" Fitz gestured toward his son.

Elegant scowled. "He ain't no mo'n a chile, suh. Whut's he know 'bout good eatin'?"

Jonathan jumped up, seized her fat arm and pushed her through the doorway. "I'll show yo' whut I knows 'bout eatin'." She whooped with joy as he followed her.

Fitz drained his glass. Calcutta, standing beside his chair, was fast asleep. Fitz raised a foot, planted it against Calcutta's rear, and sent him flying across the porch. Calcutta tripped and fell, but he was up quickly. He scooped up the tray and glasses and fled.

"They's a letter from Melanie on yo' desk," Benay said.

"Now why'nt yo' tell me that befo'?" Fitz quickly made his way to his desk and brought back the letter, which he read with obvious interest and satisfaction.

"She doin' fine," he said. "An' she happy, I reckon. Got fine marks."

"An' no mention o' gentleman friends," Benay commented.

"She sho' ain't like Jonathan. Reckon she mo' like her grandma."

"Yo' mama so straightlaced she couldn't bend over," Benay said. "Don't want my daughter that strict."

"My mama couldn't he'p it," Fitz said. "Comin' from Boston whar she lived with all them high-speakin', devil-fearin' folks, she jes' couldn't he'p it, Benay. I knows. I was brought up like that."

"You can speak like a Bostoner," Benay said. "Heard you. Nevah fo'get the time yo' come to my papa's plantations to buy horses. My cousins, so high-falutin' they figgered anybody who didn't have they boots polished ev'y mo'nin' wasn't fit to be with. Well, yo' told 'em, in that no'thern voice, whut yo' thought of 'em. Reckon that's when I fell in love with yo'."

Fitz grinned at the memory. "Kin speak that way, I likes to. But don't sound natural no mo'. I lives in Virginny an' I speaks like I belongs heah."

"Sure sound funny you talk no'thern," Benay admitted. "Fitz, whut we goin' to do Melanie comes home talkin' no'thern?"

"She was raised heah, Benay. She comes home she talks like us. Whut bothers me, whut we goin' to do with that gal? Whut folks is near ain't one of 'em got a son fitten for her to know."

"She still young," Benay dismissed the problem. "We got plenty o' time."

Calcutta returned with the refreshed drinks and withdrew to the reception hall to be out of Fitz's range. Calcutta was very sleepy by now. He'd drunk the liquor off the tray, finished what had been left in the glasses, and sampled the new drinks. One more round and he'd be staggering.

Fitz finished his drink in two great swallows. "Thinks I bettah go have a look at the hosses, Benay. An' I wants to see fo' myse'f how the tobacco crop is farin'."

"Doin' well. Weather's been good," Benay said. "But I don' know as much 'bout tobacco growin' as you do. So bes' you go see."

Fitz wandered down to the stables. He sent a boy to fetch Hong Kong, and while he waited, he had two horses saddled. When Hong Kong trotted toward him, Fitz swung into the saddle and indicated Hong Kong was to follow him.

They cantered over to the racetrack where half a dozen horses were being worked out. A chestnut mare caught Fitz's eye.

"That one"—he pointed out the animal— "looks promisin'. Whut you think?"

"Mighty fine mare, suh. Got us a black filly do better. Ain't prime yit, but when she is, ain't nuthin' I knows of kin beat her."

"Good," Fitz said. "How many new colts we got?"

"'Bout thutty, suh. All mighty good-lookin'."

"That's fine. Let's go over an' study on the tobacco plants."

"They prime, suh. Eve'thin' jes' fine fo' growin'. Soon we starts toppin', suh."

The tobacco rows were alive with slaves, loosening the earth, trimming the suckers at the base of each plant. The children were assigned to hunt for hornworms and to do the weeding.

Fitz pulled up suddenly. He sat there on the horse, while he studied a young slave at the end of a row of tobacco plants. The slave was leaning on his hoe while he wiped sweat from his glistening and magnificent torso with a piece of cloth. He was a tall youth, splendidly proportioned, with muscles that rippled when he worked. While his skin was a dark brown, his features were more delicate than those of the average slave. His face was narrower, his nose not wide or spread, his lips much thinner, and there was a certain grace about the man, even as he stood there in the hot sun with rivulets of sweat rolling down his body.

"That's him?" Fitz asked.

"Yas, suh," Hong Kong replied cautiously. "That Nina's boy."

"Whut he called?"

"Named him myse'f, suh. Like yo' pappy, I calls him fo' someplace whar ships go. Kinda liked Dundee, suh, so I named him."

Fitz nodded. "Yo' calls him whut yo' likes. He's jes' a no-good bastahd to me."

"Yas, suh." Hong Kong made no issue of it.

"He livin' with yo'?"

"Yas, suh. Sho' do. Like yo' said, we brings him up."

"He ain't treated any better'n any slave?"

"He wuks all day. Treats him like anybody else, suh."

"Looks o' him, yo' woman feeds him too good. I gave him to yo' when he was borned, I said yo' was not to give him an easy life. I want him wukked hard as he kin, jes' short o' killin' him, and I don' want him eatin' too much. Hates that boy, Hong Kong. Hates him so bad I could kill him now, 'cept then he wouldn' suffer no mo'."

"Does whut yo' say, suh," Hong Kong said, without the slightest intention of obeying the order if he could help it.

"He slothin' right now. Yo' rides ovah an' tells him to get usin' that hoe an' he bettah not stop I sees him."

"Yas, suh." Hong Kong spurred his horse and rode over to where the boy stood, now beginning to industriously use his hoe. Hong Kong pulled up.

"Dundee, come over heah," he said.

Dundee dropped the hoe and trotted over to stand beside the horse, looking up at the man he called his father.

"Massa got no call to say this crop not comin' real good, Papa."

"Now yo' listens to me, boy. Massa sees yo' leanin' on yo' hoe agin, he sends yo' to the whuppin' shed sho'."

"I jes' restin' fo' a minute——"

"Nex' time yo' see him 'round heah, yo' gets mighty busy, heah?"

"Sho', Papa. But I ain't slothin'. Yo' knows that."

"Massa, he don' know that. 'Members now, yo' sees him, yo' wukkin' hahd. Bettah yo' sees him fust, yo' gits the hell outen his sight."

Dundee hurried back, picked up the hoe, and went to work at top speed. Fitz, satisfied his edict was carried out, used his quirt unnecessarily hard on the flank of his horse. Hong Kong had to ride hard to catch up with him. They'd not progressed far on their return to the mansion when the overseers' horns began blowing over the fields and the slaves promptly gathered for the return march to their quarters.

"Tomorrow we'll look at that filly yo' tol' me 'bout," Fitz said.

They parted at that point, Fitz to ride home where he would turn his horse over to a slave, Hong Kong to ride directly to the stables and then, on foot, head for his cabin.

His cabin was larger and far better equipped than most. There was a double bed for him and Seawitch, but the small separate room where Dundee slept, had only a layer of straw spread on the floor. Anything better than that would mean great trouble if Fitz happened by.

Seawitch, busy at her cooking pot, looked up with a happy smile as Hong Kong came in.

"Sees yo' ridin' with massa. How he, now he come back?"

"Ornery." Hong Kong hung up his ancient straw hat and moved to the washbasin to clean up. "We rides ovah to the 'bacca farm an' he sees Dundee leanin' on his hoe an' calls it slothin'. He tells me to git the boy wukkin' hard, an' say yo' feeds him too good."

Seawitch straightened up from her work over the stewpot. "Whut he wants? Effen the boy wuks hard, he eats good. Has to. Cain't wuk hard yo' don' eat good."

Hong Kong shrugged. "Tol' the boy to git when he sees massa comin'. Feeds him like always, Seawitch."

"What fo' he hates the boy so much? Jes' 'cause he Nina's sucker, ain't no call to hate him."

"Yo' 'members how it was with massa an' Nina. Nevah did see two people love so much. Didn' make no diff'rence when massa marries mist'ess. She know whut goin' on. But when mist'ess get knocked up an' Nina same time, massa mighty proud he got two suckers comin'. On'y

[62]

when Nina's sucker borned, after they cut him outen her, he black."

"I think that no-count Themba raped her," Seawitch said. "Yo' figger massa killed Themba?"

"Reckon he did, an' Themba had it comin'. No-count nigger who studied on bein' better'n massa. Cain't be done. Not now. Not yit, an' mayhap nevah."

IN THE DAYS THAT FOLLOWED, THE NEW SLAVES were documented and assigned mates and cabins. The bachelors were initiated into the big lodge, which was kept locked during the night to keep them from roaming about.

The tobacco-cutting season was at hand. Dundee was among the cutters, choosing plants whose leaves were quite yellowed, indicating that it was ready for wilting and curing.

Once cut, each stalk had to be hauled to the drying sheds and hung at least a foot away from the next so the air could circulate well and the curing process given the best chance to work.

It was hard labor, even with the cooling breezes of autumn. Dundee didn't mind, however.

For a slave, he was singularly content; hard work was second nature to him.

Once the tobacco was cured, the leaves were stripped from the stalks and carefully and tightly packed into hogsheads. These would eventually be taken to the railroad siding fifteen miles north and be on their way to market.

Dundee was fully aware that he would gain nothing by working harder than other slaves, and to them it didn't matter if a spoiled leaf, or an infested one, got into the hogsheads. Dundee considered that a crime. They were betraying their own labor, the endless backbreaking work, if the results of that work wasn't good.

He looked up to see Fitz and Jonathan riding his way. He quickly stood up and bowed his head as he'd been told to do by his father and mother.

Without a word said, Fitz raised his riding crop and struck him across the face as hard as he could. The quirt cut deeply into the flesh and blood ran down Dundee's cheek.

He didn't raise his arms to ward off another cut with the whip. He didn't move an inch, and his expression showed neither surprise nor pain. He just stood there like a statue.

"Get back to wuk," Fitz said.

Dundee obediently turned away. The whip cut the back of his neck and he stood, his back still toward the two mounted men.

"Turn 'roun'!" Fitz ordered. "Turn 'roun' an' face me, yo' good-for-nothin' black bastahd."

Dundee turned, still expressionless. Jonathan looked on with wonder plain in his expression. Fitz moved his horse closer to the slave and, for a moment, Jonathan thought his father had gone mad and was about to run the man down.

"This kind o' wuk ain't hard 'nuff fo' yo'," Fitz said in angry, clipped tones. "Yo' gets yo' ass down to the stables an' clean 'em. That's all yo' do from now on. Clean the stables. Clean 'em till yo' smell like the stuff yo'll be shovelin'. An' if I see one speck o' dirt or manure, I'll whup yo' myse'f."

Dundee could only stand there, tasting the blood that had run down into the corners of his mouth.

"Answer me, yo' goddamn stupid nigger!" Fitz roared. "Yo got a tongue, ain't you?"

"Massa, suh, I does whut yo' tells me."

"Then git down to the stables. Run all the way. You sloth, you gits whupped. Now git!"

Dundee began running toward the stables, a full half-mile away. Fitz and Jonathan rode not far behind him.

Jonathan said, "Papa, why yo' treat him like that? He wa'n't slothin'. Whut's he done?"

"He got borned, that's whut he done," Fitz said. "Don't ask questions, but I hope he does somethin' that I kin whup the skin off his stinkin' back."

"All right, Papa," Jonathan said. "He sho' must have done somethin'——"

"Shut yo' goddamn mouth!" Fitz shouted. "An' min' yo' own goddamn business."

Jonathan shrugged and fell silent. They followed Dundee to the stables, where an overseer stopped him. Fitz rode up to them.

"This buck shovels manure all day," he said to the overseer. "That's all he does an' I don' want to see one crumb of it about any stall. He sloths, yo' got my permission to whup him. He sloth too much, tell me an I'll do the whuppin' myse'f."

"Yas, suh, Mistah Turner, suh." The overseer gave Dundee a violent push toward the stables and followed that with a hard kick to spur him on.

Dundee entered the stables and looked about. He had no idea of what he was supposed to do, but he automatically picked up a shovel and began cleaning the floor. The stables were almost spotless and there seemed little to do. He opened one of the stalls and wondered if he was supposed to lead the horse into the open and get at the stall itself, which did seem to require some work.

The overseer cuffed him alongside the head. "Yo opens a stall do' once mo' an' I takes the hide off you, boy. Yo' asks me 'fore yo' lets a hoss loose. These heah is thoroughbreds an' wuth twenty times as much as yo' are."

Dundee nodded, but he didn't know what to say. The overseer thrust the shovel at him and then left. Dundee took time, now that he was not observed, to find a pail of water and wash the dried blood from his face. He was bewildered, inclined to think of himself as so stupid he could not fathom what his master wanted of him, or why.

He knew full well that while he could understand many things, he could neither read nor write and he couldn't talk like white folks.

Once he'd mentioned this to Seawitch and for the first time in his life, she'd slapped him hard.

[68]

"Yo' talks like white massa an' he kill yo'. We niggers, an' we slaves, an' we don' talk like them folks. All yo' gots to learn to say is, 'Yas suh,' 'Yas missy, ma'am,' an' then do whut yo're told."

Dundee hadn't made any reply, but still his mother's answers were not of a sensible sort. If he wanted to speak better, what was wrong with that?

Sorely puzzled, he set about learning how to do this new kind of work. Left to himself, he did stop to rub his hand along the muzzle of a mare and had his arm nibbled by the animal. Dundee laughed happily at that, and carried a forkful of hay to dump it in the stall.

He moved on to the next stall. The overseer, passing by, saw him pet the horse. He came hurrying into the stable and if he'd been carrying a whip, he'd have used it. As it was, he used his fist. Dundee staggered back from the force of the blow and looked so completely bewildered that the overseer realized a man could not obey orders he never received, nor do work with which he was entirely unfamiliar.

"Yo touches one o' them thoroughbreds agin, I tells Mistah Turner an' he cut yo' up some. Nevah mind inside the stalls. If I wants 'em clean, I says so." He peered about the stable. "Yo' got the flo' clean anyway. Now yo' git yo' black ass up that ladder an' clean the loft. Ain't been cleaned in twenty yeahs, I reckon. Go on, move yo' ass or I moves it with a kick."

Dundee climbed the ladder and found himself in a spacious loft. A little light entered from a window encrusted with grime; he could see fairly well. This was no place to tackle with a hoe or a shovel and he again didn't know what to do. He decided that he must sort out everything up here, keep what seemed useful and throw away the rest, or leave it for the overseer to dispose of.

What Dundee did not know, and never would, was that this was where he had been conceived. His father, Themba, had been good at handling thoroughbreds, especially in preparing them for racing.

Dundee began cleaning the debris left by Themba. There were some old clothes, so tattered as to be unusable. Not much else. But when he had everything gathered and ready for possible burning, he noticed a loose board in a wall where it met the flooring. He pried it open and withdrew several newspapers, so old they threatened to crumble into dust. Puzzled and curious, he continued to search this hiding place and before long he had removed three bound books and several notebooks containing practice scrawls in Themba's hand. The books were primers.

Dundee sat cross-legged in the loft, scanning the books, turning pages he did not understand. He recognized the ABCs, and understood that here, in his hands, was the means of learning.

Reverently, he closed the books and tried to decide what to do with them. They certainly must not be destroyed. He tucked them back into their hiding place. He spread one of the crumbling newspapers out to peer at line drawings of men with black faces being hanged from a tree branch.

This frightened him, but did not deter him. He considered asking Hong Kong about the books, but decided that would be the wrong thing to do. His father and mother were manumitted, free people, but his father still adhered to the laws governing the conduct of slaves. If Dundee told him about the books, no doubt he'd be ordered to destroy them at once.

Sitting there alone, in a quiet broken only by the restless movements of the horses below him, he had a strange feeling that these books were going to change his life. He carefully folded the newspapers and put them back in the compartment behind the wall. Whenever he could find the time, he would climb up here and try to learn how to discover the meaning of those tantalizing words. How to say them, form them, and read them.

He found a great, quiet satisfaction in that.

He descended to the stable and decided there was nothing more to be done; it was impossible to clean an already spotless place. He stepped out into the afternoon sunlight and heaved a great sigh. If all he had to do was keep this one stable clean, his life was going to be uncomplicated and easy. Now he stood looking down at a row of stables.

He'd never been allowed to visit this section of the plantation, and he marveled at all these buildings just to house horses. In the adjoining fields more horses were grazing contentedly.

There was also a fenced-in oval, a racetrack, though Dundee wasn't certain just what it could be. Lining the fence were the two overseers in charge of this part of the plantation, a few specially privileged slaves, and a woman he'd never seen before. A white woman, beautifully dressed.

Remembering the warning to work hard, Dundee looked about for someone who could give him further orders. Recognizing the overseer who had already given him orders, he began walking toward him.

At that moment a horse and rider were circling the track wildly. The horse veered sharply, so unexpectedly and at such great speed that the rider was first whipped to the left and then, as the animal reversed itself, was thrown out of the saddle into the middle of the track.

The rider scrambled to his feet and ran for the fence. Dundee, watching the riderless horse plunging madly and in great danger of injuring itself, ran to the fence, vaulted it, and raced out onto the track. When the wild horse plunged by, he leaped, grasped at the bridle, and dug his heels into the dirt track as he tried to slow the animal down.

The horse tore free and took off again. Dundee watched him, standing in the middle of the track as if he intended to meet the animal head on as it finished circling the oval again.

At the rail, everyone watched him and held their breaths. The overseers were too fascinated to order Dundee back. Jonathan, who had been thrown by the horse, moved quickly over beside his mother.

"That slave mus' be crazy!" he exclaimed.

"Don't be too sure o' that," Benay said. "His papa was one o' the best handlers I evah saw. Knew how to talk to hosses, he did, an' they listened."

The horse slowed somewhat as it came around the track and saw him standing there, blocking its way. The animal lowered its head, snorted loudly and picked up a little speed, though it was running far slower than the first time Dundee had made a pass at it.

Dundee leaped aside just in time, but not so far he couldn't fasten a grip on the bridle once more. This time he allowed himself to be dragged along the track, despite the pain in his feet.

Tiring, the horse came to a stop, but still raging and trying to break the grip. Dundee was talking softly, talking only sounds that made no sense, but his voice was soft, coaxing. He slowly passed his free hand along the horse's neck, down its magnificent head. The horse's flanks still quivered with fear and excitement, but gradually the rippling ceased and it grew calm. Dundee kept on talking, stroking the animal, beginning to apply a little pressure so that the horse began obediently walking beside him. By the time they reached the gate, the horse was quiet and accepted an overseer's control as Dundee gave it up. Dundee lowered his head, for he was in the presence of the white masters. He began walking toward the stables.

"Hold on, boy!" a voice commanded.

Dundee stopped. He turned to see the younger of the two men who had gotten him into this trouble and this new assignment of duties.

Dundee kept his head down, folded his hands before him and never looked up.

"Whar yo' learn to handle a hoss like that?" Jonathan asked.

"Don' know, massa, suh. Don' rightly know."

"Yo jes' run out theah an' stopped the hoss?"

"Reckon, massa, suh."

"Yo' prob'ly saved that valuable hoss from bein' hurt bad."

"Don' know, massa, suh."

"Yo' knows who I am, boy?"

"No, suh, don' know nuthin'."

"My father owns this plantation and he owns yo'."

That explained why the two men had looked so much alike. Dundee wouldn't comment on that.

"Yas, suh, he owns me, he does."

"Do yo' like hosses?"

"Cain't say, massa, suh. Nevah been neah a hoss befo'."

"I can't believe that. Yo' did exactly whut yo' was supposed to do."

"Yas, suh, massa, suh."

"Yo' wuk 'roun' the stables, heah? Havin' yo' wuk 'roun' the hosses. Yo baits 'em an' yo' waters 'em. Yo walks 'em an' maybe yo' rides 'em after a while. That's all yo' do, wuk 'roun' the stables. Yo' don't shovel manure. Now git about yo' business."

"Yas, massa, suh, I goes."

He walked away, never having once raised his head to look this young white man in the eye. A slave does not look up at any white. That had been drilled into him.

"Hold on," Jonathan called again, and Dundee came to an instant stop. Jonathan approached him.

"I goin' to ask yo' somethin' an' yo' gives me a true answer. Understand?"

"Yas, suh, massa, if I kin."

"Why did my papa hit yo' with his quirt?"

"Don' know, suh."

"He jes' hit yo fo' no reason?"

"Yas, suh, massa, suh. I done nuthin'."

"Get busy," Jonathan ordered.

Dundee walked away, wondering what kind of strange men these were. Shrugging, he thought instead about stopping the horse. It did seem strange to him that he hadn't been afraid. Lots of things frightened Dundee, his fear of the lash was so great he winced when he thought of it.

Benay had already left the track, so Jonathan mounted a calmer horse and rode back to the mansion. There he discovered Fitz in the library, at work on the plantation books.

"Sit down," Fitz said. "We got us'n a fat price fo' that last batch o' yearlings we sent No'th. Bes' price we evah got."

"Papa, yo' 'members that slave yo' hit with yo' quirt?"

Fitz looked up quickly. "Why yo' ask, son?"

"I was tryin' to tame that two-year-old chestnut we got so much trouble with. She threw me an' I think she was achin' to tromp me to death. That slave jumped the fence an' stopped the hoss. I got the hell out'en theah. I wouldn't have tried to stop that spooked hoss. Like to git killed I tried that. Then that slave jes' walk up to the hoss an' tame her by talkin'. Jes' talkin'. Nevah did see anybody handle a hoss like he did, Papa."

"I knows all 'bout that. Yo' mama was there an' she saw it."

"Whut's that boy's name? You knows?"

"Name Dundee."

"Why yo' hates him so, Papa?"

"None o' yore goddamn business. Tol' yo' that befo'."

"Reckon yo' did. Tol' him he wuk with hosses now. Sho' gots a way with 'em."

Fitz glared at his son. "Times yo' think yo' own this heah plantation and I wuks for yo'. Wants that slave crawlin' in the dirt. Wants him wukkin' so hard he ain't got nuthin' lef'. Wants no wench to git near him. Wants him starvin'."

"I asked yo' befo', why? You hates him that much, they has to be a reason."

"You git down theah now and tell him to get to cleanin' the stables. All of 'em. Don' want him messin' with my hosses."

"Papa, he kin save that chestnut whut threw me. You say yo'se'f maybe the hoss ought to be shot, but it's one o' the best hosses we got. Wuth too much to throw away. That slave kin handle her."

Fitz was thinking back to Themba, the boy's father. But it was true, that chestnut was an extremely valuable animal. So far, no one had succeeded in fully breaking her. If Dundee could do that . . .

"Tells yo' whut," Fitz said. "He busts that hoss, yo' tells him whut to do. He don' an' I send him to shovelin' manure. He got two weeks."

Jonathan happily agreed. "I'll let him be. Let him do it in his own way. Like yo' said, Papa, he don' git it done, he goes back to the stable."

"I tells Hong Kong 'bout it," Fitz said matter-of-factly.

"Why Hong Kong?" Jonathan asked, and Fitz knew he had said more than he intended.

"Hong Kong his papa, that's why."

"Papa, Hong Kong got no balls. Mos' ev'y-body know that. How he Hong Kong's son?"

"Don' know. Maybe Seawitch's son. Them slaves sleepin' 'roun' makin' suckers. How I know who his papa is? Don' ask so many goddamn questions."

Jonathan nodded and arose. "Beholden, Papa, fo' lettin' me have that boy. What's he name?"

"Dundee. Don' yo' give him any freedom. Hates him. Maybe I kills him some day. You lets him git frisky, I whup him good."

"Sho', Papa, I see he wuks more'n the rest of 'em. Long he wuks 'roun' the hosses."

Jonathan left the library and made his way upstairs to his mother's private room. It was a strange room. Jonathan's grandfather had brought his wife to the plantation in 1820. She'd been born and raised in Boston. Coming to a primitive country like this, to an enormous house furnished at the whim of a man who knew little about decorating, she felt like an alien in a strange land. So Captain Jonathan Turner had imported a room from Boston. Anyone who stepped into it would surely believe he was in New England.

Benay had come to like it, because the room was somewhat isolated, quiet and rather dark. She liked to come and sit here and think. It was wonderful to be alone sometimes. And even at midday, the room seemed pleasantly cool. Jonathan knocked on the door and Benay, startled that anyone would come here, called for him to enter.

"Sit down, Jonathan," she invited him. "It's nice of yo' to come callin'."

"Got somethin' settin' on my mind an' it don' set right, Mama. Yo' saw whut happened at the track."

"I was theah. I saw it. That hoss too crazy to live, yo' asks me."

"That mare's wuth plenty money, Mama. I sure wasn't handlin' her right, but that slave, he know how. Yo' 'member seein' him?"

Benay nodded. "Scared me near to death seein' yo' fall and the hoss trampin' 'roun'."

"The slave is named Dundee an' he lives with Hong Kong an' Seawitch, them two manumitted slaves. Ev'ybody thinks Hong Kong his papa, but I knows Hong Kong ain't got no balls an' he ain't nobody's papa. Whut's it all 'bout? Papa sho' don' like to talk 'bout it. Gits mad ev'y time I mention that slave."

Benay, who'd been idly sewing, laid aside the basket and the material. "Heah's whut happened, son. The night yo' was born, so was Dundee. His mama was a slave named Nina. Some say her papa was an Ayrab prince or king. I don't know whut, but Nina was light-skinned, a very pretty gal an' she smart. Yo' papa loved her, took her as his wench. He treated her fine an' she loved him back 'bout as much as a slave gal could, reckon. Nina was knocked up same time as me. Yo' papa he got struttin' 'roun', sayin' he was havin' two suckers an' he was proud o' both. But Nina's sucker was black, as yo' can see. Nina, she died. She buried out yonder 'side Captain Turner an' his wife."

"But whut he hate Dundee fo', Mama? Hate Nina, I kin see that, but why Dundee?"

"His papa was a slave name of Themba. Big, strong man who could train racin' hosses. Bes' in the world, reckon. Yo' papa killed him fo' whut he done to Nina."

"He rapes her?" Jonathan wanted to know.

"Cain't say. Nobody knows. Nina, she never say anythin'. But from the night Dundee was bo'n, yo' papa hated him. Sometimes I get the idea he goin' to kill the po' boy. It ain't right. I knows it. Yo' papa knows it too, way down deep. But he cain't he'p the way he feels. Like he gots to take it out on somebody and the on'y one lef' is the boy."

"Sounds crazy to me, Mama, hatin' a chile who nevah had anythin' to do 'cept get borned."

"That's how it is, son. Ain't no way yo' kin change yo' papa."

"I'm goin' to turn the boy loose on the hosses, Mama. Gots to see whut he kin do. Mayhap he like his papa, an' kin make 'em do whut he wants."

"Don' go too far with Dundee," Benay warned. "Yo papa stands fo' so much an' then he riles hisse'f, an' he sure ain't nice to be 'roun'."

"I'll be keerful," Jonathan promised. "Goin' down to the stables an' see how that boy gettin' on."

"Jonathan, don' tell the boy Hong Kong ain't his papa."

"Won't," Jonathan agreed. "Don' want nuthin' achin' him. Papa say pretty soon he goes back to cleanin' stables."

Jonathan left the mansion in time to see a strange vehicle being dragged behind two big horses. It was like a small house mounted on the wagon, but its sides were open and heavily barred. He was about to stop the man driving it when Fitz came rushing out. He excitedly signaled the driver to halt and then Fitz walked around the structure and nodded in full approval.

"Whut in hell that thing?" Jonathan asked.

"It's a cage for lockin' up niggers who goin' to git whupped in the mornin'. Saw one in Lynchburg an' had one made up fo' me. Cain't be gettin' up all hours to do the whuppin'—got mo' impohtant things to do. We lock 'em in this cage till I gets ready."

"Papa," Jonathan asked, "you 'spectin' trouble on Wyndward?"

"Whut makes yo' think that fool way? I don't 'spect any trouble. This ain't bought 'cause I think there be trouble. But o' co'se it'd come in mighty handy they was. Boy! You—" he pointed at Calcutta, who was standing at the foot of the veranda observing the prison on wheels as if it had been made particularly for him.

"Yas, suh," he shouted. "I comin', massa, suh."

"Calcutta," Fitz said, "you been slothin' so long, you ain't much good no mo'. Reckon bein' so goddamn lazy yo' gots to be locked up maybe fo' a yeah or so. Yo' opens that do' in the cage an' yo' gets in."

Calcutta's teeth chattered. "Massa. I ain't slothin'. I wuks ha'd, I does. I wuks harder, I do. Don' put me in that thing, massa, suh."

"Get in theah," Jonathan said angrily. "Move yo' ass, Calcutta. Yo the mos' slothful boy we got an' you needs to be shown the error of yo' ways. Git in that cage."

Calcutta trotted over to it and pulled open the door, but stood there, not having the will to get in.

Jonathan walked up behind him, secured a

grip on the back of his neck and the seat of his pants, lifted him, and threw him inside. He closed the iron-barred door and fastened the padlock. Then he stepped back and howled with laughter.

"Papa, that sho' is somethin'. Whut'll we do with him now?"

"Let him stay theah fo' the night," Fitz declared. "Needs to be took down a few pegs. Sleeps mos' times an' he got no time fo' wuk. An' he a drunk, 'sides."

They left the cage where it stood, so all the slaves could see it. With Calcutta a prisoner, the slaves would quickly get the idea what it was for.

Fitz and Jonathan walked toward the house, moans from Calcutta following their every step. Fitz was laughing and enjoying it. Jonathan glanced at him.

"You don' think niggers is folks, do you, Papa?"

"They's animals, son. That's all they is—animals whut kin talk. Ain't that whut yo' thinks?"

"I ain't sho', Papa. Reckon yo' is right."

"It's whut yo' grandpapa thought. He treated the slaves proper, fed 'em good, didn' use the whips less'n it was needed, but then he used it till the bucks an' the wenches yelled their haids off."

"Too bad he burn with his ship," Jonathan said. "Wouldn' mind sailin' to Africa to bring back a cargo o' niggers."

"That ain't been legal fo' yeahs," Fitz said. "Good thing, too. Gettin' mo' niggers in Virginny than we got white folks. Reminds me, hear tell yo' mama goin' to have a big soiry pretty soon. Las' one befo' the wintah, reckon."

"Ain't said nuthin' to me 'bout it."

Fitz smiled. "Way she is. Knows I hates all them folks millin' 'bout, eatin' all that food an' drinkin' my whiskey an' rum. So she don't say anythin' till after the folks gets invited an' no way I kin stop it. I don' get mad. Yo' mama, she a wonderful woman. Bes' in the whole world. Jes' makes her think I mad. Then she don' say nuthin', I gets a little too much rum an' mayhap pinches a nice ass heah an' theah." Fitz paused, frowning suddenly. "Whut you aimin' to do 'bout that gal on the Fisbee place? One you knocked up."

"Nuthin', Papa. She got no call to come to me. She tuk me, I didn't take her. 'Sides, she jes' a fat slob."

"I don' know, son. Mayhap she make trouble fo' you someday."

"Worry 'bout that when it happens. Mayhap her sucker ain't mine. Way she acted, she been fuckin' fo' heahs, anythin' she gets on top o' her."

"We'll give her as much trouble as she tries to give us," Fitz said. "Listen to Calcutta howl! Got him so skeered, reckon nex' time he runs fo' drinks, he runs real fas'."

"Gettin' on, Papa," Jonathan reminded him. "We goin' to need drinks 'fore long. Got nobody else knows how to mix whiskey an' watah. I bes' let him out."

"Didn't think o' that. Let him out so's he stops shakin'. Way he is now, he couldn't carry a glass half full of watah."

Jonathan went back to the cage. He had the padlock key in his pocket. From various vantage

[82]

points, slaves were standing about looking at the spectacle of a slave in a cage. They didn't know exactly what it meant, though many of them could guess. After having been locked in a slave jail before going on the vendue table, they knew what bars signified.

Jonathan unlocked the door, swung it open. Calcutta, huddled in a far corner, began to whimper.

"Git yo' black ass outen theah," Jonathan ordered crisply.

Calcutta crawled out, his eyes wide in terror, rolling slightly as they watched the cage door for fear it would slam shut on him. He finally tumbled to the ground.

"Now git on the wagon seat an' drive this contraption down to near the whuppin' shed," Jonathan commanded.

Calcutta backed away. "No, suh. No, suh, I ain't goin' neah that thing. I skeered o' it, I is."

Jonathan pointed at the wagon seat. "Git it down theah or yo' goes with it, locked inside, an' yo' don' git out fo' a week. Git!"

Calcutta advanced timidly, then suddenly he sprang, grasped the side of the wagon, and scrambled onto the seat. He picked up the reins, slapped the horses, and howled at them. As the wagon began to move, he looked over his shoulder at the cage directly behind him and shuddered violently.

Jonathan walked down behind the wagon. When Calcutta brought it to a stop, he got down as fast as he could move.

"You sho' don't sloth 'roun' this thing," Jonathan commented. "Sees you don' sloth bringin' drinks. Mastah waitin' fo' yo, to fetch rum an' watah. Run, yo' black imp, or I cages yo' agin."

Calcutta moved like greased lightning. Jonathan signaled to Dundee, who had watched the proceedings. Dundee came running.

Jonathan said, "Gots to git this thing offen the wagon, Dundee. Yo fetches all the boys yo' needs an' set it down nex' to the whuppin' shed."

"Yas, suh, massa, suh." Dundee sprinted away, calling to slaves who were on their way back from the fields. At Dundee's orders, they put their shoulders to the task, hauled the cage down, and dragged it over to rest beside the small shed where the whipping was done. The work finished, Dundee dismissed the men with the same authority an overseer would have used. Jonathan began to see signs of leadership in this remarkable slave.

"Come heah," Jonathan ordered. Dundee quickly ran to stand with bowed head before him.

"Talked to Mastah Turner, Dundee, an' he say yo' kin keer fo' the hosses an' he'p train 'em long as yo' don't sloth. Yo' gots to wuk hard, 'specially when he 'roun'. He say yo' got two weeks an' by then yo' bettah show him whut yo' kin do."

"Yas, suh, massa." Dundee dared raise his head. "Thanks yo' I do. Wuk ha'd and yo' goin' to be proud o' me, massa, suh. Loves hosses, I do. Been pettin' that brown hoss gives yo' trouble. Gits her real gentle. Kin I ride her, massa, suh?"

"Think you kin do it, Dundee?"

"Knows it, suh. On'y way to gentle her so's yo' kin ride her 'thout gittin' throwed."

"All right. Yo' kin wuk that hoss eve'y day. I comes down to see how yo' doin' an' it bettah be bettah'n good, yo' heah me?"

"Heahs yo' massa, suh. Thanks yo' agin, I does."

"Get busy," Jonathan said.

He walked slowly back to the mansion to be in time for the late afternoon drinks on the veranda.

[5]

THE COFFLE PURCHASED AT THE FISBEE PLANTA-
tion had been secluded from the other slaves
in an old tobacco-curing shed. Fitz knew he had
got no bargain in these slaves. They'd been badly
treated, worked far too hard, not fed enough, and
locked up too long. The bachelors especially were
a rebellious lot.

Perhaps they'd be more amenable if they
were well rested and well fed before Hong Kong
set them to work in the fields, Fitz thought. The
females had given no trouble and had easily inte-
grated with the other female slaves. Some had
already chosen a mate to live with in one of the
cabins. The children had been turned over to
Seawitch to feed and build up.

It was early winter now and most of the

slaves were at work in the curing sheds. The artisans, carpenters, bricklayers, and blacksmiths were hard at work, getting things prepared for spring. No one loafed. The overseers and the drivers were too handy with their whips for the slaves to rest too much.

Hong Kong had been hearing hints that the Fisbee slaves were in a mood to rebel. Kinder treatment at Wyndward was not sufficient to overcome the hatred they had acquired from the harsh treatment at the Fisbee place.

"Don' like it none, suh," he told Fitz. "They ain't 'xactly bustin' things, but they's talkin' all the time an' they keeps they eyes out fer me or the overseers. Gots me idee they fixin' to maybe run."

"They been talkin' runnin' to any o' the ol' slaves?"

"Not yit, suh, I knows of. Thinks they's skeered to do that. Mos' wouldn't listen to 'em anyways."

"Do whut yo' kin 'bout 'em," Fitz said. "If they needs whuppin', we whup 'em."

"Yas suh. I see whut I kin do."

Later that day Hong Kong drifted down to the quarters where the Fisbee coffle were beginning to grow fat from good food and idleness. They knew that would come to an end soon and they were in a mood to listen to the talk of Toby and Isaac, the leaders of the group.

Hong Kong walked into the long shed and shouted for the men to assemble. When they were gathered about him, he told them they were now in prime condition to go to work. Tomorrow those who wanted a woman would be assigned cabins. Others would go into the regular bachelor barracks, and they would be ready for work when the overseer's horn blew at dawn.

"We's sick," Isaac said, with a broad grin aimed in the direction of the others gathered about.

"Yo' puts us to wuk," Toby added, "an' we drops. Ain't ready yit—yo' tells massa so."

Hong Kong studied the pair intently. Others would follow their lead unless this was broken up quickly.

"Yo' heahs whut I say. Any man not ready to wuk tomorruh gits whupped. Gits it laid on heavy. Thutty lashes anyways."

"Who gits to do the whuppin'?" Isaac asked with that same independent attitude.

"I is the driver," Hong Kong said. "I do the whuppin' an' I lays it on."

"Yo' whups me an' I kills yo'," Toby threatened.

Hong Kong approached the man and suddenly lashed out with his fist, hitting him squarely in the face. Blood spurted from the slave's nose. With a shout of rage he hurled himself at Hong Kong. He was met with another blow that sent him hurtling backward into the arms of his coworker Isaac. In Isaac's grip, Toby failed to break away. Hong Kong wasn't certain whether that was due to Isaac's strength or Toby's cowardice.

"Yo' wants mo'," Hong Kong said, "I kin see yo' gits it. Won't repoht yo' fer whuppin' this time, but after this, yo' gits it good. Be ready at sunup."

He walked out, trembling a little, thinking he was getting a little too old for this. He knew by instinct that the pair were very dangerous, and could well disrupt the entire plantation if they weren't stopped.

When he reached his cabin, Seawitch was serving up a large bowl of stew for Dundee, who hadn't stopped talking about his work with the horses since he came home.

Hong Kong sat down and toyed with the stew, and Seawitch knew something was wrong.

"It's those bastahds from Fisbee's," Hong Kong explained. "Two of 'em real bad ones. Talkin' up runnin'—even rebellion. Trouble is, them boys been treated so bad befo', they listens too good. Don' wants to go to Massa Fitz. Not yit. He say whup 'em an' I skeered they makes mo' trouble."

"Knows the two yo' talkin' 'bout, Papa," Dundee said. "They's real mean. Thinks yo' tell massa an' he sees they don' make no trouble."

"Son," Hong Kong said, "it ain't easy bein' manumitted an' bossin' all them slaves. They's near sixteen hundred now, an' they gits randy no tellin' whut's goin' to happen."

"Mayhap they listens good to the preachin' Sunday," Seawitch offered. "Ain't seen none o' them at the meetin'. Thinks yo' tells 'em to go nex' Sunday an' sees they listens good. Mistah Whitehead, he a mighty pow'ful preachin' man. Skeers me some, he do, talkin' 'bout goin' to hell an' such."

Hong Kong nodded and began to eat. "That's a good idee, Seawitch. 'Bliged yo' thinks of it. Whut yo' think, Dundee?"

"They's goin' tuh be trouble, yo' don't do somethin', Papa. They runs, an' comes fo' to steal hosses, an' I kills 'em, I does."

"Stop talkin' that way," Seawitch ordered brusquely. "They's 'nuff killin' been done heah."

"Whut yo' talkin' 'bout, Mama? Ain't no killin' heah I knows of."

"Befo' yo' was bohn, Dundee. They was killin' then."

"Things diff'rent them days. Twenny yeahs ago," Dundee said.

"Not much diff'rent," Hong Kong said. "On'y mo' slaves heah."

He finished his meal, but he was still restless and worried. "Takin' a walk," he told Seawitch. "Ain't goin' to be long."

He left the cabin and made his way the half-mile to the curing sheds. He could see the lights of cooking fires and that provided some sense of relief. They'd not be cooking if they intended to escape.

He had no intention of going into the shed and facing them. All he wanted was to be certain there were no plans for running or rebellion. He circled the shed once, saw no signs of anyone, and turned his steps toward home.

The pair came out of the tall grass so quickly that Hong Kong didn't have time to raise a hand. He was struck with a club that sent him to his knees.

One of them kicked him in the midriff. Hong Kong tried to get up. On his feet, he would whip this pair. But they gave him no chance. They beat at him from head to foot until he was a mass of blood, almost unrecognizable.

"Now," Isaac said with considerable relish, "we kills yo'."

He was raising the club for one more blow when they heard someone moving about in the dark. A figure materialized out of the gloom.

"Whut in hell's goin' on?" he called out. It was a white man's voice. The pair fled, dropping the club in their haste. It was an overseer who had happened by. He had a good look at the fleeing pair, but then all of his attention was directed at the half-dead man on the ground. He made a quick examination to be sure he wasn't dead and then went racing to the shed, threw open the door, and ordered two men to rip the door off its hinges and bring it at once as a stretcher.

He saw the guilty pair trying to merge with the others, still panting from running from him. He made no attempt to accuse them. The slaves all about him were surly and set to make trouble. He backed out of the shed and directed the two men as they ripped the door from its hinges.

Seawitch screamed when Hong Kong was brought in. Dundee knelt beside the man he called his father, loosening the blood-drenched garments. Seawitch fetched water and rags. She cleaned his face gently. Hong Kong was beginning to regain consciousness. He muttered something. Dundee paid no attention. He got his father's shoes off, untied the rope around his middle, and pulled down his trousers. He reached for a water-soaked rag, but his hand remained poised in the air. Then Dundee caught himself and went back to work, cleaning the man he had always loved as his father. He was still working on him when Fitz and Jonathan walked into the cabin. Hong Kong was conscious by then.

"Whut bastahds did this?" Fitz asked. "Tell me, Hong Kong!"

"Ain't nuthin' I cain't take keer o' myse'f, suh. Bettah yo' stays outa it, suh."

"Stay out of it, hell! Who did this?"

The overseer, who had also entered, nudged Fitz. "Knows who did, it Mistah Turner. Saw 'em runnin' an' when I gets to the shed where all them Fisbee niggers are kept, saw 'em agin, pantin' like they runs mighty fas'."

"All right, come with us. Wants you to pick 'em out. Hong Kong, wants you to look at 'em when you feels good 'nuff, an' you tells me they's the ones."

"Yas suh," Hong Kong said wearily. "I'se all right, suh."

"Reckon," Fitz said. "You always was one o' the toughest men I evah knowed. Whut you doin' by the shed this time o' night?"

"Lookin' an' listenin', suh. Feared they was goin' to run tonight. Reckon they saw me comin' an' they was waitin' fer me."

"You gets ten extra silvah dollahs fo' this, Hong Kong. You was tendin' my business an' you mos' got killed doin' it. Seawitch, you takes mighty good keer o' him."

Not once did Fitz look at Dundee, who had withdrawn to a corner of the cabin. But Dundee glanced up at Jonathan and saw the young master's face crinkled in a look of intense rage. Dundee was glad he wasn't be in the shoes of the pair who had nearly killed Hong Kong.

When the whites cleared out, Seawitch closed the door and went back to tending her husband. Hong Kong had closed his eyes, seeking sleep to escape the wracking pain that afflicted every inch of his body.

Dundee arose, dumped out the contents of the washbasin, added more water, and rinsed the cloths, which he took outside to hang up and dry on a tree limb. Seawitch followed him.

"Wants to talk to yo', Dundee. Yo' gots to listen."

"Listenin', Mama. Knows what yo' goin' to tell me. Hong Kong cain't be my papa. Always wondered why he nevah shucked down front o' me. Sees why now. He ain't my papa. Is yo' my mama?"

"No, son. Massa Fitz, he gives yo' to us to raise."

"Wants to know who I am. Please."

"Yo' mama name Nina. Nevah was a bettah gal on this heah plantation. She light—say her papa was some kind o' king. Not in Africa. Othuh place. Knows nuthin' 'bout that 'cep' she no plain nigger."

"Whar she now?" Dundee asked.

"She daid. She dies when yo' was borned. Night like that I nevah wants to see agin. Young massa bo'n that night too. Yo' an' him both bo'n and massa kill yo' papa. Not Hong Kong. Yo' papa name of Themba. Wukked like yo' is now, in the stables with the horses. Massa kills him."

"He rapes my real mama?"

"Reckon."

"Whut makes masssa so mad at me?"

"Massa, he loves yo' mama like she his woman. When she borned yo', an' yo' a nigger, massa gits so mad I thinks he kills all us niggers."

"Whar my mama now?"

"Tol' yo', son, she daid."

"Knows that. Finds her in the cemetery, I does."

"Son, she in white cemetery. She lay 'side ol' massa and' mist'ess. She buried like she they chile. Mastah Fitz, he buried there someday an' he lay 'tween Nina an' mist'ess after she die too. Massa he loved them both, an' he say he goin' to lie 'tween 'em fo' sho'."

Dundee hugged her, keeping his face away from her so she wouldn't see the tears.

"Yo' mad at us, Dundee? We yo' mama an' papa fo'evah, yo' lets us be."

"Loves yo', Mama, an' Papa too. Cain't love my real mama 'cause I nevah sees her. Glad my real papa, he daid. Glad massa kills him, I am. He live I kills him myse'lf. Wants to walk some."

"Yo' cain't, son. No slave gits to stay outen his cabin at night."

"Goes anyway, Mama. They's all down by the curin' sheds. I hides I sees 'em. Gots to walk. Cain't he'p it. Gots to walk."

"Don' go far, Dundee," Seawitch warned. "Dont git in no trouble. They's 'nuff o' that now."

Dundee wandered into the night. His brain was whirling, his emotions in a state of confusion he could not cope with. All he wanted to do was walk and walk. It made no difference if he was caught and punished. He was unable to be still.

Fitz, Jonathan, and the overseer had stopped by the mansion, where Fitz handed Jonathan a rifle, gave another to the overseer, and strapped on a revolver himself.

"Near killed Hong Kong," Fitz told Benay. "Two bastahds from that Fisbee coffle. Goin' to whup 'em good in the mornin'. Now we takes 'em out an' cages 'em. Nevah thought I'd use that cage so quick."

"Be keerful," Benay begged.

"Ain't no need to be keerful," Fitz said. "They makes trouble, we shoots 'em. Hong Kong said they gon' to kill him. They gits whut's comin' to 'em."

The trio walked the long distance to the curing sheds. They moved up to the one housing the Fisbee coffle, so quietly that when they stormed through the empty doorway, they surprised Isaac and Toby hiding bundles they'd prepared for running.

"Stir up the fires," Fitz ordered. "Git some kindlin' on the ashes. Wants to see whut's goin' on heah."

The fires sent a reddish glow through the shed. Most of the slaves had drawn back as far from the whites as they dared. Isaac and Toby stayed where they were, trying to hide their bundles under their beds of straw.

Jonathan kicked at the mound under the straw, exposing the bundles. He faced the pair.

"Yo' was aimin' to run an' that's a hangin' offense. Yo' runs, or yo' don' run, gettin' ready to, same as runnin'. Ain't that right, Papa?"

"Sho is." He glanced at the overseer. "Fetch the spancels an' neck irons."

"Whut we goin' to git whupped fo', massa

suh?" Toby asked. "We don' run. No suh. We swears it."

"Bettah yo' did run an' got caught," Fitz said. "Hong Kong dies, yo' get hung by the balls an' whupped 'till nothin' lef' on yo' bones. He don' die, yo' gits hung reg'lar like. Shuck down!"

"Massa, suh," Toby cried out in terror. "Don' whup me. Please, massa, suh. Wasn' goin' tuh run."

"Yo' gets whupped an' no goddamn diff'rence you ready to run or not. Yo' gets whupped 'cause you near killed a fine man. Yo' tries to whup him one at a time an' he whales yo hides off with one han'. Hates cowards. Hates 'em bad, an' you both cowards. Shuck down or I'll do it with a knife."

They quickly shed their clothes and stood shivering in the cold night air. The overseer returned with the iron chains and neck rings, which they'd left outside the shed. He applied them deftly, and the two naked bucks were now incapable of harming anyone. Fitz shoved one of them ahead of him, Jonathan kicked the other into moving. They were marched down to where the cage was located beside the whipping shed. Fitz kicked open the door and herded the pair inside.

Fitz picked up a stout stick. "Kneel down," he said angrily. "Kneel, yo' black bastahds, or I'll use the snake on yo' right now."

The long, plaited whip hung from a nail. Beside it was a wide, thick cowhide whip. The cowhide whip was preferred by the slaves, for it didn't cut the skin. With the plaited whip, a body could be almost stripped of flesh.

The pair knelt, and Fitz kicked Toby. "Raise yo'se'f so yo' squattin'," he ordered. "Raise up!"

Toby obeyed, terrified, wondering what Fitz was about to do. Fitz ran the stick behind Toby's knees and in front of his elbows, until his knees were up against his chin, then secured a rope and tied Toby's handcuffed wrists in front of him. Squatted there, Toby was unable to move except to the left or right; if he did, he would promptly fall over and be unable to get up.

When Isaac was similarly trussed, Fitz kicked Toby over on his side, grasped one leg, and pulled him out into the night. Jonathan hauled out Isaac in the same way. The overseer opened the cage door at Fitz's order, picked up the two slaves, and flung them into the cage. The door was slammed shut and the padlock hasp closed.

Fitz gave orders to the overseer. "Yo' stands heah all night with the rifle. Effen one of 'em gets loose, shoot him."

"They ain't gettin' loose," Jonathan said in grim satisfaction. "Yo' gets 'em in a buck like that an' they stays that way 'till they dies, yo' don' free 'em."

"I watches 'em good," the overseer promised.

Fitz and Jonathan walked through the night in silence. Jonathan ran his fingers through his thick hair and glanced sideways at his father.

"Yo' sees whut Dundee was doin', Papa?"

"I sees."

"Nevah saw a man 'thout balls befo'. That evah happens to me, I hope I daid. But Dundee saw. Couldn' he'p but see. Must know Hong Kong not his papa. Whut yo' think Seawitch done, he asks her?"

"She tells him whut happened," Fitz said. "Nuthin' else to do."

"Feel sorry fo' Dundee. Hopes it don' make no diff'rence he wukkin' with the hosses. Doin' real good he is."

"Knows that. He jes' like Themba. Talks to hosses he does."

"Whut yo' aimin' to do 'bout him now? Yo' hates him so much he sho' cain't come to yo'."

"Whut makes yo' think he come to me?"

"Seawitch tells him his mama love you, tells him you love Nina, he goin' to be real mad or he goin' to like you. Don' know which, Papa, but sho' ain't no call fo' yo' to hate him no mo'. He ain't no ord'nary slave. No plain fool nigger. He smart, an' he know hosses like I nevah knows anybody to know 'em."

"Don' know whut I do now," Fitz admitted. "You go on, son. I'm walkin' some mo'."

"Walk with yo', Papa."

"I said I walks by myse'f. Get the hell home an' don't bother me no mo'. Ain't in no mood to be bothered. Git!"

Jonathan shrugged and turned toward the mansion. He was whistling as he walked. Jonathan had a good idea where his father was going.

Fitz walked slowly, his head bent in thought. The early winter night smelled of hay, sweet, almost sickening. Fitz chuckled to himself, thinking of his father. Jonathan Turner had been afflicted with a strange obsession after he left the sea and his trading in slaves. The stench of the holds seemed to have entered the Captain's nostrils to stay. He was forever complaining about it and thinking of other smells to cover up the stench in his memory.

Fitz thought about Nina too. When Dundee

was taken from Nina by a surgeon's knife and she died without ever seeing her child, Fitz had gone mad. He concentrated his hatred on Dundee because, he knew now, there wasn't anybody else to hate after he'd killed Themba. All through the years his hatred had lasted, always there. Nina's child, who should have been his, should suffer in the place of his father. That was what impelled him. He felt almost ashamed of it now.

He neared the cemetery, where he often went to stand by Nina's grave and remember her. He came to an abrupt stop. Someone was kneeling at the foot of that grave. A man who wept openly, even noisily. Fitz turned around, bent his head, and retraced his steps. Dundee was alone with his mother for the first time. It was not a moment to interrupt. Besides, Dundee was a slave, and no slave must see his master wipe tears from his eyes because he had come upon a black man crying at the grave of his mother.

AT BREAKFAST THE NEXT MORNING FITZ WAS IN A
fine mood. He ate his grits, swimming in redeye
gravy, his usual four eggs, and thick slices of ham
along with Elegant's fine biscuits.

Benay said, "Wants to talk to yo', Fitz."

"Sho'," he agreed good-naturedly. "Soon's I
finish whuppin' them two bastahds."

"I wants to talk to yo' 'bout them, Fitz."

Fitz looked up quickly. He rarely tolerated
any interference with his plans for his slaves. If
punishment was required, there was no bending
his will.

"Whut 'bout them?" he asked suspiciously.

"Wants yo' don' kill 'em, Fitz."

"Sho' I kills 'em. They's no goddamn good an'
all they do is make mo' trouble I don' kill 'em."

"Whup 'em good," Benay insisted, "then gets rid o' them, but ain't no call to kill 'em. Hong Kong ain't daid."

"Near was," Fitz grumbled. He glanced at Jonathan. "Whut yo' thinkin', son?"

Jonathan shrugged. "Same as Mama, reckon. They rates whuppin', but not hangin'."

"I says they hangs," Fitz said harshly.

"Makes trouble, yo' does that," Jonathan warned.

"Trouble? From who? The slaves? Whuppin' first, then hangin' skeers the hell outen 'em. 'Sides, them two sonabitches rate hangin'."

"Yo' could sell 'em," Jonthan suggested. "Ain't no sense killin' stock, they's good o' bad. They's in good condition now, bein' fed an' not put to wuk. Lets the whup marks heal an' we gets a good price, we keeps our mouths shet 'bout why we sells 'em."

"Ain't one to throw 'way good money," Fitz admitted, "but them two gots to swing. Can't do anythin' less."

"I asks yo' agin, Fitz, don' kill 'em," Benay said. "I askin' real nice now. Yo' pay me no heed an' I asks agin, but not in a nice way. Yo' papa, he kills 'em an' that's nuthin' to him. But they's not animals like yo' say. They's people, an' they don' kill nobody so they don' need killin'. Fair's fair."

Fitz dropped his knife and fork noisily on his plate. "Looks like yo' two been schemin'. Ain't no reason fer it. Them two sonabitches was readyin' to run. Got they sacks full an' we don' come las' night, they be gone by this mornin'. Runnin' means hangin'—yo' knows that."

[102]

"Knows it," Benay said. "But, like Jonathan say, why throw away good money?"

Fitz looked from one to the other. "Looks like I eats an' sleeps alone, I don' do whut yo' say, Benay. An' my son mad at me. Thinks it ain't right, I do, but cain't fight both o' yo'. I whups 'em good, but I don' kills 'em."

"Thank yo', Fitz," Benay said.

Fitz finished his coffee and pushed his chair back. "Come 'long, son, an' we gets this business ovah with. Benay, yo' listens good, yo'll heah them hollerin' they haids off, the whup smacks they bare asses."

Fitz grumbled to himself all the way to the whipping shed. They stopped by the cage to examine the trussed-up pair, lying on their sides and moaning with pain from the restraint of their outraged muscles.

Calcutta, who rarely missed anything that might be exciting, stood by the cage. The overseer, sleepy-eyed, handed Fitz his rifle and went home to bed.

Fitz said, "Calcutta, yo' runs to the firs' stable an' finds Dundee an' brings him heah on the double."

Calcutta, swelled with pride because he had an assignment somewhat above toting glasses of whiskey, bobbed his head up and down.

"Yas suh, massa, suh. I fetches Dundee, I does. Whar he at?"

"Tol' yo', yo' bastahd. In the stables. Yo' gets him back heah in five minutes or yo' gets whupped 'fore these two sonabitches gets the lash."

Calcutta shuddered and ran, but his long,

loose strides could never be called fast. Even Fitz chuckled as he watched the skinny, long-legged slave trying to fulfill his order for haste.

"Get them two out heah," Fitz shouted at two slaves who stood nearby. "Get 'em into the whuppin' shed and tie 'em to the whuppin' posts. Hop!"

These were two slaves who had been on the plantation for years and who had immediately recognized Toby and Isaac as dangerous men. They fell to their task willingly and none too gently. One of them seized Toby's wool and dragged him across the ground. The other subjected Isaac to a different means of locomotion. Totally unable to stand or walk, he was rolled over the ground. In the shed, both were untied, the restraining sticks removed, the manacles freed from their wrists and ankles.

Still unable to stand, they were roughly hauled to their feet, screaming in pain as their cramped joints moved under this treatment. They were quickly and efficiently tied to the whipping posts. Both were crying for mercy, swearing they were good slaves and would make money for their master. They would never again disobey or harm anyone.

"Shut up!" Fitz roared at them. "Yo' makes any mo' yellin' an' yo' gets twenty extra. No call fo' yo' to yell like that till the snake bites yo'. Whar in hell that Calcutta an' Dundee?"

"Whut you send for Dundee fer?" Jonathan asked.

"Wants him to do the whuppin'."

Jonathan shook his head. "Knows that boy, Papa, an' he ain't goin' to do it."

"He Hong Kong's son and these bastahds near killed Hong Kong. On'y right he cuts 'em."

"He a slave too, Papa, an' he ain't 'bout to whup 'nother slave. Knows him."

"He goin' to do whut I say."

Dundee came into the whipping shed confidently. He knew he'd caused no trouble and if there was a whipping, he'd not be the victim.

Fitz took down the plaited whip and presented the handle of it to Dundee.

"They neah kills yo' papa, Dundee. Yo' whups 'em thirty lashes an' they passes out, yo' keeps on whuppin. Wants 'em skinned real good, I do."

Dundee's bent head didn't raise up, nor did he make any motion to accept the whip.

"Take it!" Fitz roared in renewed wrath.

"Cain't, massa, suh," Dundee said unhappily.

"Tol' yo', they neah kills yo' papa. Now yo' neah kills 'em, y'heah me?"

"Cain't," Dundee repeated.

"Yo' heahs whut I say?" Fitz shouted. He cupped Dundee's chin in his hand and lifted his head up. "Yo heahs me?"

"Heahs yo', massa. Cain't do no whuppin'."

"Dundee, yo' my slave. Yo' does whut I say. Else yo' gets whupped."

"Whups me, massa, suh," Dundee said quietly.

Fitz let go of him. "Got a mind to whup yo' myse'f."

Dundee began peeling off his shirt. Fitz muttered something and turned away from him. He grasped the whip, let the lash snake out, and drew it back.

"Massa, suh—" Hong Kong entered the shed.

"Massa, suh, yo' favors me, yo' lets me whup 'em."

"Reckon nobody's got a bettah right." Fitz handed over the whip. "Yo' son agin' me, Hong Kong. I say he whups 'em and he say he won't. Yo' raised this boy to be a ball-less wondah?"

"No, suh. I be ball-less like yo' say, but Dundee he raised mighty good, suh. Yo' cain't ask one slave to whup 'nother. Me, I a free man. I hates them two an' I whups 'em real good."

"Go to it," Fitz said.

"I kills 'em?" Hong Kong asked.

"Far's I keer yo' kin kill em' twice, but mist'ess say she want no killin'. Let's 'em live, barely."

The whip lashed out and Toby screeched. He was given five lashes, each of which bit off sections of skin and made the blood run down his ebony hide. Isaac yelled louder than Toby, then it was his turn. After ten lashes each, there were no more howls. Both men were unconscious, though their bodies writhed in agony each time the whip landed. After thirty strokes, Fitz signaled it was enough.

"Cut 'em down, sluice 'em, an' throw 'em in the cage. We decides whut to do with 'em tomorruh."

"I tends to it," Jonathan said.

"Got somethin' else yo' tends to," Fitz said calmly. He hung up the plaited lash and took down the wide cowhide whip, which he handed to Jonathan.

"You gives Dundee fifteen good strokes. Hong Kong, yo' ties him up."

Hong Kong sadly escorted Dundee to one of the whipping posts and tied him. Fitz signaled Hong Kong to leave the shed with him. After the two unconscious slaves were removed, Jonathan closed the door. He walked up to Dundee.

"Yo' heahs whut my papa say."

"Yas suh, massa, suh."

"Wants yo' to howl like them two bastahds yelled."

"I howls, massa, suh."

Jonathan stepped back. He swung the cowhide hard. It sounded like the crack of a large calibre gunshot and Dundee let out a yell which he would have emitted even without orders. Nothing stung like that cowhide. Now Jonathan stepped to one side. The cowhide swung again, this time to wrap itself noisily around an empty whipping post. Dundee gasped in wonder.

"Yell, yo' black sonabitch!" Jonathan snapped.

The cowhide hit the post thirteen more times and with each explosive blow, Dundee howled at the top of his voice. Then Jonathan freed him. "Yo' runs now. Yo' runs so fas' my papa cain't see yo' carryin' on'y one big welt."

Dundee raised his head and looked Jonathan straight in the eye. "Massa, suh, thanks yo' I do."

Then he fled from the shed, keeping out of Fitz's way except to allow one fleeting glimpse of the big red welt across his back. Jonathan came out of the shed.

"Yo' gettin' handy with that whup," Fitz complimented him. "Nevah heard him howl like that befo'. Hopes yo' didn' make him a crip. He mighty handy 'roun' them hosses."

"I gives him whut he got comin'," Jonathan said. Noticing Hong Kong's woebegone expression, he deliberately winked at him. Hong Kong quickly grasped his meaning, and a smile crossed his swollen face. Jonathan stood beside the cage and studied the two blood-soaked men inside.

"Yo' sho' whups 'em good, Hong Kong. Goin' to the stables, Papa. Yo' comin'?"

"Got wuk to do in the curin' sheds. Hong Kong, wants yo' to bring all that Fisbee coffle heah an' lets 'em see whut they gets, they tries to run. Soon's they looked, yo' herds 'em to the tobacco fields an' starts 'em cuttin'."

"Yas suh," Hong Kong said. His smile broadened as he passed Jonathan, though the effort was painful.

Jonathan made his way to the stables and found Dundee busily engaged in currying the brown mare, which he gave more attention to than the other horses, for some reason he didn't know himself. The splendid animal responded to this kindness and care. It was obvious that the horse respected this slave, and liked him as well. When Jonathan came closer the mare raised her head, bared her teeth, and gave vent to a shrill whinny to demonstrate that this liking for the slave did not include anyone else.

"Dundee," Jonathan said.

Dundee turned around, hung his head. "Yas suh, massa, suh."

"Wants yo' to sweah yo' nevah tells anybody whut I jus' done."

"Sweahs it, massa, suh."

"Now we talks 'bout this heah mare. Think she ready fo' timin'?"

"Sho' is, massa, suh. An I sweahs she fas'. Fas'es' hoss yo' evah did see, suh."

"Good. Put a saddle on her an' I gets the

timin' clock. Don' want anybody else to see how good she runs."

"I rides her, massa, suh?" Dundee looked up in astonishment.

"Yo' kinda heavy, but she carries yo' real good, she carries a jockey bettah. Yo' rides her."

"Yas suh," Dundee said happily. "I rides her."

Jonathan was at the track when Dundee led the mare through the gate. He mounted the animal, a big man on a normal-sized horse. An incongruous sight to a racing lover like Jonathan.

Dundee didn't let the animal warm up. He rode her to where Jonathan stood, the stopwatch in his hand. Jonathan studied the face of the big timing device, raised his hand, brought it down, and Dundee sent the mare running fast. Jonathan watched the brief run and marveled at what he saw. The horse had speed and stamina. Plenty of both. Something else too, a willingness to win, to outrun any other horse—at least with Dundee on her back or close by. Jonathan was pleased with himself.

As Dundee flashed by, Jonathan studied the time and shook his head. Dundee rode back and, still astride the horse, did what no slave was ever allowed to do. He asked a question.

"Whut she do, massa, suh?"

Jonathan wasn't even aware that Dundee had broken this rule. "Fo' minutes . . . little ovah, Dundee."

"Fo' minutes?" Dundee repeated.

"Yo' kinda heavy, like I say. Gets a hundred pounds on her an' a good jockey an' she cuts that to two."

Dundee's face broke into a braod grin. "She runs like that, suh, an' she wins. Yas suh, massa, suh, she sho' wins."

"Exercise her, Dundee. Be keerful. Nobody else rides her. Racin' season comin' in the spring an' we races her."

"Massa, suh, yo' takes me when yo' goes racin', suh?"

"If yo' takes keer she don't bust a laig an' she in fine shape, yo' goes."

"I thanks yo' agin, massa, suh. I asks 'nother question, massa, suh?"

Jonathan nodded. "I guess you can."

"Why yo' treats me so nice, massa, suh?"

"None o' yo' goddamn business," Jonathan exploded in righteous wrath.

"Yas suh, massa, suh," Dundee said seriously. But he thought it was because of his mother, and Dundee was grateful to her at that moment. He hesitated, made a half-turn, and paused to take another chance.

"Whut now?" Jonathan asked, ashamed of himself for showing all this kindness to a slave.

"Massa, suh, I lives wid Hong Kong an' Seawitch. Likes it fine. But wants to be close to this hoss, massa. Yo' say so, I sleeps near roof. Up the ladder, suh. Room 'nuff fo' me an' I watches the mare, suh."

"All right," Joathan agreed. "It's a good idee. But yo' see Hong Kong an' Seawitch when yo' can. Understand?"

"Yas suh, massa, suh. I goes. Loves them, I does."

"An' yo' can move 'roun' the stables, even at

night," Jonathan said. "Overseer says yo' git, tell him I say yo' kin move 'roun'."

"Yas suh, massa, suh. I tells him."

"An' 'member whut I say 'bout that whuppin'. Nobody knows."

"Yas suh, massa, suh."

"Good night," Jonathan said.

Dundee watched him walk away with considerable awe. No white man—or woman—had ever wished him good night before. He scratched his wool and made up his mind that somehow, no matter what he had to do, he was going to learn how to read and write and understand white masters.

At supper, Benay was at her most charming. "I'm proud o' yo', Fitz."

"Whut yo' proud fo', Benay?" Fitz asked innocently.

"Not killin' them two bucks. Reckon they sho' deserved it, but it ain't right. Used to think it was, but I grew up an' I changed, reckon. I thanks yo' fo' doin' whut I asked."

"Don' I always?" Fitz asked.

"Well, there have been times. . . ."

"Cain't think o' any, far's I knows. Yo' asks, I does. Goin' to sell them two fo'-fi' dollahs each. Sends 'em to cane fields in Louisiana. That'll teach 'em."

"Jus' so long yo' didn't kill 'em," Benay said with satisfaction. "Now I got somethin' else needs talkin'."

Fitz laid down his knife and fork, leaned back. "Now whut? If yo' wants me to go to church, I ain't goin' to do it. Ain't old 'nuff to be skeered o' dyin' yit."

"The nearest church is thirty miles," Benay said. "That ain't whut I mean. Pretty soon goin' to be Christmas. I wants to give a big soiry. Tol' yo' befo', but didn't know when. Now wants it to be over Christmas."

"Suits me," Fitz agreed. "Jonathan, whut yo' say?"

"Me?" Jonathan asked indignantly. "Since when I gets to say anythin' 'bout whut goes on heah?"

"Yo' sho' is quick 'bout comin' up with the truth," Fitz said good-naturedly. "Yo' gets to say nuthin'. Benay, yo' gets to have the biggest an' bes' Christmas party evah in all Virginny. Invites all the folks from Norfolk an' Lynchburg, an' Richmond."

"Reckon I gets writin' the invitations now," Benay said happily. "Whut 'bout my cousin Clarissa?"

"Sho' we invites that little whore. Her daddy too. He a prime sonabitch—wants him to see how much we got. Riles him some an' maybe I gets the chance to bust his face effen he gets mean."

Jonathan chuckled. "Likes to meet this heah Clarissa, Mama."

"Yo' stays 'way from her, Jonathan. She like a bitch in the heat all the time."

"Whut makes her so goddamn horny," Fitz added, "she married to Horace Apperson. The Major's son, an' he keepin' two young bucks fo' to pleasure him. Don' like gals, reckon. Not as much as he likes them two bucks. Clarissa, sho' goin' crazy these days, got nobody to get in bed with."

"Serves her right," Benay said. "She a wicked gal, Jonathan. Yo' stays 'way from her. But wants

[*112*]

her to come. Wants her to see all my new dresses an' my hats an' shoes from Paris."

"Tell yo' whut," Fitz said. "Yo' an' Jonathan talk 'bout this soiry an' whut yo' wants fo' it. 'Bout time Jonathan learns somethin' 'bout society."

"Whar yo' goin', Papa?" Jonathan asked, not at all pleased to be given a part in planning the big party.

"Look 'roun' some. Makes sho' them two bastahds still in the cage. Back soon's I kin."

Fitz left by way of the kitchen, where Elegant sat astride a tall stool, hiding it completely under her ample size. She began to struggle to get to her feet.

"Stays wheah yo' is," Fitz said. "Yo' gettin' kinda ol' an' yo' sho' is fat, Elegant, so yo' don' need to get up any mo'. Fine suppah tonight."

He saw a mound of biscuits, still warm, and helped himself to three of them, stuffing two into his pants pocket. He ate the one in his hand and nodded in approval.

"Elegant, whar that shif'less Calcutta?"

"Eatin' on the back steps, reckon. Sends him thar, suh."

Fitz nodded and went out. Calcutta, sprawled on the back steps, was enjoying his plate heaped with food. When he saw Fitz, he came to his feet, spilling half his supper.

"Kinda s'prised yo' wasn't asleep," Fitz said. "Now yo' listens to me, y'heah? Come near 'leven o'clock— Kin yo' tell time?"

"Yas suh, massa, I tells time real good, I does."

"Well, I doubt it, but anyway, 'bout 'leven, yo' goes down to the cage an' yo' unlocks the do' an' lets them two bastahds out. Lets 'em run, but shucked down like they is now. Yo' tells 'em they goin' to hang in the mornin'. On'y way to save they black hides is to run. Yo' waits five, ten minutes, then yo' yells they got away."

Calcutta got the gist of what he meant, but the reasons behind it were a total loss to him. He couldn't ask a single question. All he could do was obey, though he didn't like the idea of turning that pair loose. They could easily turn on him. He made up his mind to be very careful about the way he handled this assignment.

Fitz strolled out into the dark, finding familiar paths and walking along them. As he often did, he went to the white folks' cemetery and stood at the foot of his father's grave.

"Reckon things goin' mighty fine, suh," he said. "Got five hundred mo' slaves than yo' had, an' three hundred mo' acres. Fisbee place all busted to hell. Thinkin' o' buyin' it. Don' know whut fo'. Got so much now cain't handle much mo'. But yo' always say buy whut yo' kin get cheap."

Fitz stepped over to the foot of his mother's grave. He bowed his head for a moment.

"Mother, things haven't changed much. The plantation is still run by slaves and they are whipped when they do wrong. I have to handle them just as Papa did, or they'll run away with the place. But Benay and I are doing fine—so are your grandchildren. Melanie is beautiful. Benay made me send her to Boston to be educated. Benay thought I was against that, but actually I was all for it, and I reckon I put the bee in Benay's bonnet that caused her to send Melanie there. That's about all, Mother. I like to come here and talk to you this way. Northern talk. I haven't forgotten it and I never will. Good night, now."

He wandered on, feeling very good about things. He stopped to peer into the cage where Toby and Isaac lay groaning with pain. They didn't see him and he made no attempt to make his presence known to them. Instead, he continued on to the cabins where his overseers lived and got one of them out of bed.

"Yo' heahs o' any paddyrollers 'roun' these days?" he asked.

"They's always 'roun'," the overseer said. "Always lookin' fo' runaways. Right now they combin' the No'th Patch, suh. Thick woods theah. All runaways go theah. Lookin' fo' three runs from Major Apperson's place."

Fitz nodded and left. He found Calcutta on the back steps trying to finish his supper.

"Yo' sets 'em free," Fitz said. "Yo' tells 'em bes' way to run is by No'th Patch. Heah me?"

"Yes suh, massa, suh. No'th Patch, suh."

"Sees yo' don' run with 'em, Calcutta. Yo' does an' I hides yo' good."

"Massa, I nevah runs. Sweahs I nevah does. Likes it heah, massa, suh. Nevah runs, suh."

"Yo' does whut I tol' yo' an' tells nobody, I gives yo' one silvah dollah an' three big drinks o' rum."

Calcutta's delight showed on his face. "Yes suh, sho' craves rum, suh. Sho' does."

"Yo' ain't tellin' me somethin' I don' know."

Fitz continued on into the house. Benay and

Jonathan were still at the table, discussing plans for the soiree. They didn't look up as he passed the door on his way to the library, where he ate the biscuits he'd carried in his pocket.

Shortly after eleven, when he and Benay were in bed, half asleep, they heard Calcutta's shrill cries. They cut through the night silence and brought everyone in the house awake.

Fitz pulled on his pants, worked his feet into boots, and ran downstairs. He quieted Calcutta, produced a silver dollar from his pocket, and pressed it into the slave's hand. Then he went to the dining room and from the massive sideboard took several bottles partly filled with rum and bourbon. He selected one with about three good-sized drinks and brought it to Calcutta.

"Fine yo'se'f a warm place, drink it all up, and go to sleep," he ordered.

"Yes suh, massa suh."

"An keep yo' damn big mouth shut, heah?"

Fitz returned to the bedroom. Jonathan was in the hall, wondering what it was all about.

"Them two bastahds got loose," Fitz reported. "S'pects some sonabitch slave picked the lock an' opened the do'. Looks into it tomorruh. Right now I wants to get my sleep. Good night, son."

Soon after breakfast two mounted men rode up the drive. They were leading two pack horses, over which were slung the bodies of Toby and Isaac. Fitz went out to meet them. Benay and Jonathan remained standing on the veranda.

"Paddyrollers," Benay said contemptuously.

They saw Fitz reach into his pocket and place money in the hands of the two disreputable-looking men. Then he watched while they rode away, taking the bodies with them.

Fitz returned to the porch, looking grave. "Them paddyrollers said the two slaves come bustin' outa some bushes naked as a whore's ass. They said they acted like crazy men, wouldn' stop. So the paddyrollers shot 'em."

"Yo' had nothin' to do with this, Fitz?" Benay asked.

"Me?" he countered. "Whut I have to do with it? I sleepin'. Pays 'em twenty-five dollahs like the law says an' they buries them two."

"Seems like yo' had the fifty dollahs mighty handy," Benay commented.

"Carries money in my pockets all the time," Fitz protested. "Yo' knows that."

"First time I heard 'bout it," Benay said. "Times when yo' gets kinda sneaky 'bout things, Fitz. I don' like it none."

Fitz drew his arm around Benay's slim waist and led her into the house. "Loves yo' mo' ev'y day," he said. I tells myse'f that ain't possible, but finds it is. Now wants to heah all 'bout the soiry yo' an' Jonathan talked 'bout last night."

They sat down in the drawing room, Fitz very attentive. A few minutes of this and Benay's mind would be diverted and a family squabble avoided.

"Well, we decided bes' to have it beginnin' on Christmas Day. Take all week right to New Year's. Whut yo' think on that, Fitz?"

What he thought of it would have precipitated the crisis he was trying to avoid. He took a long breath and nodded his head slowly, like a man making up his mind.

"Benay, that the bes' idee I heard. Evah since I come to this plantation, we always give the slaves that week off. Nobody wuks, 'ceptin' the house slaves, we give presents an' new clothes an' we lets 'em have a meetin', make a mighty fine brew with stuff we gives 'em. If they gets a little drunk, they don' get whupped fer it. An' no whuppin' that week nohow."

"I'm delighted to heah yo' say that, Fitz. I know it's been the custom since I got heah. Wants it to go on, please. Our slaves wuk mighty ha'd all yeah long."

"Slaves' masters wuk mighty ha'd all yeah too," Fitz reminded her. "Well, that bein' settled, reckon I gots to go down an' see how the curin' goes on. We got some extra fine Orinoco this yeah. Our factory in N'Awleans says it bring a good price."

"I'm glad ev'ythin' is doin' so well," Benay said, now mollified and bubbling with enthusiasm for the party which Fitz had sanctioned.

"Cain't figger which crops brings in mos' cash. Times I think it be slaves, but then 'bacco brings fine prices, an' we sells our thoroughbreds . . . well, whut the hell! It all goes in the same pot. We's rich, honey. We's mighty rich."

Benay looked at him coyly. "We might not be quite as rich when I gets through buyin' fo' the party."

Fitz arose and bestowed a healthy kiss squarely on her lips. "Yo' spend all yo' likes, honey. Makes no mattah how much. Keeps yo' happy, is all I asks. We's two lucky folks an' we might's well tell ev'ybody 'bout it. Spends all yo' wants."

"Yes," Benay said softly as Fitz left the room.

"We are lucky. Times it skeers me we so lucky. An' I seen luck like ours change to some'hin' else. An' when I thinks 'bout it, skeers me so much, I start shakin'."

Fitz didn't hear her. It would not have mattered if he had, for he'd have laughed at her fears, and she knew it. No'hing she or anyone else might say would convince him things would ever change for them.

[7]

PREPARATIONS FOR THE WEEK-LONG EVENT BEGAN right after the tobacco crop was pressed into hogsheads and taken to the railroad. Fitz had turned over the delivery to Jonathan, and remained home. The day after the caravan departed, Fitz realized his mistake. Benay put him to work on the party.

Her invitations, sent all over the state, had drawn acceptances from all but a very few who pled sickness, travel, or plain old age.

There would be days when the festivities would move outside, providing the weather held and the temperature didn't drop too low. So Japanese lanterns were to be strung all over the front of the estate, with long tables set up for refreshments, and a dance floor constructed outside.

The slaves were kept busy, some at their customary tasks, others helping prepare for the party.

"Papa always tol' me we gets mo' suckers bo'n in September an' October than any othah month," Fitz remarked.

"Oh?" Benay said, pausing in her decision as to where to place bunting in the drawing room. "Why's that, Fitz?"

"Fo' God's sake, don' yo' know when the slaves don' wuk, they screws all the time?"

"I wish you'd be a little more considerate of the language yo' use, Fitz."

"Whut's the matter with whut I said? It's true, ain't it?"

"Yes, Fitz, it's true." Benay gave up. There were more important things to be done than arguing with Fitz.

While all these preparations were in progress, Dundee was kept busy at the stable. He spent hours with the mare, and he found another yearling that showed promise and to which he became attached.

He had left Hong Kong's cabin, over the protests of Seawitch, who didn't like Dundee being on his own.

"Boy's too young fo' that," she told Hong Kong.

"Boy's sma't, Seawitch," Hong Kong told her. "He gits 'long fine. Yo'll see. Bes' let him have he own way. Else Massa Jonathan gits mad at us."

"Yo' tells Dundee he comes to see me ev'y day he kin. Wants to see how he doin' an' how he feels."

"Sees him I tells him," Hong Kong promised. "No call to fret ovah him now. He doin' real good."

[122]

"Stays that way, I don' fret. Gits pesterin' too many gals, I busts him, yo' don't."

Dundee had carefully prepared the loft in the stable. He'd been given a blanket which, along with the one he used at Hong Kong's cabin, provided all the warmth he needed. On an exceptionally cold night he could add burlap sacks stuffed with hay, or appropriate a horse blanket. He had a chair, with the legs cut almost off so he could occupy it without banging his head on the slanted roof of the loft. And he had fashioned a small table, ostensibly to eat from, but Dundee had planned it to be a table on which to write and read. He had already examined every page in the books once belonging to his father. Each picture had a word below it, and he guessed that word had something to do with the picture. But he still couldn't pronounce the words, and he was afraid his guesses might be all wrong.

His problem was to find someone to talk to—someone he could trust. Once he knew the letters, how to form them into words and how to understand the whole business, he'd be able to read.

He knew from past years that every Christmas the slaves were allowed to gather and hear a manumitted preacher tell them the story of Christmas. The time was approaching when the meeting would be held. Somehow he had to get the preacher aside. It wouldn't be easy. At any meeting of slaves, a white master was required by law to be present.

To be found with books and newspapers, even though he couldn't read a word, would mean severe punishment and confiscation of the books. Besides, if he did learn how to read and write, and they discovered it, he'd quickly be put on the vendue table. The only way to save himself from such a fate, if he was caught with the books, was to make himself invaluable on this plantation. Therefore, he worked hard and long hours. He was bringing the mare along, and the yearling as well. In the late spring, when the racing season began, he hoped to have both animals ready. If they could win a great deal of money, his situation here would be doubly secure. He kept telling the mare she had to win. He told her that a dozen times a day. Maybe she understood, maybe not, but it didn't do any harm.

On Christmas Eve afternoon all work ceased and the start of the joyful season began. The slaves all gathered before the mansion. Fitz, Jonathan, and Benay supervised the accumulation of mounds of clothing, dresses for the women, shirts and trousers for the men. And each slave received a small special gift—chewing tobacco, handkerchiefs, sandals, small flasks of whiskey, for the men, shoes, petticoats, ribbons, cheap perfume, more handkerchiefs, and colorful scarves for the women. There were so many slaves gathered that even Fitz was not only impressed, but a little frightened. The sea of black faces seemed to stretch as far back as he could see.

Overseers stood ready to hand out the gifts as the slaves made ten lines, shuffling forward to receive their presents.

Later in the day, carts trundled along the slave quarters, handing out sides of bacon, dried fish, tea, grits, and flour—everything needed for a fine Christmas dinner.

Finally another cart brought in treacle, bay leaves, powdered ginger, and the required barrels and vats for making home brew. For once, the slaves were allowed to drink. Of course there was always danger of rebellion when they were drunk, or half drunk, but this part of the festivities had never gone awry at Wyndward so far. A rebellion would mean the food, drink, and dancing would have to be abandoned, and the slaves thought that too high a price to pay. Fitz was confident that the only thing to come out of the Christmas party was more suckers. In the long run, the expense was repaid many times over.

By late afternoon, the guests would begin to arrive. Christmas was rarely an occasion to stay home, unless that family gave the party.

Everything was prepared. Enough food was in the larder to feed an army. Fitz had laid by several kinds of hard liquor in kegs. Wine would flow in profusion. Every facility in the mansion would be taxed, and some guests would have to travel daily to the village, miles away, to be accommodated at the tavern and the inn. Nobody objected. Wyndward's fêtes had been famous since the days of Captain Jonathan Turner and his northern-bred, haughty, aristocratic wife. In those days, Captain Jonathan could have charged substantial fees for the privilege of coming to Wyndward to see this strange-speaking lady from the North.

Before the guests began to arrive, Fitz, Benay, and Jonathan held their own little ceremony. With snifters of forty-year-old brandy—which none of the guests would get—they toasted one another's health. Benay read aloud a letter from Melanie. She was terribly lonely over the holidays, she said, but a classmate had invited her to her home in a town called Worcester, and she would survive.

"She quite a gal," Fitz said, while Benay wiped a tear from her eyes. "Figgerin' on goin' No'th 'bout graduation time an' seein' her."

"Fitz, yo' don't mean that?" Benay set her glass down, flung her arms around Fitz, and kissed him. Jonathan grinned and enjoyed the moment.

"Hol' on now," Fitz said. "Didn' say yo' was comin'."

"Yo' try an' leave 'thout me," Benay said, "an I takes the Christmas present Jonathan goin' to give yo' an' shoots yo' daid."

"Whut present?" Fitz demanded.

Jonathan went to the long table and handed his father a flat, gaily wrapped parcel. Fitz tore the colorful paper away and opened the plush-lined box to reveal a pair of matched dueling pistols, the likes of which he'd never seen before.

"Sweah," he said softly, "I nevah saw such beauties. Mus' be a hundred yeahs old, Jonathan."

"Near," Jonathan said. "They's antiques. Trouble is, Papa, they don't shoot. They's jes' an ornament."

Fitz removed one gun and hefted it. "Yo' thinks I shoot one o' these, son? They's meant to look at. Not kill anythin' with. Yes suh, been wantin' somethin' like this all my life."

"We're both glad yo' likes yo' gift," Benay said. "Now s'pose yo' shows us whut yo' bought fo' us."

Fitz looked puzzled. "Now why should I buy anythin' fo' yo' two? I'm the mastah heah. Folks impo'tant as me takes gifts, don' give 'em."

"Yo' shows me whut yo' been hidin' in that bottom drawer o' yours or I sweah I take a club to yo'," Benay threatened.

"Well, go look in the drawer," Fitz said. "Mayhap somethin' theah."

Benay was out of the room before he finished talking. Fitz pulled open a drawer in one of the drawing-room tables and handed Jonathan a gift.

"Kinda like whut yo' gives me, son. Hopes yo' likes this. An' nevah uses it."

Jonathan hefted the large, heavy box and eyed his father questioningly. He opened it carefully and pulled out a huge handgun.

"Like it, son?" Fitz asked.

"Papa, wheah yo' gets this? Ain't been no guns like this 'roun' heah."

"No suh. Got it special. Shoots a forty-four an' the cylinder kin be removed an' 'nother ready-loaded one put in. This heah is a brand-new gun. It's called a Dragoon, made fo' the army an' used in the Mexican War. Got power, an' range beats anythin' so far."

"Papa, long's I live, I'll nevah part with this gun, no, suh."

"Figgered mayhap yo' need it someday," Fitz added, with a worried glance in the direction of the door, lest Benay hear him.

"Whut yo' mean, Papa?"

"Nevah kin tell," Fitz said. "I keeps gettin' a feelin' in my gut things is changin'. When I come heah in 1820 with yo' grandpapa, wasn't so many folks, so many slaves. Don' like it, this change. Means trouble. Feels it in my bones."

Jonathan had no opportunity to comment, for

Benay came rushing into the room, holding up a string of pearls. She made Fitz put them on and didn't utter a word of complaint when he was all thumbs at this task.

She ran over to a mirror and admired her gift. "They's real, I knows that. Kinda like they's alive, an' they feels so good on my skin."

She ran to embrace Fitz and kiss him again. Then she presented her gift to him. It was an antique sword, the haft inlaid with gems. Drawn from its scabbard it gleamed and, like the pearls, seemed alive.

"From me an' Jonathan," she said. "Leastwise, he picked it out, 'cause I don't know much 'bout swords."

"I thanks yo'," Fitz said. "Both o' yo'. We livin' in modern times now an' it good to have somethin' from out o' the past. Yo' surely comes with me to Boston, Benay."

"Whut 'bout me?" Jonathan asked.

"I'm makin' yo' head man o' Wyndward Plantation, son. Yo' acts in my place an' yo' gives the orders an' yo' takes the blame anythin' goes wrong. Whut I'm sayin', yo' a man now."

Jonathan wagged his head. "Thinkin' myse'f, I been a man fo' a long time, Papa."

"Whut yo' means bein' a man is knockin' up that po' little gal on the Fisbee place. What I mean yo' a man, yo' takes ovah heah, complete."

"Knows whut yo' means, Papa. Mighty proud yo' trust me."

"It ain't spring yet," Fitz said. "Mayhap things change 'fo' then. Now I got to git myse'f dressed fit fo' our guests. They be heah any minute, I reckon."

By evening, thirty people had arrived. While the festivities were slowly gathering steam, with more and more guests arriving, another meeting of considerable importance was being held in the old curing shed where the Fisbee coffle had been kept. It was a large shed, holding better than a thousand people. There were no chairs. The speaker would stand on a half-barrel, placed at the end of the shed. Night air, growing chilly, came through the open spaces that all curing sheds have, but none of the men and women noticed it.

Hong Kong and Seawitch were among those closest to the spot where the speaker would stand. Dundee stood beside them proudly.

They were all astounded to find that the speaker was being escorted by Massa Fitz, marching side by side with the minister who had consented to give a Christmas sermon. His name was James Whitehead, and no man had been better named, for he possessed a thick head of hair, all of it white as a cotton ball. He was a rangy man, but well proportioned. His black skin seemed to enhance the whiteness of his hair. He wore a frock coat, a black slouch hat, dark trousers, and black shoes. He also wore the collar of the clergy above the plain black shirt front.

Fitz raised both hands to quiet the murmuring voices. "This heah," he said, "is the Reverend Jimmy Whitehead. He a reg'lar preacher an' he comes heah to give yo' goddamn sinners a way to repent. While he speaks, my son will be at the rear o' the shed to see they's no talk o' rebellion. This is Christmas an' we don' expect no trouble. That's all I got to say, 'ceptin' I wish you a merry Christmas."

This astounded them more than the appearance of the clergyman. When Fitz left, the slaves parted to form a channel along which he strode with his customary martial steps. He passed Jonathan, who stood in back without a word, but caught up with him after he had cleared the shed.

"Yo gettin' kinda soft, Papa. Way yo' talked."

"Mayhap it make these bastahds wuk a little harder," Fitz said. "Don' do no harm, that's sho'."

"Hope the preacher don't git too windy. Wants to be back when Clarissa comes."

"Yo' stays heah 'till it's ovah. That preacher says one word 'bout rebellin', yo' stops him right then an' kick his ass offen this heah plantation."

"Yo' s'pect he talk rebellion?"

"S'pects he a real preachin' man an' all he do is put the fear o' hell into them po' souls. Feels a little sorry for 'em sometimes, 'specially when it Christmas. Clarissa comes, I sends her down heah an' yo' kin celebrate Christmas. Yo' don' know how, she teaches yo' mighty fas'."

"She skeers the hell outa me, Papa. Don' send her down heah."

Fitz laughed. As he walked back to join the now somewhat noisy festivities at the mansion, Jonathan stepped back into the shed.

The preacher had apparently been talking for a few minutes. There wasn't a sound to be heard except his voice, and a little shuffling of feet not used to sandals. Every slave gave his undivided attention to the preacher, who gave them a hell-and-damnation sermon that made even Jonathan wince once or twice.

Then, unexpectedly, the preacher began another subject. The gist of it surprised Jonathan, and probably most of the slaves present.

"I tol' yo' 'bout the Lord an' 'bout forgiveness," he said in a voice that filled every inch of the shed. It was a resonant voice of high quality, commanding attention by its tone and volume alone.

"Yo' ain't free. Yo' is slaves an' yo' wuks fo' a mastah who owns yo' body an' soul. No ... I changes that. Nobody owns yo' soul 'ceptin' yo' an' yo' God. Mind that now. Yo' lives to hope bettah days comin' an' they shorely are. They be changes goin' on yo' don' heah 'bout. Yo' got any sense, yo' minds yo' mastah an' yo' does yo' best fo' him. Any man or woman who talks rebellion is a fool. Yo' my brothers an' sisters. Yo' don' have to rebel, brothers an' sisters. The day is comin' when yo'll be free. The day is comin' 'cause it has to come. I don' say it's comin' 'cause of anythin' the Lord does, but reckon He have a hand in it some way. Bes' thing yo' kin do is obey yo' mastah an' he takes fine keer o' yo'. This heah plantation the bes' o' any I evah been on. That all I got to say, I reckon. Go in the right way an' yo' ends up bein' right, an' that means yo' don' git too anxious. I say the day comin'. Yes, brothers an' sisters, yo' 'members my words. The day comin'."

The assembly broke into its usual chant and then there was singing while the preacher walked slowly through the crowd, shaking hands, accepting kisses from some of the women, patting children on the head.

As he walked away from the shed, Jonathan fell into step with him.

"Kinda likes whut yo' said, Preacher Whitehead. Yo' is a man with mo' sense than mos' white preachers."

"I thanks yo', suh. Meant whut I said in theah."

"Know yo' did. Whut's it 'bout, the day comin'?"

Reverend Whitehead stopped and there in the evening shadows, he talked to Jonathan man to man.

"Mastah Turner, suh, I goes No'th sometimes. I heahs things ain't said down heah. They's a lot o' folks up theah who say slavery gots to stop. They's awful mad 'bout it sometimes, an' they's hotheads who talk of settin' all slaves free, yo' wants it or not."

"It won't happen," Jonathan said. "I ain't agin yo' Reverend. But it won't happen fo' a long, long time."

"But yo' agrees it will?"

Jonathan nodded. "Reckon so. Time comes, we takes keer o' things. Likely I be an ol' man it happens."

"I don' think so, Mastah Turner, suh. It come sooner'n we think."

"Why yo' tells them not to rebel?"

" 'Cause it do no good an' on'y gits 'em killed. An' white folks too. Rebellion begets revenge an' they's mo' whites than they's blacks, suh. And the whites has guns. Yo' kin see I on'y talk sense."

"Sees it all right, but mighty nice o' yo' to tell 'em that. Wants yo' to come to the house an' have yo' suppah, Reverend."

"In the kitchen?" he asked with a smile.

"Reckon. Yo' is black and they's rules."

"Yo' thinks I git mad yo' say this? Used to, but no mo'. Tells yo' why. I likes white man's food too much."

Jonathan joined him in a laugh, and almost took the old man's arm. He checked himself in time. If Reverend Whitehead noticed, he made no comment.

As Jonathan walked the minister up the path under the Japanese lanterns, the guests outside stopped all conversation and stared at them. No one spoke to Jonathan. He looked about and laughed out loud.

"Reverend," he said, so everyone could hear him, "I think it bein' Christmas an' all, it might be nice if yo' gave us white folks a little sermon an' maybe a blessin'. Think yo' could do this? I'd consider it a special favor."

"That's whut I wear this collah fo'," Reverend Whitehead said. Somewhat nervously, Jonathan thought.

"Now, Reverend, we makes this a solemn occasion an' they won't be no foolin' 'round. This ain't the right day fo' that. Now if yo' feels it ain't yo' place to give us yo' good word, yo' kin say so an' no hard feelin's."

Fitz and Benay met them as they entered the house, now crowded with guests. In the drawing room, which had been converted to a ballroom, there was music and dancing.

"The Reverend just gave a sermon to the

slaves an' he one o' the wisest men I evah did heah," Jonathan said. "Man with mo' sense than I got an' more'n mos' anybody heah has got. Was thinkin' he might give us his benediction, this be-in' Christmas."

Reverend Whitehead was indeed nervous, but trying not to show it. The guests were crowding about, those outside forcing their way into the house.

Fitz looked about at all these familiar faces. He considered the idea for a minute and then raised his arms high. "Whut's Christmas 'thout a preacher sayin' his blessin'? An' he sho' come to the right place. Sho' did. We need his blessin'. Ain't one o' us ain't a hellbound sinner. Reverend Whitehead, we welcomes yo'."

Benay had listened to this open-mouthed, but now she joined in with her husband and son. She declared the whole idea to be a fine one. Christmas would not be complete without a brief sermon.

Fitz and Jonathan escorted the old man to the bandstand that had been erected at the rear of the room. It was slightly elevated and made a fine pulpit for an occasion like this.

"Go to it, Reverend," Fitz said. "Ladies an' gen'mun, I asks yo' give the preacher yo' 'tention an' yo' respect."

"He's a nigger!" someone exclaimed.

"Sho' he is," Fitz said. He was enjoying this. "But see that collah he weahs? That's a preacher-man's collah an' it ain't no differunt than white preachers weah. That makes this gen'mun the same as any preacher. Reverend, go to it, like I said."

Reverend Whitehead quieted his fears and

prayed his hands wouldn't shake. He was a simple man, but a devoted and devout one, and in this place, under these absurd conditions, he decided to do his best.

"This heah is Christmas, the day our Savior was borned. It be a special day fer all o' us folks, colored o' white. It a day we rejoice, for on this day, a thousand eight hundred an' fo'ty-six yeahs ago, the worl' changed fo' the bettah. Mayhap not fer some, but they will sho'ly be more changes to come. It good to see all folks havin' a fine time an' enjoyin' good food an' drink. I comes straight from talkin' to all the slaves on this heah plantation and I tells yo' they be havin' they kind o' fun too. They's happy——"

"He's a liar," someone shouted. Fitz whirled about to see that Major Apperson had pushed his portly frame through part of the crowd to get closer.

"I says this nigger's nuthin' but a damn liar. Ain't no slave happy."

Fitz said quietly, "The Major will shet his goddamn mouth, or I kicks his ass outa this heah house. Mind now, means it."

Reverend Whitehead decided to cut it short. When Fitz signaled him to continue, the old man slowly dropped to his knees and clasped his hands before him.

"I asks yo' all prays with me," he said. "Prays to the Lord on His birthday."

No one moved. Fitz mounted the bandstand and stood beside the kneeling black.

"This heah Christmas an' we got us a real, genuine preacherman to give us his blessin' an' not one o' yo' sonabitches even willin' to kneel.

Now I asks yo' to kneel, all o' yo', an' that means yo' too, Major."

"The man is a nigger," Major Apperson objected. "We don' kneel to niggers."

"Sho' he is," Fitz agreed. "'Bout as black a nigger I evah did see. But he a preacherman. We not kneelin' to him, or don' yo' know that? Reverend, I gives ev'y slave on my plantation one silvah dollah today. How much they gives yo'?"

"They gives me whut they kin."

"See?" Apperson shouted. "How much yo' payin' him, Fitz?"

"I takes no money. I takes nuthin'. Them po' folks got nuthin' to give me but love," said Whitehead.

"Y'heah that?" Fitz shouted.

"He's lyin'. All niggers are liars," Apperson persisted.

Fitz leveled a steely glance at the Major, who had by now battled his way almost to the bandstand. Jonathan moved half a step to leap off the stand, but Fitz seized his arm and stopped him. He then turned to the kneeling minister and helped him to his feet.

"Turn yo' pockets out, Reverend."

Whitehead obeyed, promptly producing a handkerchief, a small prayer book, a notebook, a short pencil, and a pocket knife.

"Who yo' callin' a liar, Major?" Fitz asked. "Now I wants the Reverend to kneel agin an' we all prays with him. Any sonabitch don' wan' to do that, he takes his ass outa heah right now an' he don' come back."

Benay knelt. Jonathan, feeling slightly foolish, knelt too. Slowly, a few at a time, the guests also knelt until Apperson and three others remained standing.

"Turn out o' heah," Fitz shouted. "I means now, or I kicks yo' asses out. This heah a prayer meetin' an' this heah minister kin' 'nuff to give us his blessin'. If he be black or white, it don' make no diff'rence when he's talkin' to ... to ..." Fitz pointed a finger dramatically toward the ceiling. Then he too knelt.

Three men walked out. Apperson slowly knelt.

"Bless this heah gatherin'," the old man said. "Fo'give all sinners among these kin' folks, O Lord. Mayhap they on'y believes in Yo' come Yo' birthday, but that more'n mos' do. An' they means it. Amen."

Fitz helped him up, handed him his possessions, and whispered to Benay, who promptly scooted off to return quickly with a small canvas sack of silver dollars. Fitz handed it to the old man and bowed slightly. It was a severe effort, but he managed it. No sonabitch was goin' to say he faulted this old man, he was thinking.

"Now," he said, "my son, he goes 'bout my guests an' passes the hat. S'pect aftah this heah mighty fine sermon an' prayer, the collection will be mighty good too. Jonathan, yo' tells me whut sonabitch be bastahd 'nuff to give lessen five silvah dollahs so's I kin call him a cheapskate an' a man who don' understan' what a sermon on Christmas is."

The donations were extremely good. Reverend Whitehead was led off to the kitchen by Jonathan, who explained the circumstances to Elegant. She promptly brought out the best. The kitchen was full of wonderful smells and good food.

Reverend Whitehead ate as if he hadn't for some time. Once Elegant thought she saw him wipe away a tear, but when she looked again, he was smiling and getting his teeth into a whole breast of chicken.

"Nevah comes on sech folks like heah," he said. "Thinks they take me befo' all them fine folks to make a fool o' me. But it ain't so, sistah. It shorely ain't so. I rich. Nevah saw so much money befo'. They sho'ly God-fearin' folk. Yas, real God-fearin'."

"Ain't one o' them been to church in ten yeahs," Elegant said, and added hastily, "that don' mean they ain't God-fearin' in they own way. Kinda way I don' evah unnerstan', but they fine folk, Rev'rend. Now yo' eat up an' I fixes a basket fo' yo' to tote. Wheah yo' from?"

"Does mah preachin' in Manteo, sistah. Got me a ol' sto'. Used to be a saloon. I preaches theah fo' them what kin come. Ain't many."

"Yo' walk heah?" Elegant asked.

"Sho' ain't got no mule, sistah."

Elegant opened the back door. "Calcutta, yo' lazy sloth, yo' gits in heah fas' or I tans yo' ass good."

Calcutta came quickly. Elegant knew how to cuff him behind the ear so that his head rang for five minutes afterward.

Elegant said, "Yo' hitches up the light wagon an' yo' drives the Reverend wheah he wants tuh go. Reverend, yo' sees he keeps he mouth shet. He talk too much, give him a good slap on the ear. He

[138]

a liar an' a drunk an' a sloth, but he kin drive a hoss."

"Thank yo', sistah," Reverend Whitehead said. "I beholden."

"Yo' be lucky yo' comes to the right plantation, suh."

"I waits outside fo' the wagon," Reverend Whitehead said. "I thanks yo' agin."

Elegant waddled over to hold the door open and her guest departed, bent over by the weight of the basket of food.

"Yo' talk to me, suh?"

The voice came out of the darkness and Reverend Whitehead stopped to peer nearsightedly about. He knew from the furtive voice this was a slave.

"Don' be skeered," he said. "I kin he'p yo', I does."

Dundee came timidly out of the gloom to approach the white-haired old man. In his hand, he held one of the primers he'd found in the loft.

"What's to ask yo' he'p, suh. Got me this heah book an' wants to know what it say. Knows whut the pictures 'bout, but cain't read whut it say under 'em. Yo' he'ps me, please?"

The minister moved closer to study the young man standing respectfully before him. "Yo' a slave. Knows that. Knows yo' learns to read, yo' gets whupped an' they sen' yo' 'way. Knows that?"

"Yes suh, knows it. Gots to read, suh. An' write. Gots to learn how. Ain't nobody to show me."

"It cain't be done in fi' minutes, standing heah in the dark. Wheah yo' sleep?"

"Got me a loft, suh, in the stable."

"Yo' lives theah, 'thout nobody to see?"

"Nobody, suh."

"Wagon comin' fo' me. Nigger, got him a fancy name. They say he slothful. He a house servant. Knows him?"

"Be Calcutta, suh. Sho' is slothful."

"Big cook say he drive me home. He listens yo' tells him stay 'way from the house 'till 'nuff time go by he could took me to town?"

"Busts his neck he don' do like yo' say, suh."

"Then I comes with yo' an' tonight we studies an' I shows yo' how to read some. Be my Christmas present to yo'. Shorely got to give somethin', 'way I been treated heah. We waits fo' this boy to come with the wagon an' yo' tells him to drive off like I with him an' he don' come back fo' a long time."

Calcutta, on the wagon, slowed up when he saw the figure come out of the dark. Dundee got aboard and in undiplomatic language gave Calcutta his instructions, followed with a warning that he'd burn in hellfire if he didn't do exactly what the minister wanted. For added emphasis, Dundee told him he, personally, would break his neck. Calcutta drove off, his big eyes rolling in fear. Dundee was sure there was no need to worry about him. None of the white folks knew that Elegant had given the order for Calcutta to use the wagon.

Dundee led the minister to the stable. It was easy. No whites were about. The overseers were all home enjoying the Yuletide evening with their families.

"Whut yo' do when yo' leaves?" Dundee

asked. "Cain't fix fo' yo' to ride a wagon tomorruh."

"I walks," Reverend Whitehead said. "Been walkin' all my life, seems."

In the loft, barely big enough for both, the old man and the young man settled down to study the first primer by the light of a lone candle.

"Now yo' sees this heah pitchur? What's it look like to yo', son?"

"Sho'ly is a hoss, suh."

"All right. Now see the word below the pitchur? It made o' letters o' the alphabet which yo' gots to learn. The letters spell the word whut the picture means. Now gimme that othah book—that one. This heah's the alphabet an' 'fore mornin' yo' going' to know it so yo' kin say it over an' over 'thout lookin' at the book."

So the lessons began. They continued until just before dawn, when Reverend Whitehead made his escape from the plantation without being seen. Laden with his basket of food and the weight of his silver coins, he softly sang his favorite hymn as he walked. He was a happy man. Perhaps the only black preacher ever to give a sermon to whites—and he had managed to cause Dundee to break through the first elements of learning. Dundee was quick to understand, an exceptionally smart student. For Reverend Whitehead, it had been one glorious Christmas.

Dundee, meanwhile, was reciting the alphabet to the mare while he baited and watered her before taking her out for a morning airing. He had discovered that letters form words, and words told what the pictures were. It was like a bright ray of sunlight through a pitch-black stormy sky.

An overseer was approaching the stable and Dundee promptly fell silent. That was going to be one of the hardest things about learning—to keep others from discovering he could read and write.

"Yo' sho' wukkin' early," the overseer commented.

"Cain't leave a hoss in a stall too long, suh. Needs airin'. Yo' got time, suh, we runs the hoss an' yo' sees how fas' she is this mornin'?"

"Mr. Jonathan he gives me the timin' clock so I kin check. Saddle up an' we see how good she is."

The horse was not only good, she was surprising in her speed on this crisp dawn. The overseer was beside himself with joy, for the better the horse ran, the better his Christmas bonus.

For Dundee, it had been a double-barreled Christmas. The mare had come through and Dundee knew the alphabet. He doubted he'd ever have a better Christmas than this.

$\{$ 8 $\}$

JONATHAN WENT LOOKING FOR CLARISSA. IF HER
father was present, she must also be here. As he
passed his father, Fitz seized Jonathan's elbow
and, without a word, piloted him out of the drawing room and down the hall to the library, where
he closed the door behind them and locked it.

"Whut's wrong, Papa?" Jonathan asked in a
worried voice. When his father did something
this precipitously, it meant trouble.

Fitz sat down at his desk and motioned Jonathan into a chair close by. "Now why in hell yo'
brings that preacher into the house, son?"

"Had a mind to listen to him. Real good
preachin' man, Papa. Heered him down at the
curin' shed an' liked whut he said."

"Whut he say?"

"Tells all the slaves rebellin' was evil an' gets 'em on'y hung. Says they wuk fo' us like always."

"Whut else?"

"Well, he says they's bettah days comin' fo' the slaves, days of freedom. Any slave thinkin' rebellion, or runnin', shorely should change his mind, he says."

"Likes to heah whut yo' thinks 'bout it, son. Tell me, an' no lyin'. Wants to know jes' whut yo' thinks."

"Mayhap he's right. Plenty talk up No'th 'bout slaves be set free. Saw a newspaper the other day, named the *Liberator,* an' it sho' was whompin' up slaves bein' set free."

"Saw it too. We lucky slaves cain't read. Yo' catch one of 'em readin', yo tells me quick."

" 'Members that, Papa. But yo' cain't blame 'em fo' wantin' to be free."

"Son, I was black an' wukkin' fo' no pay an' whupped by mastah, I'd run. I'd bust loose no mattah whut I had to do. But I ain't black, an' I ain't a slave. An' yo' was wrong bringin' that ol' man to the house to preach."

Jonathan looked mystified. "Papa, yo' made them listen to him. Yo' said they listens or they leaves."

"I was backin' yo' up. Couldn't let folks think yo' outen yo' mind. I didn', them bastahds out theah'd laugh yo' outen the house. Nevah do that agin."

Jonathan nodded. "I promise. But I say it wan't a bad idee, Papa. Mayhap it done some good, even. Mayhap one or two of 'em out theah learned somethin'. Yo' got to admit the preacher was good."

"Better'n any white preacher I heerd. Come to think o' it, haven' heerd one in yeahs."

"How long befo' yo' thinks they so much trouble 'bout slaves, we gots to let 'em all go free?"

"We'll *nevah* let 'em go free. Not lessen they's nuthin' else we kin do. They so many blacks in the South now maybe they wins a war if one starts. Holdin' 'em down bes' way to keep that from happenin'. 'Sides, we sho'ly cain't afford to pay 'em. Costs 'nuff we feeds 'em an' puts clothes on they backs. Got to have slaves, son. We be outa business in six months we don' have 'em."

"Papa, yo' was raised in Boston. Yo' under yo' mama's thumb an' she don' believe in slaves. How yo' believe so strongly 'bout slavery now?"

"That's easy to say, son. Without 'em, no hoss fahm, no 'bacco growin', no sellin' slaves fo' profit. On other fahms, no cotton, no sugah cane, nothin'. Gots to have 'em. Ain't no question 'bout that. My papa he showed me an' he make me know we got to have slaves. An' he tol' me how to treat 'em. Yo' gives 'em one inch an' they takes a mile."

"Yo' mighty good to them today, Papa."

"That's diff'rent. This Christmas an' they takes they gifts fo' presents. They don' think o' whut we gives 'em as pay. That's the diff'rence. An' we gives 'em lots o' freedom fo' one week. They dies mighty young, they don' get time to rest."

"Got me an idee trouble's comin' faster'n we think, Papa. They's too much talkin' 'bout it up No'th."

"Heahs that too. I ain't goin' to Boston come spring jes' to see Melanie. Wants to find whut goes on an' how them No'therners feels 'bout us. I comes back an' I kin tell yo' how long it'll be fo' they's trouble."

"Wish I could go."

"Who takes keer o' the plantation we all goes?"

"I ain't askin', Papa, on'y sayin'."

"Knows that. Now we gets finished with this talkin', bes' we go back to our guests. Seen Clarissa an' her ma come in. Clarissa lookin' pretty good fo' an ol' whore like she. 'Members whut she was like an' sorta gits me horny lookin' at her."

"Think it do yo' any good, Papa?" Jonathan said with a chuckle.

"She gets on her back fo' anybody who ain't ovah a hundrud yeahs old. Yo' wants her, yo' jes' walks up an' puts a hand on her rump an' she ready. But be keerful, she a bitch. She got no likin' fo' any o' us, no mattah how she kisses us an' say how happy she be to see us agin."

"She married to Major Apperson's son. Whut he say 'bout it?"

"Tol' yo' he craves young bucks."

"How she marry a man like that?"

Fitz exploded into laughter. "They's a pretty good story theah, but no time fo' tellin' it now. We gets her to marry him, thinks he a big, strong man an' mos' rich. That sonabitch gets tired pickin' a daisy, he do. On'y thing he do good is goin' to the barn with the two twin bucks. Hates us, he do, as much as his papa, an' that's some hatin'."

"Why yo' asks him heah, then? Lessen it be Clarissa yo' askin'."

"She yo' mama's cousin an' on'y right we asks 'em. 'Sides, I thinkin' maybe we gets some way so

[146]

the Major buys the Fisbee coffle. They ain't wuth a goddamn an' he buys 'em not knowin' that, I laugh fo' a week."

"Yo' got an idee, Papa?"

"Wukkin' on it. Now we goes out theah an' acts like we loves all o' them bastahds."

Jonathan saw Clarissa a few minutes later. In a sultry way, she was an attractive woman. She was given to low-cut, tight gowns exhibiting about as much as she dared. She didn't notice Jonathan, but she gave a series of shrill little cries as she rushed toward Fitz, to envelope him in an embrace while her mouth sought his in a kiss far too long for a kissin' cousin.

Benay stood by, wearing a benevolent expression. She accepted Clarissa's embrace and fond greeting with what seemed to be genuine pleasure. Then Clarissa saw Jonathan.

"I do declare if that ain't little Jonathan. Yo' must be Jonathan all grown up. Reckon yo' is quite a man by now."

Jonathan was gasping before her hug and kiss were over. He was also aware that her inquiring tongue had created an embarrassing tumescence.

Clarissa looked triumphantly at Benay. "He a man all right. Finds that out fo' myse'f. Fitz, yo' don' look a day older."

"How's Horace?" Fitz asked.

She glared at him. "Reckon' yo' knows how he is."

"He heah, or down to the barn?" Fitz asked with a malicious grin.

"Yo' go to hell, Fitzjohn. Yo' sho'ly ain't no saint."

"Comes to whut Horace is, I am."

"Stop yo' fightin'," Benay scolded. "This is Christmas an' no time fo' it. Clarissa, yo' mos' welcome."

The music started and Benay seized Fitz. "Dance with me or I kick yo' shins black. Yo' ain't dancin' with that whore."

Jonathan hastily made his way through the crowd before Clarissa could catch up with him. But outside, in the cool air, he wondered why he'd done that. Clarissa was old enough to be his mother, but she was certainly desirable. And obtainable.

The dancing was on in earnest now. Fitz cared little about it. Mostly he sat with Benay, when she wasn't in the arms of some man on the dance floor. Jonathan was supposed to carry the honors for the family by dancing with every woman in the room. Most were dowagers, charmed by a young man dancing with them. The waltz brought bodies into good contact. Some of the ladies were breathing hard when Jonathan escorted them off the floor, and there were times when he experienced some difficulty in concealing from his partner that she aroused him too. Before the evening was over, Jonathan was thinking urgently of Domingo. He'd not seen her in the last few days, he'd been that busy.

But he had social obligations now.

He dutifully fought off desire and went back on the dance floor with a portly woman, drowned in perfume and with a passion that made her dance too close, except when they were on the side of the dance floor where her husband sat, talking cotton.

Clarissa was everywhere, it seemed, dancing with everyone. Jonathan, watching her seductive behavior and wondering again if he was man enough to take her on, couldn't know that her aim was to get Fitz in an embarrassing situation if she possibly could. Clarissa had listened with anger when Fitz berated Major Apperson. She had little liking for her father-in-law, but she hated Fitz and resented the way he had insulted the Major.

The evening had progressed well so far. The women were slowly tiring, but the men, fortified with good rum and bourbon, were going strong. Benay had gone to the kitchen to confer with Elegant on preparations for tomorrow's picnic, which would have to be served at all hours, a combination breakfast and noontime dinner.

Fitz sat with his chair tilted back against the wall, comfortable, glowing from the effects of the rum, and for the moment, quite alone. Clarissa made an excuse to her partner and left the dance floor to sit down beside him.

"It's a fine party, Fitz. A real credit to Benay. Eve'ybody havin' a good time, reckon."

"Reckon," Fitz replied.

"I been kinda missin' yo', Cousin Fitz. We were mighty good fren's once an' I 'members yo' rapes a gal makes her want mo'."

"I gettin' old," Fitz said. "So be yo'."

"Now, Fitz, neither of us is too old to enjoy one 'nother agin."

"Whut's the matter with Horace? Don' he treat yo' right, Clarissa?"

"Horace is no good. Yo' knows that."

"Reckon' yo' right. Saw him come in little

while ago an' he went right upstairs to bed. Reckon them two young bucks dreened him good."

Clarissa fumed, but took care it didn't show. She would endure anything if it would get Fitz into her snare.

"I kin slip outa bed an' Horace nevah knows it yo' wants to meet me, Fitz. I'd show yo' things ain't changed an' yo' not that old."

"How I get 'way from Benay? Sho' don' wants her to know I be cattin' 'roun' with yo'."

"Benay 'bout ready to fall asleep now. Been watchin' her. She goin' to sleep real sound an' yo' have no trouble slippin' outa bed. Been thinkin' 'bout the way yo' loves a gal evah since I got here, Fitz. Cravin' to meet yo'. Be like ol' times."

"Tell yo' whut," Fitz said. "Benay sleep like yo' say, an' I sees a chance, I come to meet yo' 'bout two o'clock."

Clarissa began to breathe hard. "Wheah, Fitz? Tell me an' I be theah."

"Knows the shed wheah we grows 'bacco seedlin's?"

"Yes."

"Got a little office theah, got a ol' sofa. All we needs, eh, Clarissa?"

"Fitz, right now I wouldn't need that."

"Be keerful," he said with a quick look around. "Saves it fo' latah. Now yo' gets to the dancin' fo' Benay gets back."

Clarissa wet her lips and nodded as she arose. She got a man to dance with her and she was off, to disappear into the crowd.

Jonathan sank wearily onto the chair beside his father. "Papa, yo' gots to get out theah an' dance some. I wore out. Feel like I been dreened by ten whores."

"They's one out theah jes' asked me to meet her."

"Clarissa?" Jonathan asked.

"Who else gets so horny she asks a man to meet her?"

"Yo' aimin' to do it?"

"No suh, I ain't."

"Too tired or too skeered?" Jonathan asked with a grin.

"I ain't nevah too tired fo' that, but not with Clarissa. She a schemin' little bitch. Ain't nuthin' she wouldn' do to make trouble. Heahs me give the Major hell an' I teases her 'bout that half-woman she married to. She mad inside. Mad 'nuff to make some big trouble, an' I sho' ain't takin' no chances."

"Yo' tell her you aims to meet her, Papa?"

"Tol' her I meets her at two o'clock in the little office we got at the seedlin' shed. She kin stay theah 'till 'doomsday, she waits fo' me. Clarissa up to somethin' sho', an' she don' get me into no trap."

"I sho' stays 'way from theah too," Jonathan said. He sighed and nodded in the direction of a portly woman who was beckoning coyly. "Things bustin' up fo' the night, but gots to dance so that ol' lady go to bed thinkin' I be nex' to her. I don' see yo' agin, good night, Papa."

Benay emerged from the kitchen to find Fitz as she'd left him. His chair tilted against the wall. She sat down beside him.

"Yo' ought to dance some, Fitz. Ain't right yo' jes' sits heah."

"Yo' wants to dance, I dances with yo' an' nobody else. Jonathan doin' all the dancin' an' gettin' them ladies all wukked up. I too damn old for that any mo'. 'Cept with yo'—I nevah gets too old I cain't take care o' yo, Benay. Loves yo, I do, an' nobody else."

"Things gettin' kinda quiet. The orchestra looks like they 'bout to drop. Thinks I call it a night, Fitz. Folks be too tired tomorruh fo' the picnic."

"Fo'got the picnic."

"Elegant, she goin' to see that long tables be fixed an' ready. Right under the Jap'nese lanterns. Hope the weathuh don' get colder. Was real nice today an' maybe tomorruh too. Yo' wants to go to bed, I takes keer o' things heah an' sees yo' pretty soon."

"I be waitin'," he said.

He stopped for a few minutes to down another straight rum and talk horses with a rancher who raised cattle and needed good workhorses. They settled on a price quickly, for they were both tired. Fitz went upstairs to bed.

The second floor was crowded with guests. Others would sleep downstairs wherever they could find a comfortable piece of furniture to fit their bodies. Nobody looked for solid comfort. Benay and Fitz's soirees were worth any amount of discomfort.

Benay finally came into the bedroom, exhausted. She sank onto a chair beside the bed where Fitz lay propped up against a mound of pillows.

"Gettin' kinda ol' myse'f for these kind o' parties. Nex' yeah we cuts down on the invitations."

"Agrees," Fitz said. "Yo' lookin' tired, but yo' lookin' good too."

"I thanks yo', Fitz." She moved over to sit before the mirror, where she took down her hair and began to brush it.

"I goin' to meet Clarissa at two o'clock in one o' the sheds," he said.

"Like hell yo' are." There wasn't a break in the application of the brush.

"She say she all heated up an' wants me to dreen her."

"She be gettin' dreened when she ninety," Benay said.

"Yo' don' mind I goes to see her?"

Benay swung around to face him, still applying the brush. "Got a headache, Fitz. Real bad 'cause I so tired. I takes a sleepin' powder tonight."

Fitz chuckled. "Yo trusts me not to meet her."

"Yo' ain't crazy 'nuff to give that bitch a chance to say yo' rapes her."

"She got somethin' on her mind, Benay. Cain't figure whut it is, but she goin' to get mighty cold in that shed, she waits fo' me."

Benay laid the brush on the bureau. "She got a mighty hate fo' us, Fitz. Mayhap she an' her papa-in-law got somethin' fixed up. Nevah saw a man so mad yo' made him kneel fo' that black preacher. An' Fitz, I got to say yo' handled that well. Knows yo' nevah expected our crazy son to bring a black preachin' man to say a prayer fo' all of us."

"Gave him hell fo' it. Got to teach him he cain't do them kinda things. Firs' time in Virginny

[153]

a nigger preacher say prayers to a white congregation."

"I think it was nice. Proper an' nice. Made me feel good, Fitz."

"Wondah whut that gal got in mind."

"Whutevah it is, it ain't good," Benay said. She disrobed and slipped into her nightgown. Then she entered the bathroom, came out with a glass of milky-looking fluid. "Got to have a good sleep tonight. Wakes me 'bout eight."

She drained the contents of the glass and got into bed beside him. He put his arm around her and kissed her gently before he blew out the lamp.

"Yo' is a trustin' woman, Benay. Likes that, I do."

"Got to trust yo', Fitz. Couldn' love yo'-like I do if I didn't."

"Go to sleep," he said.

"Trusts yo', I do," she said, and wrapped both arms tightly around him.

Jonathan wandered out into the night, hungry to make love to a woman. He could have rousted Domingo out of bed, but he was thinking of Clarissa. He strolled down toward the curing sheds and sought out the one where seedlings were grown. He stepped inside, but he couldn't see a thing. It was one of the darkest rooms he'd ever been in. He closed the door.

"Clarissa?" he whispered. "Yo' heah?"

There was no answer. He guessed he might be a bit early, so he sat down on the sofa, stretched out on it to test its softness and size, both of which proved ample. He was seated on the edge of it

[154]

when the door squeaked slightly as it was opened. He heard it close softly.

"Fitz?" Clarissa's voice came out of the gloom. "Yo' heah, Fitz?"

He got off the sofa, scraping his shoes as he did so. Clarissa uttered a small cry and came toward him in the darkness, waiting for him to find her. Jonathan wrapped his arms around her and brought his mouth down against hers. Instantly she responded with a tongue that all but choked him.

"Ain't got nuthin' on under my wrapper," she whispered. "Fitz, yo' loves me. Yo' always loves me. Now show me yo' does."

Jonathan hadn't uttered a word. He pushed her down on the sofa and he was prepared for her so that he had only to enter her. She grasped his buttocks and wrapped her legs around his. Her body moved beneath his.

"Yo's bettah than evah," Clarissa whispered. "Yo' meets me agin tomorruh?"

"Sho'," Jonathan said hoarsely.

He pushed her from him and stood up. He heard her get up from the sofa slowly. She fumbled about for him in the dark and her hand touched his face. Suddenly she turned her fingers into claws and raked her nails down his cheek.

Jonathan cried out in surprise and pain. He raised a hand to his face.

Clarissa said, "Now yo' marked good. Tomorruh I says yo' rapes me an' I proves it by sayin' I scratched yo' face good. Waitin' to see Benay's face when she sees the scratches. That's whut yo' git fo' insultin' my father-in-law an' fo' makin' fun o' me. Yo' raped me, Fitz. It was a nice rapin', an' I cain't say I didn't enjoy it, but nobody's goin' to know that. Yo' jes' took this po' li'l gal an' yo' throws her down, tears off her clothes, an' yo' rapes her."

She stepped back, fumbled for the door, opened it, and ran out. Jonathan didn't move for several minutes. Then he quietly walked to the mansion and went to his room, where he carefully inspected his face. There were some swollen places where Clarissa's nails had tried to penetrate the skin, but hadn't succeeded. This late in the day he was greatly in need of a shave, and the layer of whiskers had protected the skin. Jonathan grinned amiably to himself, blew out the lamp, and went downstairs and out the front door without making any noise. He made his way along familiar paths to the cabin where Domingo lived alone, a special consideration, for she was Jonathan's acknowledged pet.

He opened the door and she sat up, startled and afraid. He moved toward her.

"It me. No cause to start yellin'."

"Massa, suh, I waitin' all night fo' yo'."

He lay down beside her. "Came 'cause this heah jes' aftah Christmas an' I ain't given yo' a present yit."

"Wants no present, massa, suh. Jes' wants yo'."

"I know. That's my present. I needs dreenin' an' when we gets through, I wants somethin' else. Tells yo' later. No time now . . ."

It was half an hour later when he finally rolled off her bed and put his clothes on. Domingo blew out the candle which had softly illuminated their tryst, and peered at him in the early dawn.

"Loves yo', I do," she said simply.

Jonathan smiled at her. "Knows that. 'Preciates it. Yo' good as any white gal. Bettah, I reckon, mos' times. Now I wants yo' to fin' me a young buck, 'bout my size. Bring him heah an' I tells yo' what fo'. Now get yo' little ass outen that bed an' find him quick."

"Massa, suh, yo' ain't makin' me go to some buck?"

"No, Domingo, yo' mine an' nobody else's. Wants him fo' 'nother reason. An' they ain't much time."

She scrambled out of bed, drew on the thin, cheap dress, and scampered out of the cabin. She had no idea why Jonathan wanted a young buck, but she couldn't ask him. As long as he didn't intend to mate her with another slave she was happy. It didn't matter why he wanted this buck. She knew one, a man who'd often sidled up to her suggestively. He was a bachelor looking for a mate, but all he dared do was hint that he wanted her, for he knew full well that she belonged to the young master and it would be deadly if he took her against her will.

She invaded the bachelor quarters as if she belonged there. Some of the sleepy slaves stared at her. Two of them reached long arms in her direction, but she went on by until she found the man she wanted. She shook him awake.

"Massa say I fetches yo' quick," she said. "Yo' comes with me now."

The slave got off his straw mat and slipped on his shirt. He had slept with his trousers on. She seized his hand and pulled him along until they were clear of the quarters. They loped through the dark to her cabin.

"Whaffo' yo' drags me?" He resisted slightly. "Yo' ain't gittin' me in yo' bed, Domingo. Young massa hangs me, I pesters yo'."

"Young massa hangs yo', yo' don' run fastah."

At the entrance to the cabin, the buck pulled himself free. He could see Jonathan sitting on the edge of the cot, a piece of furniture privileged to only a few slaves. The sight of the young master unsettled him so that he started to turn and run away.

"Get in heah!" Jonathan called out sharply.

The slave walked into the cabin, hesitantly and fearfully. "Massa suh, I ain't comin' to pester Domingo. Sweahs I ain't. She say I comin' 'cause yo' wants me, but sweah I don' pester her."

"Knows that. Cut off yo' balls yo' does. Wants yo' fo' somethin' else. Yo' do whut I tells yo' an' I gives yo' two silvah dollahs."

"Massa suh—" The slave's face broadened into a smile. "Likes that I does. Whut yo' wants me to do, suh?"

"Jes' stand theah fo' now. Domingo, gimme yo' hand."

She raised her arm and he seized her hand and ran her nails against the palm of his hand.

"They's sharp," he said. "Domingo, now yo' puts yo' hand 'gainst this heah buck's cheek. Lemme see—the right cheek. Go on, put yo' han' theah."

She obeyed him, no less puzzled than the buck.

[158]

"Now yo' claws his cheek. Yo digs yo' nails deep an' yo' draws blood."

Domingo stared at him as if she believed he'd suddenly gone bereft of his senses.

"Do it!" Jonathan ordered sharply. "Scratch his face good, like he tryin' to rape yo' an' yo' fightin' him."

Domingo dug her nails into his cheek. The slave cried out in pain, but quickly subsided as Jonathan lit the candle and inspected the wounds. Four deep scratches ran down his cheek. Jonathan laughed happily. He placed two silver dollars in the palm of the slave's hand and gave five more to Domingo.

"Gots one mo' thing—whut's yo' name?"

"N'Awleans, suh."

"All right, N'Awleans," Jonathan said. "Now yo' comes with me to the kitchen an' I tells yo' whut to do latah on."

Jonathan slapped Domingo lightly on the rump, caressed her face affectionately, then led the buck to the kitchen.

Elegant, who never left her private domain, had a cot close by the stove. Jonathan shook her awake and she sat up with flailing arms to ward off any assailant.

"Massa, suh!" she exclaimed. "Whut wrong? Whut I done?"

"Yo' ain't done nuthin' 'cept cook the bes' food in the worl'. This heah is N'Awleans. Wants yo' to let him stay heah. He behaves hisse'f or I takes the whup to him. Come mornin', yo' puts a white coat on him, gives him a tray with somethin' on it. Now Elegant, yo' knows Mist'ess Clarissa?"

"Sho' does, massa, suh."

"Good. When she come down an' goes out to the picnic table, yo' lets her sit down fo' a few minutes an' then yo' points her out to N'Awleans heah. He takes the tray, goes down theah, an' serves Mist'ess Clarissa. N'Awleans, yo' makes sho' she sees yo' face. Wants her to see yo' scratches up real close. Then yo' gits the hell outen theah fas' as yo' kin. Wait—she goin' to look at yo' face an' mayhap she gonna let out a yell yo' kin heah in Richmond. All yo' does is smile. Jes' a little smile befo' yo' gits the hell out. Yo' goes straight back to yo' quarters an' yo' stays theah. Kin yo' do this?"

"Yes suh, massa, suh. I kin do it."

"Yo' does it real good, jes' like I tells yo', yo' gets two mo' silvah dollahs. Now yo' tells me jes' whut I wants yo' to do."

"I weahs a white coat, I goes down totin' a tray, an' I serves this mist'ess Elegant show me. I smiles an' then I gits the hell out."

"Good. Elegant, yo' baits him good too. All he kin eat an' the bes' food yo' got. That's all fo' now. Do jes' whut I say."

Jonathan guessed that about forty-five minutes had elapsed since he'd encountered Clarissa. He walked through the darkness back to the shed to inspect it and make certain no trace of the assignation remained.

As he opened the door, he tensed. "Who in theah?" he demanded.

"Come on in, son," Fitz said.

"I be damned," Jonathan said with a laugh. "I sends her away long ago, Papa. Hopes yo' ain't mad."

"I mo' glad than mad. Couldn't sleep thinkin' 'bout Clarissa. Don' know I comes down heah to dreen myse'f, or jes' to tell her to get the hell home. Benay, she sleepin' sound. Tells her 'bout Clarissa an' she say she know I don' go to see her—she so sho' she takes a sleepin' powder. Yo' mama a fine woman, son. Mighty fine."

"But yo' 'members whut Clarissa like. She mighty good, Papa. She know whut to do an' she got plenty juice in her."

Fitz nodded. "Reckon I'm glad she ain't heah. Now I don' have to fight with myse'f not to love her up some. Yo' does it fo' me."

"Papa, yo' said yo' was skeered Clarissa do some bitchy trick on yo'."

"Whut she do, son? Anythin' yo' feels bad 'bout?"

"Papa, she gets up an' scratches my cheek, hard she kin. She say I rapes her—she mean you—an' she goin' to tell ev'ybody they comes to the picnic table."

Fitz whistled. "She a bitch all right. She yell her haid off an' mayhap some thinks she truthful. Whut yo' aimin' to do 'bout it?"

"She thinks it yo' who give her that lovin'. In the dark she don' know who the hell got on top o' her. But she calls yo' name an' she say she goin' to make yo' sorry. She 'spects yo'll have scratches on yo' face which yo' didn' have las' night. But there ain't no scratches on you. She goin' to be one crazy gal wonderin' who she spread her laigs fo'."

"Son, yo' takes aftah yo' grandpapa," Fitz exclaimed, delighted. "Sho'ly do. He full o' tricks like that."

"Thank yo', Papa."

"Got me a trick o' my own. Been thinkin' how I gets rid o' that no-'count coffle I bought fo' a song offen the Fisbee place. Goin' to make Major Apperson buy 'em, ev'ything go like I wants. Tells yo' 'bout it tomorruh. Bettah we get to bed now. Mornin' soon."

"Sho', Papa."

They began their walk along the path up to the mansion. They didn't speak until they were almost there.

"Papa," Jonathan said, "Clarissa theah waitin' fo' yo' whut yo' think yo' do?"

"Don' know, son. Rightly don' know. 'Members her, I does. She pretty good?"

"Tol' yo', she hotter'n hell."

Fitz nodded. "Wonders whut I do she theah waitin'. Sho' wonders."

In the morning, Fitz and Jonathan, accompanied by a mystified Benay, waited in the reception hall until they heard Clarissa on her way downstairs. They quickly withdrew into the dining room so she would pass by without seeing them.

Clarissa looked cheerful, and quite lovely—a fact that Fitz noticed without commenting on it. In fact, she looked better at forty than she had at twenty. Probably screwed better too.

Jonathan nudged his father. "Yo' goes now an' sits 'side her."

"Whut's goin' on?" Benay asked her son after Fitz had left to join Clarissa. They saw Clarissa waiting impatiently until Fitz sat down. She looked keenly at him and frowned deeply.

Jonathan said, "Mama, shall I bring yo' to the table?"

They walked down, arm in arm, and Jonathan seated himself on the other side of Clarissa. She stared at him. There wasn't a mark on his face. He'd made certain of that.

Jonathan could see New Orleans coming down the walk carrying a tray somewhat precariously, for he was not adept at work around the house. But he managed it quite well. He walked around the head of the table at which a dozen guests were already seated. He bent down to place a plate before Clarissa, letting her have a good look at his scratched cheek. At the same time, he obeyed Jonathan's instructions to the letter. He gave Clarissa a slow smile, just enough that it looked like a knowing smile, that of a conspirator.

Clarissa uttered one piercing screech and slid off the chair under the table, where she lay in a dead faint.

{ 9 }

"WHUT IN THE WORLD HAPPEN TO CLARISSA?" Benay asked. "She in her room screamin' an' carryin' on like she out o' her min'."

"Cain't figger it out myse'f," Fitz said. "Jonathan, yo' got any idee whut in hell got under her skin?"

"Me?" Jonathan asked. "Whut I knows 'bout it? All of a sudden she jes' starts yellin' an' she slid outen her chair an' under the table. Firs' I thought she drunk, but Clarissa not up long 'nuff to get drunk. Reckon she jes' kinda crazy."

Benay said, "Reckon both o' yo' is lyin'. Got that feelin'. But it bein' Clarissa, I ain't askin' any questions."

"Her papa madder'n hell," Jonathan observed.

"I asks him whut's wrong an' he neah eats my haid off. Papa, knows yo' don' like the Major. I don't either. Ain't a man yo' kin like. He cheats anybody he kin. Don' like a man like that."

"It a shame the way he cheats," Fitz agreed. "Man cain't stand to let somethin' he wants get away from him. Wondah if he buys the Fisbee coffle from us."

"Fitz, yo' says yo'se'f they ain't wuth nuthin'," Benay said.

"They shorely ain't, but we sells 'em like prime stock——"

"How yo' goin' to do that?" she asked. "Major Apperson a smaht man."

"Sho' he is, but smaht men sometimes get so greedy they fo'get they smaht. Thinkin' on this. 'Specially whut we gots to do while he here."

"Reckon Clarissa goin' to stay?" Jonathan asked.

"Now whut's that to yo', son?" Benay demanded suspiciously.

"Nothin', Mama, 'ceptin' Papa wants to deal with the Major an' she don' stay, mayhap he don' stay."

"I see. Yo' ain't settin' to satisfy that gal in any way, is yo'?"

"Don' reckon she likes me, Mama."

"I'm glad to heah that. How long yo' figure we keeps these folks, Fitz? Las' yeah it was fo' days."

Fitz munched an already well-chewed cheroot reflectively as he stared into space in deep thought.

"Asks yo', Fitz——"

"Heerd yo', Benay. Thinks this be the las' day. Cain't afford to keep 'em any more'n that. An' I wants 'em to know it."

"Cain't afford . . . ?" Benay began in amazement.

"Wants Major Apperson to think we got money trouble. Not so bad we goin' bankrup'. Jes' we kinda short o' cash right now. Obleeged yo' lets folks know that."

" 'Nother of yo' tricks, Fitz, ain't it?"

"Kinda like that. Been achin' to teach the Major a lesson since he got so goddamn sassy dur-'in the preachin'. Won't hurt nobody but him. An' Clarissa."

"She my cousin, Fitz. She my blood relation —an' seein' she is, I does whut yo' says if it makes her hop."

Fitz smiled and nodded. "Sweah it will."

"All right. I begins to pass the word," Benay said.

"Do it easy-like, an' be sho' the Major or Clarissa heahs yo'."

"I'm goin' up to see Clarissa now. I'll start with her. Yo' gents wants to tell me somethin' 'fore I talks to her?"

"Me?" Fitz said. "Whut I got to tell?"

"Mama, I don' know whut in hell made her screech that way. Don' look at me. I done nuthin' to Clarissa."

Benay gave a curt nod and went into the house. Fitz and Jonathan, idling some time away on the ample veranda, remained where they were, idly watching their guests, some still at the long table gorging on Elegant's fine food. A few others were playing croquet. Many of the men were still talking money crops and drinking from Fitz's ample supply of whiskey and rum.

"Thinks they gettin' kinda tired," Fitz said. "Ev'y yeah they stays less an' less time. Folks too damn greedy. Got to make money fas' an' ain't got time fo' a little fun, even if it free. Reckon Benay gets a earful from Clarissa?"

"Papa, she wouldn' tell anybody whut happen. She ain't even sho' whut did. Thinks yo' pestered her las' night, but yo' face not scratched. Reckon' she looks at me too, thinkin' maybe it was me, an' I ain't scratched either."

"But that buck sho' scratched," Fitz commented in sheer delight. "Now let's yo' an' me talk some business. Heah's whut I wants yo' to do."

"I'm listenin', Papa."

"While I talkin', keep yo' eyes offen that Mrs. Palmer down theah in that dress looks like it go down to her knees. This impohtant business."

"Said I was listenin'."

"Wants yo' to call out 'bout a hundred bes'-lookin' bucks an' line 'em up jes' back o' the house. Put 'bout twenny good-lookin' gàls with 'em an' have the gals each hold a sucker. Anybody asks yo', say yo' jes' keepin' count, but yo' tells them bucks an' gals they goin' on the vendue table soon's we gets 'em to market."

"Thinks I knows whut you plannin' to do. I don' tell the slaves they goin' to be sold 'till the Major someplace neah wheah he heahs whut goes on. Them gals sho' goin' to raise hell. Cry an' wail, an' the bucks goin' to look like they jes' lost they woman. That whut yo' wants?"

"Yo' gettin' smaht as me," Fitz said. "Anybody asks, don' say we takin' a coffle to market in a couple o' days. Let 'em think so, but don't tell 'em so."

"Whut we goin' to do then, Papa?"

"Day after tomorruh I spancels all them slaves an' starts walkin' 'em to the city. Passes Major Apperson's place, but keeps goin', like I don' wants him to see the coffle."

"An' I takes that coffle from the Fisbee place."

"On'y at night. Yo' starts day after me, but I stop at Colonel Coldwell's plantation an' bed the coffle down fo' the night. Yo' takes the Fisbee coffle way 'roun' the Colonel's place an' gets ahead o' me while I restin' at the Colonel's. Be keerful not to go close to Major Apperson's place. Yo' gets into the city ahead o' me an' yo' puts the Fisbee coffle in the slave pens. Be sho' nobody sees 'em yo' kin he'p it."

"Whut yo' doin' with the good slaves, Papa, yo' on the way to the city too?"

"When we leaves the Colonel's place, I turns that coffle ovah to Hong Kong an' he tells them slaves I changed my mind an' they goin' back to Wyndward. Hong Kong gets them theah, they gets two days off even after New Yeah's. An' maybe I gives the bucks a keg o' rum an' the gals some ribbons. See 'bout that later. Yo' knows whut to do now?"

Jonathan nodded doubtfully. "Cain't figger how yo' goin' to get Major Apperson to buy that coffle so he don' fin' out they Fisbee slaves an' wuth nuthin'."

"Yo' looks an' yo' listens an' I show yo' how

to cheat a man who oughta be cheated. Don' even tell Benay whut we doin'. She thinks we takin' slaves to the vendue table, she don' ask no questions."

"Goin' to like this," Jonathan said. "Goin' to like it mighty good, Papa."

"Major thinks we got money trouble, he goin' to get firs' in line to try an' cheat us. Knows him, an' goin' to teach him a lesson an' maybe take that bitch daughter-in-law down some."

"He goin' to be awful mad, Papa. Someday he kin be a dangerous man he gets mad 'nuff. Yo' heerd that befo'."

"Evah since I come heah. Way I sees it, he talks like he big, dangerous man, but talkin' ain't actin'. Mayhap he got no mo' sap than that son o' his."

"I gets things goin' fo' the Major decides to take po' little Clarissa home. Yo' thinks she evah gets ovah this, Papa?"

"Not 'till she gets in bed with somebody. Wonder she goin' to worry she carryin' a black sucker? Now that'd be somethin'. Yas suh, that sho' be somethin'."

Although the slaves were officially on a holiday, this could be canceled at any time. Jonathan began to select the best-looking bucks and women with babies. He didn't tell them they were going to be sold, but when he lined them all up, they began to grow suspicious.

Presently some of the guests drifted down to see why so many slaves were being lined up. Jonathan gave them no information, merely saying Fitz wanted to check up on some of the slaves.

When he saw Major Apperson sauntering his way, Jonathan called Hong Kong aside and told him to warn the slaves they were now a coffle and would be moved out tomorrow. Till then they would be spanceled and segregated from the other slaves.

An instant wail went up when Hong Kong passed the word. Major Apperson stopped at Jonathan's side.

"Yo' makin' up a coffle, Jonathan?"

"Coffle? Reckon not, suh. Jes' countin' our slaves an' this be the firs' batch of 'em. Goin' to count ev'yone fo' New Yeahs. Like we takin' inventory."

"I see. That's a strange way of doin' it. Why the irons?"

"We always spancels 'em heah, suh. So we don' count 'em twice. Bes' way to do it, suh. Now yo' excuses me. Gots to see they locked up proper. Tomorruh we counts fi' hundred mo' an' by the time they goes back to wuk, we gots 'em all counted. Way we does it, suh."

At Jonathan's command, Hong Kong marched the dejected-looking slaves to one of the big barracks and stood aside while they filed in.

Major Apperson observed all this. "Been hearin' yo' papa got money troubles," he said.

Jonathan shrugged. "Firs' time I hears 'bout it. Co'se the factor in N'Awleans is kinda slow payin', but that don' mattah . . . much."

"Yo' didn't get paid fo' yo' 'bacco crop?"

"Didn' say that, Major. Said he kinda slow."

"Oh, I see. Jonathan, whut happen to Clarissa?"

"Don' know, suh. Mayhap she drinks too much the night befo'. Hope the po' gal ain't still sick."

"Somethin' mo' than that happen to her. She won' tell me a thing, but she so mad, I knows it somethin' somebody done to her."

"Clarissa kinda free way she dances. Make a man get the hots fo' her. Maybe one of 'em said somethin' Clarissa didn' like. Seen it happen befo', suh."

"Ummm, yes, I suppose so." The Major walked away, and Jonathan ambled over to join Benay and Fitz on the veranda.

Benay said, "Whut's that slut up to now?"

"Who yo' talkin' 'bout, Mama?" Jonathan looked about the grounds.

"When yo' mama call a woman a slut, she means Clarissa," Fitz said.

"Whut she doin'?" Benay lazily repeated the question.

"Jes' now she talk to that group o' women by the long table," Fitz observed. "Then she goes to whisper to 'nother group an' she makin' 'nother visit an' mo' whisperin'. She up to somethin' sho'."

"Didn' take her long to get ovah bein' sick an' faintin'," Jonathan said.

"Thinks yo' two know mo' 'bout that than yo' lets me know. Look, she's hurryin' off now."

"I be damned," Fitz said. "Some o' them ladies she talked to are gettin' up an' movin' casual-like after her."

"See whut they's up to, Fitz," Benay said. "Don' wan' to get mixed up in it myse'f, but yo' kin tell me, yo' finds out."

"They's headin' down by the whuppin' shed,"

Jonathan observed as he and Fitz walked in that direction. "Reckon Clarissa goin' to whup a slave fo' they pleasure?"

"Son, she capable o' anythin'. 'Members way back, fo' I married Benay, I goes to her papa's fahm to buy hosses. Meets yo' mama theah, but I sees Clarissa, she a young gal then, makin' a buck shuck down in one o' the barns. He don' do like she say, she lashes him with a hosswhup. An' aftah he shuck down, she raisin' her dress an' showin' her tits so she kin see him gettin' a hahd-on. That po' buck thinkin' she crazy."

"Reckon that buck wasn't much wrong 'bout that."

"I sends the buck away an' I gives Clarissa hell, but she jes' come to me an' gets her arms 'roun' me."

"Whut yo' do then, Papa?"

"None o' yo' goddamn business, son. Walk easy now. Gettin' kinda close."

They heard a sharp cry of pain, a woman's cry, and that puzzled them further. Moving cautiously, they rounded the end of a shed. From that vantage point, they had a perfect view of what went on.

Clarissa and a half-dozen other women were standing outside the cage. Locked in it was a beautifully proportioned buck, young and virile, and naked. Clarissa had a long pole and with this she prodded at the buck's legs, letting the pole slither up and down.

The buck cowered in a corner, bending his knees and trying to cover up. Clarissa seized a young female slave by the arm and hurled her in the direction of the cage. The slave cried out again. It had been her voice that Fitz and Jonathan had heard.

"Shuck down!" Clarissa ordered.

"Mist'ess, ma'am, don' wants to," the girl said imploringly.

"Shuck down or I rips yo' dress off an' whups yo' till they ain't no skin lef' on yo' black ass. Shuck down, I said."

Reluctantly the girl pulled off her dress and stood naked. Clarissa's eyes were bright and her voice came in hisses. Her audience stood back, but seemed to be enjoying every moment of the spectacle.

Clarissa turned toward the group. "Heerd tell, big buck like this hung so heavy ain't no white man kin get as big. Goin' to find out now."

She used the pole to prod the buck again. He looked beseechingly at the naked girl as if she could help him, but she could only stand there, as helpless as he.

Clarissa swung the pole and struck the girl across the back. "Get up theah right agin the cage. "Yo, nigger—comes close an' lets the gal finger yo'. I said come close, or yo' gets the whuppin' o' yo' life."

Fitz whispered, "He sho' hung heavy."

"Yo' gettin' horny, Papa?" Jonathan asked.

"Like yo'? That whut yo' means?"

"Kinda. Whut yo' goin' to do 'bout this, Papa?"

"Well now, thinkin' on it."

"Yo' sho' thinkin' slow."

"Know whut she goin' to do nex'? She goin' to throw that gal in the cage an' makes the buck rape her while they looks on."

"Papa, yo' standin' heah an' lets that happen? Mama goin' to be awful mad."

Fitz glanced sideways at his son. "Why yo' remin' me o' that right now? We runs down theah an' befo' Clarissa kin run, I gets hold o' her while yo' opens the cage do'. We sho' cain't miss this chance, Jonathan. Yo' ready?"

"When yo' gives the word."

"Let's go!"

Fitz gave voice to a rebel yell and Jonathan joined in. The women screamed and fled as fast as they could run, skirts flying, hats tilted off their heads by the very breeze they created in their haste.

Too stunned to move in time, Clarissa was picked up by Fitz. She kicked and screamed while Jonathan held the cage door open. Fitz threw her into the cage, then Jonathan slammed the door and snapped the padlock shut.

Wild-eyed, Clarissa pressed herself in a corner of the cage and warily watched the buck, who was too startled and confused to do anything but stand there, naked, with no sign of any passion, for he was far too frightened.

"Whut holdin' yo' back, Clarissa?" Fitz asked in a loud voice. "Yo' wants to see how he hung, made it kinda easy fo' yo'."

Clarissa couldn't speak. She was half bent over, hands pressing hard against her pubic area as if she expected the slave to leap at her and begin raping.

The terrified slave took a tentative step toward her. It was possible he thought he might get past this screaming, crazy woman and escape.

Clarissa let out a wild screech of terror and

kept trying to cover up, as if she too were naked. The slave backed up, but Clarissa's screams continued.

They were loud enough to attract the attention of the guests, who came running, not certain if they were hearing a cry for help or the anguish of someone badly injured. Major Apperson was in the foreground, with Benay not far behind. The Major came to a halt, speechless. Clarissa was still screeching, the slave was cowering back, covering himself up with his hands. The female slave, still naked, turned her back.

"Whut in hell this 'bout?" Major Apperson roared. "Whut yo' doin' to this gal?"

Fitz said, "Ain't doin' nothin', Major. Clarissa was tauntin' the buck to get him horny an' see whut happen. She whups a nakid gal to reach in an' fondle the buck."

"Whut she doin' in the cage?"

"Think she wants to see how he hung bad as all that, I gives her a chance. I jes' invited her to step into the cage an' see whut the buck will do. That's whut she wanted, seems like."

Clarissa gave one final shriek and fainted.

"Jonathan, drag her out," Fitz said. He turned to the naked slave girl. "Put yo' dress on an' go back to yo' cabin."

"Yas suh, massa, suh." She slipped the dress over her head.

"Ain't blamin' yo' none," Fitz said. "Get the hell outa heah."

The girl fled. Jonathan unlocked the cage door, grasped Clarissa's right leg and pulled her out. He carried her over to where the Major stood, fuming and cursing under his breath.

"Thinks a good hidin' do this li'l gal some good," Jonathan said.

"I don' believe a word o' any o' this." The Major was supporting Clarissa, who now managed to stand weakly, weeping and clinging to him for protection.

"Bes' yo' do, Major," Fitz said. "We got lots o' witnesses."

"I'll get to the bottom o' this," the Major threatened.

"It'll be the bottom whar yo' finds yo' answers," Fitz said "Nevah seen anythin' lower then whut Clarissa done. Yo' calls me a liar an' I takes off my coat an' whales the holy hell outa yo', Major. Saw Clarissa sweet-talk six-seven o' these ladies to come an' watch. They witnesses to eve'ythin' that happens—nevah saw ladies so disgusted. Yo' takes her outa heah now, Major. Don' wants nobody like Clarissa on my proppity."

Major Apperson glared at Fitz. "Suh, I been insulted by yo' too many times. I declare yo' tricks me once mo' I calls yo' out. Ain't takin' no mo'. Warnin' yo'. Come along, Clarissa. We ain't stayin' on this crazy man's proppity longer'n we kin get off it. An' stop yo' bawlin'. Cain't stand a woman who bawls her haid off."

He half-dragged her along and at the front of the mansion he ordered his carriage brought. No one said much, not out loud, though there was a great deal of whispering.

"Is it true whut yo' said she done?" Benay asked.

"Ask the ladies who were theah, Benay. Nevah saw anythin' like this. Yo' evah see anythin' worse, Jonathan?"

"No suh, nevah did. The po' slave, all shucked down while Clarissa pokes him with that theah pole. Then makin' the gal slave shuck down an' orderin' her to touch the buck. Like to make me puke, Mama."

"Well, I'm glad the ladies who were tricked into watchin' this were as disgusted as yo', Fitz."

"They closed they eyes when Clarissa makes the gal shuck down an' go to the cage. Easy to see they couldn' stan' lookin' at a thing like this."

Several women in the crowd mentally blessed Fitz.

Fitz shouted to the naked buck still in the cage, uncertain what to do and fearful he'd be transferred to the whipping shed next door.

"Yo' get outa that cage, boy, an' yo' runs to yo' cabin or yo' quarters. Ain't yo' fault whut happen. Get an' run!"

The slave jumped from the cage, broke into a run and rapidly made distance from that place of embarrassment and torture. Fitz watched him go.

"Sho' hung heavy," he said, half aloud.

"Whut did yo' say?" Benay asked.

"Said he sho' runs fas'. Tell yo' one good thing 'bout this crazy business. We sho' gets rid o' the Major an' Clarissa."

"I'm disownin' her as of right now," Benay said. "She may be my cousin, but cain't stand her no mo'. No man safe 'roun' her."

"Yo' sho' is right," Fitz said.

"An' that includes yo', Fitz." Benay linked her arms under those of her husband and son. "Kinda wish I was heah. Must have been interestin'."

They strolled back to the mansion. The party's tone had softened and there was little activity. Major Apperson and Clarissa, still clinging to him, waited for their carriage to come from the vicinity of the stables. When it pulled up, he gallantly stepped aside so Clarissa could get in. When she hesitated, he brought his hand up and half-raised, half-pushed her onto the seat.

As the carriage began to move, there was a wild shriek and Horace, Clarissa's husband, came running after it, arms waving while he kept shouting for them to wait. Behind him came his young twin slaves, also waving their arms. Someone laughed shrilly. The Major stood up in the carriage, which had stopped to take on Horace and his pets. He was shouting and waving his arms angrily. The carriage started up and he fell back onto the seat.

"He sho' mad," Fitz said happily.

"Kinda feels sorry fo' him," Benay said.

"Kinda worried 'bout him too, Papa," Jonathan added. "He say he calls yo' out they's any mo' trouble."

"Wait'll he finds out whut he bought at the auction nex' week," Fitz said with a loud laugh. "This heah raise his dander some, but when it goin' to cos' him money, he goin' to be crazy. Wants a drink now. Feels I needs it."

This episode seemed to put the finishing touches on the Christmas celebration. The guests began getting ready to leave. Those who didn't have to travel far were ordering up their carriages. Others were preparing for a morning departure.

In the early evening, after a light supper, which all of the remaining guests also enjoyed, Benay and Jonathan sat in the wicker rockers on the veranda. It was not yet dark and it was pleasant on this unusually warm December day.

"Jonathan, it true the Major say he calls out Fitz?" Benay asked.

"True 'nuff."

"Yo' evah heahs the Major been in othah duels?"

"Been in five, six. Knows he killed two men. Heerd he spends lots o' time practicin' with his pistols. Got me worried some."

"What's Fitz goin' to try nex' to make him mad?"

"We trickin' him into thinkin' we sells a prime coffle. Papa starts out with prime slaves, but he turns back. I takes the Fisbee coffle, ain't wuth a damn, an' I gets it to the slave market an' gets the coffle locked up. Don' know how Papa goin' to trick the Major when them po'ly slaves gets on the vendue table."

"Yo' papa will think o' somethin'," Benay said. "Reckon' he already has. Whut yo' think Fitz do, he gets called out?"

"Fight," Jonathan said.

"Yo thinks he got a chance o' stayin' alive?"

"Not much of a one, Mama. Worries me, it does."

"It worries me too, but I can tell who it don't worry. Yo' papa."

[10]

Two days after the Christmas party, Fitz kissed Benay and climbed into the ornate stagecoach his father had bought years ago.

"Major Apperson goin' to have spies out watchin' fo' me," he said. "This heah coach somethin' nobody kin miss. 'Sides, it bettah than a carriage. Not so much dust inside."

"Fitz," Benay said, "I'm worried. Yo' tricks the Major again, he got to call yo' out or he looks like a fool. An' Clarissa goin' to egg him on. Nothin' she like bettah than to have her father-in-law kill yo'."

"Ain't no reason to worry," he said. "Got me an idee—had it fo' yeahs—the Major is a coward."

"Even cowards have to fight sometimes," Benay argued. "An' he mighty good with duelin' pistols."

"Now stop yo' worryin' or I gives up this whole damn business an' busts my heart I don' have this chance to whup the Major's pocketbook. That's whut he cain't stand."

Benay stepped back and watched the procession begin its long journey. The slaves, roped and manacled, were certainly a prime lot. The procession had no sooner vanished in the great cloud of dust it created than Jonathan began assembling the Fisbee slaves.

They'd been on Wyndward now long enough for them to come back from the sorry condition in which Fitz had found them, but they were still thin and slow, having been brutally beaten into a state of submission that made them resemble zombies. Even the children were listless.

Overseers and drivers began getting them ready. No one else was working. The holidays were still in force and the slaves were enjoying their furlough from hard labor. Like the folks who attended Benay's soiree, the slaves were apt to gather in small groups to discuss things. Every one of them knew about what had happened to Clarissa and there was much quiet laughter over the predicament in which Fitz had placed her. The buck she had locked in the cage and the naked girl attained prestige among their group.

Dundee was not among those lazing away the days. His duties at the stables had not been relaxed in any way. Still he found time to study and wonder how those letters could be formed into words that matched the pictures he recognized. It was extremely slow and he needed help. He hoped the Reverend would find it possible to slip back onto the plantation soon.

That evening Jonathan was ready to lead the Fisbee coffle. During the afternoon Benay had gone down among those slaves and given them extra food and party leftovers. She regarded them as still being in a poor state of health and stamina. When Jonathan came out to begin the trek, he discovered that every wagon on the plantation had been brought out and loaded with slaves.

"Don' think Papa like this, Mama," he said.

"Don' keer he likes it o' not. Yo' walks them po' souls all that way an' half of 'em dead fo' yo' gets theah. They rides."

"Reckon yo' right," Jonathan said.

Benay kissed her son and stood and watched the procession of wagons vanish in a cloud of dust. Now she was in full charge of the mansion. There were many things to do and she was glad of that. If she remained unoccupied, she'd worry far more about the Major's threat to call Fitz out; for she knew if he did, Fitz wouldn't disregard the invitation.

Dueling had gone into a sort of limbo for many years now. But there seemed to be more and more talk of it. The newspapers did not neglect any story of a duel, though they were careful not to print names. Dueling was against the law, but no one paid much attention to that.

Jonathan and his coffle reached the city twelve hours sooner than he expected, for almost all the distance was by wagon. Not until they were within easy range of the slave market did he compel the coffle to walk the rest of the way.

Jonathan knew why this group of slaves had not come back to sound health, as most coffles do. They'd all been sick. Many of the slaves at the Fisbee place had been lost to cholera, which had swept the area. Some of those who recovered were still suffering from the long-term effects of the deadly disease.

Jonathan was half tempted to ask his father to call it all off. On the Major's place, these slaves were not going to be treated gently. Especially since they'd be the pawns in an affair that would cost the Major a small fortune.

Jonathan installed the coffle in the slave pens, where they would have to wait twenty-four hours before they'd be sold. How that would be accomplished Jonathan didn't know. These slaves, on the vendue table, would be promptly identified as worthless misfits, but Fitz was seeking a great deal. And somehow, Jonathan was sure, he would get it.

Jonathan spent the rest of the day buying the usual clothing for the slaves. Because he felt sorry for them he indulged in somewhat better quality than he otherwise would have done, and arranged that good food be supplied the coffle.

So far he'd not even tried to find his father. It wouldn't be difficult, for Fitz always stayed at the Capital Hotel. When Jonathan had completed his work, he went there and checked in. His father was waiting for him in the café.

Fitz was feeling rather good when Jonathan joined him. This was the fanciest hotel in town and had the best and largest bar. The furnishings of the rooms were expensive and plush. Chairs were padded, tables were of ample size, and so were the drinks. Food was also served here, prepared in one of the finest kitchens in the South.

Waiters bustled about. The long bar was elbow to elbow with patrons. There was an excitement about the place which Jonathan enjoyed.

"Sit down, boy," Fitz said affectionately. "Figured yo'd get heah 'bout this time. Been heah a li'l early myse'f. Nice place to do yo' waitin'."

Jonathan smiled. "'Specially since they brings yo' rum and watah a hell of a lot faster'n Calcutta brings it."

"Well, why not?" Fitz asked. "Man's got to get 'way once in a while, an' when he do, he be a fool not to celebrate his freedom. I'll ordah mo' drinks."

He raised his arm and a waiter appeared like magic. It was evident this table was closely watched so the service would be superlative. Jonathan recalled the big bills left on the table for tips. No one ever accused Fitz of being cheap.

"Yo' got the coffle locked up," Fitz said. "Made sho' o' that by payin' the slave pens a visit. They looks bettah'n I 'spected, an' sees yo' fitted 'em mighty good with clothes."

"Papa, feels sorry fo' them, I do. They's goin' to face hell on the Major's plantation. He goin' to take it out on them, sho'."

"That's they headache," Fitz said. "They's slaves. Whut they 'spect? Comin' heah, headin' the prime coffle, saw the Major's spies watchin' us. They's satisfied the coffle I sells tomorruh is sho' prime. Hong Kong he turns 'em back aftah I was sho' the Major was satisfied. Yo' nevah seed slaves get so happy when they finds out they's goin' back to Wyndward. Mos' like a second Christmas present."

"Reckon," Jonathan said. "Now how yo' figure on makin' the Major buy the coffle? Think he not goin' to check up on yo'? 'Specially since yo' let him think we near busted, and we gots to sell that coffle."

"Talked to the banks this mornin' an' tells 'em mayhap I gots to borrow a lot o' money, which made they tongues hang out. Tells 'em I short o' cash, till the N'Awleans factors pays me fo' the last 'bacco crop. Was watchin' an' saw the Major go into the banks. Comes out smilin' like he got a special whore waitin' fo' him in his room."

"Nothin' fo' me to do tonight?" Jonathan asked. "Mayhap we sits heah mos' the night an' jes' talk."

"Well, got some figurin' to do, son. An' got two, three men comin' on business. Yo kin stay till maybe nine. Likes yo' company, o' co'se. How's Benay?"

"Worryin' some 'bout the Major callin' yo' out."

Fitz frowned slightly and swallowed his drink in one gulp. He signaled for more. "Been a mite worried 'bout it myse'f, hearin' how the Major is pretty good with duelin' pistols. Asked some questions 'bout the duels he had. Seems like he shoots a little faster'n the count mos' times. He does, I gots to let him have the firs' shot or I be worse than he. Countin' on he bein' a coward."

"Mayhap he a coward come to things like business dealin', but he sho' ain't no coward comes to fightin' with pistols. He spends lots o' time practicin'. An' do yo' no good askin' to fight with rapiers, 'cause he even bettah with them."

"Don't keer to gets stuck with no rapier," Fitz said. "Gots to be guns. Way I heers it, he calls me out, I gets to call the weapons an' the terms. That right?"

"Whut I know 'bout it, that's right."

"Seems like I got to get out o' it some way."

"Cain't be done. Man who won't fight sho' ain't considered much of a man in this heah city, Papa. Mayhap we thinks o' somethin'."

"Yo' gets an idee 'preciate yo' tellin me, son."

"I will, Papa. Mama worries some 'bout the men yo' meets on business. Knows yo' does this kinda business in yo' bedroom."

"Man got to get dreened good once in a while. Don' mean I thinks less o' yo' mama. Jes' gots to get dreened."

"Reckon mayhap she knows that too, Papa. When I see yo' in the mornin'?"

"'Bout ten, reckon. Meet me heah for breakfas' befo' we goes to the market an' skins Major Apperson alive. Maybe yo' wants me to fix it so yo' has some business tonight?"

"Too tired, Papa. Yo' got in yesterday. Me, I still eatin' the dust."

"Good fo' a man to get hisse'f dreened," Fitz reminded him. "My papa was a great one fo' that. Could handle three, fo' a night an' wake up like he been sleepin' like a baby all night. Sho' had powah, that man."

"Right now I ain't got any," Jonathan confessed.

"Son, I don' insist. Knows yo' tired an' that ain't good yo' talkin' business all night. But yo' wants to re'lize yo' lives on Wyndward an' not many gals comes theah. Yo' got to be thinkin' 'bout that. Domingo fine, but yo' needs white gals too. Cain't go through yo' life like Hong Kong do."

"Knows that, Papa. I keeps lookin'. Mayhap I sees a gal someday soon. But not tonight. Wants to roll into bed all by myse'f. Pesterin' me tonight wouldn't do any good."

"Well, got some business right now," Fitz said. "Yo' finish yo' drink an' sign the check. Sees yo' in the mornin'."

"Good night, Papa," Jonathan said. "Hopes yo' business turns out real nice."

As Fitz left the café, Jonathan saw an attractive woman meet him in the lobby and they both went off in the direction of the stairs. Jonathan had an idea it would be a very good business conference.

He suddenly felt alone and he disliked the feeling intensely. He ordered a piece of pie, coffee, and a glass of brandy. He dawdled over these items, not wanting to go to his room.

Settling back, he saw a couple at a table halfway across the room. He'd been mildly attracted by the girl, whose back was toward him, because of her long, beautiful hair. The man opposite her, facing Jonathan, was not ordinary. He was a tall, slim, fair-skinned man with light brown hair, dressed completely in white—ruffled shirt, waistcoat, formal coat, pants, shoes, and even his string tie were white. Jonathan, not given to great interest in men's fashions, wondered why a man would dress like that.

Just then the girl turned around. Jonathan sucked in a quick breath. She was strikingly beautiful. She wore lipstick to shape her mouth, and he suspected she used rouge, but so cleverly it did not give her cheeks an artificial look. He didn't know, from this distance, what her eyes were like, but they had a direct look to them, like someone unafraid. Her chin was rounded, her nose delicate in proportion, and she had small ears adorned with what seemed to be diamond earrings.

Every move she made was graceful and leisurely. And she sat erect. She was attentive to her companion, and seemed to be enjoying their conversation. Jonathan had to see her at closer range. He felt impelled to do so. He signaled the headwaiter.

"Who that man, look like he been dipped in milk?" he asked.

The headwaiter smiled. "Don' know, suh. Jes' came in yestiddy."

"Gal his wife?"

"Reckon not. Saw 'em git separate keys they checked in. She sho' a looker, Mr. Turner, suh. Cain't keep my eyes off her. Pity, they leavin' day after tomorrow."

"She good-lookin' all right. I sign the check now."

Jonathan scribbled his name at the bottom of the check, finished the few drops left in his brandy glass, and rose and sauntered across the café. When he came to the girl's table he paused and looked at her very deliberately, without the slightest embarrassment.

"I begs yo' pa'don," he said, "but yo' the mos' beautiful gal I evah did see."

Then he walked on, without looking back. The girl stared after him. Her companion broke into laughter.

"You're getting better and better, Daisy. Now you draw the yokels all the way across the room. I thought this one was going to kneel and kiss the hem of your skirt."

"Oh, shut up," she said. "I think that was very nice."

"Well, he was a gentleman about it, but these country boys are sometimes pretty rough you get to know them that well."

"I have no intention of getting to know him."

"There's no time for him anyway, Daisy. We've got to be back at work in a week and it's still quite a trip to the Mississippi."

"I'm ready," she said. "Don't get the notion that I'm going to fall in love with any man who tells me I'm beautiful."

Jonathan climbed the stairs to his floor, unlocked the door to his room, and went in. Suddenly he was more lonely than he'd ever been. The image of that girl remained etched in his mind. He could close his eyes and see her face as plainly as if she stood before him.

He began to remove his coat, but hesitated and, instead, drew it on again and made his way down to the lobby. He looked into the café. The couple were no longer at their table. He sighed, knowing he'd probably never see her again.

He bought a newspaper and a cigar and set-

'tled himself in one of the chairs. He was deeply interested in the probability of a war with Mexico. Incensed at the description of what the Mexicans had done, he considered, mildly, inquiring about joining the army. Someone settled in a chair close to his own. He folded the newspaper to find the rest of the article and stared into the face of the girl.

"Good evening," she said. To Jonathan it was a voice dressed in silk. "I wish to thank you for that compliment you gave me in the café."

Jonathan jumped to his feet. "Ma'am, I meant it."

"Please sit down," she said. "Do you live in Richmond?"

"No ma'am. Comes heah fairly often."

"You live in the country then?"

"Yes, ma'am."

"On a farm?"

"Ye—es, yo' could call it that, ma'am."

"I suppose you keep slaves?"

"Yes ma'am, we do."

"I must tell you I don't believe in slavery."

"Yo' privilege, ma'am."

"You're quite a good-looking young man. May I ask how old you are?"

"Twenty, ma'am," he lied smoothly.

"I'm nineteen."

He believed her. "Yes ma'am," he said, uneasy around a girl for the first time in his life.

"You seem lonely. Are you?"

"Sho am. Been sittin' heah waitin' to get so tah'd I goes right to sleep I goes to my room."

"My name is Daisy."

"Pleased, ma'am. I'm Jonathan Turner."

"Jonathan Turner," she said. "It has a nice ring to it. I'd be delighted to share a bottle of champagne with you, sir."

Jonathan was on his feet instantly, reaching for her arm. "My pleasure, ma'am."

As she came to her feet, she stood close, facing him. They were exactly the same height, which made her rather tall. Her eyes were a deep blue, he saw now, and they were eyes that smiled at him, as her mouth did, and he smiled back.

"I like you," she said frankly.

"Yo' say I pays yo' a compliment sayin' yo' beautiful, but yo' jes' pays me the greatest compliment I evah been told in my life."

Jonathan ordered the best champagne in the house. It was quickly chilled for them. Too quickly. Jonathan would have preferred it take far longer. They talked in generalities, not getting into anything personal. Mostly they spoke of Richmond and Virginia—and New York, where she was from. Jonathan was dying to know all about her. He was aware that she was highly sophisticated, well educated, and likely had people of wealth in her family.

"I thanks yo' fo' yo' kindness," Jonathan said. "Nevah thought I'd be talkin' to yo'. Made me feel real good."

"You may escort me to my room," she said. She opened her handbag and gave him the key.

"My pleasure," he said. "Reckon it be a long time fo' we see one 'nother agin."

"Quite likely, Jonathan."

They climbed the stairs in silence and walked along the corridor of the second floor to her room. Jonathan inserted the key, opened the door.

"Yo' wants me to light the lamp fo' I go?" he asked.

"I'd be pleased."

He left the door open, struck a match, and applied it to the two lamps on the long bureau. He also lit the small lamp beside the bed. When he straightened up from that task and turned, she was standing directly behind him. She studied him curiously, as if there was something about him that puzzled her.

"Somethin' wrong, ma'am?" he asked, fearful she was going to tell him to go.

"No." Her voice was low, barely audible.

"Then why yo' lookin' at me like that?"

"I'm not sure," she said, her eyes never leaving his face. "Don't be frightened."

"I'm frightened yo'll disappear right in front o' me." He managed a smile, but being this close to her, smelling her perfume, was stirring him up so he could hardly contain himself.

"I won't. I'm real." She stepped closer to him and her arms went around his neck. "Must I make all the advances, Jonathan?"

With a cry of delight, he gathered her to him and covered her mouth with his. Her legs spread slightly to allow room for his tumescence. Jonathan's hands moved slowly down her back, exploring and caressing. They finally stopped and rested against her buttocks, squeezing them gently, pressing her closer to him.

Her fingertips moved lightly along his face, traced the outline of his ears, then continued on down his neck. They moved down to his chest, slipped beneath his coat, then lower until they reached his hips. All the time her lips moved against his, savoring the taste of them. Her tongue entered his mouth and touched his. Their passions were fully aroused now. Jonathan bent over her, arching her body, forcing her to spread her legs more. Her hands slipped between his legs and caressed his genitals.

"Cain't stan' no mo' o' this," he moaned. "Gots to have yo'."

She freed her mouth. "What are you thinking of me?"

"I loves yo', Daisy."

"Do you think I'm a whore?" There was no offense in her tone.

"No," he groaned. "Even if yo' was, I want you."

"Because I got you all stirred up?" Her hands continued to fondle his genitals.

"'Cause yo' the mos' beautiful, mos' lovable woman I evah held in my arms."

"Held many, Jonathan?" Somehow, without seeming to stop what she was doing to him, she had his trousers open. Her hands were inside them.

"None like yo'. Cain't take much mo' o' this, Daisy. Yo' drivin' me crazy."

She moved her fingers the length of his erection. "You're a lot of man, Jonathan. I just want you to know I never invited a man to my room before."

"Yo' a virgin?" he asked.

"Do you think I am?" While she spoke, she planted kisses on his neck and his earlobe.

"I so crazy fo' wantin' yo', I cain't think. Holy God, woman, yo' goin' tuh keep me wukked up like this, then kick me out?"

"No," she replied. "A virgin might. But I'm not a virgin. I'm not wanton either, darling Jonathan. I've been in bed before, but only twice. Do you believe that?"

"Anythin' yo' says, I b'lieves."

"Does it bother you?"

"Not a goddamn bit."

"Aren't you wondering about that handsome man who was at the table with me?"

"Some. Right now not much."

"I have not been in bed with him. He's my uncle. Do you believe that?"

"Tol' yo', b'lieves anythin' yo' says."

"That's all I want to know. We've wasted enough time talking. Help me undress."

"Nevah undressed a woman befo'. Not sure I know how."

"I'll teach you." She slipped her hands free of his trousers and stepped back, picked up the ends of the large bow at her neck, and handed them to him. "Just pull them and you'll loosen the bow."

He did so, and saw the row of buttons which the folds of fabric had concealed.

"Unbutton them," she commanded.

He obeyed and she pulled the fabric free of her skirt, slipped her arms out of the garment, and tossed it on a chair. She pointed to the buttons which ran the length of the skirt.

Jonathan started unbuttoning them and was on his knees by the time he reached those near the hem. The skirt fell free. By now, he was more curious than awkward and he pulled the cords on the petticoat. She stepped free of it, kicked it aside, and let him loosen her drawers.

When they dropped, she repeated the procedure without the slightest embarrassment and pointed to her corset. He stood up, untied and unbuttoned the corset cover, freeing her breasts. He moaned and drew her close.

Once again they embraced passionately, but she pushed him away when he tried to place his organ in her.

"Patience, Jonathan," she cautioned.

"I ain't got any mo', Daisy. Yo' drivin' me crazy."

She smiled and removed her corset and stood naked before him. "Now I'll undress you."

"Like hell yo' will," he exclaimed. "I nevah been teased like that befo'. Know you done it deliberate. Liked it too. But now I wants yo' an' I got tuh have yo'."

His clothes were off before she lowered the covers on the bed. He picked her up, dropped her onto the bed, and lay beside her. "I'm near crazy fo' want o' yo'."

"I want you too."

He gave a cry of delight, for she had moved to the center of the bed and with legs spread, body arched, arms extended, she was ready to receive him. They were young and eager and strong. Their love-making lasted half the night before exhaustion took its toll and they were content to lie side by side in the darkness.

"Day after tomorrow my uncle and I have to take a train to Memphis," she said.

"Got business theah?" Jonathan asked dreamily, as if it didn't matter at all.

"I work on a riverboat. We have a minstrel show. My uncle is the interlocutor."

"Thinks that's fine." Jonathan wondered what an interlocutor was.

"I sing and dance," she said. "I'm an actress."

"Nevah met an actress befo'," he said.

"I was on the stage in New York a couple of times. I wasn't bad, either, but the man who owned the show thought he owned me and I didn't like him."

"Tell me his name an' nex' time I in N'Yawk I kills him."

She laughed and snuggled closer to him. "I'm really not a bad girl, Jonathan. I went to bed with you tonight because I like you very much. You're good-looking, you're clean, even though you're only a farm boy. I was lonely and you were lonely."

"Wish we could be lonely ev'y night," he said. He was tired. Before meeting her he'd been barely able to keep his eyes open. Now he was on the verge of passing out. He held her to him and fell asleep. The last thing he remembered was her warm, lovely kiss.

When he awoke, he turned on his side and discovered he was alone. He sat up and gasped because this was not his room. Then he remembered. He could smell the perfume of her and it all came back to him. He smiled and stretched luxuriously and then looked at his watch on the night table. It was after nine.

He got out of bed, half dressed, and raced down to his room. He shaved, washed, and dressed in ten minutes, then ran down the steps, hesitating at the entrance to the dining room long enough to see that Daisy was not there. Then he dashed out to the street and kept going until he reached the slave market to find his father already there. The auction had begun some minutes before.

"Whar in hell yo' been?" Fitz asked. "Look in yo' room an' yo' bed not used."

"Tells yo' 'bout it latah," Jonathan said.

Fitz surveyed him critically. "Yo' got yo'se'f dreened las' night."

"Papa, it's mo' than that. She so beautiful— yo' cain't imagine——"

"I kin imagine. Yo' tells me latah. They's goin' to announce the sale o' our coffle any minute."

"Is Major Apperson heah?"

"Been heah since the firs' slave put on the table. Now yo' does nuthin'. No mattah whut happen, yo' keep yo' mouth shut."

"Don' feel like talkin' anyways, Papa."

"Gots to meet this gal, she hits yo' hahd as that."

"Meets her sometime, sho'," Jonathan said with a sigh.

"Aimin' to see her agin?"

"Aimin' to see her fo' the rest o' my life, Papa."

"Well, yo' fo'gets that gal fo' now. 'Bout to begin the auction an' it wuks right, ought to be some fun. Yes suh, some fun."

The auctioneer had disposed of a woman and her sucker, bought together by a man who looked as if he would treat them well. The auctioneer now banged his gavel.

"Call yo' 'tention to this nex' numbah, gents.

An' ladies." He bowed in the direction of half a dozen women present. "This heah a coffle from the plantation o' one o' our bes' planters. I refers to the honorable Mistah Turner. He is auctionin' some o' the bes' stock he got an' ain't nobody but knows whut that means. The bigges', an' stronges', an' healthies' slaves evah to come on this heah table. They's a hundred an' eight o' these pe'fec' specimens, an' anybody heah likes to bid on the whole coffle is invited to do so."

Major Apperson called out, "Five thousand."

"Five thousan'," the auctioneer bellowed. "Five thousan' fo' a hundred an' eight bes' stock. Sellin' them fo' that is a crime, gents. A crime."

"Twenty thousand," someone shouted, and all eyes turned to a rangy-looking man in a big Texas hat, wearing a leather jacket and riding breeches.

"Twenny thousand." The auctioneer sounded happier. "Now that mo' like it."

"Twenny-one thousand," Major Apperson said. "Wants to see this heah coffle, yo' don' mind."

"Thirty thousand," the man in the big hat shouted. "Ain't no need to bring 'em out. Knows whut they looks like. Knows whut all Wyndward Plantation stock looks like. Thirty thousand, and I aims to go higher."

Major Apperson hesitated. He was suddenly wary. "Kin I ask who biddin' agin me?"

"You kin," the man said. "I'm from Texas and aimin' to bring back a good starter stock on a ranch I jes' bought down theah."

"Thirty-one thousand," Major Apperson called out.

The Texas shrugged. "Wants 'em, I sho' do, but gettin' a little high. Guess I pulls out, suh. My compliments to yo'."

He walked briskly away, in the direction of Fitz and Jonathan. As he passed by, his hand flicked out and Fitz pressed a wad of bills into it. The Texan kept going.

Fitz said, "Likes to stay heah an' see the Major bust his gut, but 'fraid he get so mad don' know whut in hell he doin'. Bes' we jes' kinda walk out o' heah. Meets yo' at the hotel, son. Wants to see that gal o' yo's, but got a little business to do firs'."

"Papa, yo' were in business all night. How yo' able to last till now?"

"Takes practice, son. Takes practice. That's whut my daddy always said an' I ain't up to his record yet. Not by far, I ain't. How yo' like the gen'mun from Texas?"

"Nevah saw him befo'."

"Met him yestiddy. Comes from Norfolk. Nevah saw Texas in his life. The Major is walkin' down to the pens. We gets away now, but I bet we heahs him yell he sees whut he bought. An' all legal. He cain't say he got cheated. Nevah guaranteed the condition o' the coffle. He sees healthy ones, he eyes gettin' bad."

They walked away hastily. They didn't hear the Major cry out. "Maybe he fainted, like Clarissa do," Jonathan suggested.

"Maybe he lookin' fo' a gun, too," Fitz said. "Don' wants to meet him while he so mad. Yo' stays 'way from him too."

They entered the hotel. Instantly Jonathan

looked about for Daisy. "I stays down heah fo' a while, Papa," he said.

"Saves me askin' yo' to. Business I got's private."

Jonathan sat down. Major Apperson might come along with a gun, but Jonathan was willing to risk that.

Suddenly she was standing at the foot of the stairs beckoning to him. Jonathan kept himself from running to her, for he must assume some sort of decorum. Perhaps she would ask him to her room again.

"Good mornin'," he said.

"You bastard!" she exploded. Her face was full of fury that vied with her beauty, but never succeeded in conquering it. "You rotten son of a bitch!"

Jonathan stared at her open-mouthed, unable to utter a sound.

"So you're just a farm boy. A young, healthy farm boy who has a few slaves. You have two thousand slaves, and your farm is Wyndward Plantation, and your father is one of the richest men in the country. A farm half as big as the state of Virginia."

"But—whut's the diff'rence?"

"You, the handsome rich boy who has any woman he wants. You got me, but it was under false pretenses. I thought I was falling in love with a nice boy. I wanted to be in love with you, but not the million in money, or the acres you and your family own. I never want to see you again as long as I live."

She slapped him across the face so hard that

it actually rocked him, and then she fled up the stairs, crying audibly.

Jonathan turned and walked back into the lobby. He sat down again. This time he wished Major Apperson would come through—with a gun.

{ **11** }

THE MORE HE THOUGHT ABOUT IT THE MORE UNFAIR Daisy's attitude seemed. What if he was a rich man's son? It was a crazy way of thinking.

Slowly Jonathan's anger began to rise. He got to his feet and went directly to her room. The door was wide open, and he stepped into the room. A maid was cleaning it.

"Wheah the lady who had this room las' night?"

"Don' know suh," the maid replied. "I comes to make up the room an' she ready to leave. Ev'-ythin' packed an' all."

"Thank yo'," Jonathan said. He knew where she was—in her uncle's room—if he was her uncle. He hurried to the lobby and asked the desk clerk which room the man occupied, giving a good description of him. It was a room just down the hall from Daisy's. Jonathan hurried back to the second floor. He knocked on the door, then banged on it; then opened it. The room was made up. They were both gone.

Downstairs again, he demanded how two people could leave the hotel and not be seen from the lobby. He was told that when there was a great deal of baggage, a carriage would pull up to the side portico and the guests would leave by that route, which did not require them to pass through the lobby.

Jonathan returned slowly to his own room and sat down, trying to figure out his next move. There didn't seem to be any.

He went to his father's room, carrying a gun case.

Fitz lay on the bed, fully dressed, propped up against the pillows. He looked tired, almost drawn. Jonathan placed the box on the bed.

"Don' know, Papa, if yo' kin trick the Major agin, but I brought along the dueling pistols I gave you for Christmas jes' in case."

Fitz opened the box, removed one of the guns. He sat up, swung his legs off the bed. He cocked the gun, pulled the trigger. There was a loud click. Then he held the firing mechanism closer to his eyes and studied it.

"Firin' pin been cut down jes' 'nuff so it don' hit the cartridge. Cain't see that less yo' look awful close. Yo' got an idee how we wuk this duel? Yo' brought the guns, so maybe yo' got somethin' in mind."

"Got nuthin', Papa. Jes' figgered maybe we could use 'em."

"If we kin get 'way with it. Yo' been down to the slave market?"

"Not yit, Papa."

"Figgered that's wheah yo'd be."

"Know this gal I tol' yo' 'bout? She gone."

Fitz laid the guns aside. "Gone wheah?"

"I don' know fo' sure."

"What got into her to do that? Yo' bust her maybe?"

"She was no virgin, Papa. She tol' me so."

"Befo' or after?"

"Befo', Papa. She was hones'."

"Must be some reason she runs out."

"I nevah tol' her who I was. My name, yes, but nuthin' else. Seem she thinks I a po' boy off'n a fahm an' she kinda like that. But she finds out I'm yo' son an' they's lots o' money, slaves, an' acres. That make her madder'n hell."

Fitz frowned. "Whut she want? To get raped by a man who ain't got nuthin' but dirty fingernails from muckin' in the ground?"

"Don' know whut she thinkin', but she cleared out. Nevah gave me a chance to say anythin'."

"Yo' didn't speak up, she gives yo' hell?"

"She slapped me an' then she runs fo' I gets a chance to say a word. Went to explain but she gone."

"An' yo' don' know wheah?"

"Not 'xactly. She an actress. Sings an' dances. Man with her is her uncle an' he an . . . word I nevah heard befo'—somethin' to do with a minstrel show."

"Interlocutor?"

"That's it, Papa. Whut in hell he do?"

"He act like the caller at a square dance. Tell folks whut to do. Saw two o' three minstrel shows. They's mighty good. Jokes an' singin' an' dancin'. Done by white folks who put blackenin' on they faces so they looks like niggers."

"She say somethin' 'bout a riverboat."

"That makes sense. Minstrel shows play on Mississippi riverboats. Won't be hard to find her."

"Don' think I care, Papa."

"Whut yo' sulkin' fo' then? Thinkin' yo' had her in yo' bed——"

"Her bed, Papa."

"Whut in hell's the diff'rence, long as yo' had her?"

"She sho' was beautiful. I must o' been dumb as ... as Calcutta mayhap. Lets her get away, I did, an' she nevah comin' back. Don' know whut to do, Papa. Looks like a fool I chases her."

"Goin' to tell yo' somethin', Jonathan. It was jes' like that with me an' yo' mama. I goes to her papa's hoss fahm to buy some stock an' I sees her an' I feel like I been hit on the haid with somethin' heavy. Knew I was bound to ask her to marry me. I didn't. Not at first. Somethin' happened ain't none o' yo' business. I went back to Wyndward an' I moped aroun' fo' weeks till my papa tell me, fo' God's sake, go get her even if I has to pull her back by the hair. But I didn' go. I was too goddamn proud. Then I sees her agin, at a hoss race. She look even bettah than I 'members the way she looked when I first saw her. She a mighty beautiful woman now, but twenny yeahs ago she could look at me an' I cain't even talk, let alone move. Crazy? Sho', but it happen. I still so goddamn proud I say hello an' good-by. But yo' mama, she a hell of a lot smahter'n me. Whut I didn' know was, she love me much as I love her. So she comes to Wyndward, walks up to my papa, an' tells him she goin' to marry me. My papa grab her an' dance with her an' tell her she jes' the kind o' gal he wanted me to have. So, whut could I do? They was agin me. Tell yo' whut—when I saw her theah with Papa, I near fainted. Then I get some sense an' I goes to her an' I asks her to marry me."

"Thinks this gal come to me like that, Papa?"

"Yo' ain't been 'roun' her long 'nuff. She proud too. Yo' mama said pride didn't mattah when she knew she wanted me. Yo' go to find this gal. Not now. Not right away. Firs' yo' thinks 'bout her. Yo' begins to see her when she ain't theah an' yo' kin heah her voice like it callin' to yo'. That kinda crazy feelin' won't go 'way. Then yo' goes an' finds her."

Jonathan's woebegone expression grew lighter and he actually smiled. "Good advice, Papa. Soon's I know fo' sho' I cain't do 'thout her, then I goes."

"Right now," Fitz said, "yo' goes down to the slave market and see whut the Major had to say 'bout gettin' his ass trimmed."

"Sho', Papa, I goes now."

"Gets the chance," Fitz said, "kinda pass the word I be in the hotel café tonight. Don' wan' the Major to get hisse'f all tired out lookin' fo' me."

"Tells 'em, Papa. Hopes yo' think o' some way to get outa this heah duel. Kinda like to take yo' back to Wyndward alive."

"That's how I'd kinda like to go back. Gettin' me an idee. Not wuth talkin' 'bout yit. Yo' go to the slave market. Come right back."

The slave market was empty, but the auctioneer was still there, totaling his books.

"Glad to see yo' agin." He held out a fat, sweaty hand. "Hopes yo' bringin' mo' business soon."

"At the reg'lar time," Jonathan said. "Whut Major Apperson do he see the coffle he bought?"

The auctioneer pushed his once white hat to the back of his head and wiped his brow with a soiled handkerchief.

"Now I heerd some fancy cussin' in my life, but nevah anythin' like whut he said. Cain't figger how yo' papa made him think the coffle was prime an' not the dregs o' whut came offen the Fisbee place."

"Why, Papa didn' even tell the Major he was comin'. An' he sho'ly nevah tol' him the coffle was prime. Yo' did."

"I nevah saw the coffle. I thinkin' they like all the othah coffles yo' papa bring to market. All prime."

"Papa nevah touted the coffle to anybody. If the Major thinks it prime an' bids, that his fault, not ours."

"Who the man who bid it up? Not that I keers, Jonathan. Bigger price, bigger share fo' me. Puts the money in yo' papa's bank tomorruh."

"That fine. Major say anythin' made sense?"

"On'y that when he sees yo' papa again, he kills him."

"Obleeged, suh. That's whut I wants to know."

"Tell yo' papa to be keerful, Jonathan. Major Apperson fight duels befo', an' that's whut he'll do 'bout yo' papa. Call him out sho'."

"Reckon he will."

"Yo' papa evah fight a duel befo'?"

"Five . . . no . . . lemme see, now. They was six, I think. Papa killed ev'y one o' them. Papa mighty good. Pistols or rapiers, but he likes to duel with swords. An' he likes axes too, sharpened like a razor. Takes a mighty strong man to duel with axes. Reckon the Major ain't got the guts fo' that."

"Reckon. Well, gots to run now. Tomorruh we got two big coffles to sell. Thank yo' kindly fo' yo' business, an' tell yo' papa hopes he don' git hisse'f killed."

Jonathan nodded and left. He knew very well that within the hour Major Apperson was going to hear the false story of Fitz killing six men in six duels. Maybe it would scare Apperson so he wouldn't issue a challenge. But Jonathan doubted it. Everyone in Richmond knew, by now, how Major Apperson had fallen into a trap. The story of what happened would make Fitz more popular than ever and the Major a laughing stock.

Jonathan hurried back to the hotel. With every step he thought of Daisy.

When Jonathan entered his father's room Fitz was shaving. His face well lathered, he put down the brush and stood looking at his son, who stared into space.

"Yo' sho' got it bad," Fitz said.

Jonathan looked up. "Whut? Whut yo' say, Papa?"

"Heah I am, gettin' myse'f lookin' real nice case I gets killed tonight, an' yo' sits theah thinkin' o' this heah gal. An' I bets that the Major shoots me, somebody got to tell yo' 'bout it, yo' standin' right theah an' seein' me drop." He picked up the straight razor and carved a neat swath through the lather on his cheek.

"Major madder'n hell, Papa. He paid an' the money be in yo' bank tomorruh. I tells the auctioneer yo' kills six men awready in duels an' yo' likes to fight 'em with axes. That near busted him —I knows he go straight to the Major an' tells him."

"He goin' to call me out, yo' think?"

"Knows it, Papa. Ev'ybody in Richmond laughin' at him. On'y way he kin stop that is by killin' yo'."

"Duelin' against the law in Richmond. He know that?"

"Don' think he keers, long as he kin call yo' out. They's places wheah yo' kin fight a duel an' no trouble."

"It goin' to be fought right downstairs in the café, son. On'y way I kin win. I stands up to him in a fair fight an' he drops me sho'."

"Yo' gots to fight him he calls yo' out, Papa."

"Knows that, but don' mean theah has to be shootin'. Yo' stop thinkin' 'bout that gal long 'nuff an' I tells yo' whut I got in mind."

"She beautiful, Papa."

"An' I goin' to get myse'f full o' holes. Yo' cares? Yo' cares she beautiful."

"Don' think o' her no mo', Papa. Whut yo' goin' to tell me 'bout this heah duel?"

Fitz explained his plans in detail.

"It risky as hell, Papa. They's too much kin happen make yo' plan bust up."

"Yo' think of anothah way, son?"

"No suh, I cain't. Hep's yo', bes' I kin. We gets away with it, sho' a miracle."

"Glad yo' mama not heah. She be havin' a fit."

"Bets Daisy mo' beautiful than Mama was," Jonathan said dreamily.

"Yo' listens to me, Jonathan. When I gets through killin' the Major, I kills yo'. Ain't no gal evah look as pretty as yo' mama."

"Bets Daisy do."

"Who the hell Daisy? Oh, the gal yo' dreamin' 'bout. Reckon I goin' to have me a daughter-in-law a hell of a lot sooner'n I evah thought."

Jonathan wagged his head. "Likes the way yo' worries 'bout this duel. Yo' thinkin' 'bout Daisy more'n the Major. One mo' thing, Papa. I gets Daisy to come to Wyndward, yo' acts polite an' nice. Yo' don' pinch her ass like yo' done at the party."

"She theah?" Fitz asked in mock surprise. "I pinches Daisy?"

"God damn, Papa, think 'bout gettin' killed, will yo'? Leave the thinkin' 'bout Daisy to me."

Fitz toweled his face and slapped on bay rum. Then he lay down on the bed again and closed his eyes.

"Call me 'bout six. Reckon the Major come 'bout eight an' I wants a nice, quiet suppah fo' I shoots him. Ain't worryin' none whut yo' do.

Man can't get hisse'f in trouble dreamin' 'bout a gal." Fitz settled himself for a nap. He opened his eyes again. "Not lessen she married."

Jonathan returned to his own room with a new worry on his mind. What if she was married? What if she'd lied about the man in the milk-bottle suit? Was he really her uncle? Perhaps they were married. Perhaps she'd lied to him because she wanted a taste of variety that one night. Jonathan began to grow angry and, in his mind, he cursed her, until he decided it wasn't possible she could have lied about that. And he felt good again.

He too dozed the afternoon away. He awoke later than Fitz had stipulated, and again he rushed to get dressed. Fitz was already up, dressed and ready.

"Leave the pistols heah," he said. "Don' wants him to think I brought 'em special. Time comes I says we fights the duel right now, he say ain't no guns an' yo' fetches these."

"Got the cartridges goes in 'em. They's real bullets, Papa."

"Hope them theah firin' pins cut down 'nuff."

"Tested 'em, Papa. They's cut down to 'bout a hair 'tween the hammer an' the ca'tridge. Nobody evah goin' to notice till aftah. Then whut happens?"

"Wuks way I thinks, won't be no back talk. Reckon we go down now. I'm hungry."

The café was packed when they arrived. People knew the Major would come and there'd be trouble between him and Fitz. Nobody wanted to miss it.

There was a reserved table for Fitz and Jonathan, with a waiter in attendance. They sat down as if they noticed nothing amiss. They ordered whiskey and water to be served before a hearty meal of steak and potatoes. They ate slowly and carried on a conversation concerned mostly with Daisy.

"Thinks I go after her, Papa."

"Yo' waits till we got the seedlin's started. Bes' yo' don' go headlong aftah her anyways. She means whut she said 'bout 'thinkin' yo' picks her up 'cause yo' rich an' yo' beds down with any gal. Maybe she in love with yo' too. Now that bein' the case, she waits an' gets hungry an' horny fo' yo', then yo' finds her an' she mos' easy to bring home."

"Think Mama yell 'cause I too young?"

"She does, yo' asks her how ol' she when we married. An' me too. I was eighteen."

"Yo' shorely on my side, Papa."

"Got to be. An' yo' bettah be on my side, 'cause the Major jes' comin' in now an' he look like he ridin' at the head o' a regiment. How he evah get that title anyways? Nevah was a war I knows of he coulda fit in."

"Gives it to hisse'f, reckon. He's comin' ovah, Papa. Hang onto yo' balls."

Fitz threw back his head and roared with laughter. When Major Apperson stood beside the table, Fitz was still laughing. He looked up as if he saw the Major for the first time.

"Evenin', suh," he said affably. "Heah yo' bought yo'se'f a mighty fine coffle today."

"Stan' up!" Apperson shouted. "Stan' up, yo' crude, double-crossin' sonabitch."

Fitz pushed back his chair, then thought better of it and sat down again to finish his cup of coffee, infuriating Apperson even more.

"Stan' up or yo' a mis'able coward," the Major roared.

The crowd around the table was thick, but quiet—and very interested.

Fitz rose. "I standin', suh, at yo' pleasure."

Apperson drew back his hand and slapped Fitz smartly across the face. Fitz's calm expression never changed.

"Now that wasn't nice, Major. Yo' hits a man when his hands are down. Yo' jes' fires up an' hits him. Like this!"

It was no slap. It was a punch that sent the Major reeling backward to fall against a table. There were plenty of willing hands to keep him from collapsing to the floor.

"I'm aimin' to kill yo', Mistah Turner, suh. I'm callin' yo' out."

"Suits me," Fitz said.

"My friends will call on yo', suh."

"What fo'? We don' need no friends to call on us, Major. All we needs is two pistols an' we settle it now."

Major Apperson looked apprehensive for the first time.

"We do not fight duels like that, suh."

"Now yo' listen heah," Fitz said. "Yo' jes' called me out. Means I gets to say whut weapons we uses, when we fights, an' wheah. So I says we uses duelin' pistols, we fights now, soon's my son brings the guns down. An' we fights heah."

"That's—agin the law," Apperson said.

"Whut the hell we cares 'bout the law? Yo'

gettin' nervous, Major? Jonathan, go fetch the guns."

"I ain't usin' yo' guns," the Major said. "Don' trus' yo', Fitz. Yo' tricked me too often. Don' trus' nuthin' 'bout yo'."

"Don' have to," Fitz said quietly. "All yo' gots to do is fight me now. Gives yo' a chance to 'xamine the guns. Ev'ybody in this heah saloon kin do the same. They's as fine a pistol as evah been fired. Used 'em 'bout a yeah ago in Norfolk. Bullet whooshed by me so close I could feel the breeze."

"Whut did the othah man feel?" someone asked.

"Nuthin'," Fitz said. "Got him right through the heart. I was a little slow then. Firs' time I evah let the othah man get off a shot."

"Yo're tryin' to scare me," the Major accused. "Yo' nevah fought a duel in yo' life. I ain't skeered o' yo' an' yo' damn braggin'."

"Suit yo'se'f," Fitz said. He sat down again and asked for another cup of coffee. He was drinking it when Jonathan returned with the dueling pistols. He placed the box on the table and opened it. There were a few murmurs of appreciation for such fine guns. Jonathan placed a box of cartridges on the table beside the guns.

"Way I sees it," he said, "the Major kin have his pick an' anybody he says so, gets to load both guns."

The Major picked up one of the guns and spent five minutes examining it while Fitz felt the sweat roll down his face. Fitz drank his coffee, holding the cup in a steady hand, acting as if the duel meant little to him.

"Looks like fine guns to me," someone observed.

"Satisfied," the Major said. "Kin kill him with these easy as my own."

Fitz wiped his lips with a napkin and arose. "We gets it ovah with, Major. I got to get some sleep. Goin' home tomorruh an' it a long ride."

Fitz picked up the second pistol casually. He walked toward the bar, the crowd parting to let him through. He was followed by the Major, protesting about the place of the duel.

"Cain't fight heah, suh. Too many folks, in too close. We misses an' we kills somebody don't aim to kill. Don' like this nohow."

"Major," Fitz said, "yo' wants to put a stop to this, yo' 'pologizes an' yo' admits yo' nothin' but a man blowin' steam an' no fire back o' it. I claims my rights as bein' the man called out. Now yo' jes' takes that loaded pistol. Ain't nobody else goin' to get hurt 'cause we won't miss."

Fitz turned, jabbed his gun hard against the Major's slightly protruding stomach.

"We fights this way, suh. I puts my gun against yo' belly. Yo' puts yo' gun 'gainst mine. Bartender, got a bung startah?" He raised his voice. "Yo' got one, bartender?"

"Got one, Mistah Turner, suh."

"Good. Now when I says so, yo' start countin' to ten. Each time yo' counts—slow-like—yo' bangs the bar with the bung startah. When yo' gets to ten an' bangs the bar the tenth time, the Major an' me, we shoots."

"Yo're crazy!" Major Apperson cried. "It's suicide."

[216]

"Might be. Man don' 'spect to live fo'evah, suh."

"I refuse!"

"Cain't, Major, suh. Yo' calls me out, 'member? I says how we fights an' this is how. Bartender, yo' kin begin bangin' the bung startah."

The crowd drew back. The Major's face was ashen, his eyes darting about seeking some ally to come out and say it was no way to fight a duel. No one said a word.

"One!" the bartender shouted, and the bung starter made a great noise.

"This is insane," Apperson protested.

"Two!" the bartender's makeshift gavel hit the bar again.

The count went to four. Apperson hadn't drawn a breath since the first count. The bartender called out five. The crowd had grown very quiet. There was a loud click. The Major stepped back, his gun slanting to the floor. The hammer was down. He'd fired at the count of five. Now he moved back several steps until the crowd held him there. He looked about. There wasn't a friendly face in the saloon.

Fitz said, "Yo' gun misfired, suh, but yo' was a little too soon, reckon. Yo' gets no second chance. I aims to be fair an' I don' shoot till the bung startah lands fo'—or is it five—mo' times."

The gavel came down with the bartender's count of six. Fitz slowly raised the pistol and pointed it squarely at the Major's stomach. It was held in a steady hand. The muzzle must have looked as big as a cannon to Apperson.

The count reached eight. Fitz kept the gun level.

"No!" the Major cried out. "No—please! Don't shoot, Fitz. It's murder. Yo' cain't shoot."

"Kin," Fitz said calmly. The count was delayed slightly. Fitz nodded and the gavel came down to the count of nine, came up again for the final count.

Apperson turned his back and fought with the men holding him back. He was howling like a madman, clawing at them, kicking and pleading at the same time.

The gavel came down and the bartender shouted, "Ten!"

The crowd tensed. Major Apperson, his back still toward Fitz, froze into immobility. When nothing happened, when no shot was heard and no bullet plowed through his back, he turned around. Fitz slowly lowered the gun.

"Had 'nuff," he said. "Let him go."

Someone picked up the pistol Apperson had dropped. Jonathan accepted it, unloaded it, and placed it carefully in the box. Fitz gave him his and Jonathan unloaded and put that one away also. He closed the box and walked casually out of the café.

Fitz sat down. "Coffee's cold," he said. "Wants some pie. Nevah had time fo' my dessert. Wants pecan pie, waitah, or I shoots yo' an' the cook."

"We gots peach pie, Mistah Turner, suh," the waiter said.

"Likes peach pie. Bring the whole goddamn pie. Duelin' makes me hongry. An' make that a pot o' coffee if yo' please. An' a double brandy."

They began the journey home the next day.

Both occupied the high seat on the ancient stage-coach Fitz's father had once bought for show. Jonathan allowed it was about as comfortable as a wagon or a carriage, but not by much. But they had so many things to talk about they hardly noticed it.

"Yo' think the Major guesses whut happened las' night, Papa? Or do yo' think he shakin' so much all he doin' is changin' his wet pants?"

"Felt sorry for him, I did. Made a big fool out o' hisse'f 'fore all them people. Brought it on hisse'f, he did."

"Mayhap the Major won't bothah us no mo', Papa. He too scared o' yo' now."

"Well, son, Major Apperson, he a strange man. Nevah gets the bes' o' me an' yet he keeps tryin'. Mayhap he tries agin."

"He all done, Papa," Jonathan prophesied. "Nobody evah trusts him agin. He nuthin' but a blowhard an' a coward."

"Still, he a man to be watched, Jonathan. Don' fo'get, he pulled the trigger when the count was five. Jes' like I knew he would. Now a man who do a thing like that ain't above shootin' somebody in the back."

"Yo' aimin' to tell Mama all 'bout it?" Jonathan asked.

"Might's well. She finds out anyways. An' son, I ain't sayin' that the Major was the on'y man scared 'nuff to wet his britches las' night. There was a mighty small tolerance 'tween the hammers of them guns an' the ca'tridge. Hopes when I said we push the guns against each other's bellies an' then shoots, he back off. But he didn'. Reckon he didn't know how to do it 'thout bein' called a coward. Yo' don' mind we talks 'bout somethin' else?"

"Sho', Papa. I tells yo' 'bout Daisy."

"Hell, I been hearin' 'nuff 'bout that gal. Maybe I takes her to bed 'fore yo' do."

"Yo' does an' we uses diff'rent pistols," Jonathan said good-naturedly.

"Yo' don' know it, boy, but we gots trouble we gets home."

"What kinda trouble?" Jonathan glanced at his father's set face and knew this was no joking matter, whatever it might be. "Ain't heerd o' any trouble."

"Ain't heerd 'cause nobody's talkin' 'bout it. Bes' it kept a secret, but we goin' to have a meetin' o' all planters close by soon's we get back. They's trouble hatchin'—big trouble. They's a Underground Railroad wukkin' somewheres not far off our place. An' they's talk o' rebellion."

"Whyn't I heerd 'bout it?" Jonathan asked.

"It ain't on our plantation. But mos' othahs go that kinda trouble. Don' show, but lays back an' ready to bust loose. Yo' knows whut a rebellion's like. 'Specially them niggers gits hold o' guns an' axes an' knives. Had one our place yeahs ago. Yo' mama's papa gets his haid sliced clean off, an' plenty othahs died that night. We busted it quick an' we hung some o' the bastahds, but behind our backs the talk nevah stops. They gets a leader an' all hell goin' to bust loose."

"Wyndward nice an' quiet, Papa."

"Sho' it is. We treats our slaves good. We don' wuk 'em ha'f to death. Don' pay to do that. On'y kills 'em off, an' they expensive propitty. Reckon near ten or fifteen planters come to the meetin'. We exchanges whut we knows an' see they's a plot behind it. Almost' jes' as impohtant, the Underground Railroad. They losin' lots o' slaves."

"Papa, I thought there was a national law jes' comin' outa Washington says all escaped slaves gets caught, they's got to be sent back to they owners. An' anybody he'ps a slave, or hides him, gets arrested."

Fitz cleared his throat and spat over the side of the coach. "Yo' evah heah a no'thern gen'mun sendin' back a slave? They passed that law to keep us quiet down heah."

"Read a copy o' the *Liberator* couple o' weeks ago. They sho' agin slavery."

"Don' know whut in hell they talkin' 'bout. Up theah in the No'th, don' have half a million niggers at they backs. Don' have big plantations take a thousand men to wuk. Lots o' folks down heah don' believe in keepin' slaves, but yo' don' heah them talkin' that way. They sees whut's goin' on an' how we need slaves an' they keeps they mouths shut."

"Don' get mad, Papa, I knows we gots to have 'em jes' like yo' do. But whut if yo' turned black an' yo' wuks fo' a man treats yo' right 'nuff. but pays yo' nuthin' an' kin whup yo' if yo' makes a mistake? Yo' puts yo'se'f in his place an' yo' wonders. Knows I do sometimes."

"Yo' got it all wrong, son. Folks is made to do certain things. Some be bankers, some doctors, some planters like us. An' some have to do the hahd wuk, an' niggers was born fo' that purpose. They serves us 'cause that's the way it is. I black, I be no diff'rent I am now. I knows it my place to serve an' I does it."

"Rather talk 'bout Daisy," Jonathan said.

"Reckon yo' does, but slaves is mo' impohtant, Jonathan. We ain't got them we ain't got nothin'. But, seein' yo' wants to talk 'bout that gal, yo' got things standin' in yo' way too. Firs' of all, how yo' knows she give a goddamn 'bout yo'? Whut yo' knows 'bout her, anyway?"

"Don't mattah, Papa."

"An' whut yo' aimin' to do 'bout Domingo? An' mayhap that gal—whut her name? Belle?— on the Fisbee place makes trouble."

"Heerd tell when yo' marries Mama, yo' didn' sen' Nina 'way."

"Loved 'em both, I did. An' they both knew it. Yo' mama an' Nina kin' o' women yo' don' meet often. But aftah a while, I didn' sleep with Nina no mo'."

"Wondah if that's whut made her go to Themba an' get herse'f knocked up?"

"Themba rapes her. Yo' understand that, Jonathan. Themba rapes her an' I kills him fo' that. Nina loved me. She wouldn't think o' goin' to 'nother man 'thout she comes an' tells me first. Don' want yo' talkin' 'bout Nina. She 'bout as good a gal yo' kin fin', black or white. Nevah fo'gets her."

"Got to admit, Papa, I don' know Daisy well 'nuff to be sho' how she feels 'bout Domingo. An' mayhap Domingo gets mad I marries Daisy. Belle—now that's diff'rent. She a no-good slut. Wouldn' marry her no mattah whut."

"We sho' got troubles," Fitz lamented. "Goin' to be glad to get 'way from it all."

"Yo' goin' to Boston soon?"

"Fo' Melanie's graduation. Come spring."

"Wish I could go with yo', Papa. Times I

miss Boston. Liked school up theah. Skeered the hell outa me at firs', but got used to it. Folks sho' diff'rent up theah."

"Sho' are. Know whut I misses mos'? Talkin' like they do."

"We don' go back we goin' to fo'get whut it like to talk no'thern."

"Let's try it," Jonathan suggested. "Papa, do you really believe it's necessary fo' us—there I go—*for* us to talk so much like the slaves?"

"The slaves talk like southern people because that's all they've ever heard. With you and me, yes, we must speak as our friends and neighbors do. Otherwise we'd be setting ourselves apart. We may be rich, Jonathan, but isolation bears too heavy a price. Do you think I'd have heard about the Underground if I used my Boston voice around here?"

"When will you call a meeting of the planters?" Jonathan asked.

"Soon as we get back. I talked to them a week ago."

"Do you think Major Apperson will come?"

"He's entitled to. He's a planter and belongs to our organization."

"What of the Fisbees? Last I knew, they were still on the plantation, but they have neither money nor slaves . . . nor even crops."

"They don't count. I won't ask them."

"Think I'll take a nap," Jonathan said. "Mind if I pull up and let you handle the coach for a while?"

"It's best we spell one another. I want to be home tomorrow. No stopping at Colonel Coldwell's place this time."

"You mean I don't get to see his wife?" Jonathan asked in mock dismay.

Fitz said, "You got two gals now. Any more than that and you'll have trouble for the rest of your life. Pull up and let me take over."

Two hours later, they changed places again. It wasn't until dusk, when they began looking for a likely place to rest for the night, that they were both on the high seat again.

"Papa," Jonathan remarked, "if yo' plannin' to go 'no'th fo' Melanie's graduation, it'll be plantin' time. Bes' I be heah to run things."

"Yo' got othah plans?" Fitz asked. "Co'se yo' gots to be in charge."

"I wonderin' when I go to get Daisy."

Fitz said, with a slow shake of his head, "Yo' go fetch the gal any time yo' wants. She comes, she be welcome. She throw yo' out, I'll get drunk with yo' an' take a week off to visit ev'y whore-house in Richmond."

"Reckon them riverboats runs all yeah, Papa?"

"Not lessen they puts 'em on sleds. Maybe way down in Louisiana they runs, but they sho' cain't get No'th in the winter."

"Then I bes' go soon's I kin. Don' know whut in hell boat she on, but reckon I kin find her."

"She as good-lookin' as yo' say she is, yo'll find her. An' one mo' thing."

"Yes, Papa?"

"I'd be damn sho' her uncle ain't the kin' whut sleeps with his niece."

"Been thinkin' 'bout that too. Reason why I wants to go see soon as I kin."

[12]

THERE WAS PLENTY TO EAT AND ALL THE LIQUOR a man could hold, but it was not a festive occasion. Twenty-two planters were present, from distances as far as a hundred miles. Ron Craig from Craig Plantation, Hugh Lister from Montclair Farms, Robert Harper, who owned the thousand-acre Melody Plantation—almost all were big planters with great sums of money invested in land, buildings, machinery, and slaves. Most of all in slaves.

Fitz presided, because it was his home where they met. Every man there respected him for his honesty and his ability to lead. Jonathan was not as well known, but as he took his part in the proceedings, they all came to realize he was as astute as his father.

Somewhat unexpectedly, Major Apperson put in an appearance, but only because of the vital circumstances of the meeting. He greeted Jonathan with a cold nod. He didn't look at Fitz, but he had a low and respectful bow for Benay, who was supervising the refreshments. And he took a back seat, as if he didn't wish to subject himself to the gaze, and possible contempt, of his fellow planters.

Fitz addressed the delegation. "It's a pleasure to see you-all agin. Makes me have a mind to call these kin' o' meetin's more often. We all in the same business—in the same boat—an' trouble fo' one is trouble fo' all. Today we don't talk crops or market prices. We talks slaves, 'cause slaves are the bigges' investment we got an' they kin' give us the mos' trouble."

"More'n jes' trouble, Mistah Turner, suh. They's bound to git mighty dangerous, we don' hide 'em when they needs it."

"Mistah Craig," Fitz said, "that's whut I was gettin' at. Reckon we all used to think the Abolitionist Society jes' a lot o' Sunday saints more worried 'bout temperance an' Sunday school than slaves. Mayhap once that was true, but ain't no mo'. They's satisfied temperance ain't goin' to wuk, Sunday school takes keer o' itse'f. But—there's slavery. Slavery, gen'mun! It's somethin' they kin wuk on. They's even one group, the American Colonization Society, whut is bent on sendin' slaves back to Africa. Now ain't that somethin'? Yo' kin get one slave who wants to go back, yo' show him to me."

"I ain't evah heered one say he wants to go

back." Major Apperson decided to risk getting into the meeting.

"Ain't nobody else evah did either," Fitz went on. "But we all heers little whispahs, bits o' information, the way some slaves are actin', an' we knows they's an unrest we cain't afford not to control."

"Whut yo' offerin' in the way o' advice, Mistah Turner?" someone asked.

"Well, suh. If slavery evah gets into politics, they's goin' to be pure hell to pay. This heah country is goin' to be so divided nobody knows whut the hell side they on. On'y way we gets to fight this is to make sho' we got no trouble, so they's no newspaper writin' an' no talk 'bout how the po' slaves are gettin' whupped ev'y goddamn day an' twice on Sunday 'cause they's no wuk on Sunday an' we gots mo' time for whuppin'."

"How we do that, suh?" Hugh Lister asked.

"Firs' thing, we kinda scared. Any man heah who thinks we ain't skeered, kin'ly raise his hand." Fitz looked over the crowd and saw no hands raised. "So I say this first, an' it mighty impohtant. No slave must evah think we ain't secure. Let 'em get the idee we skeered, they goin' to raise hell. So . . . we bes' be so strict not one nigger gets away with anythin'. We be so stern an' rigid in dealin' with 'em that we don' have to do much whuppin'. But if whuppin' is called fo', use it, an' use it quick's yo' kin. Let all the niggers see it done, yo' kin arrange that."

"Uses the whup, I thinks it needed," Major Apperson said.

"On'y when yo' sure, suh. On the other hand,

when a slave does somethin' good, then yo' rewards him. A dollah, or a new shirt or a bottle o' beer. Or a day off. Whutevah seems bes'. Reward them whut does good, whup the hell outa them whut busts the rules. An' we don' stand fo' no slothin'. That the wu'st sin of all. Whup 'em they don' wuk good."

One man stood up. "Whut we do 'bout black ministers comin' to hold services? Got one moseyin' 'bout my place, tryin' to git my slaves to listen to his preachin'."

"We needs mo' o' that," Fitz said. "Glad yo' brings it up. Had a preachin' man heah some time back an' he teaches slaves to do they wuk like they tol' tuh do an' nevah sloth, an' nevah even thinks o' runnin'. Now it bein' Christmas, I lets him talk. Sends my son down to listen to the preachin' an' make sho' no talk of rebellion. Wasn't none, was they, Jonathan?"

"No, suh," Jonathan declared. "That preachin' man do good. The slaves listen to him an' they do whut he say. Thinks we ought tuh have him come heah ev'y Sunday. Mayhap some o' yo' folks needs him too an' we kin sen' him to yo'."

"Whut yo' think 'bout lettin' 'em dance?" another man asked. "I gives one o' 'em a banjo once a month an' he plays an' ev'ybody dances an' has a good time. Seems to me they wuks harder next day. Don' allow it often, but they sho' looks forward to it."

"Dancin's fine, yo' don' let it turn into a meetin' where some slaves kin talk rebellion. Reckon won't do any harm an' sho' don't cost much to let 'em have theyse'ves a good time ev'y Sunday."

"Sounds to me like we babyin' them too damn much," Apperson said. "Ain't objectin' to whut yo' said, suh, but we gives 'em all yo' talk 'bout an' they thinks they emancipated."

"Nevah let 'em think they anythin' but a slave," Fitz agreed.

Jonathan had been staring at one of the big windows. It was raised about an inch. Once he thought he saw the extension of a shadow against the brush outside, as if someone moved stealthily.

Fitz went on. "One mo' thing gettin' outa hand. I'm talkin' 'bout the Underground Railroad. I ain't lost no slave yit, but I heers lots o' yo' did."

"Five my place," Ron Craig admitted.

"Lost one day 'fore yestiddy," another planter said. A third had lost a pair during the week and still another had lost seven in one day.

"Lets all the slaves know 'bout this an' they all think o' runnin'," Fitz said. "They's 'nuff o' that 'thout the Underground comin' in to he'p 'em run. Reg'lar runners don't get far. The paddyrollers see to that, but paddyrollers cain't do much agin the Underground 'cause they don' know whar it is or who behind it. An' neither do we."

Jonathan stepped close to his father and whispered. "Papa, thinks somebody outside listenin' below that window. Yo' keeps talkin' an' I slips outa the house an' gets 'roun' to the back. I see anybody, I grabs him or I yells fo' he'p."

"Get out theah quick," Fitz said. "Don' let anybody heah know whut yo' doin'. They raise too much hell an' whoevah listenin' gets away."

"I jes' walks out like yo' give me a message or an errand. Keep talkin', Papa."

Jonathan slipped out of the room and made his way through the dining room and the kitchen. Elegant was seated on her high stool close by the stove, dozing. She wasn't aware of his existence. There were no other slaves anywhere within sight. Fitz had seen to that.

Jonathan reached the corner of the house and risked a quick look down along the side of the house where the partially open window was located. He saw a man kneeling below the window, his back toward Jonathan. There was no doubt that he was eavesdropping.

Jonathan crouched, moving very slowly and warily. It was a slave, Jonathan was sure. He moved forward again, as close as he dared. If he had no start on a dash to collar the slave, he might lose him. The element of surprise was vital. Jonathan took a quick breath and began running lightly forward. The slave straightened slightly. Jonathan wondered if his father was delivering some wild statement that held the attention of the eavesdropper. In any event, Jonathan was no more than half a dozen yards from the slave when the man whirled about. He froze in surprise and terror for a moment and then took off. But it was too late. Jonathan gained on him, went into a headlong dive, and pulled him down. He held the man flat against the ground and lashed out a punch that rocked him enough to make him dizzy and docile.

Jonathan yanked the slave to his feet and propelled him across the grounds to the front door. He shoved him into the meeting room.

"He listenin' like yo' said?" Fitz asked.

"Kneelin' right undah the open window, Papa."

"Seen him befo'?" Fitz scanned the trembling man and failed to recognize him, though with all the slaves he kept, it was quite possible this was one of his. No one at the meeting recognized the terrified slave.

Jonathan said, "Nevah saw him befo' I knows of, Papa. I sends fo' Hong Kong. He knows ev'y one."

"Sen' Calcutta, an' whup him he don' get Hong Kong heah in ten minutes."

Jonathan hurried out to find the family servant, who was usually fast asleep somewhere.

Fitz seized the slave by the throat. "Wheah yo' from, yo' sonabitch?"

"Wuks heah, I does," the slave said.

"Like hell yo' do. Why yo' listenin' below that window?"

"Wasn't listenin', suh. Was weedin' grass, suh. Like the overseer tells me."

"Whut overseer tells yo' to do weedin' at night?"

"Don' know his name, massa, suh."

"He tells yo' whut to do, yo' knows his name. Stop yo' lyin' or yo' gets fifty lashes 'stead of twenty."

"Massa, suh, I ain't lyin', I ain't. Wasn't listenin'."

"We'll wait till Hong Kong gets heah." Fitz addressed the group. "Hong Kong manumitted an' head drivah heah. He hones' as kin be. He tells us whethuh this heah miserable no-good bastahd lyin'. If he is, we all goes to the whuppin' shed an' he gets it till they ain't no meat lef' on his bones. Then we throws him out in the woods someplace an' lets the animals finish him off."

"Bes' we hangs him aftah yo' lashes him, Mistah Turner," someone suggested.

"If they's anythin' lef' wuth hangin'," Fitz agreed.

The door opened, and Hong Kong entered quickly. He took one look at the quaking slave and grabbed him by the neck, his big hand closing to shut off his air.

"This heah nigger don' belong our plantation, Mistah Turner, suh. Sho' he listenin'. Wants I strangle him right heah, suh?"

"Take him down to the whuppin' shed," Fitz ordered. "Get out the rawhide. We all gets theah in a few minutes. Tie him to the whuppin' post."

Hong Kong dragged the terrified man out of the house. Fitz resumed his control over the meeting. "Don' know whut he up to, but sho' don' belong to one o' us. Maybe he a spy, sent by one o' the small farms 'roun' heah. We fin' out. An' this is somethin' to make yo' all re'lize whut the hell is goin' on. Things ain't peaceful, somebody send a spy."

"Thinks it be somebody runnin' the Underground, Fitz?" Craig asked.

"Reckon. He runnin' an Underground close by, he got to know if we heahs 'bout it. We goes down to the shed an' we makes this nigger talk. After that we decides whut to do 'bout it. Seems we was not dreamin' o' trouble comin'. It heah."

In the spacious whipping shed, Hong Kong had already tied the slave to one of the posts.

Hong Kong held the plaited, end-knotted lash, waiting for orders.

Fitz said, "Shuck him down some."

Hong Kong ripped the slave's shirt off his back. Then he retreated and let the whip snake out before him.

"Give him a good one," Fitz said. "Make it cut deep. Sees if that loosens his tongue."

The whip hissed and struck, drawing blood instantly. The slave screamed in pain. Fitz walked up to him, grabbed him by the wool, and lifted his head up.

"Nex' time yo' gets two, yo' don' answer. Then yo' gets fo', an' six an' eight. Aftah that yo' half daid an' we hangs yo'. Tell me who sent yo' heah."

"Massa suh, don' whup me no mo'. Don' hang me, please, massa suh!"

"Then answer me!" Fitz shouted.

"I tell yo' an' I gits hung. I don' tell yo' an' I gits hung. No mattah whut, I hangs."

Fitz nodded and turned to the highly interested group. "Yo hear whut he says? If he caught he gets hung, if he say who sen' him."

He turned back to the slave. "Yo' tells us an' yo' gets ten lashes an' we don' hang yo'. I lets yo' run. So now yo' got one chance to live. Yo' bettah take it now, 'cause I won't ask agin."

"Massa suh, I tells yo'. Don' whup me no mo'."

"Yo' tells us who sent yo' an' yo' gets only five mo' lashes. Gots to whup yo' fo' whut yo' done. We spancels yo' to the post till we finds out yo' tellin' the truth. Yo' is an' yo' kin run. Yo' lies an' yo' gets the meat whupped off yo' an' then we hangs yo' upside down till yo' daid."

"Massa suh, yo, lets me run please. . . ."

"Hong Kong, give him two mo'."

The whip cracked suggestively and the slave howled, though the whip hadn't touched him.

"He Mastah Fisbee, suh," he confessed hastily.

"Fisbee nuthin' but scum!" someone shouted.

"Ain't s'prised myse'f," Fitz admitted.

"Fisbee got no mo' slaves," Major Apperson said ruefully, "An' them he had was sho' pitiful, as I finds out."

Fitz started to laugh and the others joined in.

"Mus' be Abolitionists payin' him," Jonathan said. "On'y thing he kin do, bein' so busted like he is."

Fitz said, "Hong Kong, yo' keeps this bastahd heah till we decides whut to do. We fin' out he tellin' the truth, yo' gives him five mo' an' then yo' turns him loose an' lets him run. Makes sho' he keep 'way from the east woods. Paddyrollers theah all the time now. Don' wants him comin' back heah, daid or alive. Bes' he gets far away."

"Yas suh, Massa Turner," Hong Kong said. "I shows him wheah to run."

"Reckon yo' know which way," Fitz said with a grin. "Ain't much this heah man don' know 'bout whut's goin' on, gen'mun. He one damn good man."

"He knows 'bout the Underground?" Major Apperson asked.

"I kin speak, suh?" Hong Kong said.

"Yo' kin say whut's on yo' min', Hong Kong," Fitz said.

"Knows they's a Underground 'roun' heah, but don' know wheah, suh. Like this heah bastahd say, could be Fisbee farm, suh. Heerd tell some slaves seen 'roun' theah, an' the Fisbees they got no wuk fo' slaves no' mo'. Reckon it could be the place."

"Good. Yo' watches this bastahd, Hong Kong. We be back fo' mornin', an' yo' keeps yo' mouth shet 'bout this, heah?"

"Don' know nuthin', suh. Knows nuthin' 'cept got me a nigger wants whuppin'. Killin', he lies 'bout whut yo' ast him."

Fitz led the group out of the shed toward the stables. They didn't talk about their mission because there would be too many ears, even at this time of night. It was essential that no slave learn anything about this plot to enable them to flee from slavery.

When they reached the assortment of buggies and carriages, they talked quietly, with a watchful eye out for any possible eavesdropper.

"We has to move right away," Fitz said. "That nigger don' come back like he s'posed to, they knows somethin' went wrong an' they clears out. We kin reach the Fisbee place in two hours an' not have to ride hard. But we takes a vote now on whut we do when we gets theah."

"We hangs any slave we sees is hidin'," someone suggested.

Fitz shook his head. "Cain't see that. Slaves wuth too much. We turns 'em ovah to whoevah owns 'em. Lets him do whut he wants, but I don' believe in hangin' 'em 'less they done mo' than try to run."

"Who gives a goddamn 'bout the slaves?" another voice spoke up. Fitz thought it was Robert Harper. He was perhaps the most belligerent man in the group; not a man to punish a slave without good reason, but his punishments were known to be very severe.

"Well, whut we give a damn 'bout?" Fitz asked.

"We hangs the Fisbees. Don' know how many they is, but we finds out they runnin' that Underground, we hangs 'em right there."

"Don' go 'long with that," Fitz said. "They gets a fair trial. We ain't a lynch mob."

"Ain't no court goin' to hang 'em," Robert Harper said gruffly. "We gots to, so we teaches anyone else a lesson they don' fo'get."

"See when we gets theah," Fitz said. "Thinks that buck tellin' the truth, but nevah kin tell fo' sho'. One thing we don' wan' to do is hang the wrong man. We leaves now, gen'mun. Rides easy an' we stays togethah bes' we kin. Anyone gets to the Fisbee place ahead of the rest, waits till we all theah."

It was agreed by a series of assenting murmurs and the men spread out in returning to their own conveyances. Fitz and Jonathan hurried down to the stables. Dundee, busy deciphering words in the primer, heard them coming. Hastily hiding the book and the pencil and paper, he scrambled down the ladder and was engaged in filling water buckets when Fitz and Jonathan came in.

"Yo' gets us the carriage, an' fast, heah?"
Fitz said.

"Yas suh, massa, suh," Dundee said. He fled
from the stable for the barns, where the vehicles
were kept.

"Think that bastahd slothin' 'roun' heah?"
Fitz asked.

"Papa, he the bes' wukker we got. By spring,
he goin' to have that mare ready fo' the big track
an' maybe three more 'sides that. All fine racin'
hosses. Ain't nevah seen a man train so many in
one season. An' so well."

"Got a mind to have Hong Kong whup him
jes' to show othah slaves they bes' wuk hard."

"Wouldn't do it, Papa. Dundee a little diff'-
rent. He smaht an' he wuth a lot to us. Goin' to
make us a lot o' money sho'. Yo' whups him an'
he ain't goin' to care much what happens.
Hosses win or not. Way he is now, thinks the
hosses belong to him. That's how good care he
takes o' them."

"Well, all right," Fitz said, knowing he had
never intended to carry out the threat anyway.
He knew quite well the kind of work Dundee was
doing and it closely matched the kind of work
his father had done years before. Themba had
been a genius around horses. A rebellious, dangerous slave otherwise, but he could make horses
do his bidding, and without cruelty. Dundee had
the same skill.

Dundee drove the carriage up, hopped down
and stood by with his head bowed. As he passed
the slave, Fitz could see, in the gloom broken
only by lantern light, some of the characteristics

[237]

of Nina, whom he had loved so dearly. Fitz half-raised his hand to touch Dundee's bowed head, but restrained himself. Jonathan, falling behind his father, patted Dundee on the head. Dundee looked up and dared to smile, but only fleetingly. He let go of the horses and the carriage rolled away, to stop first at the mansion so Benay might be advised that they'd be gone most of the night, and the reason for it.

When he returned from delivering the message to Benay, Fitz had changed his mind about the tactics of this expedition.

"Jonathan, drive back to the whuppin' shed. We takes that nigger with us. Got me an idee, an' we needs him."

"Whatevah yo' say, Papa," Jonathan said. He began driving the brief distance to the whipping shed.

"Whut yo' think 'bout Major Apperson comin'?" Jonathan asked on the way.

"Reckon this heah business as impohtant to him as to us."

"Don' trust him none."

"Neither do I, son. But we all stick togethah in this, or maybe we all go down when them Abolitionist Societies begins to drive us crazy. Anyways, yo' got mo' than the Major to worry yo' when we gets to the Fisbee place."

"Yo' means Belle? Reckon they finds she been helpin' ship slaves No'th, they hangs her too?"

"She carryin' my gran'son an' nobody goin' to kill him. Don' give a damn they hangs her, but cain't do that 'thout killin' the sucker. Yo' sees yo' chance, yo' gets her away from theah.

Don' wan' to fight fo' her, but sho' will it comes to that."

Jonathan pulled up before the whipping shed and Hong Kong emerged to find out what was wanted of him.

Fitz said, "Get him off'n the whuppin' post, spancel him good, an' gets him in the carriage. Yo' comes too. We's takin' him 'long with us."

"Yas suh, I fetches him," Hong Kong said.

The terrified slave was bundled into the back of the carriage with Hong Kong sitting beside him. Jonathan whipped up the horses and planned to catch the others long before they reached the Fisbee place.

Vehicles left well away from the suspected plantation, the planters assembled quietly and walked toward the large, once opulent mansion.

When they all came to a stop, Fitz advanced the plan he'd concocted. "Way I figger, when that slave don' come back, old man Fisbee an' his son goin' to come lookin' 'roun' the slave quarters to see if he came back 'thout lettin' them know. They'll run if they thinks we comin' to bust up his Underground—if he has one. So if they comes out, I sends in the spy. When the Fisbees ask him 'bout whut happened, we got us a full confession o' his guilt."

"That'll make it easier to hang 'em," Bob Harper said with satisfaction. For a small, almost frail-looking man, he seemed exceptionally blood-thirsty and belligerent.

"So now we all hides," Fitz continued. "It bein' good an' dark tonight, they'll nevah see us. Be sho' not to light any lanterns. Hong Kong, yo' brings that spy an' yo' tells him whut we want.

He gets a chance to run, he he'ps us. He don't, he gets strung up. Tell him that an' make sho' he understands whut yo' talkin' 'bout."

"I tells him so he unnerstans, Massa Turner, suh. He so scared now he do whut he tol'."

"Take him close to the house. When anyone comes out send him into the open so he kin be seen, but he don' say a word, even when they call to him. They gots to come an' get him an' that's when they ask him questions."

"I do whut yo' says," Hong Kong assured him. He unlocked the slave's irons and removed them, with a soft and deadly warning that he would die instantly if he tried to escape or warn the Fisbees.

Fitz motioned Jonathan to follow him and they went off to take a position from where they hoped they would hear the Fisbees talk out their guilt without knowing it.

"Got to get Belle outen theah," Fitz said. "Reckon yo' kin get inside the house an' get her?"

"Got to try, Papa. Bettah go now, befo' the Fisbees comes out an' the fun stahts."

"Make sho' she ain't hurt none. Wants that sucker to get born in one piece."

Jonathan made a circle of the house. The back door was not locked, and Jonathan opened it quietly. There was faint candlelight from one of the front rooms and, once inside, he could hear voices. He stopped and listened. They were male voices—two men, he estimated. That meant only Fisbee and his son Matt, were here, which made things easier.

He had no idea where Belle slept, but most likely it was on the second floor. The back stairs creaked under his weight, but when he paused, he heard no sound of anyone stirring. He kept going. On the second floor, he was faced with six closed doors. He was aware how floors creaked in these old houses so he moved carefully, with his back against the wall so all his weight would be closest to the soundest part of the floor.

The first three doors revealed only empty rooms, but when he carefully opened the fourth one he heard slow, steady breathing of someone fast asleep. He entered the room, moved to the bed by sense of feel, with his hands out before him to warn of any furniture that might make a tell-tale noise if stumbled.

He reached the edge of the bed and this time he did stumble against it. Belle sat up, still half asleep, but thoroughly alarmed. She saw a bulky figure hovering above her and opened her mouth to emit a yell, but Jonathan's hand clapped down over her mouth.

"It's me, Jonathan," he whispered. "Come fo' yo', Belle. Cain't stand it bein' 'way from yo'. Dreams o' yo'. I had to come."

He experimented slightly by removing his hand just enough so if she yelled, he could stop it before the sound emerged. Instead, her arms raised, went around his neck, and pulled him down onto the bed and onto her body.

"Yo' wants me like I wants yo'," he said in the same kind of whisper. Hoarse, very low, as if it indicated his pent-up passion.

"Now!" she whispered. "Now, Jonathan. Been waitin' yo' comes like this. Get in bed. Needs yo' too."

"Cain't. Yo' folks heahs us. An' jes' one night

ain't 'nuff. Been thinkin' we goes off to New Aw-leans, maybe. Now! Tonight! Got a carriage wait-in', pocket full o' money an' wants to be with yo' in bed."

She nodded assent and he removed his hand completely. She got out of bed.

"No noise," he warned. "Don' want no fight with yo' folks. On'y wants yo'."

She nodded again and hoisted up her cotton nightgown, pushing her naked body against him and giggling. Jonathan exhaled slowly, but did nothing. She put on a slip of some kind, over it a dress which had been balled up on a chair. She pulled on white stockings and started to put on her shoes, but Jonathan signaled her to carry them. It was working better than he expected. Belle seized him in a hot, passionate embrace. Her lips sought his, and he returned the kiss. Her hands moved down to his genitals. He responded immediately. It wasn't much of an effort.

"We gots plenty time fo' mo' o' that," he said. He fondled her breasts, pushed his erection into her pubic area, then cautioned her to be silent. He picked her up, told her to put her arms around his neck. She obeyed, clinging to him while he made his slow, careful way to the back stairs, down them, and finally out into the open. He hoped none of the posse would be in sight and that no one would call out. Belle was far from intelligent, but she had sense enough to realize that if Jonathan was not alone, there was trouble, and she would do her best to warn her brother and father.

Still carrying her, enduring her partially suppressed giggling and occasional nip at his ear-lobe, he managed to reach the area where the carriages were hidden. They were none too visible in the darkness, but the outlines were there. Belle suddenly realized this was some sort of trick. Before she could yell, Jonathan smothered the cry again. He dumped her bodily into the carriage.

"Yo' makes one sound an' I knocks yo' stiff. Understan', Belle?"

"Yo' bastahd!" she said. "Yo' double-dealin' sonabitch. Yo' damned liar. Yo'——"

"One mo' word an' yo' gets rapped right on the chin. Yo' listens to me. Yo' papa an' brother runnin' an Underground Railroad. Don' lie an' say it ain't so 'cause we know it is. They's goin' to be arrested an' held fo' trial. Don' want yo' mixed up in it. Feels too wahm fo' yo', Belle. Whut I said in the bedroom wasn't no lie."

"Yo' goin' to hang my papa an' my brother?" she asked.

"They won't swing. Nobody wants to kill 'em. On'y make things worse'n they are now. On'y wants to bust up this station on the railroad."

"Yo takin' me back to Wyndward, Jonathan?"

"Sho' will. My papa says I got to do right by yo'."

"That was a lie 'bout goin' to New Awleans?"

"Well—yes. Fer now. Latah we kin go. Now all I asks is yo' keeps quiet till this ovah with. Kin I trust yo', Belle?"

She nodded. "Don' know why I say yes, but I does. Wants yo', Jonathan. Wants yo' bad. Yo' get back to me quick as yo' kin."

"Won' be long," he promised. He stepped into

the carriage and kissed her passionately, hoping it would keep her content for a little while.

He left her there, merged with the darkness and made low hissing noises until his father's whisper directed him. They knelt behind brush, as did the other members of the group. Hong Kong had the slave by the neck in an everlasting threat to strangle him if he made a sound.

They heard a door open. One man came out to the porch and looked around. "Matt," he called, "get yo' lazy ass out heah an' go see if that no-good nigger is back yit, an' so goddamn stupid he don' know 'nuff to come an' tell us whut he found out."

Hong Kong gave the slave a push and the slave advanced slowly. He was acting exactly as he'd been ordered to.

"Massa, suh," he called out, "I's back, massa, suh."

"Whut in hell took yo' so long?" It was the elder Fisbee talking. "Yo' bettah have somethin' to tell me or yo' gets the skin whaled offen yo'."

"Heerd 'em talkin', massa."

"Whut they say? Did yo' hear 'em talking 'bout the Underground?"

Things happened very fast after that. Fitz gave one shout and charged. The elder Fisbee on the porch did his best to get into the house, but he failed by a second or two. Fitz had him. He dragged him across the porch and into the open before the mansion.

"Matt Fisbee," Fitz called out. "We comes to get yo', we comes shootin' an' with a rope. Yo' comes out quiet an' I sweah yo' ain't goin' to be hurt by us."

"They'll hang yo'," Fisbee managed to yell. "Kill 'em, Matt. Kill 'em all——"

Fitz wound an arm around Fisbee's neck, squeezed hard, held it there a full minute and then let go. Fisbee dropped to the ground, unconscious.

"Matt," he called out. "Yo' Papa is on the ground at my feet. In ten seconds I puts a bullet in him, yo' don' come out."

Fisbee, on the ground, began to move. He tried to sit up. Fitz put a foot against his chest and pushed him back down.

"Yo' heered me, Matt?"

Fisbee gave a cackling laugh. "Hates me, he do. Yo' kills me, he a happy man, that no-good bastahd son o' mine."

"Shut up or I puts my foot right through yo' mis'able face," Fitz warned. "Yo' comin', Matt?"

"Come an' git me, yo' got the guts. Knows who yo' are. Yo' cheatin', no-good——"

"Theah's 'bout fo'ty o' us," Fitz warned. "Mos wants to hang yo', but gives me they word yo' gets turned ovah to the sheriff. We come get yo' an' yo' gets shot, or yo' gets hung or maybe yo' gets both."

"Let's go get him!" someone shouted. Several men started forward, but dropped to the ground when bullets began to whiz over their heads. Jonathan slipped away in the dark and headed for the rear of the house by a roundabout route. He could hear Fitz trying to talk Matt out of the house. Several more shots were fired, all from Matt's gun.

Jonathan reached the back door. It was still open, just as he'd left it. To go in and try to locate

Matt in the dark would be dangerous. Everything had happened very fast and perhaps Matt Fisbee hadn't found the time to do any real thinking about his situation. When he did, he'd do his best to escape. By the front door would be plain suicide, so he'd no doubt try the back. Jonathan picked up one of the wooden kitchen chairs and drew back into a corner just inside the door to the front of the house where Matt was still firing and daring them to come and get him.

Jonathan waited. He could hear his father's voice again, but not what was being said. Matt Fisbee fired half a dozen quick shots to keep all heads down. As Jonathan had guessed, Matt was now going to make a dash for it. He had no other recourse. By now, he knew there were far too many men out front to fight.

He came through the kitchen door in half a crouch, as if he expected someone might be just outside. Jonathan brought the chair down as hard as he could. It struck Matt across the back and sent him sprawling. Before he could get up, Jonathan had kicked the revolver out of his hand. Rather than take a chance Matt might have another gun, he kicked him on the chin. Matt Fisbee was no further trouble.

"This is Jonathan," he shouted through the night. "Yo' all kin come in now. Matt's takin' a nap."

They came, all of them, to light lanterns and candles they found in the house. The elder Fisbee was dragged in and forced to the floor beside his unconscious son.

Fitz said, "Jonathan, take a man an' see whut yo' kin find in the barns an' in the slave barracks. Ev'ybody else fan out some and sweep the plantation fo' any signs of runaways. Look ev'ywhere, 'specially if they's any new diggin' or maybe a cave somewhar on the hillside. Got to be slaves heah an' we got to find 'em."

"Let's string the two of 'em up until they tells us wheah they keeps the runaways," Bob Harper suggested.

"Gave 'em my word, no harm," Fitz said. "Means it."

There was some grumbling, but no one disputed Fitz's authority. Jonathan took Bob Harper along. No one else. The two of them would handle any slave situation they encountered.

The cabins had no floors, no furniture except for a small open stove with a hole in the roof for the smoke to escape. There were no windows. The doors were flimsy, and of course could not be locked from the inside.

In one of the cabins they found two female slaves, one with an infant no more than three months old, and five male slaves, all young and valuable to their masters.

Harper lined them all up while Jonathan made them identify their masters. Harper said, "We looks 'roun' heah we finds a whuppin' shed sho'. Says all o' these gets whupped good befo' we sends 'em back to they own plantations."

"No way to do it, Bob," Jonathan said firmly. "These slaves belong to yo', would yo' like to have 'em come back half daid from whuppin'? Bettah they punishment lef' up to they masters. That's whut we do—sen' 'em back an' let they masters take keer o' it."

"An' whut we do with the Fisbees? I say

hang 'em, but yo' papa agin it an' reckon mos' othahs agin it too. Me, I say once yo' hangs 'em, they won't do that agin."

"Papa is right," Jonathan insisted. "He thinks we hangs too many o' these, on'y gives the Abolitionists mo' to argue 'bout slavery ought to be abolished. They gettin' mo' pow'ful eve'y yeah, Bob. Rile 'em an' it on'y gets worse fo' us."

"Ain't like it used to be," Harper grumbled again. "Twenny yeahs ago we'd string up the whole lot of 'em an' be done with it. But reckon they's some sense in whut yo' say, an' whut yo' papa thinks. Ev'ybody else goes 'long, I does too."

"March 'em out," Jonathan said, "while I search the house. Cain't tell whut I'll find theah."

One of the runaway slaves tried to get up from a layer of straw on the ground serving as a bed, but he was unable to do so.

"Get up," Jonathan ordered, "or I gets yo' up with the toe o' my shoe."

"Massa, suh," one of the women said. "He whupped so he near die, massa, suh."

Jonathan ripped the man's shirt down the middle and turned him over to reveal a back so lacerated it had begun to fester. The whip had been knotted, possibly with a metal tip, which had acted almost like a knife.

"Yo' mastah whup yo' like this?" he asked.

"No suh. Massa don' whup me, suh. Comes heah an' I gits whupped fo' makin' noise."

"White massas gits drunk," the woman explained. "They goin' to whup all o' us till we mos' die, suh. On'y they gits tired aftah lashin' him."

"Yo' tends to him, yo' women. Wash him

good an' I gets him a clean shirt an' cloth to bandage him. Keep him nice an' clean all the way to wheah he come from."

"Yas suh, mastah suh, we keeps him clean."

"This be some Underground," Harper commented angrily. "The Fisbees half-kill the slaves they tryin' to sneak No'th. Sho' am goin' to let it be known whut happened heah."

"I'll be right back," Jonathan said.

He hurried to the house, went in and lit a lamp. Then he seleced several shirts from Matt Fisbee's clothes closet and two pair of pants. From Belle's more ample supply of clothes he appropriated dresses for the female slaves. He paid special attention to the room usually designated as the library, where plantation records were kept and business was transacted. Here there was only a dilapidated desk and a chair in the process of falling apart. Little work had been done in this room. Jonathan pulled open drawers, spread whatever papers he could find on the desk, and studied them in the lamplight. There were half a dozen letters that interested him. He tucked them into his pocket. Opening another drawer, he came upon a flat wooden case which, when opened, revealed empty spaces where small guns had been kept. Possibly derringers.

Jonathan raced for the front door, threw it wide, and ran out. "They armed—got guns——" he shouted.

He heard a muffled shot, a cry of pain. Then the two Fisbees apparently broke free and began to run. But they underestimated the numbers of the posse and they were quickly stopped, but not before one of them fired another shot, which went wild. Then they were knocked to the ground and held there.

Jonathan joined his father. "Saw where they kept they small guns," he explained. "Got a plush lined case o' them, but came 'cross it too late."

"Ed Mallory got winged. Nothin' serious. Sho' got us a pair o' low snakes."

"Papa, they worse than that. Shows yo' whut I means." He borrowed a lantern from a man nearby, held this so Fitz could read the letters Jonathan gave him.

"Found 'em in the desk," he explained.

"They ain't even snakes," Fitz shouted. "Reckon they less human than slaves. Listen, gen'mun, these heah letters are from a branch of the Abolitionists. Says they pays the Fisbees fifty dollahs fo' eve'y slave they sends No'th. They low as paddyrollers. Lower, reckon."

Jonathan said, "Mo' than that. Finds slaves they got hidin' till they gets on the Underground. The Fisbees whupped one of 'em so he near daid. Cuts him bad an' lets the cuts fester. Mayhap he dies befo' we gets him back to his master. Fisbees got drunk an' whupped the slave fo' the fun of it."

"So they steals slaves, whups 'em fo' no reason, gets cash money fo' each slave they gets on the Underground." Fitz walked over to where the two men lay on the ground. He kicked the elder Fisbee in the ribs.

"Git up! Stand on yo' feet, yo' no-good bastahd. An' that goes fo' yo' son. Both o' yo' git up so's we kin see whut two low-down skunks looks like."

"Knows whut to do with these two," Bob Harper said. "We whups slaves fo' doin' nuthin' sometimes, but we nevah whups 'em 'cause we likes to heah 'em yell. Reckon these two like whuppin' othahs so much they goin' to enjoy bein' whupped theyse'ves."

Fitz raised his voice. "Hong Kong—come here."

Hong Kong came at a run from the fringes of the posse where he'd quietly listened to everything that went on.

"Wants yo' to whup these two till they cain't screech no mo'."

"Yas suh," Hong Kong said with a satisfaction he couldn't hide. "Heerd tell long time ago, the Fisbees kills some slaves jes' to heah 'em holler."

"Put some heft into the whup then," Fitz ordered. He turned to the others. "Makes it mo' hard to bear, a nigger whups 'em."

"Whut we do with 'em aftah they whupped?" someone asked.

"Been agin hangin' 'em," Fitz said. "Agin it fo' anybody 'cept slaves who riots. We whups these two an' that done, I heads fo' home an' don' give a damn whut happens aftah that. Leaves it to all o' yo'."

The two shrilly protesting men were dragged down to the slave cabins, where the whipping shed was quickly located. Fitz and Jonathan didn't join them, but they could hear the screeching of the pair as Hong Kong laid on the whip with a vengeance.

"Reckon they hangs 'em, Papa?" Jonathan asked.

"They got it comin," Fitz said. "An' the man who handles the rope will be the one they shot an' tried to kill. Me, I want to go home. Soon as Hong Kong gets through, we go back."

"Papa, whut yo' father do with two critters like the Fisbees?"

"Whups 'em, hangs 'em, an' watches 'em die."

"Why yo' don' wan' to see that?"

"Had 'nuff o' it. Mayhap I gettin' old. Don' know, but killin' I got little appetite fo' 'cept somethin' special. Things changin', reckon."

"Sho' are, Papa. Got no guts fo' hangin' either."

"Whut yo' do with Belle?"

"Throws her in our carriage. Question is, whut we do with her now?"

"Kicks her ass outen heah, guess. Jes' don' wan' her baby gets hurt."

"Brings her back home, Papa?"

"Reckon that bes'. Benay takes keer o' her, but when yo' sucker bo'n, we kicks her ass so she goes off an' wheah I don' give a damn."

They reached the spot where they'd left the carriage, but it was no longer there. They searched among the other conveyances until they realized that Belle hadn't waited for them. She'd stolen their best carriage and a pair of their best horses.

"Papa," Jonathan said, "it my fault. Nevah figgered she'd do this. Didn't think she had 'nuff brains."

"Jes' as well," Fitz said. "Now we rid o' her an' the baby not harmed. Wondah, though, whut happens that baby grows up."

"Kinda interestin' to see him," Jonathan mused. "Or her, if it a girl."

"Won't be so interestin' he come to see yo' with a gun or a knife in his hand. Belle goin' to teach that sucker to hate yo' long 'fore he even sees yo'. But nothin' we kin do 'bout it now. Whut we gots to do is get somebody to give us a ride home."

"Papa, yo' says so I goin' to hunt fo' Daisy right aftah we gets back."

"Bes' time o' yeah," Fitz agreed. "Needs yo' mos' in the spring when yo' mama an' me goes No'th. Been meanin' to ask. How yo' gets Belle out o' that house 'thout her makin' a hell of a lot o' noise?"

Jonathan laughed. "Tells her I comes to take her 'way an' we gets married an' goes to Wyndward to live."

"She sho' like that."

"She like it so much she tries to get me into bed right then an' I has a hell of a time keepin' her from rapin' me. Reckon now she know it nothin' but a trick, she madder'n hell."

"Wouldn't be s'prised," Fitz agreed. They began walking toward some of the posse who were on their way back from the whipping shed, from which the screeches of the Fisbees had ceased.

"On'y thing," Jonathan said somewhat ruefully, "she all skinned down, she jumps on me, an' I ain't got ovah it yit."

"We gets back, yo' got Domingo."

"Thinks o' that too. Reckon I stay 'roun' fo' a few days 'fore I set out to find Daisy. Bes' I go lookin' fo' her with nothin' on my min', an' sho' got somethin' right now."

❴ 13 ❵

JONATHAN ARRIVED IN MEMPHIS LOOKING THE PERfect gentleman-dandy. His mother had informed him that if he was to court the girl he was in love with—who barely knew him—he should be attentive to his wardrobe. A tailor in Richmond had agreed. The end result included tight pale-blue trousers with a wide green stripe, a high stiff collar with a black cravat, a checked waistcoat, a dark purple frock coat, and a high hat and gloves. Fortunately, no one in the lobby of the Memphis hotel seemed to find this excessive.

Jonathan was in such a hurry to begin tracking down Daisy that he sent his bag to his room without inspecting the premises, and immediately set about questioning the elderly desk clerk. At the mention of a showboat the clerk told him coldly he was entirely uninterested in such frivolity, and hadn't the slightest knowledge of any showboat. His attitude that showboats were not to be discussed in polite society was not an auspicious beginning for Jonathan.

He didn't press the clerk, but went out of the hotel into a bustling city of fifteen thousand, a size comparable to Richmond and perhaps Norfolk. There was a helmeted policeman ambling along one of the principal streets and Jonathan stopped him.

"Suh," he said, "I'm lookin' fo' a riverboat, sort of. Got a minstrel show aboahd an' one o' the dancers is a gal name o' Daisy. Yo' knows anythin' 'bout a boat like that, suh?"

The policeman shook his head. "All kinds of riverboats dock here. Showboats, passenger boats, log rafts, flat bottoms, we get 'em all. Knows there are showboats, but I don' know much 'bout 'em. Maybe down at the docks yo' might find someone who knows more'n I do."

"Thank yo' kin'ly," Jonathan said. "Goes down theah now."

"You new in Memphis?"

"Yes suh. Jes' got in."

"You be mighty keerful down at those docks. They's lots o' bad apples down there an' they spend all they spare time lookin' fo' somebody dressed like yo'. They'll take the clothes off yo' back, you ain't keerful."

"Goes anyway," Jonathan said. "Mos' impohtant I finds this gal."

"Must be, the way you go at it," the policeman said. "She mus be pow'ful pretty."

"She is," Jonathan said with a sigh. "Thank yo' agin, suh."

He ambled down the street toward the river, where he could already see teeming activity. Boats of all shapes and sizes were maneuvering in a manner that seemed to threaten the safety of all, but there were no collisions. The noise reached him a few blocks away. Stevedores were hurling bales of cotton about; trunks, crates, barrels, all were being moved.

There were also loafers, men sitting about on the pilings or leaning lazily against rows of packing cases waiting for shipment. Jonathan scanned the boats tied up and those close enough to study, trying to guess if any were showboats. He thought not.

Two men, roughly clad in baggy, soiled pants and work shirts laced up with leather thongs, were eying him with considerable interest. Jonathan walked up to them and put his questions as concisely as possible.

"It be a showboat an' gots a minstrel show aboahd. They's a gal named Daisy dances in the show. She got light hair an' a pretty face."

"What you want with her?" one man asked. They were both about Jonathan's age, lithe, tough, and, Jonathan guessed, dangerous.

"That my business," Jonathan said. "I pays yo' if yo' knows wheah that boat is."

"How much?" the second man asked.

"Ten dollahs. Pays yo' now."

The first roustabout nodded. "Fair enough. But how much if I takes you straight to this gal?"

"Knows her?" Jonathan asked in surprise.

"Knowed Daisy fo' more than a year. Prettiest gal I ever saw. Like you said, she got blue eyes, light hair. She about eighteen. For twenty, I take you to her."

"Now? Right now?" Jonathan asked, scarcely believing his luck.

"She stays in a hotel close by. Whenever the showboat is docked for repairs, she stays there. Saw her two-three days ago."

"Take me there," Jonathan said.

Only one of the pair walked with him along the dock, but when Jonathan glanced back, he saw the second man scuttling down closer to the river where a path followed along the dock.

Where the wooden platform of the dock end-end, they turned down a dirt path leading to a squalid section of small houses, even smaller cabins, and cheap saloons. Jonathan seized his companion's elbow, and brought him to a stop. "Mistah," Jonathan said, "Yo' lies to me 'bout this gal, I goin' to take it real personal. Thinks all yo' aftah is my money an' yo' don' know this heah gal nohow."

"Why, what makes you think that?" the roustabout proclaimed with great innocence. "Knows Daisy for years. Tol' you what she looked like."

Jonathan suddenly reached out and closed a big hand around the roustabout's throat, pushed him against a wall, and held him there. He waved his free hand, in the form of a fist, before the man's nose.

"Yo' thinks I some country boy comin' to the city fo' the firs' time in my life, yo' makin' a big mistake."

The roustabout tried to tear himself free and succeeded in yelling for help. His companion darted out from around a nearby corner. The man Jonathan held managed to land one short punch to Jonathan's belly, but there was little force behind it for he'd not had room enough to really swing the fist. Jonathan raised one big hand and brought it down on top of the greasy cap the roustabout wore, stunning him. Jonathan stepped back, crashed his fist against the man's chin and, as he sank to the ground, partly supported by the wall, Jonathan turned in time to meet the second man, who was drawing a huge knife. Jonathan had never seen anything like it. The blade, flashing ominously in the sunlight, was as deadly a weapon as he'd ever come across.

The roustabout made a wide, slashing sweep with the blade, which Jonathan avoided with ease, but the next one came so fast it almost landed where it was meant to, against his throat.

He managed to put considerable strength behind a punch that hit his opponent low in the stomach, a painful and disabling blow. The roustabout howled in pain and backed away. Jonathan took quick advantage. He seized the man's knife arm, twisting it savagely until he dislocated it at the shoulder. When he let go, it hung limp and useless. The knife had fallen to the ground. Jonathan picked it up and examined it while the roustabout cursed the pain in his shoulder. Jonathan pushed him over against the same wall which now propped up his unconscious partner.

Jonathan held the knife against the roustabout's throat. "Thinks yo' knows wheah this gal

I named is. Thinks yo' heered o' that showboat. Thinks yo' tells me now or I slit yo' throat little by little, like this."

He eased the keen blade along the skin and blood began to seep down the man's neck. He was wild-eyed with fear now.

Jonathan touched the flat of the blade into the light flow of blood and held it up before the roustabout's eyes.

"Yo' blood, suh. Nex' time I cuts deep. I askin' once mo'. Yo' knows Daisy?"

"Don' know her. Swear I don'. But think I saw her once on a showboat like you said. Minstrels aboard, singin' an' dancin'. Reckon this gal be the one. Ain't many showboats aroun'."

"I do thank yo' kin'ly," Jonathan said. "I asks that yo' thanks yo' partner fo' me. Reckon I needs somethin' to 'member yo' two sweet characters by, so I'm keepin' yo' knife."

"That's a Bowie. It cost me a lot of money."

"Yo' objectin' I takes it?" Jonathan pressed the point of it against the man's partially bared chest. "Sho' is sharp, suh. Sho' cain't tote a blade like this 'thout a scabbard."

He tore the man's shirt partly off to expose the leather holsterlike container for the knife. It extended down the man's thigh and was looped so his belt passed through the loop and kept it in place. Jonathan cut through the belt and pulled the scabbard free.

"Sho' kin cut," he observed. "I now asks yo' where is this heah boat an' whut it called. I asks once——"

"It's named *Sarah.* It berthed in Baton Rouge, givin' shows all winter. Saw it every time we sailed by. Went aboard once to gamble. I want my knife back. It was made to order and you can't buy one in a store."

Jonathan calmly pulled his belt free far enough to inset it through the holster loop. He pulled down his pants to a point where he could nestle the blade against his thigh. The roustabout thought for a fleeting instant of trying to surprise Jonathan, but then Jonathan's head lifted. The roustabout took one quick look at those icy eyes and decided against it. Jonathan patted the man's cheek and smiled.

"I thanks yo' kin'ly fo' the knife. Ain't got time to search yo'—mayhap yo' carryin' a gun too."

He brought up his fist in an uppercut, seized the man as he started to fall, eased him down, and then walked casually away. His next stop was at the hotel where he had just registered. He sent up for his bags while he checked out and arranged to be taken back to the riverfront by carriage. There he bought transportation on an elaborate riverboat due to sail for New Orleans in three hours, with a stop at Baton Rouge.

Jonathan paid for the best cabin aboard, stopped by the salon to purchase a bottle of good bourbon. Armed with this, he went to his state-room and there removed much of his clothing, including the newly acquired knife, which he placed in one of the bureau drawers. Then he took a healthy pull at the bottle of whiskey, lay down on the bed, and thought about Daisy. He didn't think the roustabout had lied, but he might have been mistaken. If not, she was aboard a ship named *Sarah* that was docked for the winter in Baton Rouge.

He heard the preparations being made for departure, but he wasn't interested enough to go on deck. The journey so far had been tiring—train rides, stagecoach rides, and once a buggy and driver for a short stretch. Certainly this part of the country was being rapidly settled, too quickly for transportation to keep pace. For now, it was smooth and easy. The riverboat would soon dock at Baton Rouge, a matter of a day and a half.

With a third of the whiskey gone, Jonathan began to feel hungry. Someone moved down along the corridor outside the staterooms sounding a gong. Jonathan assumed that to be a way of calling the passengers to the table.

He found the dining room on the boiler deck. It was large and richly appointed with tables for four, spotless linen, silver service, and fine china. Jonathan shared a table with two well-dressed men, both cotton factors.

"Turner?" one asked. "From the Wyndward Plantation, suh?"

"Yes suh," Jonathan said happily, pleased he'd found someone who knew about his family. To be recognized this far from Virginia seemed to him nothing short of an honor.

"Yo' wouldn' be Cap'n Turner's son? No—too young . . ."

"Grandson, suh," Jonathan said. "Same name as him."

"Well now, that's a coincidence meetin' yo' on the Mississippi, suh. My name is Tomkins, suh. Bill Tomkins, an' my friend heah is Beau Madden. We factors, an' I used to handle yo' grandpa's 'bacco shipments. Fine Virginia bright he raised, suh. Calls fo' drinks, this heah meetin'."

They settled down to enjoy a fine meal and their beverage. Conversation centered around the price and quality of cotton, which Wyndward did not raise.

"We raises 'bacco, hosses, an' slaves," Jonathan explained. "Good money crops, an' prices don' go up an' down like cotton."

"How true, suh," Tomkins agreed.

"Whut brings yo' all this way from home?" Beau Madden asked. "Kinda young to travel this far, ain't yo, suh?"

"I'm near twenty," Jonathan said. "An' I come heah lookin' fo' a gal I met once. Thinks she 'roun' heah someplace."

"Lots o' good-lookin' gals 'roun' heah," Tomkins chuckled. "Whut her name?"

"Daisy," Jonathan said.

"Her las' name, if yo' please."

"Don' know it, suh. Jes' Daisy."

"Ain't goin' to be easy findin' her, yo' don' know her whole name, Mistah Turner. Glad to he'p I kin, but needs mo' than a firs' name."

"She a dancer," Jonathan explained. "Yo' travels the river much?"

"Up an' down all the time," Beau Madden said.

"Mayhap yo' hears o' her then. She with a minstrel show on a boat name of *Sarah*."

The two men exchanged quick glances. They suddenly became interested in eating.

"Yo' gen'mun heahs o' her?" Jonathan asked, puzzled by their sudden change of attitude.

Beau looked up first. "Bill, bes' we tell him. Fo' his own good."

Bill Tomkins nodded, pity in his eyes. "The gal Daisy, she sings an' dances with a minstrel show on a boat named *Sarah*. Cain't be no mistake. Gots to be the gal yo' means, Mistah Turner."

"Wish she wasn't," Beau added.

Jonathan turned white. "She daid? Somethin' happen to her?"

"How long yo' knows her?" Beau asked.

"'Bout two-three hours. Meets her in Richmond. Nex' day she gone."

Bill Tomkins was the possessor of a double chin and an ample paunch. Both of these shook as he drew a breath for the explanation.

"This boat, the *Sarah*, ain't jes' a showboat. A pleasure boat. Folks go to see the show an' to gamble. Lots o' gamblin' goin' on. The show is only to get folks aboard."

"It's what goes on aftah the gamblin' stops, we don' like to tell yo' 'bout, Mistah Turner."

"Well, tell me," Jonathan urged. "No mattah whut it is, tell me."

"The *Sarah*, kind of a fancy whorehouse, suh." Beau wagged his head. "Las' thing they does at night, soon's the gamblin' stops, is to auction off this gal Daisy."

"Auction? Like on a vendue table?" Jonathan asked with a note of rapidly growing horror.

"Her uncle a no-good bastahd lookin' fo' nuthin' but money. Who bids the highes' gets Daisy fo' that night."

"I kills him," Jonathan said, half under his breath.

"Now yo' listen heah, Mistah Turner," Bill Tomkins warned. "Her uncle owns the boat an' eve'ybody wukkin' on it. Got some mighty tough crew an' gamblers. They eats yo' alive, sho'."

Jonathan felt he couldn't stay there another moment. He arose, pushed his chair close to the table. "Obleeged tō yo', gen'mun. Don' like whut yo' tells me, but reckon it the truth all right. Don' know whut I do now. Gots to think on it. I kin do yo' a favor, yo' kin call on me any time."

He bowed slightly, walked out of the salon, made his way to his stateroom and sat down on the edge of the bed, nauseated. He told himself, coldly, that he should have known. Should have guessed. She's known him a few moments and invited him to her room. It had been a wonderful night making love to her, but he realized, that in his more or less youthful innocence, he had not recognized her for what she was.

It had been easy to find her, which meant she was well known up and down the river. It was even possible those two roustabouts knew her too, though he doubted it. Daisy would not come that cheap.

Still, she had been sufficiently a lady to fool him. Perhaps that meant something. She might sell her body to a man practically every night in the week, but not of her own free will. Jonathan remembered her handsome uncle—if that's what he was. Perhaps she was not only under his evil influence, but dominated by him and forced to do his bidding, with no regard as to what she might wish.

"I be goddamned," Jonathan said half aloud. "I comes all this way an' I ain't goin' back. Got to see fo' mahse'f. An' let her tell me herse'f."

He removed most of his clothes and drank until he fell asleep.

In the morning he didn't feel too well. He didn't see either Tomkins or Madden again; they must have disembarked sometime during the night or early morning. The boat had made several stops.

He had his breakfast late, alone. After he put away a solid meal, he felt better. He paced the deck, breathing deeply, and for the first time began to enjoy the scenery as the boat continued its slow journey.

He climbed up to the hurricane deck, which acted as the roof of the boiler deck, where all amenities were located. He walked that deck, descended to the lower deck and watched the boilers, the engines, and inspected the twin stacks from which smoke belched.

The time began to pall by afternoon. He tilted one of the wooden deck chairs back against the cabin wall, closed his eyes, and dreamed about the Daisy he'd known. The lovely, soft-spoken girl in the Richmond hotel. Whatever she was, she was not an ordinary whore. No matter what she was, she was lovely, desirable, and capable of haunting his memory, inspiring in him a savage desire to possess her. To love her and receive her love in return. She was capable of that, he knew. She was warm and affectionate and beautiful. She was what he wanted, and before his dreaming time was over, he knew also that he was going to take her away with him, if she consented to go. It made no difference how he set her free of her uncle. He would manage somehow. Anything that stood in their way would be removed.

As he finally disembarked from the riverboat, he was able to see the *Sarah*, docked well down the area. She carried huge banners proclaiming the virtues of the minstrel show and the restaurant.

Jonathan hired a carriage and paid the driver for speed. He checked into a hotel, for it was too early for the performance to begin on the *Sarah*. But he could at least return to the dock as soon as he registered at the hotel.

He paced the dock, but there were no signs of Daisy or her uncle. Possibly they lived ashore and only came to the boat for the show and the gambling later on. He did learn, from the posters at the foot of the gangplank, that the boat would sail promptly at seven and return to the dock at midnight. Jonathan tortured himself. Did the highest bidder for Daisy's favors remain aboard with her, or was he expected to take her to a hotel?

There was now plenty of time, so Jonathan walked back to the hotel. Baton Rouge was not as large a city as Richmond or Memphis. It had more of an air of newness about it, as if it was now in the first stages of rapid growth. It did have buildings as high as five stories, however, and there were quite a few people on the streets.

The roads were dry and dusty. In wet weather they would be seas of mud. But the stores seemed well stocked with merchandise. They also appeared busy.

Jonathan's hotel room was comfortable, facing the dock, so he could see the *Sarah* tied up to her berth. He changed clothes, putting on cream-colored trousers, a pure white waistcoat, a ruffled shirt with a string tie, and a long, pale brown frock coat. Under these clothes he had strapped on the Bowie knife, which still fascinated him.

At twenty minutes of seven, he strolled down to the dock. Men and women were getting aboard. The calliope was calling with its loud, raucous voice, barely in tune. It was a popular entertainment, Jonathan could tell by the crowd on the dock. As he stepped from the gangplank, two large, rough-looking men studied him momentarily. About the deck, he could see members of the crew, standing idly at the rails, but alert and suspicious of everyone who came aboard. Possibly there had been trouble with the law, or some rival showboat.

Then the gangplank was raised. The *Sarah* began to back out into the river, her whistle drowning out the calliope. Like the boat which had brought Jonathan here, she was a sidewheeler. She had a substantial stage with draw curtains, and kerosene-lamp-lit footlights. The benches for the audience were well filled. Jonathan took a seat at the rear. He spoke to no one and stayed wary of the ship employees. By the look of them, they'd tolerate not the slightest nonsense, which didn't make Jonathan's prospects any brighter.

He had no plan of action. Whatever happened would have to be handled as the situation of the moment called for. Once Jonathan ran his hand over the haft of that giant knife snug against his leg. It was a comforting weapon to have.

A three-piece orchestra stopped all the whispering in the audience. They played for ten minutes before the curtain parted and Daisy's uncle appeared, resplendent in a red suit, the coat glistening with sequins. He made a brief welcoming speech as his eyes roved over the audience. If he saw Jonathan, there was no recognition.

The show began, a typical minstrel show of old jokes, dancing by men in blackface which any four-year-old plantation child could have done better. But entertainment was scarce here and the audience enjoyed it all. So did Jonathan, who had never seen a show like this before.

Midway, the pace changed. Daisy emerged and Jonathan closed his eyes. The moment he saw her he could feel the warmth of her naked body straining against his. He knew at once that he would not go back to Wyndward without her. No matter what she was, how many men she'd bedded, she would be his. If he believed he had even a remote chance of getting away with it, he would have walked up on the stage, taken her by sheer strength, and carried her off the boat the moment she docked. But it couldn't be done. As the performance continued, the hefty-looking members of the crew had moved closer to the stage and stood with their arms folded as if they were eunuchs and this was an impenetrable harem.

Daisy wore a knee-length dress, made bouffant by several petticoats beneath it. She performed a solo dance, which was graceful if not especially original, though neither Jonathan nor the audience was aware of it. Then she was joined by a blackface man from the half-circle of minstrels and they did a soft shoe, changing into a tap dance which drew a great deal of applause. Jonathan's was the loudest.

The show was finally over. Daisy disappeared and didn't come on again. With the show over, the audience left the theater section and went about the boat seeking food, beverages, and the gaming tables, which were heavily patronized.

Jonathan strolled toward the end of the hurricane deck where the entrance to the cabins was located. Two burly men lounged there and Jonathan changed direction. He didn't wish to arouse the slightest suspicion before he'd decided on a plan of action.

There were two gambling rooms, one of which was for men escorting women. Here the games were not large, but in the other room, catering only to men, the stakes were much higher and the action far livelier. Jonathan decided on Faro, a game he knew fairly well. In the space of twenty minutes, he lost almost fifty dollars. He played more heavily. If he'd been regarded with some suspicion before, it was no longer evident. The guards took him for a sporting man who would likely lose every dollar he came with.

The time was passing too slowly. Jonathan was getting bored and restless. He wondered when the auction would start. He assumed that the other girls in the show would be auctioned off too, but for a price much below what Daisy would bring, he was sure.

Jonathan drifted back toward the stage, where the auction would be held. One of the guards gave him a nod and a knowing smile as he entered and took a seat in the front row.

Other men drifted in until there were about thirty present. This time when the curtain parted, there was no music. The footlights were bright enough to make everything easy to see. It was Daisy's uncle who made the announcement that any girl could be had for the highest price bid. The last girl would be the most expensive, and the loveliest.

Jonathan's anger was rapidly growing into a rage he found hard to control. The first girl stepped through the curtains and stood motionless for a moment to allow the men to study her. Jonathan gasped at the scanty mist of veiling which covered her, through which every part of her body could be seen.

"Now watch this little bundle of beauty show you just a little bit of what she can do." He looked down at the piano player in the pit. "A little music, please."

The piano player started playing with the bass keys. He played slowly while the girl started to move her body in unison with the beat of the music, which increased almost imperceptibly. Her hips gyrated, slowly at first, then faster. Her arms raised and she held the folds of fabric in her hands. As they moved outward and upward, the fabric separated and she was completely naked. She had changed her steps somewhat and now her ample breasts made rapid circles. The audience bellowed approval.

Jonathan had never seen anything like it. He wanted to jump up on stage, get through that curtain, and rescue Daisy before she had to perform. The bidding stopped at fifty dollars. The girl went down the steps to be collected. As a middle-aged man, scarcely five feet tall, came to claim her, one of the guards picked up a long black velvet cape from a stack on a chair and walked over to the girl. He faced her as he put it around her shoulders, drew it close in front so it would overlap, using it as an excuse to let his hands slip beneath the cape and fondle her ample breasts. Her escort knew better than to protest and the girl was apparently used to it. Then, to Jonathan's surprise, the guard accompanied the two from the room. Anyone observing the trio would see nothing wrong with it. The auction continued.

One girl, huge in every respect, was greeted with catcalls and whistles and stomping of feet. She smiled and blew kisses at them. It was apparent she enjoyed it as much as they. Her dyed hair was piled on her head. Her face, though heavily made up, was beautiful. When Daisy's uncle walked over to her, she turned to him, took his face between her hands, and gave him a moist, lingering kiss as he moved into her. Jonathan's disgust heightened as the two gyrated, to the continued yells and calls for the bidding to start.

Finally Daisy's uncle pushed her away, pretending reluctance. She pouted, then turned to the audience and with a slow gyration of her hips, plus a knowing wink, grasped the folds of the diaphanous fabric and held it away from her so she was entirely nude. Her enormous breasts reminded Jonathan of Colonel Coldwell's wife. He shut that memory out of his mind fast and forced his attention back to the auction. Each time there was a bid, the girl gave a further indication of her prowess so that the bidding would go higher. She got one hundred dollars.

Jonathan's impatience was growing, but he noted that there was only one guard left at the entrance to backstage. Apparently there was one more girl to be auctioned before Daisy. When she emerged, Jonathan noted dispassionately that she was too thin and, though still young, had sagging breasts. She was wan, perhaps ill.

When the girl was called upon to perform, she didn't respond. Daisy's uncle spoke to her again, this time sternly. She gave him a look of disgust, turned her back, spread her legs, bent down so that her face was between them, and thumbed her nose at the audience.

Jonathan felt like applauding. Not so Daisy's uncle. He walked over and slapped her buttocks so hard that she fell. He pulled her to her feet. She spat at him. Amazingly, a man stood up and bid twenty dollars for her. He seemed delighted with her performance.

"Take her," Daisy's uncle said, and kicked her down the stairs. Once again, she fell. The guard standing at the door snatched a cloak from the chair, walked over, and pulled the girl to her feet. She started to scream and claw at him. He reached down and pinched her genitals. She screamed with pain. He wrapped the cloak around her carelessly, and when she still fought, he pinched her again. She moaned and went limp. He picked her up and motioned for the man who had bid twenty dollars for her to follow. He did, eagerly. Jonathan felt like throwing up.

There was one cloak left on the chair. Daisy would be next. Jonathan had to fight to keep his hands from turning into fists.

Daisy's uncle smiled and raised his arms to the audience. "And now, gentlemen, the prize of the evening. Young, beautiful, and willing.

The curtains will part just a little so you can see what you are getting."

When they separated, Jonathan saw Daisy wearing a gown just as diaphanous as the others, but much more elaborate. It sparkled with rhinestones and was edged with ostrich feathers. Slowly, she opened the gown and revealed her nakedness. She didn't move, she didn't smile. She looked like a statue. A lovely, beautiful statue and yet she was a human being, about to be defiled.

Jonathan could stand no more. He stepped through the entrance to the stage just as the curtains closed and the bidding started. One man stood by the curtain ropes. Jonathan moved toward him. Daisy didn't even glance his way. The stagehand stepped out to intercept Jonathan. A clip on the jaw, delivered so fast the man didn't have time to cry out, dropped him to his knees and he eased forward onto the floor.

Daisy backed away as Jonathan rushed toward her. Then, with an audible gasp, she recognized him. He motioned for silence. Her uncle was making the final pitch, working up the audience to the charms they would buy in Daisy. Jonathan reached down under his waistband and pulled the bowie knife free.

Daisy's eyes grew wide and frightened, but he smiled at her and she answered with an uncertain, tremulous smile of her own.

Her uncle reached through the curtain for her hand. When she was pulled through the curtain, Jonathan was right at her heels. He kept the knife hidden. The bidding had begun before

Daisy was on stage. Someone bid two hundred dollars. Obviously Daisy did come very high.

Jonathan held the knife low, tilted it upward, and sliced through the uncle's trousers until the blade rested cold against his crotch.

"Yo' makes one yelp fo' he'p," Jonathan whispered, "an' yo' be ball-less in two seconds. I bids a dollah an' a qua'tah fo' this heah gal an' yo' bettah say that the bes' bid. Man with no balls nevah pleasures hisse'f agin. Now I takin' Daisy. Yo' tries to stop me an' yo' dies aftah I slice off whut must be mos' impohtant to a bastahd like yo'."

Jonathan sliced through the trousers, leaving the man exposed at the rear, his pants dropping into a tangle around his legs.

Jonathan kicked him clear across the stage. Then he pulled Daisy closer and they raced toward the end of the stage. A burly stagehand tried to stop him, but a wave of the knife discouraged him quickly. It had all happened so fast, no one else had as yet reacted.

They ran along the aisle to the exit and onto the deck. Four men were lined up to stop them. Jonathan looked around. Half a dozen more were coming toward them.

Without a word, he pulled Daisy to the rail, picked her up.

"No—no!" she shouted. "No—the wheel—use the port side! The other side!"

He managed to cross the deck before they got to him, and threw Daisy overside. One guard closed with him. The Bowie sliced his shoulder so that he screamed and turned away. The others

[275]

hesitated just long enough. Jonathan climbed the rail and jumped.

He landed not far from where Daisy was floundering. He reached her side. One hand held the knife. With the other he circled her waist and they swam through the dirty brown water. Someone on board began shooting at them. Jonathan pulled her below the surface, swam until his breath gave out, and then they both surfaced. They were protected now by the darkness. The lights from the showboat were receding, and they were able to swim ashore.

The mud threatened to ensnare them on the bank, but Jonathan managed to lift her and get out of the ooze successfully. He carried her further away from the bank where there were trees and soft, dry grass. He set her down carefully, then lay on his back gasping. She leaned over him, bent down and kissed him with fervor. He wrapped his arms around her. They were both soaking wet, covered with mud. Without a word, he turned, taking her with him, until he was on top of her. They fumbled with his wet clothes, tearing them off, and in the space of three or four minutes after they reached shore, he had taken her, with a wild passion that had been locked up in him too long. She responded with a willing abandon that matched his.

She opened her eyes and looked up at him. "You are mad," she said. "You are one crazy man. You are out of your mind and I love you dearly, Jonathan. I love you. I've loved you from the moment I saw you. I dreamed of you coming for me on a white charger, with spears and swords and you'd lift me onto your great steed and dash off into the night with me. And do exactly what you did."

"I dashed off," Jonathan laughed. "Sho' did, but no hoss an' no spear. On'y a knife that skeers the hell outa me even when it's me holdin' it. Daisy—I knows whut yo' uncle put yo' through. Made yo' do. Knows yo' couldn't he'p it. I loves yo', an' befo' tomorruh done with, I marries yo' an' takes yo' back to Virginia. Eveh since yo' lef', I been like a crazy man. Thinks o' yo' day an' night, an' when I couldn't stand it no longer, I come fo' yo' even if I gets killed, tryin' to get yo' away."

She was weeping. "Jonathan, whatever you wish me to do, I will do." She raised his muddy hand to her cheek and scrubbed at the tears. "Take me away, Jonathan. Hurry, before they find us."

Jonathan kissed her mud-smeared face and they laughed joyously, relieved they had escaped. But they sobered quickly when he gathered her in his arms and pressed her to him, reveling in her nakedness. She was his at last. And she loved him. She proved it with her arms pressing him close, her mouth seeking his and setting his blood racing. But they had to find safety.

Gently he eased himself free of her, urging her to cover herself with the scanty, torn garment as best she could. He fumbled for his clothes, dressed quickly, slipped his coat over her and they began walking through the darkness without any idea of where they were. They only knew where they were going.

[14]

Dundee's greatest dread was being discovered in his long, nightly study periods. He had rigged a lantern so the light was thrown downward, illuminating only his books and pads. In the course of a single month, with the help of the Reverend Whitehead, he had learned to read much of the primer he'd inherited from his father.

Reverend Whitehead, now commissioned to hold prayer meetings every Sunday evening came in a cart drawn by a mule, both purchased with the proceeds of his Christmas address to Fitz's captive audience.

"Gots to be keerful," he admonished Dundee for the tenth time. "Yo' knows whut they do they fin's out yo' studyin'."

"Wuth it," Dundee declared confidently.

"Don' aim to be a slave all my life, Rev'ren', an' when I changes, I kin do bettah, I knows how to read an' write."

Reverend Whitehead regarded his student with apprehension. "Whut yo' mean yo' not be a slave all yo' life?"

"Nuthin', suh," Dundee said quietly. "But I heahs they's lots o' white folks up 'no'th don' like keepin' slaves. Evah heah 'bout that, Rev'ren'?" He paused, his eyes searching the old man's face. "Kin yo' git hold o' a newspaper fo' me?"

"I caught bringin' a newspaper, it'll be the last day they lets me come heah, son."

"I know. If yo' don' want to do it, say so."

"I'll see whut I kin do."

"The *Liberator*, Rev'ren'?"

Whitehead wagged his snowy mane. "Yo' aimin' to git me an' yo'se'f strung up, Dundee? How I goin' to git that paper? Think they sells 'em in the sto' heah? Maybe I kin. I'll see."

"Long as I live, I'll nevah fo'git whut yo' done fo' me."

"I'm a crazy ol' man, that's whut I am. They treats yo' bad heah, yo' wants to git yo'se'f some-wheah else?"

"No suh, they treats me good. 'Specially the young massa. He papa . . . well, he doin' bettah he sees whut I do with the hosses. Mayhap I he'ps win some races fo' him, he manumits me."

"Yo' hopin' too high, son. Ain't no way he goin' to set yo' free. An' they ketches yo' readin' an' writin', they whups yo' good. They ketches yo' readin' the *Liberator*, an' they hangs yo' sho'. Whut yo' want with all that learnin'? Yo' aimin' to git othahs to he'p yo' rebel? Or yo' fixin' to run?"

"No suh, ain't fixin' to run an' ain't fixin' to rebel. Jes' wants to know whut's goin' on some-wheah 'sides Wyndward Plantation. That ain't so bad, is it?"

"Yo' asks Massa Turner an' he tells yo' how bad it is. Gots to go now. Yo' heahs from young massa he been 'way so long?"

"Comin' back. Heahs massa tellin' the over-seer."

"That's good. Been hearin' 'bout some nig-gers who wuks on a fahm no'th o' heah an' one of 'em is talkin' 'bout killin' his mastuh an' run-nin'. Crazy talk. Gits him hung fo' sho'. But they listens to him. I tell 'em they got no chance, but they calls me a crazy ol' man, skeered o' he own se'f. I ain't skeered o' me, son, but I is mightily skeered o' hangin' from a rope."

Dundee watched the old man drive off in his cart with the plodding mule pulling it. The min-ister stopped the cart to remove his hat and bow his head to Fitz, who came striding down the driveway. They talked for a few minutes and it seemed a friendly conversation.

Dundee thought of telling Fitz about the im-pending rebellion, but decided it was none of his business. Let the whites face the consequences of trouble, for they were responsible for it.

Fitz came striding down toward him and, as always, Dundee felt prickles of fear creep up and down his spine. It was a feeling he detested. He clasped his hands before him and bowed his head as Fitz came closer. He hated doing this.

A man should look another man squarely in the eye, but slaves were not men. Not the way the white folks thought.

"How's the mare comin', Dundee?" Fitz asked.

"Massa, suh, ain't no hoss kin beat her."

"I'm plannin' to race her late in May. Wants her in prime condition."

"She prime right now, suh."

Fitz said, "Dundee, lif' yo' haid an' look at me."

Dundee raised his head slowly, wondering what was coming next.

"Knows how yo' wukked to get that hoss in shape. Knows yo' got a way with hosses. Like yo' papa had. He one sonabitch nigger, but hosses listened when he talked. Yo' talks to 'em, Dundee?"

"Yas suh, massa, suh."

"They knows whut yo' sayin'?"

"Reckon, massa, suh."

Fitz looked at him for a long moment, then said, "Yo' gets all the hosses yo' thinks kin run, an' yo' keeps 'em heah. Yo' got nuthin' else to do 'cep' that. I tells the overseers yo' ain't no ordinary nigger an' I gives yo' the right to go wheahevah yo' needs to. Yo' goes to the back do' when yo' hungry an' Elegant feeds yo' good."

"Massa, suh, I's grateful."

Dundee was more than grateful. He was stunned. This man had flogged him for no reason only weeks ago.

"Yo' goes to Richmond with us when we races an' I gives yo' ten silvah dollahs to spend. If the hoss wins, I gives yo' ten mo'."

"Massa, I does whutevah yo' wants o' me."

[282]

"All I want is fo' our hosses to win. Saw yo' talkin' to yo' mama one night."

Dundee held his breath. He could be lashed for being out of his cabin at night.

"Yas suh, I talks to her. Nevah seen her, massa, but I talks."

Fitz nodded. "So do I. She a gal good as any white gal. Thass why I buries her in the white folks' cemetery. I gives yo' permission to go talk to her whenevah yo' wants. An' if yo' tells any othah niggers whut I just tol' yo', I whups yo' good."

"Yo' is kin' to me, massa. I don' talk."

Fitz turned away abruptly.

Fitz found Benay at her evening sewing. She was never one to waste time and since Jonathan's letter, she was very pleased and happy.

"Fitz, when you 'spect Jonathan and Daisy be home?"

Fitz lowered himself into a chair beside her. "Two-three days, reckon. Jonathan say she a beauty, pretty as yo', Benay, but don' believe that. Ain't nobody half as beautiful. An' I ain't lookin' fo' nuthin' either. Jes' tellin' the truth."

"Thank yo', Fitz." She sucked a slightly bleeding needle prick on the tip of her forefinger. "Worries me whut Melanie goin' to think 'bout me."

"She thinks yo' her mama, that's whut she thinks."

"I know, Fitz. When she lef', she was a warm an' lovin' girl, but it's been months now an' she livin' up No'th. Ain't no tellin' whut she thinks 'bout keepin' slaves."

[283]

Fitz looked puzzled. "Now whut in hell she goin' to be worried 'bout that? She was borned heah an' she raised by slaves. Knows all 'bout 'em. She a southern gal, Benay. Nobody kin change her from that."

"Yes they can, Fitz. It wouldn't be hard. If I came heah from the No'th, reckon I wouldn't be able to stand folks bein' slaves."

"Whut in hell got into yo', Benay? Yo' been readin' the *Liberator*?"

"O' co'se not. Don' believe anythin' they prints. But skeered o' Melanie. When we goin' to Boston?"

"Soon's Jonathan comes back an' I think he ready to run the plantation. Got to give him a chance to get over bein' married an' gives him time to staht makin' a sucker. Wants a grandson, I do. Wants to be sho' this heah plantation stays in our family long as they is a plantation."

"Hopes yo' gets whut yo' want, Fitz. I likes it heah. Yo' been mighty nice to me an' I loves yo' fo' it. Hopes Jonathan got him a gal who'll be jes' as happy."

"Reckon we wuks it all out."

"Thought o' somethin' else, Fitz," Benay said. "Readin' Jonathan's lettah agin, reads Daisy from the No'th. Wondah how she goin' to take to slaves."

"She bettah take to 'em."

"Won't be easy, she a nice gal, Fitz. She goin' to heah, soon's they comes, how the Fisbees got hung that night."

"I wasn't theah," Fitz said. "All fo' hangin' 'em. Deserves it, they did, an' they would have pulled 'em up myse'f on'y I figgers they's too much goin' on now 'bout slaves. An' the folks who he'p the Fisbees still runnin' a good part o' that railroad, hidin' slaves an' transportin' 'em. Fo' money, Benay. Not 'cause they sorry fo' the slaves, but fo' money."

"Who aims to run the Fisbee place now?"

"On'y relative lef' is Belle, an' wheah she is, nobody knows. Wants to buy the place, but cain't fin' nobody kin sell it. Waits a few mo' months. Nobody comes I kin do business with, I moves in on it anyway an' I pays latah if Belle is foun', or any othah heir. Cain't let that place go to seed. Take yeahs to bring it back. Bad 'nuff now 'cause the Fisbees did nothin' but go back an' fo'th to the outhouses. Place needs cleanin' up an' soonah o' latah I sen's in 'nuff slaves to do the job."

"Yo' gets mo' land yo' goin' to have mos' o' the slaves in all Virginny, Fitz. Think that wise?"

"Why not, we needs 'em. Hell, cain't do nuthin' 'bout it till we tries to fin' Belle."

"Whut makes yo' so sho' she comin' back af-tah whut happen to her papa an' brothah?"

"She be back. Got reasons. We talks 'bout somethin' else now. How we goin' to travel all the way to Boston? Yo' evah sailed on a ship, Benay?"

"Be skeered on a ship."

"Nothin' to be skeered 'bout. Nice way to travel. Tell yo' whut. We goes to Boston by train an' we comes back by ship to Norfolk."

"Got me pretty dresses, Fitz. Gets to show 'em off on a boat?"

"Lots o' times. Ev'ybody eats all dressed up. Rich folks travel by boat mos' times."

"All right then. I'll start packin', or thinkin'

'bout it, soon's Jonathan an' Daisy gets heah."
She smiled thoughtfully. "Goin' to be nice havin'
'nother lady in the house, she ain't too hard to
get 'long with."

"She is an' we shows her how to change.
Reckon Jonathan loves her she goin' to be fine.
Sho' wants him to have a son. This heah plantation goin' to last fo'evah, Benay. Wants one o' our
own blood to be runnin' it a hundred yeahs or
mo'."

"I hope so too, Fitz. But yo're kinda young to
be talkin' 'bout the future like that."

"I'm gettin' on to fo'ty, Benay. I ain't as chip-
per as I used to be an' I don' go 'roun' lookin'
fo' trouble any mo'. Keeps away from it, I kin."

"Fitz, s'pose I gives Daisy my personal
maid."

"Alameda?"

"Yes. She's a fine personal servant an' she
takes fine keer o' Daisy like she's done fo' me."

"Yo' gots to fin' 'nother one then."

"Got my eye on a young 'un. Name of Domingo."

Fitz whistled sharply. "That be Jonathan's
Domingo? He pesters her. Think he don' wants to
bed with her even if he married?"

"Don' know fo' sho', Fitz. But Domingo a
likely gal an' cain't tell how a No'therner goin'
to take to her new husban' rapin' a black gal when
he feels like it."

"Sees whut yo' mean. When yo' came heah
an' I pesterin' Nina when yo' didn' want me, did
it bother yo'?"

"Some, at first. But that was near twenny

yeahs ago, Fitz. Times changed some. Anyway, Nina was special. If yo' had to pester someone, I would have told yo' to pester her."

"Mayhap Jonathan got somethin' to say 'bout it. He a man now, all grown up."

"Melanie is almos' grown up too, Fitz. I cain't wait to see her agin. Worried some too, how she goin' to feel comin' home aftah bein' up No'th so long. Skeered she changed."

"Benay, she comin' home to her papa an' mama who are wuth two, mayhap three million dollahs. We rich. Melanie kin have anythin' she wants."

"That worries me too," Benay said. "Mayhap she don' want anythin' we got. Nevah had much education myse'f an' don' know anybody graduated from finishin' school. Don' know how they thinks."

Fitz arose, sat down on the sofa beside her and drew an arm around her shoulders. "Benay, yo' been livin' all this time with a man who graduated from private school. Yo' sho' ain't skeered o' me, way yo' gives me hell sometimes."

She nestled her head against his shoulder. "I fo'gets sometimes. Knows yo' kin speak proper no'thern English yo' a mind to. I cain't, Fitz. I keeps thinkin' when I sees Melanie, she goin' to speak like yo' kin, an' she goin' to think I speak funny."

"Benay, that gal o' ours says or do anythin' to make yo' feel 'shamed o' yo'se'f, she goin' to get turned on my knee an' spanked like she eight yeahs old. But it won't happen. She like yo', Benay. She nevah wants to hurt anybody an' she ain't goin' to think yo' talks funny, 'cause if she speaks Boston down heah, it'll be Melanie who speaks funny. Guess I go to bed now. Comin'?"

"Since when did I let yo' go to bed alone?" Benay asked. "Co'se I'm comin'."

Both were glad they had rested well that night, for late the next morning Benay saw a carriage turn into the long driveway. She hastily called Alameda and had her tend to her hair as quickly as she could, while she changed from the dull gray dress she'd put on for morning wear into something more colorful.

"Jonathan comin' with his new wife," she told Alameda. "Wants yo' tend to her good as yo' tend me. She likes yo' I goin' to give yo' to her. Bettah fo' yo' to learn how to dress a young woman."

"Yo' ain't so old," Alameda said, with the confidence and privilege granted a personal servant like her. "I tends her yo' says so, but ruther tend yo', missy."

"Yo'll do as yo' told," Benay said. "An' min' yo' manners."

"Yes'm, missy, ma'am. I min's 'em, I does."

Benay fled downstairs to be on hand when the carriage pulled up. Alameda hurried to the window to see what her new mistress looked like. She would please her if she could, for being a personal maid was as high as a slave could go, and with the position came good food, good hours, and nice secondhand clothes from time to time. She could hold her head higher than any of the women in slave row. Living in the big house was best of all, even if she slept on the floor outside Benay's room and now would do the same for her new mistress.

Jonathan ran to take his mother in his arms and kiss her with an affection he rarely showed. Then he helped Daisy from the carriage. Benay studied the slim, somewhat pale golden-haired girl with intense blue eyes, a perfect nose, chin, and mouth, and a tendency to smile with a warmth that could charm anyone.

"Mama, this be Daisy, yo' new daughter-in-law."

"Nevah min' the in-law, Jonathan. She my daughter, like she born to me. Daisy, I say it now. Yo' one o' the mos' beautiful gals I evah did see. Jonathan, yo' papa goin' to think 'bout makin' love to Daisy fo' sho'."

"He kin think 'bout it," Jonathan laughed. "But he try it an' I bust his face."

"I'm so glad to be here," Daisy said. "I'm going to call you Benay. Jonathan told me if I called you Mrs. Turner you'd have a real fit."

"I sho' would. Yo' ain't been in the South long, has yo'?"

"A year. A little less."

"Daisy used to wuk on a showboat," Jonathan explained. "Nevah seen one so fine. An' she one mighty good dancer, Mama, an' she got a voice I kin listen to fo'evah. Wheah's Papa?"

"Down at the stable talkin' to Dundee, 'spect. Gettin' that brown mare ready fo' racin' soon's we come home from Boston." Benay turned to Daisy and took her arm to escort her into the house. "Jonathan's papa an' me, we goes to Boston 'nother two or three weeks. Jonathan's sister graduatin' from a nice school up theah. Ain't seen her in mos' a yeah now."

"Yes, Jonathan told me we'd be expected to run the plantation while you're away. I won't be much help, I'm afraid. I had no idea how big this house was. When we were driving here, I asked Jonathan how big the plantation was and he told we'd been driving on it for an hour. I can't imagine anyone owning so much land."

They entered the house. The three most important house servants were lined up to greet their new mistress. Alameda curtsied nicely, bowed her head, and said she was very happy to meet her mist'ess.

"Thank you," Daisy said. She glanced at Benay. "Whatever does she mean?"

"I gives her to yo', Daisy. She been my maid now fo' a long time an' she the bes' we got. Now I wants yo' to meet Elegant. She our cook an' yo' goin' to be mighty keerful she don' make yo' fat. She the bes' cook in the world, I reckon."

Elegant shook from chin to toe as she tried to curtsy.

"This slave," Benay said, looking at Calcutta, "is a houseboy. He does ev'ythin' at the slowest speed in the world. Fitz says he mos' slothful nigger evah was borned."

"He sloths, missy-ma'am, yo' kicks him in the ass an' he moves fastah," Elegant said. "Yo' don' kick his ass, yo' tells me an' I does it fo' yo' with pleasure."

"He also drinks too much," Jonathan chuckled. "Sho' don' make him run any fastah."

Daisy, clearly bewildered by this odd household, maintained her poise. There was a whoop of joy behind them and Fitz seized Daisy in an embrace that made her gasp aloud. Then he let go and stepped back to study her with approving male eyes, not lustful, but taking in all the charms she possessed. Satisfied they were ample, he nodded approval to Jonathan and gave Daisy a resounding kiss.

"Nevah thought my son would bring home a gal like yo', Daisy." Fitz looked both pleased and proud. "He kinda shy 'roun' gals an' think he gets the hots fo' some gal, she goin' to be nuthin' much. Reckon I figgered yo' all wrong, son. An' welcome back home."

For the first time in his life, Jonathan was embraced by his father. It was surely nice to be home again, Jonathan thought.

It was too cool for drinks on the veranda so they had them in the drawing room, the size of which awed Daisy into a silence that lasted until Jonathan nudged her, kissed her with his eyes, and put her at ease. His folks were everything he said they were. Even better, they liked her.

"It's wonderful here. You have no idea how much. I lived on a riverboat for months and my room could be tucked into the smallest corner of this one and be lost. In New York I had a two-room flat where I could move around a little more, but it was still very small."

"Wait'll yo' sees the rest o' the house," Fitz said. "My papa built it. He was a captain of a merchant vessel—a slaver. He got rich runnin' slaves an' he dreamed 'bout this house fo' yeahs. Brings my mama heah. She a No'therner from Boston, an' upstairs is a room my papa fixed up jes' fo' her. Exactly like her favorite room when she was home in Boston. Liked it, she did. She even cried a little firs' time she saw it. Nevah befo' did I see my mama cry."

"I can understand," Daisy said. "It told her better than words how much he loved her. You've done the same for me by accepting me. I already love you and I'll love this house as you do, even though I haven't seen any more of it than this room. It's certainly impressive. You could have a ball for a hundred people here."

"Mo' than that," Benay said. "Bes' yo' go upstairs with me an' I shows yo' wheah yo' an' Jonathan sleeps. Alameda, yo' comes too."

Jonathan sat down and looked at his father. Fitz was still standing and there were deep furrows along his forehead.

"Whut's wrong, Papa?" Jonathan asked.

"Don' like way things goin' 'roun' heah. Up No'th they raisin' hell 'bout us hangin' them two Fisbees fo' runnin' an Underground. That's bad 'nuff, but they's other stations 'roun' heah an' we cain't find 'em. Some slaves gettin' away an' othahs gettin' kinda restless. Yo' knows them niggers folluhs any leader, an' they's some beginnin' to take charge on some fahms. Nuthin' yo' kin lay a finger on—or a whup—but it theah an' boun' to get worse."

"I tried to get home sooner——" Jonathan began.

"Ain't talkin' 'bout that. Nothin' yo' could do yo' was heah. Warns yo' 'cause we gots to be mighty keerful. Be ready, trouble starts, an' it will."

"No trouble heah? Yo' sho'?"

"Hong Kong, he says no trouble yit, an' Hong

Kong knows. He worried some too, reckon. Don'
say nothin', but I kin tell. Benay boun' to go to
Boston soon's she kin, an' I don' like leavin' right
now. Cain't tell her no 'cause she got her heart
set on seein' Melanie agin. I wants to see her too,
far as that goes, but it's not the bes' time fo' me
to leave."

"Papa, I'm grown now. I kin take keer o'
things. Don' yo' worry none. Whut yo' think o'
Daisy?"

"Good thing fo' yo' I didn't see her first.
She a beauty, son. Yo' one lucky man. Kin tell
Benay likes her too."

"I'm glad. Worried Daisy some, reckon, but
she the kind o' gal yo' cain't he'p but like. Worries me some, whut she goin' to think livin' with
slaves. Thinks she got to treat 'em like they human."

"She learns," Fitz assured him. "Tol' her 'bout
Domingo?"

Jonathan shook his head. "Couldn't. I gives
Domingo up. Gots to."

"Ain't like it was when I marries yo' mama.
Things changin'. Like I tol' Benay, yo' cain't see
changes, but they heah, an' mo' comin' fas'."

"Papa, yo' 'spectin' trouble soon? Whut fahm
looks like it be hit first?"

"Bob Harper's. When they hung the Fisbees,
they did it on Bob's place, an' he makes all his
slaves come an' watch. Don' know how to keep a
peaceful fahm, he don'. Gets kinda crazy sometimes. Knows they's talk goin' 'roun' all the plantations an' slave rows gettin' word they ain't goin'
to be slaves much longer. Folks up No'th comin'
to set 'em all free. Talk like that gets 'roun' an'
the slaves fret an' gets sassy. Happens heah I goin'

to use the whup mo' than I evah did. My papa was right. All they unnerstan's is bein' whupped. An' when they's trouble, yo' whups 'em mo' often an' gives 'em mo' lashes."

"They knows any slave who rebels gets hung," Jonathan said.

"Sho' they knows it, but some planters don' do it. They wants to hang 'em, but not if the slaves they proppity. Slaves bringin' a big price these days. 'Minds me, Major Apperson sold the Fisbee coffle he bought from us at big money. Got mo' than he paid us, so he ain't mad at us any mo'. That's how slaves are priced today. They be too valuable to get hung an' they knows it."

"Papa, how long yo' think slavery goin' to last? Knows it cain't be fo'evah, even if mos' othah planters thinks it will."

"Don' know, Jonathan. Long's we live, I hope. We got mo' acres than I kin count. We got near two thousand slaves. We raises mo' 'bacco than any other plantation in the state. We breeds an' raises mo' thoroughbred hosses than anyone else an' we trades in slaves. Now s'pose they say all niggers are free an' they gets paid fo' they wuk. Cain't whup 'em no mo'. Firs' of all, they starts slothin' so yo' gets no wuk outen them. An' how any planter goin' to raise the money to pay 'em, an' how many ovahseers an' drivers yo' gots to hire to see they do they wuk right? It cain't be done. We don' have slaves, we don' keep this heah plantation."

"Comin' to that?" Jonathan asked incredulously.

"Not fo' us it ain't, 'cause we not goin' to let 'em say all slaves are free."

"Got 'roun' some in N'Awleans," Jonathan said. "Hears news 'bout whut goes on in Washington. Don' seem to hear much o' that heah."

"Whut's goin' on?" Fitz asked. "Wait a minute. We talkin' so much, we gets dry." He raised his voice to a shout. "Calcutta, comes heah right now or I tans yo' hide till it blacker'n yo' is."

Calcutta loped into the room to await his orders.

"Brings us bourbon an' cold watah fo' each."

"Yas suh, massa suh. I runs."

"Don' start yo' runnin' till I gets through tellin' whut we wants. Latah, yo' brings us rum. Now yo' runs."

Calcutta left in a burst of speed. He was anxious to try the new rum, but he'd not dared open a bottle of it. He broke any former record reaching the springhouse where the whiskey and rum were kept and where a deep cold-water spring provided fine addition to the liquor.

"Crazy things goin' on in Washington," Jonathan resumed their talk. "California jes' admitted to the Union. They was a big fight California have slaves. But in Congress the politicians from the No'th and them from the South got togethah an' say California a free state. No slaves. Seems like the No'thern congressmen won. But then they passes a law says runaway slaves gots to be caught an' sent back to they owners. An' any who he'ps slaves run gots to be punished."

"Seems like all they do is give up one thing to get 'nother."

"Yo' thinks that's somethin'? In Washington they voted to abolish tradin' in slaves—but yo' kin keep slaves theah, an' treats 'em jes' like we does. Cain't figger out whut they up to."

"Too many people don' know whut in hell they doin' buttin' in our business," Fitz said. "I declare, that nigger slower than evah lately. Reckon he older'n we thinks an' he slippin'?"

"No, likely he stoppin' to sample yo' new rum."

"Wait'll he comes. Got thinkin' we bettah be kinda keerful how we breaks Daisy in to how slaves be treated. Talks to Benay 'bout it on'y yestiddy. Whut yo' think we all go to the Sunday night singin' an' dancin? He'ps her get used to niggers an' how they behaves."

"Reckon she'd like that. Knows she kinda skeered bein' 'roun' so many blacks. Ain't used to it. The niggers sho' carry on Sunday nights. An' she kin' listen to the preacher tellin' 'em how hot hell is goin' to be they gets theah."

Calcutta came into the room, precariously balancing a tray with four drinks on it. His long legs were a little more rubbery than usual and there was a wide grin on his face. He lowered the tray, presenting it to Fitz first, and the liquid in the glasses created waves from his unsteady hands.

"Set the tray down," Fitz ordered. He stood up. "Open yo' mouth, Calcutta."

"Mah mouf?" Calcutta repeated.

"Open it or yo' will when I whups yo'."

Calcutta opened wide. Fitz moved closer and sniffed. "Yo' mo' stupid than I thinks," he said. "Yo' steals my whiskey, it don' make yo' breath smell much, but rum somethin' else. It got a strong smell an' it comin' from yo' like yo' tipped the whole bottle. Yo' half drunk, Calcutta."

Calcutta remained standing, wordless, his mouth still agape.

"Close yo' goddamn mouth an' answer me," Fitz roared. "Yo' stealin' my rum?"

"No suh, massa suh. I ain' stole nuthin'. Gits a little rum on my hands, massa suh, an' I licks it off, suh."

Fitz sighed in disgust and sat down again. "Yo' the fanciest liah on this heah plantation, an' yo' the laziest nigger we got. Yo' runs back to the springhouse an' brings the bottle o' rum. The whole bottle. Whut's lef' in it."

Calcutta's relief was apparent in the relaxation of his whole body as he loped off.

"Thinks yo' goin' to have him whupped," Jonathan said.

"Calcutta thinks so too. Don' do any good. Goin' to try a new kinda treatment."

Calcutta returned with the tall bottle balanced on the tray. Fitz let him stand there for a few moments.

"Yo' stealin' mo' rum while yo' bringin' it heah?" he asked.

"Sweahs I didn', massa, suh. Calcutta don' steal, suh."

"I b'lieves yo'," Fitz said amiably.

Calcutta didn't know if he should smile or start pleading for mercy. This he didn't understand at all.

Fitz said, "Yo' ain't stealin' my rum, yo' is a good nigger. Yo' likes my rum, Calcutta?"

Calcutta said, dreamily, "Sho' does, massa, suh. Likes it, I do."

"Then drink the whole goddamn bottle," Fitz ordered.

"*Drinks* it?" Calcutta didn't believe what he heard.

"Yo' stan's theah like yo' are right now. Yo' tips the bottle up an' lets it pour into yo' mouth. Ev'y drop. Wants to reward yo' fo' bein' a nigger who don' sloth, who nevah steals my whiskey, an' nevah tells a lie. Drink it, yo' long-legged ostrich."

Calcutta obeyed the order promptly. He swallowed two large drinks, eyes tearing a little on the fiery stuff, but he bravely went at it again. He managed to finish the bottle, most of a quart. He stood there holding the empty bottle, not yet glassy-eyed, but nearing that stage.

"Whut yo' standin' theyah fo'?" Fitz shouted at him. "Runs an' brings us mo' drinks. I says yo' runs."

Calcutta tried to say something, but the words didn't come. Reeling slightly, he managed to leave the drawing room, but a few seconds later they heard a crash and then a sharp cry of surprise and concern. Elegant waddled into the drawing room, her broad face wreathed in worry.

"Massa suh, Calcutta he jes' drop in he tracks. Cain't git him to move. Reckon he daid?"

"Daid drunk," Fitz said. "Teachin' him a lesson fo' stealin' my rum. Yo' drags him out an' lets him sleep it off. When he wakes up, yo' puts him to wuk. Doin' anythin' yo' kin think of. He goin' to be mighty sick an' not know whut in hell he doin', but yo' keep him wukkin' ev'y minute. He sloths, yo' kick his ass an' gits him movin'."

Elegant gave a whoop of joy. "Massa suh, I does it like yo' say. Po' Calcutta, he ain't goin' to know whut goin' on, an' he sho' goin' to be sick."

She moved her enormous frame with a surprising grace as she left the room, chuckling to herself.

"Me an' yo' mama been thinkin' 'bout leavin' mayhap in a week," Fitz said. "That too soon, Jonathan? Thinks yo' gettin' ovah bein' married so yo' kin think o' business 'stead o' pesterin'?"

"I be ready," Jonathan declared with a grin. "Kin run this heah plantation an' pester Daisy too. Ol' 'nuff now fo' that."

When Benay and Daisy returned to the drawing room, they were talking animatedly.

"I do declare," Benay said to Jonathan, "yo' couldn't have picked a nicer gal fo' yo' wife. Wants to go to Richmond befo' we goes to Boston. Daisy needs all kinds of clothes."

"We left in a hurry," Jonathan said with a grin. "Cain't carry much on a train anyways. Obleeged if yo' see that Daisy gets whatever she needs."

Supper was a success, though Daisy was somewhat disturbed to have Alameda standing directly behind her chair to anticipate whatever she needed. If she reached for the salt, Alameda beat her to it and presented the shaker with a little giggle at her superior speed.

Other things in this household disturbed and sometimes frightened Daisy. They retired early, for Daisy was tired from the long journey and Jonathan was in a fine mood for some pestering. Daisy was as eager as Jonathan and they enjoyed one another until Daisy suddenly gasped and sat up in alarm.

"Whut's wrong?" Jonathan asked.

"There's someone in the room," Daisy whispered. "I can hear someone breathing. Jonathan —I'm frightened."

He put an arm around her and pulled her down on the bed again. "Yo' hears Alameda, that's all."

Daisy twisted her head to face him. "What's she doing in our room? And we just . . . Jonathan, get her out of here."

"She yo' pet," Jonathan said. "She sleeps on the flo' at the foot o' yo' bed."

"All the time?" Daisy asked in dismay.

"Sho'. That's wheah she belongs."

"I don't want to hurt her feelings, Jonathan, but I must say I don't like the idea of her being in the same room with us."

"Yo' wants me to, I see she sleeps outside the do'."

"It would be better," Daisy admitted.

Jonathan sat up and raised his voice to a shout. "Alameda, wake up an' get yo' black ass outen heah. Yo' sleeps outside the do' from now on. Get!"

Alameda scrambled to her feet. "Yas suh, massa, I sleeps by the do', suh. Goes right away, I does."

They heard her scramble to the door in the dark. It opened and closed quietly. Daisy breathed a sigh of relief.

"I never heard of anything like that before," she said.

"Yo' personal servant nevah goes far off 'lessen yo' sends her."

"Well, I'll certainly have her understand that I don't want her in our bedroom all night. Oh, Jonathan, I don't care how different things are here. I love you and I love the house. I even love all these black people."

"They ain't people, Daisy. They ain't human."

Daisy sat up again. "Of course they're human. Whatever makes you think they're not?"

"Slaves ain't human. That's whut I been tol' since I was born. They's made to wuk, an' to obey, an' to bring a good profit when they sold. That's all they are."

"Jonathan, they can talk and understand when you talk. They eat and breathe. No doubt they make love and are loved by someone. They have children——"

"They bettah have suckers. They don', we ships 'em off. Tomorruh I shows yo' the birthin' house whar the suckers borned. I shows yo' the infirmary. I shows yo' some o' the finest hosses yo' evah did see."

"I love to ride," she said. "I learned how when I was a little girl. Seems like forever since I've been riding, though."

Jonathan hugged her. "I gets you a little golden horse to match your hair, and silver tack, an' you rides like a princess ev'y mornin'."

"A princess," she repeated. "Jonathan, I still can't believe it. If you hadn't come I'd never have dared escape from my uncle. If he'd caught me, his guards . . ." Her voice trailed off.

"Whut would he do, have 'em beat you?"

"He would have let them take me first, then beat me. That was the threat he held over us. The first thing he makes the brutes do when he hires them is to open their trousers to see how big they are."

"If whut they got in they trousers is like the rest of 'em, they's sho' big."

"They're big. Once a girl protested because the bidding wasn't high enough. Don't know why she cared. She wouldn't get any of it anyway. Guess she was just sick of it. Like the one who thumbed her nose at the audience. She couldn't do it any more. She knew what would happen. She's dead now."

"That's whut I wondered," Jonathan said. "Why yo' didn't save yo' tips an' run off."

"Nothing got started until my uncle went to each room and got paid in advance. The guard waited till he came. The rest of the guest's money went into an envelope along with his valuables. Nothing was stolen. My uncle was too smart for that. They got everything back after they'd pleasured themselves."

"He sho' didn' leave anythin' to chance."

"Nothing. He loved brutality. The girl who complained had to submit to those brutes for punishment. He made the rest of us watch. The girl screamed until the pain made her faint. She bled to death. After the boat got started, her body was thrown overboard. Saw it twice. The second girl was so torn, she got thrown off the boat, not even dead. That's why I was afraid to run."

"He evah take yo'?" Jonathan asked, his voice tight. "I mean, in bed."

"No, but enough others did. I was lucky in a way, though. I got the older ones because they bid the highest. They didn't have the juices the younger ones had and I knew a few tricks for tiring them out quickly."

Jonathan chuckled and gathered her close.

"Yo' know lots o' tricks, Daisy baby. An' I loves ev'y one o' them. Jes' glad I knows why you did whut yo' did. Yo' gots to admit I didn' lose no time huntin' yo' down. I was bound an' determined yo' was goin' to be mine."

"I am, Jonathan. For now and always. I love you."

"An' I loves yo'. One thing mo'—we don' talk 'bout whut yo' life was befo' I met yo'. Yo' ready fo' pesterin'? Yo' wants it, Daisy? Yo' is good at it."

She laughed softly, reaching for him. "So are you, Jonathan. So are you."

{ 15 }

DAISY WAS AWAKENED AT DAWN BY THE OVERSEERS' conch horns. She sat up, startled, but Jonathan muttered an explanation and pulled her down again so they slept until after eight. Benay had held breakfast, though Fitz was absent on business at the curing sheds.

"Daisy kinda upset, Alameda sleepin' in our room," Jonathan said. "I sends her to sleep by the do'."

"I meant to explain that," Benay said. "I really meant to tell Alameda not to spend the night in your room."

"It was a little unsettling," Daisy said, her smile reminiscent.

"She means we jes' married an' we carryin' on some," Jonathan explained.

"I am sure Benay knows what I mean," Daisy said.

"I jus' want Mama to know it didn't spoil our night."

Benay said, "I need on'y look at yo' both to know." She flashed a smile—maternal, lascivious, happy. "Now, got me 'nother idea fo' yo', Daisy. He'ps yo' unnerstan' niggers. Tomorruh Sunday. Nobody wuks on Sunday, an' we has a preachin' man comes heah to preach to the slaves. Aftah the sermon we has banjo music an' dancin'. Got to admit they ain't no bettah dancers than niggers. Guess it in they blood. They got all kinds o' dances. Cakewalk one of 'em."

"Why, I used to do that on the stage," Daisy said.

"Yo' ain't seen a cakewalk till yo' sees the slaves do it. Kinda makes yo' feet shuffle some too, while yo' watchin'." She stood up and stretched luxuriously. "Time fo' me to get the gals wukkin' 'roun' the house. Jonathan, yo' papa says no need yo' goes back to wuk yit. Wants yo' to show Daisy ev'ythin' on this plantation. Monday we goes to Richmond, Daisy, an' we stays till Wednesday buyin' clothes. An' I tells yo' now, no need to hol' back on yo' spendin'. We got mo' money we kin use."

"I don't know why I deserve such good fortune," Daisy said, and there were traces of tears in her eyes.

"'Cause yo' marries me," Jonathan declared. "Come 'long now to the stables. Wants to show yo' a hoss goin' to win eve'y race she in, come spring."

They strolled down the drive to the stables, hand in hand, in the warm sunlight of a fine winter day. Dundee emerged from the first stable, bowing his head.

"This heah," Jonathan explained, "is Dundee. He the bes' slave we got with hosses. They knows whut he say, an' sometimes, thinks he knows whut they say."

Dundee made soft laughing sounds.

"Dundee, yo' kinda special," Jonathan declared. "Yo' keep yo' haid up. This my wife, name of Daisy. She likes hosses too."

Dundee lifted his head and smiled. "Massa, kin I say somethin'?"

"Sho'. Say it."

"She sho' the mos' beautiful lady I evah did see."

"Why, thank you, Dundee," Daisy said. "I'm going to return the compliment. You are a very handsome young man."

Dundee was too shocked to acknowledge the compliment. Jonathan chuckled. "Reckon he ain't heard that in all his life, Daisy. Papa say his mama, Nina, was bes'-lookin' wench he evah did see. She came from a family o' Ayrabs. Her papa some kinda king, way I hears it. Reckon that why Dundee mo' smaht than reg'lar slaves, an' kinda good-lookin', too."

"I think he's too smart to just spend his time around horses," Daisy said, in her ignorance of slavery. "Can you read and write, Dundee?"

Jonathan said, "Daisy, any slave who reads an' writes gets tied to a post in the whuppin' shed an' gets a hundred lashes befo' we takes him to Richmond or Lynchburg an' puts him on the vendue table. Slaves cain't evah learn to read an' write."

Dundee's forehead had broken out in a sweat. He knew the beads of perspiration were running down onto his cheeks, but he could do nothing about it.

"Well, I don't think that's very fair," Daisy said with a show of tartness. "By educating some of the more gifted, you can improve the lot of all the others who may never learn to read and write."

"An' that," Jonathan said, "is why we don' let any o' them learn how. Tells yo' mo' latah. But Dundee heah is special. Papa knows it too. Ain't that right, Dundee?"

"Yas suh, massa, suh, he sho' do. Treats Dundee good, he does."

"We'll have a look at the mare now," Jonathan said. "Bring her out."

The sleek, beautiful horse nibbled at Daisy's hand. Daisy crooned; she wanted to stay and make friends. But Jonathan, eager to show her all Wyndward, took her arm and guided her away. They walked down to the shaded lane past the necessary houses.

"Reckon my mama shows yo' whut they fo'," he said.

"Of course, Jonathan."

"Yo' see mama go out the back do' an' open a parasol, day or night, an' yo' know wheah she goin'. Nevah could figger out why she gots to have a parasol she goes to the outhouse."

"If she does, so will I," Daisy said with a laugh. "Jonathan, she's wonderful. All your people are wonderful. Even that slave, Dundee."

"Gots to tell yo' 'bout his mama. Papa loves her like I loves yo'. Co'se she kin nevah be mo' than his pet. Papa boun' to marry a white gal someday an' Nina knows that. But when Nina dies, Papa mourns much as if it was Benay."

"More and more," Daisy said, "this kind of life puzzles me. Isn't there ever trouble? All these slaves. You can't tell me they like being slaves."

"Trouble 'nuff," Jonathan admitted grimly. "Sometimes they rebels. All hell busts loose they do. Some runs. They's a Underground Railroad takes runnin' slaves from one place to another, each time gettin' them further No'th till they gets into a antislavery state. Sometimes they comes back, even knowin' they get whupped when they do. They finds it not much diff'rent up No'th, 'cept up theah nobody feeds 'em, or gives 'em a place to live."

"They really come back to . . . this?"

"Not all. On'y some." His eyes searched her face. "Ain't no othah way, Daisy. Bettah we nevah brought them heah, but we didn't, wouldn't be much 'roun' heah 'cept wilderness."

"I do understand," Daisy said. "At least I think I do. The main thing is that I love you. Everything else is insignificant compared to that. I want your children. . . ."

"We sho' wukkin' on that," Jonathan chuckled.

She hugged his arm and raised her head high. She was Mrs. Jonathan Turner and she was in love and she was now a respected and respectable woman, grateful to be a part of the world.

Sunday was quiet. No conch horn was blown, the fields were empty of slaves. Along slave row everyone was busy. Vegetable patches were tended; babies spent the day with their mothers instead of in the birthing house. A few sick slaves were visited in the infirmary, where capable older women cared for them.

By night it changed. Those slaves who wished assembled in one of the huge, empty curing sheds and listened to the Reverend Whitehead deliver one of his sermons on tolerance, obedience, and love. Daisy was caught up in his rhetoric and Jonathan gave the elderly preacher an extra reward, which made him beam with delight.

Afterwards, the Reverend made his way to Dundee's loft in the stable to continue his lessons. Dundee had advanced at such a pace, the Reverend was quite amazed—and growing more frightened each time he visited Dundee.

"Yo' gots to be mighty keerful, boy. Yo' knowin' too much, an' yo' slips an' says mo' than yo' means to say an' they stahts to wondah. Yo' slips agin, an' they knows yo' now a nigger who reads an' writes. Soon's that happens, they sells yo'. Aftah they whups yo'."

"Not long as I kin handle the hosses way I does, an' they goin' to win races an' make money fo' them. I be keerful, Rev'ren'. Burns the *Liberators* yo' brings me soon's I git through readin' em."

"Yo' ain't showed 'em to somebody else?"

"Knows bettah than that. Don' talk 'bout 'em either, but whut I reads, makes me think mo' than evah, slavery goin' to be gone befo' too long."

The minister nodded slowly. "Don' know that

[*310*]

good or bad, but like yo' say, ain't no way to stop it comin'."

"Wants to be ready it comes," Dundee said.

"An' now yo' bettah git ovah to the curing shed fo' the dancin'. Yo' don' show yo' face they goin' to wondah whut in hell yo' doin' by yo'se'f all the time. 'Members, yo' gits in trouble, I gits in trouble, an' I too ol' fo' any o' that."

Dundee helped him down the ladder and walked out of the stable with him. "No need to worry, Rev'ren.' Knows how to keep my mouth shut. I goes to the dancin' now, an' I thanks yo' agin fo' all yo' does fo' me."

Dundee waited until the elderly man was aboard his donkey cart and moving away from the plantation, then trotted over to where the music and shouting filled the night.

Torches illuminated the scene. A banjo, strummed as loud as possible, provided the rhythm for the cakewalk. Fitz, Benay, Jonathan, and Daisy watched the frolic.

Daisy, excited by the music, stepped away from Jonathan's side and indulged in her own version of the cakewalk, strutting with the best of them, until Benay went to her side and quietly led her back to where the men stood.

"Oh, Benay, was I wrong?" she asked in dismay.

"Ain't done, Daisy. Don't blame yo' none, but white folk cain't mix. Jes' ain't done."

"Jonathan, are you angry with me?" Daisy asked.

Jonathan said, "Co'se not. Yo' a fine dancer."

"Jes' don' do it agin," Fitz added. "Like Jonathan says, don' blame yo' none."

There were other things for Daisy to learn, some of them unpleasant. The following morning, Daisy was selecting her clothes for the journey to Richmond with Benay. She had bought a few things in New Orleans on her honeymoon, but none seemed suitable, somehow. Skeptically she held up a pale green shirtwaist which she had worn with a gray skirt, then dropped it on the bed. Alameda picked it up. "Yo' gives this to Alameda, missy, ma'am. Sho' look good on me."

"How do you know?" Daisy asked. "How do you know it looks good on you? Have you been trying on my clothes, Alameda?"

"No, missy, ma'am. I nevah does that. No, ma'am."

Daisy moved closer to the slim, lithe girl. "Since you came into the room, I've been smelling my toilet water, and I haven't used any today. You smell of it, Alameda. You've been stealing it, using it. And you've been trying on my clothes when I wasn't here."

"Missy, ma'am. I nevah does. Sweahs I nevah does."

"Now you're lying," Daisy said angrily. "You can't have the shirtwaist and if you steal any more of my toilet water or anything else, I'll tell my husband."

Alameda's affection for that shirtwaist was too great. She snatched it up. "Yo' goin' to Richmond to buy lots o' clothes. Yo' gives this to me."

Daisy's patience broke. She grabbed the garment and pulled vigorously. Alameda, without thinking, tightened her grasp on it. Daisy went reeling backward.

For a brief moment they stared at each other, each terrified. Then Daisy walked out of the room, hurried downstairs, and found Jonathan in the library with his father.

"Jonathan," Daisy said, "Alameda is impossible. She's been trying on my clothes and using my toilet water. She snatched a blouse away from me because she wants it. Must I put up with such insolence?"

Jonathan rose. "Wait heah, Daisy."

Fitz said, "He goin' to fetch Alameda an' takes her to the whuppin' shed. Sometimes the slaves gets that way—like they losin' they haids ovah somethin' they covets. Yo' lets 'em get away with it an' they gets wuss. Till they no damn good a'tall."

"Jonathan is going to *whip* her?" Daisy asked, aghast.

"Mo' than that, if I knows him. Now yo' ain't nevah seen a slave get whupped, but yo' bettah begin now. Yo' be theah to watch. Alameda knows she done wrong. Cain't let her get away with this, an' she been uppity too long as it is."

"But—I didn't mean to have her punished that much," Daisy said.

"Has to be done. Up No'th she does somethin' like that, yo' fires her. But heah we cain't do that. Cain't fire a slave, so we has to punish her. Reckon Jonathan won't give her mo' than half a dozen lashes, but she deserves twenny an' mo'. She laid a han' on yo', Daisy?"

"Well . . . not exactly. I think she pushed me a little, but I can't say for sure."

"Don' tell Jonathan. Layin' a han' on yo' means she gets fifty lashes. Yo' goes an' watches."

Daisy heard Alameda's shrill protests as Jonathan dragged her down the steps and out the door. Daisy, under Fitz's edict to go and watch, followed them down to where the big cage rested beside the whipping shed.

"Ought to put yo' in theah fo' a few days, fo' I whups yo'," Jonathan said angrily, "but got 'nother way to tame yo' down."

He kicked open the door and shoved her inside. He saw Daisy running toward them and waited for her. Silently he ushered her into the small room where two thick posts had been set up.

Jonathan pushed the terrified slave toward one of the posts. "Shuck down, far as yo' waist," he ordered.

When she hesitated, Jonathan seized the back of her dress and ripped it down to where a rope belt held it around her middle. He forced her against the post, rounded it, pulled her hands together, and cuffed them with spancels. Then he picked up the cowhide and swung it. Alameda shrieked in pain and terror. Daisy's hands arose to her lips and held there as she watched in horror. Jonathan swung the cowhide five more times before he threw it to one side. He released the slave and she dropped to her knees.

Jonathan said, "Yo' gets yo'se'f down to the cabins an' yo' takes one. Yo' picks a buck an' yo' stahts makin' us suckers. An' yo' wuks in the fields ev'y day from now on. Yo' no longer a house servant an' yo' nevah will be agin. Now on yo' feet an' get yo' black ass outen heah fo' I kicks it out."

Alameda, clutching the tattered dress to her, got up and fled, weeping loudly.

"Reckon Papa tol' yo' to come an' watch," Jonathan said.

"Yes. I . . . didn't want to. Oh, Jonathan, weren't you too harsh with her?"

"Daisy, a house servant earns her way into serving us. But she steals, or whines, or lies, she goes back to the fields. She knows this. They all do. Hates whuppin' a gal much as yo' hates watchin' it done, but has to be. Ain't no othah way. Yo' keeps 'em down or they slices yo' haid clean off they gets the chance."

Daisy moved up to him and kissed him on the lips. "I do understand. These are ways I have to learn. Maybe I took her side too much because of what I went through . . . I was beaten too."

"That happen fo' I meets yo'," Jonathan said. "We weren't alive until then, an' befo' that was nuthin'. We nevah looks back."

"Yes, my dear Jonathan, we never look back," she repeated. "What a fine and kind man you are."

"Gets yo' 'nother body servant. Thinkin' 'bout Domingo. She a fine gal an' she knows her place. Times she reminds me of how Nina must have been."

"Jonathan did you sleep with her, as your father slept with Nina?"

"Yes, ma'am, sho' did. But no mo'. Theah's nobody 'ceptin' yo', Daisy."

"Does Domingo know that?"

"She do. She knows, an' like Nina, she 'spects nuthin' from me or from yo'."

Daisy's mouth and lips were dry, but she

managed a smile. "I will not hold it against her, or against you."

"No goddamn reason yo' should," Jonathan said.

Daisy thought he sounded more like his father then ever. And who am I to talk? she asked herself.

The next morning, Fitz and Jonathan saw the two women off. Two trusted slaves occupied the high seat on the old stage, which Benay insisted on using instead of the carriage because they could pack more things into it on the return trip.

"Cain't sweah whut yo' finds at Colonel Coldwell's place," Fitz said. "The house an' the Colonel an' his wife, they all gone to pot some lately, but they old friends an' it a good place to stop fo' the night."

"Might's well tell yo'," Jonathan added glumly, "the Colonel's wife had the hots fo' me ev'y time we stops, but sweahs she nevah gets me in bed." He made no mention of the gazebo. It was something he'd rather not think about. He'd always felt ashamed of that.

"Kin sweah to that too," Fitz added. "Yo' see her an' yo' knows why."

"I'll take your word for it, gentlemen," Daisy said in mock seriousness. "But if she's beautiful, I may not come back."

"Then yo' comes back," Jonathan said. "Miss yo', I will, Daisy. Don' stay too long."

She blew him a kiss as the stage lumbered away. Fitz and Jonathan walked back to the house. It was a cool day, but not too chilly to sit on the veranda.

"Ain't seen Calcutta 'roun'," Jonathan said.

Fitz chuckled. "I tells Elegant when he wakes up, wuk him so hahd he don' know whut he doin', with that hangovah he bound to have. Sees now if he gets ovah it."

Fitz shouted for the servant. Calcutta, who must have been just inside the door, emerged as fast as he could. He stood there, a foolish smile on his face, waiting for orders.

"We wants whiskey an' cold watah," Fitz said. "An' when yo' gets heah with the drinks, I smells yo' breath. Yo' got one drop in yo' mouth, yo' goes to the whuppin' shed. Now move!"

Calcutta was back in far faster time than usual. But when he presented the tray, a good part of the drinks had slopped over and as the tray still shook in presenting it, more liquor spilled.

"Yo' nervous, Calcutta?" Fitz asked. "Yo' shakin' like yo' on yo' way to the whuppin' shed."

"No suh, massa, suh, I ain't skeered. I feels fine, I does."

"Yo're a liar," Fitz said good-naturedly. "Yo' been drinkin' so much, yo' shakin' bad."

"I ain't been drinkin', massa, suh. Yo' kin smell."

Fitz arose to sniff at Calcutta's wide-open mouth. There wasn't a trace of whiskey on his breath. Fitz sat down again.

"Fo' once yo' ain't lying. Now go back to the springhouse an' yo' kin have one drink o' whiskey. Jes' one, mind."

[317]

"I thanks yo', massa, suh. Thanks yo' agin, I does."

He walked off the veranda and into the house. Well down the hallway he paused, looked over his shoulder, raised the tray, tilted it and let the spilled liquor cascade into his mouth. Then he went on to find the drink Fitz had granted him. There was no sign of nervousness or shakiness in the way he handled the tray, or poured his own generous drink. Calcutta was well satisfied with life.

Fitz and Jonathan worked and talked business for the rest of the day. They drank copiously, ate well, and went to bed early. Neither mentioned it, but they were lonely. Jonathan thought about taking Domingo to his room, but felt obliged not to. Still, the temptation was not easy to ward off, especially since he knew Domingo was sleeping on the floor outside his room, only waiting for him to summon her.

Fitz was the first to wake up. He did so slowly, aware that he was hearing alien sounds. It was just after three.

Then Fitz thought he saw a strange light in the sky, reflected against his bedroom window. He arose and padded to the window, raising it higher and leaning far out to determine the origin of that pinkish glow.

He heard the pounding of hoofbeats. Someone was riding very fast toward the mansion. Fitz hastily put on a shirt, pulled on his pants, and laced his shoes. He was buttoning his shirt as he hurried into the corridor, to find Jonathan also in the process of hastily dressing.

"Thinks there's a fire, Papa," Jonathan said. "Mus' be 'roun' the curin' sheds."

"Thinks somebody comin' to tell us. Bettah get downstairs to let him in."

They ran quickly along the corridor to the stairs and down to the first floor. Jonathan opened the door. It was Dundee riding up.

"Massa, suh," he shouted. "Curin' shed burnin', suh. Real good, it's burnin'."

"Ride to the overseers' houses and roust 'em out o' bed," Fitz ordered. "Tell 'em to get down there quick."

Dundee wheeled the horse and galloped off, digging his hard heels into the horse's belly. Fitz and Jonathan started running toward the curing sheds. The flames were already high and smoke was darkening the starlit sky.

A score of slaves were already on hand, watching the fire helplessly. Without orders, they did nothing. Fitz began shouting for them to fetch all the pails and pans they could round up, to fill them with water. In short order, they had formed a scraggly, largely ineffective bucket line, throwing small quantities of water on a blaze impossible to control.

Jonathan said, "Papa, we ain't goin' to save this one. Mayhap we should wet down the shed nex' to it so the whole string don' go up."

Fitz nodded. "Yo' tells them whut to do. I'll see how close the fire is to the nex' shed."

It was dangerously close, but under Fitz's direction and Jonathan's exhortation, the slaves managed to keep the wall exposed to the heat and flames well wetted down. Jonathan seized a long strip of wood which had fallen away as the fire progressed. It was charred and hot to the touch, but it became useful as he pried and prodded the nearest wall down, to help it all burn to a cinder.

The overseers arrived, but there was little they could do except stand and watch. In an hour, the shed had become a mound of embers. Fitz wiped sweat off his face and neck and began to probe in the ashes.

"Whut gets me," he said, "is how a fire could have stahted heah. Ain't nuthin' heah kin staht a fire. No candles, no cookin' fires."

"Soon's the ashes cool down some," Jonathan said, "I'll look 'roun' an' see if they's anythin' shows how it stahted."

"Firs' time anythin' like this happens on Wyndward," Fitz said with a slow shake of his head. "Think they's somethin' in the wind, Jonathan?"

"Trouble, somewheah," Jonathan said. "Kin almost smell it lately."

They exchanged a long look of foreboding. Then Fitz shrugged. "Reckon we cain't do much heah. Jes' tells one o' the overseers to stay heah an' be sho' fire's all out, an' no sparks apt to set somethin' else burnin'."

They walked back to the mansion. Elegant, awakened by all the confusion and noise, had thoughtfully brewed a pot of coffee and supplmented this with some of her airy-light biscuits. Fitz and Jonathan ate them greedily while they talked.

"Looked 'roun'," Jonathan said, "soon's we got theah. Lots o' slaves theah, but none o' them was snickerin' or smilin' like they'd set the fire an' now was enjoyin' watchin' it burn. Slaves cain't hide they feelin's much. An' all I saw was they seemed skeered. So I thinks this fire set, not more'n one did it, an' nobody else knew it was happenin' till the fire was goin' good."

"Don' know who would do this," Fitz said. "If on'y one man set the fire, he musta had a reason. We ain't even whuppped none o' the bucks lately."

"Wonderin' this be some kin' o' warnin', Papa. Tellin' us they's mo' comin'."

"Mayhap it so. But whut they wants, they cain't come to us an' say so."

"Think I asks Dundee an' Hong Kong, they heers anythin' 'bout a runaway who is hidin' heah an' tryin' to stir up trouble. Or a runaway who floats 'roun' from one plantation to 'nothah talkin' rebellion or runnin' away. Man like that would be mighty dangerous."

"We fin's him, we hangs him fas' as we kin string up a rope. I'm wonderin' should yo' mama an' me go to Boston."

"Papa, breaks her heart yo' don' take her. Melanie's too. Been a yeah now since yo' saw her. I kin handle any trouble that comes."

"Yo' runs across a renegade slave stirrin' up trouble, think yo' got the guts to string him up?"

"Why yo' asks a thing like that?" Jonathan asked indignantly.

"Yo' nevah was too harsh with slaves, son. Mayhap yo' talked like yo' was, but in yo' heart yo' kinda bleedin' fo' 'em."

"Papa, mayhap I don' like it sometimes. But I do whut's needful to keep Wyndward."

Between them for a moment was the vision of the burning shed, and the thought of their absent wives. Then Fitz picked up another biscuit, lavishing it with butter and honey. "Yo' keeps yo' mouth shut 'bout this when Benay comes back. Whut yo' think 'bout how Daisy likes it heah?"

"Daisy likes it. She don' like whuppin'. Thinks she tries to stop me when I hides Alameda, but she on'y covers her face an' aftah it ovah, she says she unnerstan's why it gots to be done. Thinks she gets ovah her feelin's fo' long."

"How does she feel 'bout givin' me some gran'chillun, Jonathan?"

"Wants 'em jes' as much as yo' do. Reckon won't be no trouble theah."

"She a strong gal? Don' mean muscle strong, but kin she stan' up to mayhap a rebellion that gets mighty bloody an' makes us hang some o' the slaves? Kin she face that, do yo' think?"

"She kinda goodhearted, Papa. Likes ev'y-body, an' hates any kin' o' trouble. Jes' the same, thinks she faces up to it even if it gets bloody."

"Hopes so, son. This sho' ain't no place fo' a woman who cain't. Well, I'm kinda sleepy. Reckon I'll have me a drink o' rum outen the bottle I keeps heah. Wakes Calcutta an' sends him fo' drinks, he be back 'bout time to get up. Want to join me, son?"

"Not this time, Papa. Sleepy myse'f. In the mornin' I looks 'roun' the ashes an' lets yo' know."

Fitz nodded and went to the sideboard for the bottle. He poured himself a stiff portion, sat down again, and tried to free his mind of the idea that Wyndward, his bastion, had been infiltrated by the enemy.

In the morning, Jonathan paid Dundee a visit. He found him busily currying a likely looking roan he'd selected from a herd. This one bore the markings of a future racehorse.

"Reckon yo' bettah bring this one up," he told Dundee. "Yo' sho' kin spot 'em."

"Yas suh, massa, suh. Don' know why I kin, but I does."

"Dundee, yo' seen any strange niggers 'round' heah? Knows yo' cain't recognize all our slaves, but mayhap one who acts like he don' know much 'bout Wyndward Plantation."

"No suh, massa, nevah sees anybody acts like that, suh."

"Been thinkin' that fire las' night was set."

"Reckon it was, suh. Nuthin' theah to staht a fire."

"Jes' wonderin' if it set, who did it. Cain't figger any slave we got, would do that. Treats ev'ybody pretty good an' ain't whupped nobody, 'ceptin' a wench yestiddy who sloths an' steals."

"Cain't he'p yo', massa, suh. Wishes I could, suh."

"Well, keep yo' eyes open."

As Jonathan walked away Dundee mulled over the possibility of some Wyndward slave being rebellious enough to set a fire. He did know there's been some muttering among the bucks, but if anybody wanted to make trouble, he should be the one. By now he was reading well enough to understand every word in the *Liberator*.

[323]

Dundee's brushing of the roan's short mane grew slower as he wondered what he would ever do if he was suddenly set free. He had nowhere to go, no one to go to. Except Seawitch and Hong Kong. Going back to them, even as a free man, surely wouldn't change his way of life. Furthermore, he didn't want to abandon these horses.

Jonathan made his way to the mounds of ashes that had once been a curing shed. Not much was lost by this fire. Before the morning was done with, Jonathan would give the orders for clearing the debris and rebuilding. Carpenters and masons and blacksmiths, well-trained slaves only one step in status below the house servants, would begin work. In a week's time, there would be a new shed finished and ready for use.

Jonathan picked up a slender piece of partially charred wood and began poking in the ashes. Eventually his makeshift prod turned over a mound of partially burned wood. Tangled in the debris was a piece of half-burned cloth. He examined it carefully. It was flimsy, it should have burned to nothing, but apparently fallen timber had protected it from the flames.

He put it into his pocket. Fitz might recognize it. To Jonathan, it looked like a section of a slave's dress.

Jonathan started walking back to the house, rubbing his face sleepily. Maybe he'd take a nap, he thought, wishing for Daisy. As his fingers passed down his face he thought he smelled oil. He sniffed his fingertips again, then pulled the piece of cloth out of his pocket and held it to his nose. It had been soaked in coal oil. He quickened his pace as he headed back to the house.

Fitz threw the piece of cloth on the top of his desk. "So now we knows the fire was set. Question is, who set it?"

"Alameda wearin' somethin' like this when I shucked her down. Yo' think she got guts 'nuff to do this?"

"She goddamn mad yo' whups her."

"Madder I sends her to the fields, Papa. But cain't see she done this. Not herse'f, anyways. Ain't got 'nuff brains fo' that."

"Talks to Dundee 'bout knowin' anythin'?"

"Says he don' know nuthin' 'bout any strange slave 'roun' heah. Didn' talk to Hong Kong yit."

"I did, little while ago. Says he ain't seen or heard nuthin'."

"Papa, thinks either of 'em would admit it if they did know?"

"Reckon not. They's niggers, an' they got to stick with they own."

[16]

Fitz and Jonathan were having breakfast, waited on by Calcutta. He was in a fine mood this morning, eager and willing to serve.

"Mayhap givin' him a whole bottle puts some life in him," Jonathan said.

"Gives him all that rum ev'yday an' he rolls ovah an' dies—mos' likely out o' plain happiness."

"Reckon we got wuss niggers than Calcutta, Papa. Whut yo' aimin' to do today?"

"Seedlin's comin' 'long an' I sees to them. Then I been wonderin' we should open the field way down by the creek fo' plantin' this yeah. Got plenty 'bacco growin', but a little mo' won't hurt none. They's a biggah demand than evah fo' our bright in England."

"I goin' to time Dundee's hosses. Soon's yo'

an' Mama comes back from Boston, be time to race 'em."

Calcutta burst into the room. "Rider comin' fas', suh. He sho' in a hurry."

Fitz and Jonathan both arose from the table and hurried out of the house. Whenever someone rode like this, he was the bearer of bad news.

The rider had to pause to recover his breath, but when he spoke, he did so as fast as he could talk.

"Bob Harper's place, Fitz. They rose up befo' daylight, killin' an' rapin' an' burnin'."

"Jonathan, have Dundee saddle a pair o' hosses. I'll fetch guns," Fitz snapped.

"Thinks Bob Harper daid," the rider said. "Looks mighty bad."

"Whut's bein' done to get a posse?"

"Ten o' us rides to fetch as many as we kin. Reckon we have fifty or mo' men befo' long. Maybe by the time yo' gets theah."

"Yo' tell 'em we comin'. I'll sen' half my overseers too. Cain't send 'em all. We got some trouble too. We leaves soon's we kin."

"I goin' to warn all the small fahmers 'roun' heah. Could be them rebels tryin' to scourge the countryside much as they kin. Fo' food an' guns—an' women."

Fitz gave silent thanks that Benay and Daisy were in Richmond.

Jonathan rode up, leading a horse, just as Fitz came out of the house carrying side arms and two rifles, with boxes of ammunition. He passed Jonathan's share to him, then they rode over to the fields to enlist the help of some of the overseers.

If the slaves in the fields had any idea of what

was going on, they gave absolutely no sign. They kept on working as usual, not looking up or slowing their pace.

Hong Kong, however, sensed there was trouble.

"They's a rebellion on the Harper place," Fitz explained when he joined them. "Reckon it pretty bad. Yo' stays heah, Hong Kong. Keep yo' eyes an' yo' ears wide open. Fire heah las' night, rebellion five miles away this mornin' means could be lots o' trouble comin'. Yo' makes sho' nobody gets a chance to run."

"They runs, they gits they laigs busted, suh. Won't be no runnin' on this heah plantation."

"Depends yo' sees to that. Come on, Jonathan, now we rides."

Halfway to the Harper plantation, they were joined by four riders from other nearby plantations. They waved, shouted greetings, and kept riding as fast as they could.

Two more came riding from a side road, and all of them reached the plantation only fifteen or twenty minutes later. Before they got there they could see the low cloud of smoke. Some twenty men were already there, but Fitz, being owner of the biggest plantation, saw that he was expected to take charge right after he dismounted.

With Jonathan at his side, he walked into the house. The destruction was complete—windows broken, drapes and curtains torn down, furniture hacked to pieces with axes. All through the house was wanton and vicious destruction. In the larger parlor they found grimmer results of this rebellion. Bob Harper, barely recognizable, lay dead, his head shattered by the sharp edges of axes. His wife had been almost decapitated and there were obvious signs that she'd been raped. Their eleven-year-old daughter had been equally abused and cruelly slashed.

In the kitchen, two house slaves had been stripped and held down against the hot stove before their throats were slit.

Fitz was grim-faced as he began a hunt for weapons Bob Harper had owned. Neither he nor the half-dozen men helping him found any.

Fitz went out to stand on the veranda facing the grouped posse. He figured he had at least sixty men. Enough, he thought, but there was an added danger they should know about.

"Ev'ybody in the house been killed. Miz Harper an' her daughter, they raped befo' they slashed an' axed to death. We got us a big rebellion heah, gen'mun, an' we gots to crush it quick. They's guns missin' from the house. Don' know how many guns Bob kep' about, but all gone. Means these heah rebels got somethin' to hold us off with an' we got to be mighty keerful."

"Any nigger we sees with a gun, or a ax, we shoots 'thout warnin'," someone said.

"That's whut's got to be done," Fitz agreed. "First, we got to fin' out how many slaves run. All yo' men, 'cept Hugh Lister, staht ridin'. Don' think the rebels far off. This happened on'y 'bout two o' three hours ago. They be bunched up, sho' skeered to be ridin' or runnin' alone. So they's a good chance we gets 'em all when we finds 'em. Jonathan, yo' rides with the men. Send word back soon's yo' sights anythin' or sees anyone. Hugh an' me we'll join yo' soon as we kin."

As the men left the plantation they spread out, searching for any clue that would lead them to the hiding place of the rebels.

Hugh, a burly, stocky, powerfully built man, walked with Fitz to the slave row. Those slaves who had refused to run had voluntarily confined themselves to their cabins. There was one overseer, rifle armed, standing guard. Fitz knew him as Will Pauling.

"Count 'em yit?" Fitz asked him.

"Been tryin' to, Mistah Turner, but I the on'y overseer lef'."

"Whut happened to the others? Bob had fo' last I knew."

"They's daid. Rebellion stahted when the haid overseer sounded the conch. Gets all the slaves outen they cabins an' nothin' looks wrong. Two tol' me they was sick. I stayed behin' to see if they were lyin'. Happened when the slaves were bein' marched to the fields. Twenty or twenty-five of 'em had axes an' knives hidden in the brush 'side the path leadin' to the fields. They dropped outa line, got they weapons, an' befo' the overseers knew whut was goin' on, they was killed. One buck, he comes my way, an' soon's I sees he got a knife, I shoots him."

"He daid?" Fitz asked.

"No, suh. Had two women carry him to that cabin—firs' one in the row. Las' I knows he was breathin'."

"We sees him now. Yo' get out 'nuff slaves yo' kin trust, an' see all the bodies picked up an' put in one o' the sheds. Sees they burned one barn."

"Runs befo' they sets fire to any mo'. I did

[331]

some shootin' an' they knows I gets word out, so they lef' in a hurry. Skeered mayhap they stop at some other place an' rape an' kill, but ain't heered nuthin'.'"

"We ain't heered much either. Soon's yo' gives the orders fo' the dead folks be picked up, come back to the cabin an' bring a rope, yo' kin find one."

Hugh Lister was in the cabin before Fitz reached it. A buck lay on the straw-covered section of floor where the slaves slept. Two silent, plainly frightened women stood looking at him. He was moaning and tossing about, but he was far from dying.

Fitz handed his gun to Lister and began peeling the clothes off the slave. He looked up and ordered the women out of the cabin. When he had the buck well shucked down, straightened up.

"Looks like he got a bullet through his goddamn shoulder, an' 'nother one through his right laig. Some good shootin' by the overseer. We kin wuk on him, he don' talk."

"Hides him, he don'," Lister said bitterly. "Aftah whut we saw in the house, don' keer we strips the skin off him inch by inch."

Fitz kicked the wounded slave as hard as he could. "Wants yo' to tell us how many runs off."

"Don' know, massa. I wasn' to run, suh. Sweahs I wasn't goin' to run."

"I asked yo' a question, answer it."

"Tol' yo', massa. Don' know."

Fitz reached for the rifle Lister was holding. He used the butt to strike the slave's face until the blood ran. "Asked yo' a question," Fitz said coldly.

"Tol' yo . . ."

Fitz slowly aimed the rifle barrel squarely between the slave's eyes. "How many?"

"Reckon . . . twenny, suh, maybe fi' or six mo'. Tol' yo' don' know fo' sho'."

"One of 'em was the leader," Fitz said. "Whut his name?"

The slave tried to reach up and brush blood off his face, but Fitz used the rifle barrel to fend off that hand.

"They wasn't no leadah, suh. Sweahs no leadah, suh. Jes' eve'ybody . . ."

"Yo' lie one mo' time an' yo' is daid," Fitz warned. "They was axes an' knives hidin' 'long the path. Somebody puts 'em theah, somebody steals 'em an' gets ready to rebel. One goddam nigger did that an' yo' knows who he is."

"Massa, suh, they wasn't no leadah. If they was, I don' knows 'bout it."

"Who tells yo' to leave the rest o' the slaves an' go to kill the overseer that wasn't killed already?"

"I was on'y tryin' to tell the ovahseer I wasn't runnin', suh."

"Yo' had a knife in yo' han'. Yo' was tol' to go kill him. Who tol' yo'?"

The slave turned his head away. Fitz waited until the overseer arrived, carrying a rope. Then Fitz wasted no time. "Make a noose in the middle, get it 'roun' his goddamn neck. Yo' takes one end, Hugh takes the other. When I says so, yo' pulls an' we hangs this bastahd while he lyin' down."

[333]

The rope was affixed around the neck of the terrified slave. Fitz leaned over him.

"I asks yo' once mo'. Who tol' yo' to go kill the overseer? Jes' once I asks an' then yo' dies fo' sho'."

"Massa, suh, please don' kill me. Wasn't aimin' to run. Sweahs I wasn't."

Fitz gestured. The two men pulled the rope tight and the slave's body arched up as his wind was cut off. He clawed at the rope with his hands, trying to free himself of it before he strangled.

Again Fitz gestured and the rope was slackened. Fitz pulled the noose free enough so that the man could speak. The slave breathed in great gasps of air.

"Yo' gettin' closer to dyin' ev'y time yo' don' talk. Who tells yo' to kill the overseer?"

"Massa, suh, wants to tell yo'. I mos' daid now an' I wants to live. But I tells yo', I gits killed anyway."

"Who goin' to kill yo', we don'?"

"I says an' I dies. . . ."

Fitz gestured and the rope tightened again. The slave's waving arms indicated he wanted to speak. The rope was slackened.

"Las' time," Fitz said. "Yo' talks an' we lets yo' live. Yo' don' an' this time we kills yo'. That's fo' sho'. Whut anybody else kin do to yo' mayhap yo' kin stop, but yo' cain't stop us."

"Massa suh, it was Tubal."

"Wheah he from?"

"Don' rightly know, suh. Sweahs I don'. But he runs long time ago. He massa's long way off,

[334]

don' know he name. Tubal, he comes heah at night an' he talks to us. He say we gots to kill ev'ybody an' gits guns an' knives an' we goes killin' ev'y white we meets an' we rapes all the women befo' we kills 'em."

Fitz reached down and pulled the slave into a sitting position. "Whut's this heah Tubal look like?"

"He big man. Big buck. He got neck big an' roun' as he haid. Seen him bust a piece o' wood rest o' us needs a ax fo' to bust it. An' he say nuthin' so good as rapin' white women. Says we kin live off whut we steals an' we rapes an' keeps on rapin', till white folks git so skeered they stays inside, skeered to go out. He a pow'ful talker, massa, suh."

"Yo' were goin' with him. Tell the truth."

"Yes suh, massa, suh. He say I don' go, I gits killed. He come back, he sho'ly kills me."

"Let's finish off this bastahd," Lister suggested.

"Not now," Fitz said. "Mayhap we needs him agin. Mayhap he lies his fool haid off. That case, he dies slower'n any man evah did. We leaves the overseer heah to mind him. He so bad off now he gives no mo' trouble. He does—" Fitz glanced at the overseer—"yo' shoot him in the belly an' lets him die slow. Hugh, we bettah ride now an' find the othahs. Evah heah o' this Tubal?"

"Name don' mean nuthin'," Hugh replied. "Mos' looks alike anyhow. But this one sho' be a big buck if we ain't bein' lied to."

"If we are," drawled Fitz, looking down at

[335]

the wide-eyed, frightened slave, "we goin' to kill this sonabitch an' leave his carcass fo' wild dogs to eat on."

"Massa, suh, didn't lie. Sweahs . . ."

Fitz didn't wait to hear the rest of the protest. He and Hugh went out to where they'd left their horses and were soon riding hard to overtake the posse.

They were well spread out, riding slowly and meticulously hunting for signs to tell them in which direction the rebels had gone. Fitz soon found Jonathan and they joined forces.

"Fisbee place close by," Jonathan said. "Mayhap they gone theah."

"Mayhap. Let's cut loose an' ride," Fitz said. "On'y way to find out."

The ride to the Fisbee place required less than twenty minutes. The dilapidated mansion, the untended grounds, and the empty, unplanted fields all seemed deserted. Fitz studied the place from an obscure vantage point.

"Jonathan, I'm goin' in. Yo' stays behin'. Yo' see anythin' move, staht shootin'. Keep 'nuff bullets flyin' so I kin get the hell outa theah."

"I'm ready," Jonathan said. He dismounted and tied his and Fitz's horse before Fitz moved out from the cover and began a fast run across the open area. Jonathan kept a rifle trained on the house, and kept eying the surrounding area as well. Fitz reached the house and went in, his gun at a ready angle. When he reappeared, he signaled Jonathan to come in.

"By the looks o' this," he said, "some of 'em been hidin' heah. Stealin' chickens an' a few hogs. Bones lef' behin'. They sho' busts things up."

Jonathan kicked aside some battered pots and pans. A fire had been built in the middle of the parlor, not for the purpose of destruction, but for cooking.

Fitz went about stamping heavily on the floors in various sections of the house. He banged his fists against walls, tried doors and finally explained his actions to a sorely puzzled Jonathan.

"Place looks like hell, but it's well built. This heah house'll last 'nother hundred yeahs. Aims to own it. Don' know how or who I gots to deal with, but I gets it one way or 'nother."

"Don' go lookin' fo' Belle fo' my sake," Jonathan said wryly. "She one gal I don' wants to see agin long's I live."

"We'll see 'bout this place, land an' all, soon's I gets the time. Right now we'd bettah find the othahs an' keep huntin' down the rebels fo' they kills an' rapes at anothah plantation."

They had no difficulty in finding the others, for four quick shots directed them. They rode faster.

Suddenly they came upon a dozen men standing around two slaves who lay in the grotesque postures of violent death.

"Say they been to the Kirk plantation," one man explained for Fitz's benefit. "Say they got theyse'ves shot, but the rest o' the rebels kep' goin'. Reckon whut we finds ain't goin' to make us spend much time showin' these bastahds any mercy."

"Anybody gone there fo' now?"

"Twenny men. Hears no shootin', so reckon they too late to he'p the Kirks."

"Whut happened these two daid?" Fitz prodded one of the bodies with his foot, turning it over so he might look at the dead man's face. He was a stranger to Fitz.

The spokesman for the group shrugged. "Found 'em crawlin' away an' they tells us 'bout the Kirk place, so we shoots 'em like they damn well deserve."

"Maybe they knows wheah that bunch goin' aftah they gets through at the Kirks. Yo' kills 'em too fas'. Make 'em talk! Make 'em tell ev'ythin' they knows. Now we don' know wheah the rebels gone."

"Whut they says 'bout the Kirk place wuss than whut they does to po' Bob Harper an' his family. Gets us so mad, we kills 'em."

"Bes' go see," Fitz said. "An' keep yo' eyes peeled fo' mo' wounded niggers. Kirk has guns an' knows how to use 'em."

As they approached the Kirk house, they saw the bodies of four slaves sprawled out in death. They must have tried to rush the house and been greeted by bullets.

"Them niggers ain't runnin' no mo'," Fitz said grimly.

Inside, they found that all the male members of the family had been bludgeoned to death. The women—old Mrs. Kirk, her daughter, and her granddaughter—were alive, and in a state of frenzy, still whimpering with terror.

Hugh Lister, who had been among those who reached the house first, explained to Fitz what they'd learned.

"Kirk heard 'em comin'. He an' his two sons an' the son-in-law got to the house in time to get they guns, an' kills an' wounds a few. But they

[338]

was too many an' they gets into the house an' kills an' then settles down fo' some rapin'. Reckon the old woman clean outen her mind, an' the othahs not much bettah. Sho' goin' to need lots o' rope, we fin's these bastahds."

Fitz found the daughter the best able to give coherent answers to his questions. The old Mrs. Kirk kept moaning and rocking her scant frame, unreachable in her agony. The granddaughter, not more than twelve, was in a sort of trance, staring at nothing, understanding nothing.

Fitz turned to one of the men beside him. "Reckon yo' bes' rides to the nearest place an' fetches some womenfolk to come an' care fo' these po' souls. Cain't leave 'em heah like this."

"Fetches my own wife an' her mothah," the man said. "Gets 'em heah less'n an hour. Yo' finds the niggers did this, don' kill 'em till I gets back. Wants a crack at 'em befo' they dies."

Fitz knelt down in front of the chair in which the little girl's mother sat. Her face was still blood-smeared and her torn dress revealed bruises and cuts.

"Miz Kirk," Fitz said quietly. "Needs to know when they lef' an' wheah they gone, yo' knows. Mayhap yo' hears 'em talkin'."

"They kills Billy. They jes' kills him! An' they yells like crazy people."

"Knows that," Fitz kept his voice low. "They gets finished heah, they goes somewheah else. Whut they say?"

"Rapes me," she said. "An' they goin' to kill all us soon's they gets through rapin'."

"Whut skeered 'em off?"

"Don' know. They jes' up an' runs."

"They asks yo' any questions? Got to know, Miz Kirk. Got to fin' 'em."

"Jes' screamin' an' rapin' an' killing' . . ."

"Asks me they's gals on the Hampshire fahm," the little girl said in a monotone. "Asks me they gots guns theah."

Fitz went to the child's side and drew her to him. "Knows yo' hurt, but whut yo' jes' tol' us means mayhap nobody else gets hurt 'cause yo' he'ps us. Yo' safe now."

Outside Fitz called the men around him. "Wants two men to roun' up whut's lef' o' the Kirk slaves an' see the daid gets buried. Womenfolk be heah soon to care fo' the Kirk ladies. Been tol' the rebels asks 'bout the Hampshire plantation. That two hours ridin' an' a big one. So far they's on'y raided small fahms, but they ride now fo' somethin' like the Hampshire place."

"We bes' rides theah fas' as we kin," Hugh Lister said.

"Thinks they wait till dark," Fitz said. "Yo' sees whut happens heah, this little fahm. Fo' daid ones in the yahd an' two more crawlin' away, been shot up some. They ain't goin' to jes' charge a place now. 'Members this, gen'mun, they's got a leadah an' he ain't no fool. Cain't stand to lose six men ev'y time they tries to take a place. Thinks he waits till dark."

"Whut we goin' to do then?" Hugh asked.

"We rides to the Hampshire place, one at a time. Yo' stops half a mile 'way from the house, yo' ties yo' hoss, an' yo' waits. Soon's we all theah an' it gets dark, the rebels goin' to come sho'. We goin' to be theah waitin'."

"Bettah tell the Hampshire folks——" Hugh began.

"No. They got slaves too. They heahs we warnin' the Hampshires an' we waitin', mayhap the rebels gets word an goes somewheah else, wheah we ain't. Cain't afford to take any chances now."

"Papa, how yo' so sho' they aims to hit the Hampshire house? Sho' they talks 'bout it, but whut if they changes they minds?"

"Have to take the risk," Fitz said. "The Hampshire closest by, gives 'em the mos' to kill an' rape an' steal. Knows that family—by now they gets word whut's goin' on, an' they be ready. Worried some, sho', an' I wishes we could tell 'em, but bes' we don't. Whut we got to do is see not one o' them rebels gets away. Not a single one."

"Reckon that's the right thing to do," Jonathan said, backing up his father. "Right now we got no idee wheah they hidin'. We jes' rides 'roun' lookin', ain't goin' to find 'em in time. We lets 'em come to us, 'thout knowin' it, an' we gets 'em all."

There was a general agreement. The men began riding off, singly, well spaced so they'd make little fuss going through the countryside. Each man, warned and alert, would instantly shoot any Negro he saw skulking about.

The men thought of their own loved ones at home, and were in a frame of mind to kill all slaves. The hours passed by with no word of any further attacks.

When Fitz and Jonathan reached the Hampshire place, they heard no sound, saw no one; and yet they knew that forty men were waiting, hoping not only to repel an attack, but to kill as many of the attackers as possible.

Fitz and Jonathan had left their horses well back and had reached a point just inside the clearing before the Hampshire mansion. It was a large house, an attractive target for rebels. Lights burned in every window. Now and then, Fitz and Jonathan heard the low barking of dogs. They'd been turned loose. It made concealment more difficult for the posse, but each man was fully apprised as to what he must do, and they were all quiet, moving only when absolutely necessary.

"Got to get 'em all," Fitz said. "Cain't let 'em get away with this. They gets stirred up by whut's happenin' in the No'th. They listens to slaves who comes back an' talk goes 'roun'."

"Yo' sho' been 'spectin' somethin' like this, Papa."

"Expects mo'. Got to keep 'em down. Got to make 'em so skeered they nevah even *thinks* o' somethin' like whut happened today. On'y way we kin handle 'em."

"Goin' to hang 'em all?" Jonathan asked.

"Too many fo' that. We hangs twenny-thirty an' up No'th the Abolitionists raises hell like they nevah did befo'. That's no good, Jonathan. On'y makes word go 'roun' an' sets——"

Jonathan hissed a warning and they fell silent, clutching their rifles a little tighter, their nerves taut. When nothing happened, they assumed they had heard some awkward movement on the part of a member of the posse. Darkness was total. There was a mild breeze stirring, but otherwise no sound. Another hour went by. The posse held perfectly still. Each man there wondered, with cold dread, if they were setting a trap for rebels who would strike elsewhere, especially at his home.

They heard a dog set up barking and a few moments later, a yelp. The barking was cut off.

"They jes' fixed one o' the dogs," Fitz murmured. "They's heah. Begin to close in, Jonathan. Be keerful—no sound. Don' want them to know we's heah till they all in the open."

Lying flat, rifles beside them, Fitz and Jonathan saw the first of the rebellious slaves creep from brush and move toward the house. Not a hundred yards away they heard more movement, and they froze in place. More slaves were approaching the clearing, moving right through the posse, totally unaware of it.

There were twenty or more crawling toward the house. As these advanced, another dozen came out of the forest to follow them. Another dog barked an alarm. The lights in the house began to go out. Fitz heard windows being raised. A few seconds later shots rang out from the house. Like one man, on some kind of an unheard signal, the blacks arose, and with screams of rage, they charged.

The firing grew heavier from the mansion. Fitz pointed his rifle in the air, fired twice in rapid succession, and the posse came out of the forest behind the blacks. The rebels were trapped between two fires. If they ran toward the house, they were cut down from there. If they retreated, or tried to run around the house, they were met with the fire from the posse. At least ten of them were already down. The posse was closing in slowly, relentlessly, and every avenue of escape was gone.

One by one the slaves threw away their weapons and raised their arms as high as they could get them. Whenever members of the posse took charge of one of these blacks who surrendered, they pulled their arms behind their backs and manacled their wrists.

In fifteen minutes it was over. Fitz shouted for the Hampshire family to come out. Firebrands were found and lit. A circle of men held them aloft while the slaves were herded into one tight group.

Fred Hampshire came out to find Fitz and greet him with a bear hug of relief. "Knowed they was boun' to come," he said. "Knowed the posse was 'roun' somewheah, but didn't know wheah. Tol' my wife an' ev'ybody else, we don' heah nuthin' from the posse, reckon they outside somewheah. Made us feel safer. Co'se we wasn't *sho'* yo' was theah, but we depended on it."

"Yo' did well holdin' 'em off so we could move in," Fitz said. "Nobody gets hurt in the house?"

"Not a scratch, Fitz. We be fo'evah beholden."

"Reckon now we sees to makin' sho' this ain't goin' to happen agin," Fitz said. "Yo' knows a black named Tubal?"

Hampshire shook his head. "Nevah heerd o' the name, suh."

"Hopes he ain't one o' them on the ground."

They approached the group of sullen, terrified slaves. Fitz looked them over. There was one far bigger than the others, a near giant of a man, but if he was the leader, he gave no indication of it. If the others were asked who led them, not one would know. Or they'd point out one of the dead men. Fitz must not only be sure of Tubal's identity, but he had to make the slave admit it if he could.

"Yo'—" Fitz pointed to one of the slaves. "Step out. Means yo'."

The slave reluctantly moved forward. Fitz walked up to him.

"Knows whut yo' done an' knows whut's goin' to happen to yo'. But we don't claim all yo' niggers to blame. Mos' o' yo' too goddamn stupid to know whut to do in rebellin' this way. So yo' followed someone who did know. Yo' tells me who he be."

"Don't follow nobody, massa suh," the slave said quickly.

Fitz smashed him across the face with the butt of his rifle. The man fell, unconscious. Fitz pointed to another slave. The slave didn't stir. Fitz aimed the rifle. The man stepped out of the group quickly.

"Yo' knows whut I wants. Asks yo' once."

"Massa, suh, it be Isaac, suh. He daid. Sees him hit an' he goes down. He daid."

Fitz nodded. "Jonathan, yo' makes him point him out. Yo' ain't satisfied he tellin' the truth, kill him."

The slave, moaning in fear, was prodded into leading Jonathan to one of the bodies. Jonathan turned the dead man over with his foot.

Hugh Lister said, "That be one o' Kirk's slaves. I sells him to Kirk myse'f."

"His name Isaac?" Jonathan asked.

"Sho' ain't," Hugh replied.

Jonathan raised his rifle and fired. The slave dropped. Jonathan walked calmly back to Fitz's side.

"He lied. Who's nex'?"

"Mayhap we makes a mistake. Don' think any o' these sonabitches gots the brains to lead. Ev'y damn one too stupid to know anythin', let alone makin' a rebellion like this. Ain't nevah seen a nigger got that much sense. Line 'em up."

There were sixteen slaves left. They were herded into a line, torches brought closer. Fitz inspected them carefully. He stepped back.

"Shuck down," he ordered.

Some of them hurried to obey the order. The huge Negro didn't make a move at first, but then he seemed to accept the order and began removing his clothes.

"Goin' to hang yo', eve'y las' buck. Aftah yo' daid, we leaves yo' hangin' fo' the animals to eat. But fo' that, yo' gets a hundred lashes. Mistah Hampshire, we begs to borrow yo' whup."

"Sent fo' it," Hampshire said. "Wants to use it myse'f till I gets too tired."

Someone came through the crowd carrying a long lash with a weighted handle and a leaded tip.

"Blames myse'f fo' some o' this," Hampshire said. "Buys this heah whup an' hangs it on the wall. Nevah once used it. Gots sixty slaves wukkin' fo' me an' not one evah gives me trouble 'nuff to whup. Takes the hide clean off a man, I hears. Wants to see fo' myse'f."

"Take yo' pick," Fitz invited casually. All of

[346]

this was meant to intimidate the slaves into talking.

Hampshire selected one man out of the group. When he hesitated, Hampshire used the butt of the whip to club him into moving. When he was clear of the others, Hampshire swung the lash. The slave screamed and went down on his knees. Hampshire swung the whip again and again until the slave lay still and only faint whimpers passed from his lips.

Fitz approached the man directly to the left of the massive slave. The man was so terrorized that he shrank back and he tried to speak, but fear had frozen his vocal cords. He raised his hands in front of his face and cowered before the fate he knew was coming.

"Yo' nex'," Fitz said. "Yo' po' sonabitch don' seem like the othahs. Thinks they makes yo' run. Mayhap yo' don' get hung. Feels sorry fo' a po' mis'able man like yo'. Whut fahm yo' from?"

"Ran ... Ran ... Randall, massa, suh. Don' wants to run. Makes me run."

"Who?" Fitz asked. Then the man he knew to be Tubal made the move Fitz expected and hoped for. He tripped the man expertly, and as he fell, kicked him squarely in the face. It was a kick with such power behind it that everyone heard the slave's neck snap. When he fell, he was already dead.

Fitz said, "Tubal!"

The big slave looked up and then he sighed and his shoulders drooped. He bent his head in a token of submission.

"This heah," Fitz said, "be the slave who

runs long time ago an' goes 'bout gettin' othah slaves to rebel."

Fitz picked up Tubal's clothes, ripped them apart. Coins and bills showered onto the ground, along with gold rings and other jewelry.

Fitz indicated the loot to the other slaves. "Any slave gots money or rings, gets killed now."

"Massa, suh," one man said. "We ain't gots nuthin'. Tubal, he keeps it all. He say he goin' to pay fo' the Unnerground."

"He goin' to make hisse'f rich, that's whut he goin' to do," Fitz said. "Yo' gets nuthin' but a rope 'roun' yo' neck while he runs an' runs an' runs. Jonathan, search all the clothes."

In five of them Jonathan discovered cheap trinkets, probably held out from Tubal's greedy hands. Fitz sorted the five slaves from the line, made them stand beside Tubal.

"They gets whupped now," he said. "Ties 'em to that row o' trees." He indicated a row of old oaks.

The men were prodded with guns, kicked to their feet when they fell. One by one, they were made to encircle a tree trunk while their arms and their wrists were manacled. The remaining slaves huddled close, fearful their turn would come next.

The whip was passed from one member of the posse to another and used with a vengeance inspired by the memory of what they'd seen at the looted and pillaged farms. The night was filled with the cries of those whipped, but there was no mercy in the men who wielded the snake. Each slave was lashed into unconsciousness.

The next step was obvious. Ropes had been

procured. They were passed over the limbs of trees. The bleeding men were freed from the tree trunks, again manacled and dragged beneath the dangling ropes. The nooses were fashioned. Torches brought closer. Fitz signaled and the men were hoisted into the air. The posse turned away. No one wanted to see the agony of the dying men.

The spared slaves were herded into one of Hampshire's sheds. In the morning they would be turned over to their masters, who would inflict whatever punishment they saw fit.

Hampshire's sons passed around jugs of whiskey. Jonathan drank only a mouthful before he hurried off into the night. Fitz followed him in time to hear him retching.

"Feels like it myse'f," Fitz said. "Whut happened wasn't whut I like to see."

"The whole goddamn thing was gettin' to me right from the firs' plantation we found all them daid folks. Hangin' them whut did the killin' was no he'p."

"Knows how yo' feels," Fitz said. "But yo' agrees it had to be done. We don' hang 'em what does these things, it keeps happenin'. Folks keeps gettin' killed an' raped. On'y way to stop it is to make them who thinks they kin do this know they gets hung finally."

"Even that don't make it no easier, Papa. Knows it gots to be done. Knows why, but still . . ."

"Yo' feels the same way I did when my papa hangs rebels. Makes me sick too, but nevah lets him know it. The likes o' my papa, yo' grandpappy, mos' gone now. But when he was alive, whut he did had to be done, like we have to do this. Nevah bothered him. Did me, an' I ain't proud o' that. Even now. We goes home."

Jonathan wagged his head. "Home sho' goin' to look good. Glad Daisy not heah to know whut we did. I fetches the hosses."

Jonathan made his way through the men, his stomach still rebelling. He found the horses, mounted his own and led Fitz's. Riding past the row of hanging slaves he averted his eyes at first, then forced himself to look their way.

He brought up his horse sharply, let go of Fitz's, and rode quickly to the row of dead men. The sixth rope had been cut. Tubal was gone. Alive or dead, Jonathan didn't know. He raised his voice in a great shout that brought most of the men to his side. Fitz was one of the first. Fitz studied the length of rope in the light of a torch.

"Sho' been cut," he said. "Reckon that big bastahd daid befo' he cut down?"

"Whupped so bad mayhap that killed him an' the rope didn'," Hugh Lister said.

"Howsomever," Fitz said, "he sho' wasn't fitten to walk. He a big man. Carryin' him mighty hahd wuk. Spread out, all o' yo'. Search fo' him, but yo' finds him, don' kill him. We wants to know who cuts him down."

The search went on until after daybreak, but they found no trace of Tubal.

Finally they gave up. Fitz and Jonathan rode home slowly, exhausted, hungry, and dismayed.

"He 'live, we got mo' trouble," Fitz said.

"He strung up like the othahs," Jonathan said. "They daid. Reckon he daid too."

"Mayhap, son. But Tubal a pow'ful man. Yo' sees that neck o' his? Big 'roun' as he haid. Ain't goin' to say he daid till I sees his body an' it be cold."

"Sho' don' like this," Jonathan said.

They rode silently, nerves raw, through the quiet morning. As they approached the house, Fitz checked his horse. "Look theah, son. Evah see anythin' look so grand as Wyndward? Hopes to die heah."

"Hopes I do too," Jonathan agreed.

It was an hour after dawn. Just before the light of morning had made the stars fade, a figure had run lightly across the meadow to disappear around Wyndward mansion. If Fitz had seen that, he would have canceled all his plans for attending his daughter's graduation in Boston.

{ 17 }

THE JOURNEY TO BOSTON WAS TEDIOUS, UNCOM-
fortable, and seemingly unending. The railroad
car's economically padded benches were impossible to sleep on, Benay asserted. But finally, exhausted, she made a pillow of Fitz's shoulder,
and so they spent the night hours while the train
rolled on northward.

"Now stop yo' frettin'," Fitz told Benay
good-humoredly. "Tol' yo' bettah go No'th by
ship from Norfolk rather than this way, by railroad from Richmond."

"I'm 'fraid I'm not much fo' travelin'," Benay
admitted. "I used to think I wanted to travel
ev'ywhere, but not this way."

"It makes it any easier," Fitz said, "yo' lived
in N'Awleans, take us twelve days to Boston an'

we travels by train, boat, stage—reckon sometimes yo' walk."

"I'll try to fo'get I'm covered with cinders. My pretty dress will have to be washed two or three times to get all the grime out. I'll do my best not to speak o' the unspeakable food served us when the train stops fo' meals. I'll only remember that we're on our way to see Melanie, an' that makes up fo' all the discomfort. An' I'll also say this. We go home by ship."

"Good 'nuff," Fitz agreed. "Least yo'll get home feelin' clean."

Benay hugged his arm and looked at him lovingly. "Sho' ain't right fo' me to talk this way, darlin' Fitz, when I knows yo' plenty worried 'bout leavin' Jonathan to run the plantation."

"Worried some," Fitz admitted. "He got brains, an' he skeered o' nuthin', but don' like whut happened befo' we lef'."

"Yo' means the buck yo' hung an' got away aftah somebody cut him down?"

"That buck mighty dangerous. Reckon he a talker an' the slaves listen. An' it happens wheah we hung the sonabitch, our plantation nearest one. Whoevah cuts him down, mayhap came from Wyndward."

"Yo're worryin' too much," Benay said, "Jonathan kin take care o' anythin' that happens. 'Members whut yo' papa was like. Nobody evah fooled him an' he skeered o' nuthin'. Jonathan mo' like him than anybody else. Sho' didn' have no heroes on my side o' the family, so whut he got in courage came from yo' an' yo' papa."

"Reckon," Fitz agreed. "Jes' a bad time fo' us to leave, that's all."

"Got me some worries too," Benay admitted. "Befo' Melanie leaves to go to Boston, she kinda uppity, an' she cries too much we has to whup a slave. Yo' tol' her often 'nuff not to play with the piccaninnies, but she pay no 'tention to yo' o' me. She a mighty independent gal."

"Didn't spank her 'nuff," Fitz agreed. "Reckon too late to spank her now, she growed up."

"It's crazy to talk this way, but wonders she goin' to be 'shamed o' us, Fitz."

"'Shamed? Benay, we got mo' money than mos' folks. We runs one o' the bes' plantations in Virginia, we owns two thousand slaves——"

"Ownin' all them slaves ain't goin' to make Boston folks like us much. Yo' sho' knows whut Boston folks are like. Yo' bein' from Boston."

Fitz nodded slowly. "They's outspoken, an' they thinks family mo' impohtant than money, an' they don' like folks who gets they hands dirty in they wuk. No, don' think Melanie like that."

"Her fren's may be, Fitz, an' we embarrasses her by comin'."

"She that touchy 'bout us, then we takes her back with us an' she comes, like it or not. I ain't standin' fo' no daughter o' mine bein' so goddamn uppity."

"Well, be careful, please," Benay begged. "Wants to have her fren's like us. Yo' tells me I does anythin' wrong."

He took her hand between his. "Benay, yo' my wife. I loves yo' like I loves nobody else, an' it be like that always. Yo' cain't do, or say, anythin' wrong yo' tries to, an' anybody says anythin' yo' don' like, I busts him."

"That would get us in trouble," Benay said.

Fitz smiled. "Yo' thinkin' too much that way. Melanie goin' to be mighty happy to see us. Yo' worryin' 'bout nuthin'."

Despite Fitz's assurances, Benay's concern grew when they reached Boston. It was nearly midnight by the time they arrived at their hotel, the finest in town. Even at that hour, Boston was busy. Benay, who had known nothing larger than Richmond, was confused by the taller buildings and the quick pace. The traffic, the constant roar of noise, the lofty attitude of the desk clerks at the hotel, the opulence of the lobby—all were unsettling to her, tired as she was.

It had been agreed by letter that Melanie wasn't to try to meet their train. As they had arrived so late, they made no attempt to get in touch with her that night. And the next morning Fitz insisted they take a drive just outside of Boston. Melanie would likely have classes in the morning anyway.

They rented a carriage drawn by a pair of fine horses and Fitz set out as if he recalled every street and exit from the city, which in fact he did. Before long, they had left the city by way of Commonwealth Avenue to cross the Charles River and on to Cochituate Village. Benay was entranced by the scenery, by the birches lining the river, the thorn bushes, and the flowers.

Fitz brought up the horses as they came into sight of a stately old house, gabled, on a large acreage of lawn. Green blinds contrasted to the white paint, and red brick chimneys rose from every corner of the house.

"That," he said, "is the Eban Fitzgerald house. Built more'n a hundred yeahs ago. Got twenty-one rooms, but not much like whut we got on Wyndward. Drawin' room on the second flo' 'stead o' the first. Some bedrooms on the firs' flo'. Got an attic so big a chile kin run an' play like he outside."

"Who tol' yo' 'bout this house?" Benay asked.

"Nobody tol' me. This is wheah I was born."

"I be damned," Benay said, looking from him to the house and back again.

Fitz picked up the reins and clucked to the horses. "Now we drive to the school."

They stopped at a quiet roadside inn for their noonday meal, which Benay found delightful. But her anxiety quickened when they pulled up in front of a stately looking house on the campus of an old, renowned finishing school for girls, expensive and efficient—and staid.

Before they got out of the carriage, a tall girl in a white dress came running down the walk, waving her arms, blond hair swirling out behind her.

She was in the carriage before Benay could get out.

"Mama!" she cried. "Mama, I thought you'd never get here."

Benay hugged her tightly, then drew back. "Now yo' looks like Melanie sho' 'nuff. Yo' sounds like Melanie, but yo' too growed up. Yo' a woman."

"Whut the hell yo' think she turned into?" Fitz asked.

Melanie scrambled out of the carriage and all but leaped into her father's arms.

"Papa, you don't look a day older."

"Whut 'bout me?" Benay asked as she climbed out of the carriage.

"You're as beautiful as you ever were," Melanie said. "Maybe more beautiful. I'm so glad to see you again. It's just—just wonderful. How's Jonathan?"

"His new wife a nice gal," Fitz said. "Mighty pretty. Yo' brother 'bout as happy as he kin be."

"Sends his love, he does," Benay added. "Yo' lives in this big house?"

"It's a dormitory, Mama," Melanie explained. "There are fifty girls living here. We have our own rooms. They're really quite nice."

"Reckon," Fitz said, thinking of the fee. "Min' if I give my daughter a kiss?"

"Thought you'd never ask, Papa," Melanie teased, then threw her arms around his shoulders and kissed him soundly. "I missed you. I missed you both."

Benay beamed.

A group of girls had emerged and were walking toward them. To Benay they all looked alike—hairstyles and dresses almost identical, the same proud tilt to their heads, the same proud walk and assured manner. Melanie introduced them. Their names fell away from Fitz's and Benay's memories. The girls were very polite and stood aside to let Melanie escort her parents toward the dormitory.

One of the girls looked loftily at her companions. "I told you they'd be awkward country people. Just plain southern trash. I knew Melanie came from that kind of family the moment she entered school."

"I wouldn't say that, Rosemary," another girl said. "I sort of like her southern accent, even though she's mostly lost it."

"I can't imagine what you like about it, Angela," Rosemary said. "It's not even English. They are very ordinary people."

"Rosemary, you don't even know them," Angela said.

"I don't have to know them, Angela. They keep slaves. Did you ever think of that? They whip them and make them work until they drop dead. They buy them and sell them. It's revolting and inhumane."

"Well, I don't believe in keeping slaves," the girl named Angela admitted, "but everyone down South believes in it. You're being too harsh on Melanie's parents."

"You heard them speak. What a dreadful accent."

"Well, Melanie spoke that way when she was first admitted."

"It's to our credit that she's changed," Rosemary said stiffly. "I still say she has no business in this school."

"If they're so dreadful how come Melanie's so nice?" Angela demanded loyally. "I still say you're wrong."

"Let's find out," Rosemary said with more than a touch of maliciousness. "Let's ask the dean to see if she can get Melanie's father to make a speech at graduation exercises. I'll bet he refuses because he'll be scared, but if he does speak, I'll also bet he makes a fool of himself."

"Who'll ask the dean?" Angela said.

"I will," Rosemary said. "After all, my father gave the school five thousand dollars last year. The dean will listen to me."

The dean did listen, and quickly approved. Fitz had donated twenty-five thousand dollars only two months ago. Rosemary wasn't told that. Donations were rarely spoken of.

Fitz and Benay took their daughter to the hotel for dinner. The evening was pleasant, though Melanie winced several times when her father addressed the waiter and the captain.

Benay had quickly noted the absence of the southern accent with which Melanie had grown up.

"Mother," Melanie said, "when I got here, the girls made fun of me because of the way I talked. So I just stopped talking that way. It was easier than arguing with them. Some of the girls are very stuck-up."

"I sorta noticed that," Benay said. "To me, it sounds like they talk funny, not us."

"They just don't understand," Melanie said. "I ... I've something to tell you. I don't know how. I should have written. It's ... I think I'm in love."

"Ain't surprised, with your looks a boy comes along you like," Fitz said. "On'y when it's love, yo' don't think. Yo' knows."

"Melanie, you're only seventeen," Benay objected.

"Oh, I don't mean I'm going to get married right away," Melanie explained hastily. "It's not like that, but he's in college studying to be a lawyer. He graduates this year. I'm sure you'll like him. His name is Alan Hayes. He comes of one of the finest families in Boston. I've met his parents and they're very nice."

"Good," Fitz said. "Now all yo' needs is fo' us to like him."

"That will mean yo'll live in Boston?" Benay tried to hide her disappointment. "If yo' marry him."

"Of course, Mama. And I will marry him. I know I will. We're madly in love."

Fitz said, "Then yo' knows fo' certain."

"Of course, Papa." Melanie spoke with a trace of impatience.

"When will we meet this exceptional young man?" Benay asked.

"Oh . . ." Melanie hesitated. "Well, he's studying for his final tests now. That means he can't see me until graduation. He said he'd try to come. He has to pass his examinations, so he's real busy."

"Yes," Benay said flatly. "Knows whut yo' means."

Melanie toyed with her dessert. "There's more. It concerns you, Papa."

"Now whut I done?" Fitz asked. He was enjoying his daughter, and paid scant attention to her assertions that she would marry this Yankee.

"It's what . . . you'll be asked to do, Papa, tomorrow at the graduation exercises. The dean is going to ask you to make a speech to the whole school."

"Well, I'm real proud," Fitz said. "It's an honuh I sho' cain't refuse."

"I wish you would," Melanie said, with lowered eyes and voice.

"Whut yo' mean by that?" Benay asked sharply.

"Papa ... Mama," Melanie sighed deeply. "I love you both. Honestly I do. You're the kindest, most wonderful parents anyone could have."

"Except for whut?" Benay demanded.

"It's the way you talk, Papa. The girls used to laugh at me, and they'll laugh at you."

"Reckon they won't," Fitz said calmly.

"I know them. I even think some of the girls asked the dean to have you speak so they can ... they can make fun of you."

"Because of the way I talks?" Fitz asked, bewildered.

"They'll say you're just ... just a ... just a southern farmer."

"Whut of it?" Fitz demanded. "That's whut I am, an' I ain't 'shamed o' it."

"Don' make the speech, Fitz," Benay advised. "Don' wants our daughter to feel 'shamed."

"I makes it anyway. Melanie, yo' jes' tells any who laughs that I'm yo' papa an' whut I does, or how I does it, is right, far as yo' is concerned. Will you' do that?"

"I'll try, Papa. Honestly I will."

"Cain't ask fo' no mo' than that. Now we bes' takes yo' back 'cause yo' got things to do befo' tomorruh when yo' gets yo' diploma. Goin' to be real proud o' yo', Melanie."

"Yo' secon' in the whole class," Benay said. "Makes me proud too. Now yo' jes' don' worry none 'bout yo' papa makin' that speech. I have my way, he goin' to stan' up an' say he ain't prepared fo' makin' a speech, an' wants to be excused."

"I—I don't know what to say," Melanie was nearing tears. "I feel so terrible even suggesting it. I think I'm wrong. Yes, I'm so wrong. Make the speech, Papa, and if Rosemary makes any remarks, I'll yank her hair so hard her head will hurt for a week. You make the speech, Papa."

"I will," Fitz said simply. "Let's get yo' back now."

Returning from the school, Benay vented her feelings about the affair.

"She grew up too fas', Fitz. Listens to these gals talkin' 'roun' the school, an' they talks like nobody else on this heah earth, 'ceptin' them. They selfish. Wishes we didn' send Melanie heah. She gettin' as selfish as the othahs. Now she talkin' gettin' married. She seventeen. . . ."

"Yo' wasn't an ol' lady, I marries yo'," Fitz reminded her with a grin. "Yo' was young 'nuff to dreen a man eve'y damn night."

"Wondahs whut they say yo' talked like that befo' these gals, Fitz. Reckon they think it funny?"

"Benay, I don' give a goddamn whut they thinks. But I'll make a speech they won't fo'get in a hurry."

"They folks goin' to be theah too, Fitz."

"Good. Makes it bettah fo' me. Now yo' stop yo' frettin', Benay. Knows these folks, I do. Yo'll see whut I means tomorruh."

"Fitz, yo' kin speak this heah no'thern way. 'Less yo' fo'got it."

"Nevah fo'gets it, Benay. Whut 'bout this heah marryin' business?"

"Don' know whut we kin do."

"Melanie comin' back with us. Yo' heah her

say anythin' she don' want to go back to Wyndward?"

"No, not a word. An' that worries me, 'cause
she thinkin' 'bout goin' back, she say somethin'
'bout it."

Fitz leaned over and kissed Benay's cheek.
"She goin' back, she knows it or not. She wants
to or not. She goin' back."

"I think it best. I does, Fitz. Fo' her sake,
an' ours."

Benay was fairly satisfied with Fitz's response to the speech-making and his insistence
that Melanie come home. But in the morning,
when they were ready to leave for the graduation exercises, she was completely dismayed at
Fitz's clothes.

Benay had brought a dress especially for the
occasion, a checked muslin printed in mauve and
purple in a pattern of roses. The skirt had flounces
shaped in the cone design. Narrow borders match-
ing the flounces trimmed the bodice. The sleeves
were a wide version of the pagoda form with a
puff above the deep frill of the opening. She always had a parasol to match her costume, and
this one was lined with gathered silk muslin in
mauve and covered with the checked muslin of
the dress. A lace awning fell from the edges of
the parasol, not only giving further protection to
her fair skin, but casting alluring shadows on her
face, serving to accent her natural beauty. A bonnet, bowed attractively beneath her chin, framed
her face. Short silk gloves completed her costume.

Fitz wore a frock coat, a white shirt with a
string tie, and a huge straw plantation hat. His

shoes were black with white spats and his trousers a striped, formal pair.

It was the hat that outraged Benay. "Wheah in hell yo' gets that hat, Fitz? Yo' ain't wearin' it. I won't let yo' wear it."

"This heah," Fitz said, "is the mark o' a southern gen'mun. Figgers I look somethin' like Colonel Coldwell. Ain't as fat o' co'se, an' ain't that old, but I'm a southern gen'mun an' nobody's goin' to mistake me fo' anythin' else."

She argued and pleaded, but Fitz wore the hat, and when they walked down the aisle of the auditorium, it drew snickers. Melanie, in the front row, turned crimson with embarrassment.

There were speeches by school officials. Two prominent citizens lauded the school, the girls, and Boston, in set, dull speeches they'd probably made fifty times before. Then the Dean, a portly, well-bosomed matron with eyeglasses on a cord, introduced Fitz.

"Melanie Turner's father and mother have honored our school by coming all the way from Virginia. I think it only fitting that Mr. Turner give us an idea of what the South is like. Will you do us the honor, Mr. Turner?"

Fitz left the big hat on his chair, to Benay's relief. He walked confidently onto the stage and took his place at the center of it, standing in front of the lectern, which he disdained.

"Ladies an' gen'mun," he said, in rich southern dialect, "I comes heah to see my daughter gets herse'f graduated. Thinks this heah be a fine school an' likes ev'ybody I sees. So far."

Melanie almost covered her face with her

hands in sheer torture as Rosemary, behind her, snickered openly. So did a number of the other girls, and some of their parents cast looks of surprise at one another.

"Fin's Boston mos' int'restin'," Fitz went on. "Now you-all would fin' Virginny int'restin' too, so I tells yo' 'bout wheah we lives an' wheah Melanie grows up."

The snickering was turning to muffled laughter. Fitz heard it and his smile grew more expansive, while Benay felt like sliding off her chair.

"We gots two thousan' slaves on ouah li'l fahm. Two thousan' niggers whut we makes wuk fo' us an' we pays 'em in vittles an' a cabin, an' some clothes. They gets sassy, we whups 'em good. We keeps 'em down."

"Mr. Turner," one man in the audience called out, "do you think that's a kindly thing to do? They are human beings."

"Mistah," Fitz said, "they ain't human. We nevah says they's human. They slaves. They bo'n to serve us an' that's all they good fo'."

"I do not agree with you," the man shouted. He was angry now. "You people cannot keep men and women enslaved forever."

"Reckon yo' right 'bout that," Fitz said. "Times they dies."

"Sir!" The spokesman for the whole audience now stood up. "I resent what you are saying. I resent you."

Fitz smiled with the innocence of someone who could not be embarrassed by anything.

"Let me tell you, sir, something about slavery you have never, in your infinite wisdom, thought of. I refer to your cotton mills. All up and down this state, cotton mills are booming. Did it ever occur to you that without the cotton we raise, there wouldn't be any mills? And you wouldn't be here in this expensive school where your daughters have been educated. You gentlemen—and I believe some of you ladies as well—enjoy a cigar or a pipe of tobacco. We raise the finest Virginia bright in the world on our farm. Incidentally, that farm is half as big as the Commonwealth of Massachusetts.

"You enjoy the racetrack, no doubt, and you see the finest horses racing for you to bet on. I raise some of those horses. I have sold many of them to people who live in Boston and its environs. Do you understand what I'm getting at?"

"Mr. Turner, sir," the spokesman said, in a mollified voice, "we'll all be obliged if you will enlighten us further. We don't understand the connection."

"Without slaves, there wouldn't be any cotton, or tobacco, or racehorses, or much of anything else. Not too long ago, slavery existed right here in Boston. You can look that up in your fine libraries. White people bought and sold slaves, not for farming, but for their own personal comfort. In the South we tried to work our own farms, but they are just too big and the work is too hard. So we brought in indentured people. Criminals from Europe, families who sold themselves into virtual slavery for so many years, if we paid their expenses to reach this country. They were unable to stand up under the hard work. Then we discovered this kind of work could only be done by people who were born and lived on the outside, not in comfortable homes. People who could walk for twenty miles and scarcely draw a hard breath. People who could stalk wild animals for days and days, and not grow tired. I refer to Africans.

"So, some were brought here and they proved to be most successful. In those days, nobody had any money to pay for help. Slaves then sold for as little as twenty dollars, whereas we now get two thousand, and more, for a strong, healthy buck. To operate the kind of farms that could produce the things you people in the North need for your factories, we brought in slaves by the thousands. Now the cotton was grown, the sugarcane harvested, the tobacco cured and prepared for market. And you people up here prospered as we did. You grew rich and fat and you damned us for keeping black people enslaved. Let me tell all of you, whatever you have in the way of worldly goods, was also earned by the sweat of our slaves. If we could exist without them, and had to pay for our help, the costs of what you now buy would triple and more."

"Mr. Turner, I agree that you make sense, but slavery is not a matter we can approve of in this modern world."

"My friends," Fitz said, "I don't insist that slavery will always be necessary. One day machinery will take its place. Eli Whitney proved that. Someday there will be no more slaves, but at present slaves are necessary to us. And to you, even though you decry the existence of that system. And please do not, for a moment, believe that only Southerners are responsible for it."

"What about whipping slaves?" someone asked. "Is that really necessary?"

Fitz said, "You must understand one thing. We have enslaved people who are used to freedom. Even more freedom than you yourselves would seek. They came here under restraint. At this moment, there are almost as many slaves in Virginia as there are white people. Our slaves are physically far better than we can ever hope to be. But they are not educated, they are easily led, and without restraint, they are dangerous. They rebel. My wife's father was decapitated during one rebellion. If all of them went on a rampage, we could not long stand up to them. They must be intimidated, made to obey every small command, never permitted to ask questions. We refuse to allow them the fundamentals of an education because that would inspire them to rebellion. We have a problem, ladies and gentlemen, and it can be controlled only by the methods we use. Nothing else will suffice. We are not unholy devils. Personally, I hate to whip a slave as much as I'd hate to be whipped myself. But it is sometimes necessary. Now I think I've taken up enough of your time. Thank you very much for your attention." He turned to face the school officials. "And I sincerely thank you for giving my daughter such a fine education, amidst an atmosphere of love and tolerance and understanding."

He walked off the stage to mild applause that swiftly grew until it rang in his ears. Melanie intercepted Fitz and hugged and kissed him. Some of the men shook his hand, some looked the other way. Fitz sat down.

"Those things yo' said," Benay whispered, "nevah thinks o' them myse'f. Loves yo' fo' whut yo' did. Nex' time yo' s'prises me like that, I busts somethin' ovah yo' haid an' I sleeps alone fo' ... mayhap even a week."

"Benay, yo' has my promise nevah again to s'prise yo'. Now we mixes with these heah fine people an' reckon we meets this heah boy Melanie thinks she in love with. Saw him holdin' her hand fo' I went to speak. Nice-lookin' boy. Jonathan could take ten o' him without breathin' hard. That don' mean nothin'. Folks diff'runt up heah."

Benay's easy ways and her warmth, abetted by her beauty, attracted both men and women, and she was soon talking happily with a number of people. Fitz, cornered by a dozen important men, was busy answering questions about the economy and the prices of cotton, sugar, and tobacco.

Finally, Melanie was able to get the two of them together. With her was a young man with ruddy cheeks, only an inch taller than Melanie, slim with the slenderness of youth. He had dark brown eyes and, in contrast, rather light-colored hair. He was impeccably dressed to fit the occasion and when he looked at Melanie, it was with the kind of love both Benay and Fitz recognized as their own kind.

"Mama, this is Alan Hayes." Melanie glowed with pride.

"I'm very happy to meet you, Mr. Hayes," Benay said.

Fitz extended a hand. "A pleasure, Mr. Hayes."

"Papa, that was a wonderful speech," Melanie exclaimed. "I loved it. But when you started talking without your southern accent, I thought you were someone else."

"Ain't a bad accent," Fitz said. "Melanie speaks highly of you, sir."

"I'm honored to meet you and Mrs. Turner," Alan said. "Melanie told me her mother was beautiful. I see now where she inherited her beauty."

"You're quite right, sir," Fitz said. "Did you enjoy my little speech? It was quite impromptu, you understand."

"Oh yes. It was a fine speech. You gave us a better understanding of why you feel you need slavery. However, I hope I will not offend you, sir, by saying it is not very long for this country. It's going to end—perhaps sooner than you think."

Fitz shrugged. "When it does, we'll take whatever steps are necessary. Perhaps to preserve it, perhaps to agree that it must go out of existence. It all depends on circumstances."

"I intend to go into politics," Alan said. "My father is a congressman and that's what I aim to be."

"A fine ambition," Fitz said. "I'm sure, from what I hear, that Congress is in dire need of new blood. Young blood. I wish I could vote for you, sir."

Benay said, "Melanie, we expect you to return to Virginia with us. Yo' unnerstan's that?"

"Yes, Mama, I know I have to go back. I didn't want to, but now . . . well, I want to see Jonathan again and meet his wife and—and see everyone again."

"We leave by ship in two days," Fitz said. "Can't stay any longer than that. There's been trouble. Jonathan is there, but sometimes two heads are best when it comes to deciding how to deal with trouble. Alan, you are most welcome to come visit anytime you like."

"All I'll say to that," Benay announced, "is if yo' comes to see Melanie, an' yo' travels by railroad, we knows yo' sho' 'nuff in love with her."

{ 18 }

JONATHAN COULD FEEL TKE UNREST. SOME SLAVES refused to look up when told to do so. Some went out of their way to avoid any sort of encounter with Jonathan, were leery of Hong Kong and almost contemptuous of the overseers.

"I kin smell it," Jonathan said to Daisy. "Las' Sunday on'y 'bout half—or less—comes to the meetin'. I gets the ʒeeʹin' hey's skeered."

"Of what?" Daisy asked. "You haven't done any whipping. Not once since your father went North. These slaves have nothing to be afraid of."

"That we knows of," Jonathan amended her statement. "They's wukkin' like always, on'y they slothin' some. Cain't put a finger on it, but somethin's wrong heah."

"Maybe Hong Kong would know about it," Daisy suggested.

"Mayhap he does. Soon's they comes in from the fields, I'll go down an' talk to him. Hong Kong one fine man. Trusts him like I trusts yo'. Trouble is, Hong Kong black an' no mattah how he feels 'bout us, an' the way we treats him, he still got sof'ness fo' othah blacks. Hates to try an' make him talk."

"I don't think you could," Daisy said. "Since your father and mother went to Boston, I've come to know the slaves far better than before."

"Yo minds 'em, Daisy? Bein' 'roun' slaves? Black folks?"

"You noticed that, did you?"

"Kinda noticed. Shies 'way from 'em, yo' do."

"There are so many of them, Jonathan. What could we do if they decided they didn't like being slaves anymore and just went off? How could we stop them?"

"Couldn't," Jonathan acknowledged. "But all plantation owners gets togethah an' we stops 'em. Wheah they got to go? Walk to the No'th takes days an' they starves on the way."

"But what if they don't realize that and go anyway?"

"Now yo' knows whut skeers the hell outen us." Jonathan looked across the dining-room table at his wife. "Yo' feels good, honey? Kinda seem yo' a bit peaked."

"I feel fine," Daisy said stoutly. "Never better."

"Mayhap yo' ain't gettin' 'nuff sleep lately."

"If I'm not," Daisy said with a laugh, "I like

[374]

it that way. I do love you, Jonathan. I know what I was when you found—"

Jonathan held up his hand quickly. "Yo' ain't said a word jes' now. Didn' heah a thing. 'Cept yo' says yo' is in love with me. Mo' than anybody else in the worl' kin be in love?"

"Yes," she said. "Yes, Jonathan. More than anyone in the world."

"Yo' a liar, Daisy," Jonathan said casually. "Yo' lyin' in yo' teeth."

"Jonathan!" she exclaimed in horror. "What in the world are you saying?"

"Reckon way I feels, I love yo' more. So yo' lyin'."

She jumped up from the table and hurried over to take his head between her hands and kiss him long and ardently.

"Now yo' reckon I goes to see Hong Kong aftah that?" Jonathan asked.

"You go see him," she said. "Just get back soon. I'm going to have Domingo prepare a bath. She's a good girl, Jonathan. She's warm and attentive. I like her very much."

"Knows yo' do, an' she loves yo' right back. Thinkin' I'll ask Papa to manumit her soon's he comes back. Won't change anythin'. She won' go 'way. Nowheah to go an' nobody to go to. So she stays, but she a free nigger. We kin pay her somethin' an' do things fo' her we cain't do she a slave."

"Wonderful," Daisy said. "I used to think people who kept slaves were cruel."

"They on'y cruel to they wives," Jonathan said. "Means I won't be back till aftah yo' has yo' bath."

He walked briskly down to the rows of slave cabins and knocked on Hong Kong's door. It was opened quickly by Hong Kong. Seawitch, seated at the table, arose.

"Evenin', Seawitch," Jonathan said. "Now yo' sit. Ain't no call yo' has to get up I comes in. Me or anyone else. Yo' lookin' good these days. Like yo' gets younger."

"Me?" Seawitch cackled with glee. "Mastah, I gits old ev'y day, but I sho' likes it heah. Ain't no place I wants to git ol' in 'ceptin' right heah."

"Good! Hong Kong, I comes to ask if yo' sees anythin' makes yo' wondah somethin' wrong heah."

Hong Kong shook his massive head. "Heerd nuthin', suh. Yo' thinkin' somethin' goin' on?"

"Don' know. Jes' feels somethin'. Ain't asked the overseers whut they thinks. Mos'ly they sees nothin' anyways, 'ceptin' a slave who sloths. Been much slothin', Hong Kong?"

Hong Kong frowned deeply. "Reckon, suh, mayhap they is. Cain't notice it 'nuff to raise hell, but weedin' ain' goin' fas' as sometimes. Ketches lots o' whisperin' an' it stops quick I comes 'long."

"Know whut makes me wondah? That buck we hangs, an' who got cut down befo' he daid. Thinks he still alive. Now . . . whut his name? Tubal! Yes—Tubal. Thinks he stirrin' up all that trouble befo' an' gets away to hide somewheah an' stir up mo' trouble. Yo' hears anythin' 'bout him?"

"No suh, nuthin'. He comes heah an' I kills him. Sweahs I kills him."

"Yo' comes across him, yo' be mighty keerful,

Hong Kong. He one big nigger, an' strong. Yo' ain't gettin' any youngah."

"I kin whup any nigger on this heah plantation, suh."

Jonathan turned to leave. "Keeps yo' ears open, Hong Kong. Don' want no trouble heah while Papa in Boston."

"Keeps listenin', suh."

Jonathan made his way down to the stables. He pushed open the big door and heard Dundee scrambling about in the loft.

Jonathan climbed the ladder until his head was above the loft floor. "Whut in hell goin' on, Dundee?"

"Was sleepin', massa, suh. Gittin' dressed, I was."

"Come on down," Jonathan said. "Wants to talk to yo'."

"Yas suh, massa, suh. Comin' down."

He descended the ladder hurriedly and he stood before Jonathan with lowered head, until he recalled that he was no longer required to do so. He raised his head and looked Jonathan in the eye, somewhat fearfully. Jonathan had nearly caught him studying; he'd barely got the books hidden in time.

"Talked to Hong Kong an' Seawitch," Jonathan said. "They both fine. Now wants to ask yo' whut I asked them. Keeps gettin' a feelin' somethin' goin' on heah. Don' know whut, but worries me some. Yo' heah anythin' makes yo' wondah?"

"Stays in the stables, massa, suh. Don' get 'bout any mo'. Sees nuthin', massa, suh."

"Yo' heah 'bout a big buck name of Tubal?"

Dundee promptly shook his head. "No, suh, massa, suh. Heers he a bad niggah, but nuthin' else."

"Yo' evah sees him, yo' knows him he come by?"

"No suh. Nevah saw him, suh."

Jonathan glanced down at Dundee's right hand. "Whut that on yo' fingers, Dundee?"

Dundee raised his hand quickly and looked at the ink stains from a quill so ancient it sometimes dripped. He held his breath for a moment and then studied the fingers more closely.

"Was poundin' bent nails at the forge, massa, suh. Reckon I hits my han' much as I hits the nails, suh."

Jonathan seized his hand and lifted it up. "Yo' sho' is black, Dundee, an' this heah bruise even blackah. Hurt some?"

"On'y a li'l, massa, suh. Ain't nothin'."

"Well, like I tol' Hong Kong, yo' keeps yo' eyes open an' repo'ts anythin' looks wrong."

"Yes suh, massa, suh." Perspiration beaded Dundee's forehead. He had never been so frightened in his life.

"Oh yes, an' mayhap we goes to Norfolk fo' long. Racin' season openin', yo' makes sho' the mare in good shape."

"She ready right now, massa, suh. She ready she evah goin' to be."

"That's fine. She win an' yo' gets all the silvah dollahs yo' big hands kin hold."

"Thanks yo', massa, suh. Sho'ly thanks yo', suh."

Jonathan nodded briskly and left him. Dundee wilted against the door of the mare's stall. Then he hastily went to a pail of water and washed off the ink. He was still weak-legged when he climbed back to his loft.

He hadn't quite told the truth to Jonathan. More than once he'd seen Alameda stealthily moving about after dark. By the way she acted, she was up to no good. She broke the rules by being out of her cabin by night beyond the slave area. Perhaps she was only meeting some young buck who already had a wife.

Jonathan returned to the mansion by way of the kitchen. Elegant and two scullery maids were hard at work doing the dishes. The work came to an abrupt stop and all three stood before him, the scullery maids with their heads down, Elegant with hers raised and her big, fat face smiling serenely.

"Elegant, yo' sees or heahs anythin' goin' on don' soun' right to yo'?"

"Goin' on, suh?"

"Like mayhap yo' finds some o' yo' food stolen."

"No suh. Nuthin' like that, suh," she lied blandly. Stealing food from the kitchen had been going on now for fifty years. Sometimes she knew who was guilty, most times she had no idea. Some food had been missing these last few weeks, but that was nothing to become alarmed about.

"Well, watch out. Tells me yo' heahs anythin'."

"Yes suh, massa, I tells yo'."

Jonathan went on into the mansion. He knew Daisy was upstairs, warm and fragrant from her bath. He longed to go to her at once, but he went instead into the library, where he sat at his father's desk and tried to sort out the various suspicions scurrying about in his mind.

His father had been concerned with the escape of Tubal, that awful night of riot and blood. Wyndward had been the nearest plantation for a man like Tubal to have gone for refuge. If he traveled too far, he was likely to have been at least seen, if not caught. And if he remained close at hand, living in the forest, there should have been a few signs left as he moved about. Jonathan had searched part of the forest without finding a trace. Still, that weird feeling persisted, as if Tubal was somewhere close by and Jonathan sensed it.

He finally gave up and joined Daisy, who was already in bed, with Domingo standing by. The slave gave Jonathan a warm smile and disappeared.

"You find anything?" Daisy asked.

He shook his head. "Nobody knows nothin', sees nothin'. Still I got this feelin'."

"You're worrying too much," Daisy said. She threw aside the bedclothes. "Get in here with me and I'll show you how to stop worrying."

"Well now, that ain't a bad idea. Makes it wuth comin' home."

He quickly removed his clothes and got into bed. Their love-making was not swift, not something to be gotten over with. They lay clasped in one another's arms for a long time.

"You're still worrying," Daisy said. "I guess I haven't got the old power any more."

"Yo' got all I kin handle," he said. "Cain't he'p it. Knows mayhap I be plain crazy, but that damn feelin' won't go 'way. Wish Papa was heah."

"Darling," Daisy whispered. "You can take care of anything. Stop your fretting and take care of me."

Late in the morning, next day, Jonathan was still prowling about searching for some small thing that would confirm his still vague, even unreal suspicions. Calcutta, lanky legs pedaling as fast as he could run, which was not very fast, hailed Jonathan from a distance. He ran up, panting so hard he had to stand there and struggle with gasps as he tried to speak.

"Missy say yo' comes back quick, massa, suh. Say yo' gots comp'any."

"Who?" Jonathan demanded.

"Reckon it be man yo' calls Majah, suh. An' he chile."

"Some chile," Jonathan grunted. Of all people he didn't want to see, it was Major Apperson and his hot-blooded daughter-in-law, Clarissa.

Jonathan walked back casually. The longer he took, the less time the company would stay. Even Calcutta beat him back to the house, which amazed Calcutta more than anyone else.

Major Apperson was his usual red-faced, jovial, important self. He arose and offered his flabby hand. Jonathan shook it and then sat down. Across from him sat Clarissa, her rather attractive face wearing the kind of smile that told him amply that she was willing if he was. He ignored her.

Daisy came in, followed by a maid with a tray of drinks. They were passed around. Then Major Apperson said, "Sho' didn't know yo' papa in the No'th. Reckon he talkin' theah to stop all this heah agitation goin' on 'bout us keepin' slaves."

"I told you, Major," Daisy said, "that they went to see Melanie graduate."

"So yo' did, ma'am. So yo' did."

"Bets Melanie all growed up," Clarissa said.

"Keep yo' mouth shet while I talks business," her father-in-law admonished her roughly.

"Major," Jonathan said, "I be real busy these days. Kin'ly state yo' business, suh."

"Intendin' to, suh. Wants to 'range fo' a two-hoss race. Yo' mare an' one I bought some time back."

"Whut yo' talkin' 'bout, two-hoss race?"

"I be on the board o' directors at the race track in Norfolk an' I gets to say whut I wants an' I gets it. Kin fix it so yo' mare runs agin mine fo' fifty thousand dollahs to the winnah."

Daisy drew in a sharp breath. That was more money than she had ever heard offered as a wager.

"Cain't wait fo' yo' papa to come home. We opens the track with our race, suh. Yo' got the backbone to risk yo' hoss agains' mine? Or do yo' have to wait till yo' papa gets home so yo' kin ask him?"

"I runnin' this heah plantation, suh," Jonathan said hotly. "I does whut I thinks bes'."

"Well then, we got us a deal, son?"

"When this heah race?"

"Nex' Thursday."

"Fifty thousan', winnah take all?"

"Winnah take all," the Major agreed.

"We be theah," Jonathan said. Major Apperson smiled, offered his hand.

"Sees yo' at the track. Gets a good stall fo' yo'. Needs a jockey, gets one too."

"Gets my own," Jonathan said. "Fixin' fo' a stall is fine. We be theah."

Major Apperson seized Clarissa's wrist and hauled her out of the chair. "Stop lookin' at Jonathan like yo' in bed with him." He glanced at Jonathan. "This heah gal nevah thinks o' anythin' 'cep gettin' in bed. Don' give a goddamn who with, jes' so she gets in bed. Thinks she kinda crazy. Come on, Clarissa."

Apperson yanked her out of the room and pushed her along the reception hall. Jonathan sat back for a moment, clapped his hands and yelled for Calcutta.

"Brings us rum an' cold watah. Yo' runs, or yo' ass gets blacker'n 'tis now."

"Runs, massa, suh," Calcutta said. His first half-dozen steps were something akin to running. After that, he loafed along. These days he felt quite secure. Jonathan wasn't as apt to kick him as his father was.

"What was that all about?" Daisy asked.

"Man wants a race."

"Fifty thousand dollars is a lot of money for one race. He must think he'll win. But why?"

"Way I sees this, Major Apperson, he hates Papa like poison. Hates me too, reckon. Knows Papa away an' thinks mayhap he kin put somethin' ovah on me an' laugh 'bout it when Papa get home."

"What can he do? In a two-horse race there

can't be any cheating. It would be too obvious.

"Knows that. But he got somethin' up his sleeve. He be a member o' the board of directors at that racetrack an' he gets away with anythin' he likes. Tells Dundee he gets the mare ready an' runs her tomorrow for timin'."

"Oh, Jonathan, how awful if you lose fifty thousand dollars!"

"Nuthin' awful 'bout it. Papa don' give a damn I lose that money, but he madder'n hell the Major cheats me outen it. Gots to do some real thinkin'. When Papa be home? Knows he write in the lettah we got day fo' yestiddy."

"Won't be for a week or ten days after the race. They're coming by sail—a schooner. That's a slow way to travel."

"Nothin' I kin do then 'cept watch ev'ythin' the Major does. Keep Dundee lookin' too. He one smaht nigger an' he wants to win the race more'n I do. Reckon we kin spot whutevah the Major got in mind."

"Let's hope so. Think how proud your father will be if you manage to outwit the Major."

"Thinkin' mos' 'bout how mad he be I don't."

"Let's forget that for now," Daisy said. "Melanie is coming back with them. Please tell me about her. Do you think she'll like me?"

"Cain't he'p but like yo'. Don' know 'bout Melanie. She jes' ovah fifteen she leave an' goes to school. Nevah had to do much o' anythin', an' she kinda snooty. Like she bettah'n anybody else. Mighty pretty gal, though. Mayhap she changed. Hopes so. An' she take too kin'ly to niggers. Cain't treat 'em way she did. Mama spanks her fo' this. Papa—he thinks she kin do nothin' wrong. Reckon he did think so, he jes' tells her be mo' careful. She be Papa's li'l gal, but she don' fool Mama none."

"I'll be more than anxious to meet her now. She might listen to me."

"If yo' take down her britches an' spank her good."

"Now, Jonathan, you know I wouldn't do that. I think you ought to tell me more about Clarissa. There is an interesting woman. She couldn't take her eyes off you. Anything ever happen between you two?"

Calcutta arrived with the tray of drinks, spilled over as usual, and saved the day for Jonathan. Calcutta wondered for hours afterward why he hadn't been yelled at, even kicked, for he'd certainly been very slow. He'd had trouble with the cork on the jug of bourbon. Not that he prepared bourbon for Jonathan and Daisy, but Calcutta had been more in the mood for corn and he had to open a fresh bottle.

Jonathan was up early the next morning. After a quick breakfast, he was scolded because he didn't eat enough by Elegant's standards. He hurried to the stable. Dundee was at work, as all slaves had to be at dawn.

"Dundee, reckon yo' gets into the city sooner'n we 'spected. Yesterday Major Apperson comes. Yo' knows him?"

"Yas suh, massa, suh. Knows him, I does."

"Know whut he like?"

"Sonabitch cheats eve'ybody."

"Yo' soun' like my papa."

"Heahs him say that 'bout Major, suh. Ten times, reckon."

Jonathan chuckled and ordered Dundee to saddle the mare and get her on the track for timing. Dundee, overcome with an eagerness he couldn't hide, did so in quick time. Jonathan stood at the rail, signaled for Dundee to start the mare running and timed the run carefully.

Dundee pulled up and looked at Jonathan inquiringly. Jonathan finished making notes in a small book.

"Busted las' runnin'. She in bes' condition. I 'preciate that, Dundee."

"Yes suh. Reckon I 'preciate it too, suh. The mare has got good blood."

Jonathan heard that change in Dundee's speech. It was almost like listening to his father switch from southern to northern—or the way Jonathan did it himself.

"Wants to time her fo' a long run. Yo' gets her stahted an' goes 'roun' the track ten times."

"Yes suh, massa, suh. Ten times."

It was an unusual order, but Jonathan didn't explain, only waved Dundee to begin the race against time. As soon as Dundee pulled away and reached the opposite side of the track, Jonathan went back to the stable and climbed the ladder to Dundee's loft.

The abrupt change in speech was nothing by itself, but when Dundee agreed, without protest, to run ten times around the track, Jonathan was surer than ever that Dundee had really changed. Slaves didn't know how to count to ten.

It didn't take him long to uncover the section of wall behind which were hidden several more books than Themba had owned, along with tightly folded copies of the *Liberator* and other newspapers, paper covered with Dundee's still primitive writing, the quill and inkwell that Reverend Whitehead had brought him.

"I be damned," Jonathan exclaimed. He put everything back, except for one folded copy of the *Liberator*, which he left on Dundee's pallet. He then returned to the track in time to see Dundee's worried expression as he went by for the ninth time. Jonathan knew what he was worried about. He timed the mare and delighted in the result. Dundee rode through the gate Jonathan opened for him. He rode to the stable and removed the saddle. He cooled the mare, rubbed her down, and turned her into the stall. Then he climbed to his loft. The first thing he saw was the copy of the *Liberator* on the pillow.

Dundee let his legs dangle off the edge of the loft, down alongside the ladder. He had never been so confused in his life. By now Jonathan should have hauled him off to the whipping shed, given him a hundred lashes, chained him, and scheduled him for the vendue table as soon as possible. Yet he'd said nothing.

Dundee made up his mind. He turned around, descended the ladder, and hurried outside to proceed straight to the mansion to confront Jonathan.

He skidded to a stop. Jonathan was seated on the track rail, beckoning him over. Dundee sighed and approached him slowly. He knew what was coming now.

"Massa, suh, gots somethin' to tell yo'. Kin I talk, suh?"

"Yo' kin talk."

"Been learnin' to read an' write, suh. Kin read a newspaper pretty good. Gots me copies o' the *Liberator*."

"That a bad paper fo' a slave to read, Dundee."

"Yes suh, massa, suh. I reads it on'y 'cause it learns me words. Don' unnerstan' mos' whut I reads theah."

"Whut yo' want to read an' write fo', Dundee?"

"Tells the truth, suh. Ev'y word I says is true. Don' lie. Not to yo', suh. Knows whut yo' gots to do 'bout it, but tells yo' anyhow. Thinks I be free someday an' wants to know 'nuff so I kin git 'long. That's all, suh."

"Whut makes yo' think yo' evah goin' to be free?"

"Thinks so, massa, suh."

"Yo' reads that in the *Liberator*?"

"Knows it befo' I sees the *Liberator*, suh. Feels it in my bones, I does."

"Now yo' listen to me, yo' skalawag. Yo' should be hided till yo' raw an' then maybe strung up."

"Knows that, suh."

"But yo' risked it 'cause yo' thinks it that impohtant yo' studies?"

"Yas suh. Wuth it."

"Yo' an' me, Dundee, bo'n on the same night. Reckon it wasn't a very good night, whut I hears. Knows yo' ain't no ord'nary nigger. Knows that fo' a long time, an' my papa knows it too. Papa away now an' I in charge heah. So whut I says is whut happens."

"Yes suh. I goes down to the whuppin' shed."

"No! Ain't goin' to whup yo'. Takes yo' to meet my wife an' I asks her to teach yo' readin' an' writin' an' 'rithmetic. An' I tries to fin' my old schoolbooks fo' yo' to use."

Dundee's head was swimming. "Yes *suh*, massa, suh!"

"Yo' tells anybody whut goin' on, then yo' goes to the whuppin' shed."

"Yes suh, massa, suh."

"That all yo' kin say?"

"Massa, suh, don' know whut to say. Thinks I'm dreamin'. Yo' standin' theah an' sayin' I kin learn to read an' write an' I don' gits whupped."

"Yo' got any idee why I doin' this fo' yo'?"

"No suh, massa, suh."

Jonathan nodded. "Then I'll tell yo'. Hong Kong a fine man, bes' head driver on any plantation, but he gettin' on an' mayhap we goin' to need yo' to take his place. Hong Kong doin' fine, but if he kin read an' write an' do some figgerin', he'd do bettah. Times changin', Dundee. Don' know whut's com'n', but whutevah it is, we goin' to be ready. Wants someone we kin trust, an' reckon we gets no trouble with yo'."

"Massa, suh, sweahs I does whut yo' asks. Sweahs I fin's any trouble, I takes keer o' it. This heah the bes' plantation in the worl', reckon, an' I aims to he'p keep it so."

"Come 'long then. We walks to the big house. Goin' to tell my overseers yo' a driver now. Means yo' kin go 'bout at night an' yo' kin burn a light in yo' loft late as yo' wants. Yo' gets bettah clothes an' from now on, yo' comes to the back do' an' Elegant feeds yo' whut we eats."

"I thanks yo', suh. Ain't goin' to say it agin, but I thanks yo' an' I do all I kin fo' this heah plantation."

"Good 'nuff. Now, the firs' thing we gots to do is try an' guess whut that sonabitch Major Apperson up to. He gots somethin' in mind an' it sho' ain't good fo' us. Yo' thinks 'bout it, Dundee. We talks latah."

He led Dundee into the mansion by the front door, something that had never been done before except with house servants. Dundee was impressed beyond belief at what he saw in the reception hall, and the drawing room all but stunned him in its size and beauty.

"Yo' goes on in," Jonathan said. "I be back."

Dundee wandered slowly through the large room. Suddenly Daisy got up from a high-backed chair which had concealed her presence. She turned, saw Dundee, and screamed.

Jonathan came rushing into the room.

"I—I was frightened," stammered Daisy. "I —this slave——"

"He Dundee. Tol' yo' 'bout him befo'. Yo' knows whut he done? Learnin' hisse'f how to read an' write."

"Oh, Jonathan, you don't mean to punish——"

"Says I lets him learn how an' mayhap yo' kin he'p."

"I—help?" Daisy looked astonished.

"When yo' gets the time, yo' shows him how to read an' write good. I goin' to the attic an' brings down my ol' schoolbooks he kin use."

"I . . . teach him right here, in the house?"

"Why not? Dundee kinda special. Mayhap Papa raises hell he come home, but reckon he won't."

"Dundee," Daisy said, "we'll go into the library and talk, so I can find out just how far you've progressed."

Dundee bowed slowly. "Thank you, ma'am."

Jonathan went to the attic, located his old primers and early schoolbooks, came back downstairs, and dumped them on Dundee's lap. He and Daisy were carrying on a conversation, somewhat lamely on Dundee's part, but Daisy was patiently correcting him and there was a look in the eyes of the black man, the slave, which Jonathan swore he'd never seen before in his life.

{ 19 }

FOUR DAYS LATER, JONATHAN WAS GETTING THINGS ready for the journey to Norfolk and the racetrack there. He was still baffled. He knew there must be a trick behind the Major's plan, but so far, he'd found no answers.

"Perhaps you should tell the Major you really can't enter the race because you're needed at Wyndward with your father gone," Daisy suggested.

Jonathan thought about it. "Thing is, Daisy, I wants to go. Wants to beat the Major at his own game, whatever it is. Hong Kong and the overseers kin take care of Wyndward while we away."

"How long will we be gone?"

"To Norfolk? Day an' a half to get theah, day an' a half to get back. Day to rest the mare an' then the day o' the race. Comes back soon as it's ovah."

"Five days."

"Cain't make it any less'n that, but yo' sho' won't mind. Yo' kin buy dresses an' hats, whut-evah yo' wants."

"I'm sure I'll enjoy it, Jonathan."

Jonathan rose and stretched. "Thinks I go down an' talk to Dundee. Gots to figger out whut the Major up to, or mayhap I lose my shirt."

"Tell him not to be late for his lesson today."

Jonathan nodded and made his way to the stables. There he and Dundee inspected the mare before they wandered out to hoist themselves on-to the fence rail at the track.

"Think o' anythin'?" Jonathan asked.

"Tries, suh. Tries hard. Major say he gits yo' a jockey yo' wants him to?"

"That's whut he said, but he knows bettah than that. Knows we don' trust him."

"Reckon he say this so yo' thinks that whut he aimin' to do—gits yo' a jockey who don' wants to win ridin' yo' hoss."

"Yo' means he figgers we think that all he goin' to do, he tries to cheat us? So we don' look fo' anythin' else?"

"Yes suh. Reckon so."

"Then we has to look somewheah else fo' his trick. Now that's all he say 'cept he gets us a stall at the track. So if he knows we won't let him give us a jockey, then mus' be somethin' to do with the stall."

"Reckon, massa."

"Somehow we puts the mare in that stall, somethin' goin' to happen to her. Won' kill her, fo' then there be no race. Mayhap they gives her somethin' to slow her down?" They thought for a moment. Finally Dundee shrugged helplessly.

"Whut we have to do," Jonathan said dream-ily, "is bring the mare to the track, but 'thout beddin' her down in a stall the Major has ready fo' us. We kin do it if we got a hoss looks 'nuff like the mare to fool him an' we puts that hoss in the stall."

"Ain't, suh. The mare got white stockin's an' we got no racin' hoss like that."

"We could paint the stockin's white, may-hap."

Dundee grinned, then sobered. "Massa suh, knows a hoss stan's high as the mare, same color—but that hoss is a stallion."

"Oh, hell," Jonathan said. "That the on'y hoss looks like the mare?"

"Yas suh, on'y one. Mayhap"—his eyes gleamed a little—"I keeps a blanket coverin' the stallion so he balls don' show."

"Dundee, yo're a crook aftah my own heart. Thinks we gets away with it?"

"Ain't no othah way, suh."

"I'll fin' somethin' yo' kin use to paint the stockin's on the stallion. We leaves day aftah to-morruh. Wants yo' to go see Hong Kong an' tells him I said yo' to have bettah clothes an' new shoes."

"Tells him, suh."

"Be sho' the paint won't run, the stud gets his legs wet. Gots to fool the Major, Dundee."

"He aimin' to do somethin' to the mare sho'," Dundee said.

"Whut he thinks he does to the mare, he

does to the hoss with balls, on'y the Major ain't goin' to see them, we kin he'p it. Get busy, Dundee."

Jonathan spent the rest of the day getting ready for the trip. Bright and early the day they were to leave, Daisy begged off.

"I don't know what's the matter with me, Jonathan. I just don't feel good. I'm weak and my stomach is queasy. I can't go with you. I'm sorry, but the journey is too hard and too long."

"We kin wait an' see yo' feels bettah fo' long."

"No, please don't delay. The sooner you get there, the quicker you can come home. I'll be all right."

"Yo' runnin' a fever?" Jonathan asked anxiously.

"I don't think so. Feel my forehead. It's cool."

Jonathan passed his hand over her forehead and face. There were no signs of heat, no perspiration.

"Yo' ain't skeered to stay heah alone?"

"Now what's there to be afraid of, silly? Of course I'm not. If I begin feeling worse, I'll send Domingo for the doctor."

"Takes him a day to get heah," Jonathan said. "Thinks I call the whole damn thing off."

"You'll lose all that money. The Major won't let you back down now."

"Hell wi'h the money. He kin have it."

"Jonathan, you go to that race—and win it. Think how pleased your father will be."

"Hell wi'h him too."

"Please. It's nothing serious, darling Jonathan. I'll be all right."

"I goes, 'cause I reckon I has to. But on the way I sends Dr. Latimer heah soon's he kin make it. Means he comes tomorruh sometime. An' I pays him a thousand dollahs to stay heah till I gets back. Fo' that kind o' money he be glad to 'blige."

"All right, if that eases your mind. You know," Daisy mused, "perhaps if I got up and went along, I'd be all right. But . . . if I'm not, everything will be spoiled. Your idea is very good. Let's do it that way."

"God damn," Jonathan said vehemently. "Don' wants to leave yo' when yo' sick."

"You must, unless you want the Major to announce that young Turner was too cowardly to follow through on his promise to race his horse against the Major's. You'd never get over it."

Jonathan knelt by the side of the bed. "Yo' knows how much I loves yo', Daisy. Knows how impohtant it is fo' us to beat the Major, but even so, I wants to stay heah till the doctah comes. Sends word to the Major I be a day late."

"He wouldn't stand for it. You know that. As a member of the racing commission he'll see to it that you'll have a hard time racing any of your horses in the future. Go on, Jonathan, and win the race. For me. And please don't worry."

Jonathan rose, bent and kissed her. "Hates myse'f," he said.

She hugged him, smiling tremendously. I want to hear every word the Major says when your horse wins."

With greater reluctance than he'd ever experience in his life, Jonathan boarded the old stage for the ride to Norfolk. Dundee, driving a van pulled by four strong horses, had gone on ahead by several hours, transporting the blooded mare secretly to the racetrack. Behind the stagecoach, in which Jonathan rode alone, came another van carrying the stallion. Dundee had done a fine job with the paint, a clipped mane, and a general scrubbing down. Major Apperson, of course, knew what Wyndward Plantation's prize horse looked like. If he wasn't permitted to look under the blanket, he'd never know the difference. The stallion was younger than the mare, so he was no bigger.

It was early next morning before Jonathan reached the small village in which Dr. Latimer had his practice. He stopped long enough to ask the doctor to ride directly back to Wyndward and remain with Daisy until Jonathan returned.

"Comes back soon's the race ovah. Daisy sho' sick when I leaves. Pays yo' one thousand dollahs fo' yo' services, Doctah."

"I couldn't refuse a call to Wyndward," Dr. Latimer said. "Your father and his father did a great deal for me in times past. But I'll go only on one condition."

"Yo' names it an' it be yo'rs."

"Bet the thousand dollars on your mare for me. I know how that horse can run, Jonathan."

"Sho' does that fo' yo'. Knows anythin' 'bout the Major's entry?"

"Pretty good filly, Jonathan. Fast and strong, but I sees your mare and she runs faster."

"Yo' goes right away, please, suh?"

"Within the hour. Just take time to gather up my things. From what you've told me, I don't

[398]

think there's anything seriously wrong with Daisy. I'll take good care of her."

Jonathan felt much better after that. He resumed his journey, kept the two slaves at the reins, traveling all night, and he slept uncomfortably in the coach. Had he been accompanying the mare on his journey, he would have stopped for the night in deference to the horse.

Late the next day the procession drove into Norfolk and proceeded straight to the racetrack on the outskirts of town. Norfolk was filled with race enthusiasts, but Wyndward's reputation and standing got Jonathan a fine room in the best hotel.

As soon as he was unpacked, he went to the track, where the stallion had already been placed in the stall and well covered with an oversize blanket. If anyone noticed that the mare possessed male organs, no one mentioned it.

From there, Jonathan took along the two stage drivers and went out well beyond the track to where several caravans and horse vans were drawn up. Among them was Dundee and the mare.

"Eve'ythin' fine?" he asked Dundee.

"Sho' is, suh. She achin' to run. Kin yo' trust the jockey?"

"Bes' they come, an' honest. He rides many times fo' us an' he hates the Major like we do. Now I tells him the trick an' he gets heah befo' the race an' the mare turned ovah to him. He waits till the las' minute an' then rides the mare to the track."

"Goin' to wuk," Dundee gloated. "Knows it goin' to wuk."

"It bettah. Yo' comes back with me, Dundee, an' takes yo' place with the stallion. Wants the Major to see yo' theah 'cause he knows yo' been trainin' the mare. He talks, yo' tells him yo' got orders not to talk to anyone. An' yo' cain't let him 'zamine the mare 'cause she frisky an' ain't used to strangers. He goin' to insist, though. Yo' lets him in finally. Yo' 'members that?"

"Yes suh, massa, suh. Does I get to see the race, suh?"

"Soon as the hosses on the track, too late fo' the Major to know he bein' fooled, then yo' kin leave the stable an' go to the rail."

"We wins," Dundee said. "Got to win. Massa Fitz whale the hide off'n me we don'."

"Maybe Massa Fitz's son take the hide offen yo' too," Jonathan said with a grin. Dundee knew he didn't mean it.

When Major Apperson arrived at the stables he found Dundee apparently sound asleep with his back against the wall beside the stall door. Through slitted, watchful eyes, Dundee saw the Major and his daughter-in-law approach, but he didn't move until the Major kicked him awake. Then he jumped to his feet, snatched off his cap, and bowed.

"Yo' a Wyndward slave?" the Major asked.

"Yes suh, I'se a slave wukkin' at Wyndward, suh."

"Wants to see the mare. Open the door."

Dundee said, "Cain't, suh. Massa Jonathan, he tell me not to open the do' fo' nobody."

"Don' give a goddamn whut Massa Jonathan say. Yo' open that do', yo' lazy nigger."

"Cain't, suh. Sweahs I cain't. Massa Jonathan whup me, I lets anyone 'ceptin' Major Apperson in the stall, suh."

"I am Major Apperson. Now let me in or I'll do some whuppin' myse'f."

"Yes suh. Yo' is Major Apperson I opens the do', suh. Yes suh."

He pulled the door open. The stallion, half asleep, was munching some greenery it had discovered in the stall. Major Apperson looked down at the white stockings and nodded. He rubbed his hand against the horse's head, seeming satisfied, and left the stable.

Dundee reached into the stall and pulled some of the greenery out of the stallion's mouth. He sniffed it, peered inside the stall, and saw there was more on the floor. He'd not noticed that when he arrived at the stables, but then he'd had no reason to enter the stall and search it. The slaves who had brought the stallion here would have been responsible to see that there was no strange food in the stall.

Dundee didn't know what to make of this, but he was not worried. By now the mare was on her way to the starting gate for the first race of the day—the race to settle the rivalry between two powerful plantations.

Dundee waited until he heard the trumpet opening the racing. He glanced into the stall again, saw nothing amiss, left, and went directly to a portion of the rail at the track, where Negroes were allowed to watch.

Betting on this two-horse race was intense. With the Major picking up any bets he could cover, the odds were favoring the Major's entry. Jonathan had bet ten thousand of the plantation money and added to it the thousand he had promised Dr. Latimer as his fee.

Although Apperson's horse was good, the Wyndward mare was better. It really didn't turn out to be much of a race. The mare pulled ahead from the start and, encouraged by the skillful jockey, who was much lighter than Dundee, steadily lengthened the distance between herself and the Major's entry. She didn't even seem winded when her jockey pulled her up. She had won handily, by more than three lengths.

Dundee's throat was raw from screaming at the mare to make it an even greater win. Now he returned to the stable. He opened the stall to lead the stallion out, but the horse was quivering from head to tail. His muscles seemed to be in spasm, his eyes were dull, froth showed at the mouth. Dundee was looking at a sick horse.

Major Apperson, his face red with fury, arrived at the fastest pace he could assume. "That ain't the mare," he shouted. "Whut the hell's goin' on heah?"

"Don' know, suh," Dundee answered deferentially.

"Jonathan tol' yo' nobody else sees this—this hoss 'ceptin' me. That right?"

"On'y Major Apperson," Dundee said.

"Wheah was the mare jes' won the goddamn race?"

"Mare, suh?"

"Yo' knows whut I mean. Answer me, yo' damn nigger, or I hides yo' myse'f."

"Suh, all I know is Massa Jonathan say maybe yo' likes to buy this heah stallion."

"Stallion?" The Major entered the stall and

ripped the blanket off the shivering horse. He bent down, saw what he was looking for, and emitted a string of curses the like of which Dundee had never heard before.

"He won't get away with this," the Major roared. "I'll sue him. I'll see he nevah agin races a hoss in this state."

"Yo' aimin' to buy this heah stallion, suh? Has to tell yo' he a mighty sick hoss."

"Yes—I see that. I wouldn' buy him fo' one silvah dollah. Wheah's Jonathan?"

"Don' know, suh. I jes' a po' slave an' nobody tells me nothin', suh."

Apperson eyed him malevolently. "If I thought you had anythin' to do with this goddamn cheatin' game . . ."

"Brings the stallion, suh. All I knows."

"Ah, yo' too damn stupid to know anythin'."

The Major rushed off to find Jonathan. Dundee examined the stallion for a moment, then he picked up some of the green fodder the horse had not yet eaten and stuffed it into his pocket. He sat down, pulled his cap over his eyes, and pretended to go to sleep, as any self-respecting slave would have done, left alone this way.

Major Apperson found Jonathan in the bar at the hotel. He stormed up to him, his face beet red again. It had turned that color the moment he saw Jonathan.

"Aimin' to have yo' arrested, suh," he shouted.

"Afternoon, Major," Jonathan said. "Yo' entry sho' tried hard, but my mare bettah. Ain't sayin' that ain't a fine hoss yo' runs today."

"I provided a stall at the stable fo' yo' mare.

I went theah an' I foun'—a ringer. That's whut it was. A ringer. 'Gainst the law fo' to bring in a ringer, suh."

"Whut yo' talkin' 'bout?" Jonathan asked. "Yo' sho'ly had a stall waitin' fo' my hoss, but I put the othah hoss in it Major, suh, yo' jes don' make any sense yo' talkin' 'bout a ringer."

"Yo' put that hoss looks 'zactly like yo' mare so I be fooled."

"Tell me, suh, why I aims to fool yo'?"

"It's a trick. That's whut it is, a trick." The Major turned to address the very interested bar patrons, all of whom were horse lovers and racing experts. "All hosses fo' racin' kep' in racetrack stables fo' the race. That a rule."

"Shows it to me in writin', Major," Jonathan said. "Ain't nevah heered such a rule."

"Yo' deceived me. That's cheatin'. Yo' made me think the hoss in that stall was yo' mare."

"Major, suh, yo' still ain't talkin' sense. I wants to race my mare, I brings her heah an' I races her, but wheah I keeps her fo' the race ain't nobody's business."

An elderly, white-coated man addressed Jonathan. "I am Alex Newall, suh. I heads the racin' commission. Major Apperson has made some serious charges 'gainst yo', suh. Claims yo' fooled him by keepin' yo' mare hid, an' passin' off the mare's double."

"Mistah Newall, suh, I thinks po' Major Apperson kinda upset I wins the race, an' he owes me fifty-five thousand dollahs. I aims to collect it fo' I leaves Norfolk. Or he kin hand it in at my bank. Whut he talkin' 'bout, I don' know. He sayin' I bring in two hosses looks alike. Far as I kin see, whut if I did? But the Major makin' one hell o' a mistake, suh. Them two hosses don' look alike."

"I saw them. They's 'zactly alike," the Major said irately.

Jonathan shook his head. "Mr. Newall, suh, yo' got my leave to go see that hoss the Major say looks like my mare. Yo' takes one good look an' yo' staht thinkin' like I do. That the Major kinda excited an' don' know whut he lookin' at."

"They's no diff'rence," the Major shouted, then his face grew redder. He suddenly realized what was coming next.

"Now Mistah Turner, suh," Newall said, "Major Apperson claims the two hosses alike, but yo' says they not. Tell me the diff'rence, suh."

"Mistah Newall, suh, my mare a gal hoss. The stallion in the race track stable hung so low an' heavy, he make a fine breedin' hoss. He a stud wuth a thousand dollahs—an' I thinks Major Apperson's fahm gettin' to need new blood, he evah thinks to win a race."

"One is a mare, the othah a stallion?" Newall asked, and threw back his head and roared with laughter. "Don' know whut this all 'bout, but if the Major cain't see the diff'rence 'tween a mare an' a stallion, he sho' slippin' some."

"Reckon bes' thing to do," Jonathan said, "is fo'get the whole business. I invites all heah to step up an' order whut yo' craves. Pays fo' the whole thing. Kin afford it, winnin' so much. Major, it's yo' money payin' fo' all this, so step up an' drink yo' share."

"You—go—to—hell!" the Major shouted. He stalked out, still wondering exactly what had happened. He would spend the next twenty-four hours trying to find the answer. When it came, he would realize he was a victim of his own greed and chicanery.

Jonathan made his way to the stables. Dundee, still apparently asleep, came to his feet instantly when Jonathan spoke to him. He was grinning widely.

Jonathan said, "Hol' out yo' two han's, Dundee."

Mystified, Dundee obeyed and Jonathan let silver dollars trickle from his hands until Dundee could hold no more.

"Says that's whut I do we wins, an' we sho' won. An' the Major still don' know how we done it. Ev'ythin' wukked good. Now yo' go spen' that money. Fin's yo'se'f a wench yo' craves one. Don' get drunk. Yo' sho'ly gets in trouble yo' do that. Buy somethin'. They don' wants to sell yo' whut yo' craves, tell 'em yo' buyin' fo' me. Gives yo' a note so yo' kin buy anythin'."

Jonathan found the stub of a pencil in his pocket and enough paper to write permission for Dundee to go about the city and to make what purchases he chose. Dundee tucked it into his pocket.

"Knows whut the Major was aimin' to do, suh, so yo' cain't win the race."

"I been wonderin'."

Dundee opened the stall door and showed Jonathan the shivering, wretched animal so sick it could barely stand. Dundee produced a sample of the greenery the horse had found in the stall.

Jonathan rolled the dried grass between his

fingers, sniffed it, and let out a solid oath. "Knows whut this is, Dundee?"

"No suh, but it sho' make that hoss sick."

"This is loco weed. It can kill a hoss. Maybe it kills this one. If we put the mare in this stall an' didn' see the weed, the mare would have eaten it too, an' she'd not be able to be led to the starter's gate, let 'lone run a race. Befo' yo' spen's that money, yo' fin's a vet an' brings him heah to take care o' the hoss. The mare already on the way back home."

"Yes suh," Dundee said gleefully. "Does it firs', suh."

"We leaves early in the mornin', Dundee, so don' gets yo'se'f so dreened yo' cain't wake up in time."

"I sho' be theah yo' ready to go, suh."

"Yo' gots the papah I gives yo'. Yo' kin get 'roun' the city 'thout gettin' locked up."

"Gots it, suh. Thanks yo', suh."

"In the mornin'," Jonathan said.

Jonathan returned to the hotel. He was very tired, but too concerned about Daisy to feel elated over the victory.

So Jonathan was in no mood for pleasuring himself. He went to the dining room, ate a hearty meal by himself, and drank enough to insure a good night's sleep. Passing through the lobby he saw Clarissa, in all her finery, seated in a big chair she knew he would have to pass by on his way to the stairs.

"Evenin', Jonathan," she said.

He bent over her extended hand. "Evenin', Clarissa. Yo' lookin' mighty nice."

[407]

"I ain't mad yo' fooled my papa. Reckon he madder'n hell. Don' wants to see him tonight. Yo' busy, Jonathan?"

"Sho' am," he said. "Busier'n hell, Clarissa. Late now."

He walked away from her. Near the desk he caught the eye of a tall, rangy redhead, one of the lobby whores. Jonathan left word at the desk that he be awakened at dawn. Then he approached the girl, took her arm, and led her toward the stairs.

Clariss's outrage at having been rejected for a common strumpet was as great as Jonathan had hoped.

Upstairs Jonathan gave the girl twenty dollars. "Ain't nuthin' lef' fo' yo' to dreen. Reckon this heah 'nuff yo' kin take the night off. Or go somewheah else."

"Mistah Turner, suh," she said indignantly. "I treats yo' papa real fine an' I kin take extra care o' yo', suh. Ain't no reason to give me twenny dollahs fo' nuthin', suh."

"It fo' treatin' my papa so good. Yo' his favorite. I wasn' so tired I'd show yo' I bettah'n my papa, but not tonight. Yo' takes the money now, an' no fuss."

She wasn't certain if she had been insulted or praised, but the money she clutched in her hand remedied any insult. She kissed him hard, found no response, and let him go to his room.

Jonathan and Dundee left the next morning. The stallion rode back as he'd ridden to the city. The animal was still sick, but the vet Dundee found had done a fine job and the animal would likely survive.

They made the customary stop for the night alongside the road back, after riding as far and as long as they could. Before dawn, they were on the road again. They would be home in less than seven hours now, and Jonathan longed to feel Daisy's arms about him. They'd celebrate his victory over the Major by a lengthy stay in bed.

Dundee saw the rider first. He called down from his high seat on the stage, "Massa, suh, rider comin' fas'."

Jonathan stuck his head and shoulders out of the stage window. The rider was cutting across fields, whipping the horse into maintaining all the speed it possessed.

"Massa, suh," Dundee called down again. "It Hong Kong comin'."

Jonathan cried out, something between a prayer and a curse. Hong Kong would ride to intercept them only if he was the bearer of serious news, bad news. The coach stopped. He got out and waited until Hong Kong brought his horse up.

"Massa, suh, rides so yo' gits back fas' yo' kin."

"Whut happened?" Jonathan asked. "Mistress daid?"

"No suh. She not daid, suh. Doctah says I rides an' tells yo' to git back soon's yo' kin."

Hong Kong left the saddle and stood by the panting horse. "Yo' takes my hoss, suh, an' yo' rides."

"Whut happened? Whut the hell is goin' on, Hong Kong?"

"Cain't tell yo', suh. Jes'—cain't . . ."

Jonathan mounted the already tired horse, wheeled it and headed toward Wyndward Plantation, his heart heavy with fear. He'd never seen Hong Kong so upset. How sick was Daisy? Why the hell couldn't Hong Kong have brought a faster horse?

When Jonathan reached the mansion, Dr. Latimer came rushing out to meet him. Jonathan looked about. Everything seemed to be exactly as it had been when he left. If there'd been a rebellion, there'd be plenty of signs.

"Tell me!" he said to the doctor.

"Better you come inside, Jonathan."

"Whar's Daisy? Tell me wheah she is, damn yo'."

"Daisy is in her room. I'll tell you 'bout it after you have a big drink of rum. Sent Calcutta to fetch it. Should be ready now, he don't sloth too much."

Jonathan seized the doctor by the shoulders. "Don' stan' theah an' put me off. Somethin' happened to Daisy. Yo' tells me now!"

"All right, Jonathan. Before I arrived, and I left right after you told me to ride to Wyndward, I found Daisy—hard to say what it is. . . ."

"She sick? She goin' to die?"

"That night, the day you left, a big buck got into the house an' raped her."

Jonathan closed his eyes in horror. "Oh, my God! Knows I shouldn't have lef'!"

The doctor touched his shoulder gently. "You couldn't expect this. Nobody could."

"I sees her now, doctah. Maybe I kin comfort her. Reckon she needs me bad."

"No, she doesn't need anyone, Jonathan."

"Yo' tells me she ain't daid. . . ."

"She's alive. Come along—you can see her. But you'd better have that drink first."

"He busts her up so she dyin'?"

"No, there are only a few bruises."

Inside, a very solemn Calcutta offered a large glass of dark rum, without water, on a tray that not a drop had spilled on. Jonathan gulped it, set the glass aside, and went loping up the stairs before the doctor could stop him. At the top of the stairs, the doctor begged him to wait. Thoroughly confused, Jonathan slowed his mad rush. The doctor reached his side. He took Jonathan's arm and led him in to their bedroom.

Jonathan saw Daisy seated in a chair beside the window. She looked as lovely as the day he'd left, and she seemed unhurt.

"Daisy!" he cried out. "Daisy, forgive me. I'll never leave you again. We'll find the bastard and——"

She didn't turn her head. If she heard him, she gave no sign of it. He knelt before her. "Daisy . . . yo' heahs whut I says?"

"I don't think she hears anything, Jonathan. I don't think she sees anything either."

Jonathan looked up at the doctor in confusion. "Whut the hell yo' sayin'? Her eyes wide open."

"She's in some kind of a shock, Jonathan."

"Shock? Whut yo' mean?"

"She doesn't respond to anything. We have to take her to a hospital in Richmond as soon as we can."

"She don' know whut goin' on?"

"I don't think so."

Jonathan sat down heavily. "She looks fine. I don' unnerstan'."

"She doesn't want to remember what happened to her. It's as if her life depended on shutting this out. I've seen it before. Jonathan, there's something else. I don't know how you'll take it. I don't know if it's good or bad, or what the outcome will be."

"Yo' tells me now," Jonathan said. He couldn't take his eyes off Daisy. She was so beautiful, like the night he'd first laid eyes on her.

"I examined her, of course," the doctor said. "When you left, she was sick, but nothing serious. She had entered the first stages of pregnancy. She's going to have a baby, Jonathan."

He stared at the doctor, trying to comprehend what he had said.

"A baby," the doctor repeated. "She will have a baby in about eight months."

"But—kin she have a baby like—this?"

"Physically she is in fine shape. What ails her is in her head. Maybe having the baby will bring her back. I don't know. We know very little about this condition. We don't know how to treat it, except with kindness and all the care we can provide."

"She stays heah," Jonathan decided. "Yo' stays too. Don' care how much it cost."

"No, Jonathan. She can't be cared for properly here. We can't get her to eat. She—there's a fine hospital in Richmond. I swear she'll be well cared for there. You can come see her whenever you wish. They'll take care of her, keep up her strength, keep her very quiet and without worry. In time she may come back. I hope so."

"An' that's all? Yo' takes her away from me? Yo' puts her in a crazy house? That's wheah she goes, ain't it?"

"It's an asylum, but a special one. There are no really insane people there, only those like Daisy. There are fine doctors who know more about this condition than I do. They might be able to tell you she'll soon be well again."

"I cain't cry," Jonathan said. "She daid, it wuss, but this bad 'nuff. I tries to unnerstan' whut yo' tells me. Yo' say a buck got into the house an' rapes her. Daisy so skeered she gits the way she is."

"Something like that. I wish I could give you more assurance, Jonathan."

"Wins the race, doctah. Makes a big fool outen Major Apperson. Wins fifty thousand from him, wins mo' bettin'. Yo' gives me a thousand dollahs to bet an' yo' wins too. It now five thoussand. We wins, Doctah. But Daisy don' win."

"I know, but she has a good chance of coming out of this. I want to begin the journey to Richmond as soon as possible."

"She in any pain?"

"No. She feels nothing. There is no pain. Her mind is a blank and her body . . . is just there. But I tell you again, we can do something, with luck."

Jonathan walked slowly to stand beside Daisy. "Don' know yo' heahs me, Daisy. Yo' does, yo' knows I loves yo' an' I nevah loves anothah long as I live. Goin' to see yo' gets the bes' treat-

[413]

ment an' I prays fo' the day yo' looks at me an' knows me. No mattah how long it takes, I won't stop lovin' yo' fo' one single minute. Hopes yo' heahs me. Now I gots somethin' to do."

"When can we leave?" Dr. Latimer asked. "We'll have to get her ready. Warm clothes. Your stagecoach would be excellent. We'll arrange for drivers and travel all night."

"She gets any wuss we don' leave till mornin'?"

"No, that might even be better. Domingo has been a fine nurse, Jonathan. She will put Daisy to bed. Perhaps she'll sleep. I don't know. She may stay exactly as she is now."

"I be ready in the mornin'. Yo' an' Domingo takes good care o' po' Daisy."

Jonathan went back to her, bent and kissed her cheek. It was like kissing a corpse, except that the face was warm with life. Jonathan walked downstairs and into the kitchen. Elegant, astride her stool, was weeping quietly. She didn't look up.

"Yo' knows who did that?" Jonathan asked. "Yo' knows, Elegant, yo' tells me."

"Yes suh, massa, suh. Sees him he runs aftah he rapes. Nevah saw him befo'."

"Whut he look like?"

"Big—big buck. Hol's he haid kinda crooked like."

"Like it be stiff? Maybe like he been hung, but gets cut down?"

Elegant's eyes opened wide. "Thass whut I thinks I sees him! He runs an' he haid ain't movin'. Sideways or up or down, suh."

Jonathan nodded. "Yo' any idee wheah he hidin'?"

"Massa, I knows wheah he is I goes an' kills him myse'f."

"Reckon yo'd try, Elegant."

"Mist'ess goin' to die, suh?"

"Don' think so. Tomorruh we takes her to Richmond to a hospital."

"She sits theah 'thout sayin' nuthin'."

"Yes. Wheah Calcutta? Mayhap he knows wheah this bastahd is hidin'."

"Calcutta sweahs he don' know, massa, suh."

"Well, hidin' somewheah. Finds him if I have to search ev'y damn cabin on the plantation."

"Suh, knows yo' goin' to be mighty busy, but Elegant, she says yo' gots to eat. I makes yo' some meat 'tween some bread, suh. Yo' kin eat while yo' goes 'roun' lookin'."

"That's a good idee. I comes by soon fo' somethin' to eat."

Jonathan went to the library, opened a gun cabinet and took out the heavy revolver his father had given him for Christmas. He thrust this under his belt and went out of the mansion. He called on the overseers first. All slaves were confined to the cabins and all work had ceased. The overseers knew nothing.

"No strange niggers heah, suh," one told Jonathan. "We knows our slaves, suh, an' we knows if a stranger comes heah. Cain't figger wheah that bastahd came from."

"I kin tell yo' mo' 'bout him. He Tubal, the leader o' thet rebellion. We hangs him an' five othahs, but when we not lookin', somebody cuts

him down an' takes him 'way. He been hidin'—
knows it somewheah on this plantation. Someone from heah cuts him down."

"We searched ev'y place we kin, suh. No sign
of a slave like that, suh."

"He big an' husky. Yo' sees him, shoot him,
but don' kill him. I wants the pleasure o' that.
Reckon hangin' make his neck so stiff he cain't
turn it any. That's the kin' o' man yo' hunts fo'."

Jonathan visited as many cabins as he could,
but no slave admitted seeing a man like the one
Jonathan described.

Jonathan's anger was cold and deadly. He
moved methodically, hoping to stumble on some
information. It seemed reasonable to assume Tubal was in the area still.

Jonathan was still looking for a clue when
Dundee, Hong Kong, and the others arrived. Dundee was off the stage and running up to Jonathan
before the stage stopped.

"Suh, massa suh, kin I speak?"

"Yo' know somethin'?" Jonathan demanded.

"Suh . . . befo' we leaves, sees somebody movin' 'bout aftah dark. Movin' so nobody kin see an'
goes to the shed wheah the food is kep'. Reckon,
fo' stealin'."

"A slave who shouldn't be runnin' loose aftah dark?"

"Yes suh. It be Alameda, suh."

Jonathan gave a long sigh. "Alameda! Nevah
thinks o' her, but reckon that's wheah this buck
hidin'. So many slaves heah, nobody knows who's
who."

"Takes me, suh?"

"Don' wan' nobody. I handles this by my-se'f."

"Yes suh, massa, suh."

"Obleeged, yo' tells me."

"Reckon should done so befo' now, but don' mean nuthin' then."

"Don' yo' go blamin' yo'se'f fo' somethin' like that. No call to think yo' to blame. That's all fo' now."

Jonathan began walking back to the slave row. With slow, measured steps and a quiet fury which made his actions deliberate, with no turning away from what he had to do.

He asked where Alameda's cabin was located and he went there directly. He opened the door, gun in hand, and then he searched the premises, what little there was to search. He discovered an extra blanket, a straw bed with indentations from more than one person. Hidden beneath Alameda's clothes—which formed a sizable bundle, for in her days as housemaid she'd been given many of Benay's old dresses—was a man's shirt. By its size, there was little doubt whose it was. Jonathan left the clothes as they were and went outside. Though it was now almost time for the slaves to be brought back from the fields, Jonathan walked away from slave row, stopping only to look in the big cookhouse, the supply sheds, and the infirmary.

He found no further indication of Tubal's presence, but he never doubted that Tubal was the man he was after. He didn't quite know which way to turn. He doubted that Tubal had left the plantation. The overseers had gone out in force to block an escape, and they'd enlisted the help of the paddyrollers and everyone else who could carry a gun.

What Jonathan didn't know was that within minutes of his return to Wyndward, Tubal had left Alameda's cabin, where he'd been staying in such secrecy that the slaves who lived nearby had never seen him. Now he was hiding in the vicinity of the stables, ready to step inside a stall and risk being kicked by the horse occupying it. He was desperate. He'd had no intention of raping Daisy, though in his secret wanderings at night he often watched her through the windows of a lighted room and he had desired her, but only with the ineffectiveness that controls a slave's life. She was not for him, especially now. He wasn't inclined to press his luck. He knew what being hanged was like and he dreaded a repetition.

It was Alameda who encouraged him, insisting it would be easy to attack Daisy. Jonathan was in Norfolk, Fitz and Benay were in Boston. Who could stop him? And, she pointed out, nobody knew he was on the plantation. After the deed was done she would hide him, and when the excitement died down, he could slip away.

Now Tubal was well aware that he might not get away. Alameda had mentioned an Underground Railroad, but it turned out she meant the one run by the Fisbees, and that had been destroyed. Tubal knew there were patrols out looking for him, and escape from the plantation was quite well blocked.

What he had to do was find a safe place where he wouldn't be found until he could manage to slip away—not with Alameda, as she expected. He owed her his life, in one way, but he wouldn't be in this fix except for the encouragement she'd given him to commit this impossible crime. He knew now that he meant nothing to her, nor did the cause. All she cared about was her hatred for Benay and Daisy. She had cut him down within a minute of his hanging, to be sure, but only to make him an instrument of revenge. Hers.

Hiding in the evening shadows, Tubal was uncomfortable as well as frightened. His neck was still so swollen and sore he couldn't move his head without intense pain. Soon after Jonathan had finished his search of Alameda's cabin, he saw Dundee emerge from the first stable to go to a well for a bucket of water. He didn't know who Dundee was, but any slave should be willing to help another slave, especially when his very life was in danger.

So Tubal waited until right after dark, when the plantation activities had died away for the most part. He slipped out of a barn which he'd picked as a temporary hiding place. He ran along the row of stables to the one Dundee occupied and darted inside. The mare, a highly nervous animal, reacted to the presence of a stranger. Dundee, in the loft, was aroused by the sudden movements of the horse and he leaned over the edge of the loft to see Tubal cowering in the gloom of the stable.

"Whut yo' doin'?" Dundee asked. He knew who this must be, but he couldn't afford to show that he did. In a fight with this giant, desperate and scared, he'd be no match, Dundee knew.

Tubal looked up, relieved that the face he saw was that of a black man.

"Needs yo' he'p," he said. "Gots to hide. I'se runnin'."

"Yo' got money?" Dundee demanded.

"No, ain't got nothin', but yo' he'ps me an' I sen's yo' all I kin soon's I git No'th."

"Come on up," Dundee invited.

Tubal climbed the ladder until his head was just above the edge. Dundee wrapped his arms around Tubal's neck and began a slow pressure that turned Tubal's head to the left and kept turning it. Tubal reached up with one hand, but Dundee avoided it. Then Tubal made a bad mistake. He tried to balance himself on the ladder rung with his feet, and he used two hands to try and get at Dundee. That left him, a second later, actually hanging in air. Dundee's hold on his neck never relaxed.

Dundee kept the slave's head moving always to the left. Then, when he felt all Tubal's neck muscles had reached their limit, Dundee gave the head a hard, sudden twist. There was the sound of cracking bone and Tubal's arms, flailing in vain to find Dundee, suddenly fell to his sides limply. Dundee let go of the man and Tubal's body went crashing to the stable floor.

Dundee lay back, breathing hard. He'd been almost at the limit of his strength; he couldn't have kept that tight grip on the neck of the heavy man much longer.

When he breathed easier, Dundee climbed down the ladder and knelt beside Tubal's body. He made certain the man was dead. Then he walked out of the stable and turned in the direction of the big house.

Halfway there, he saw Jonathan coming from

[420]

the house of an overseer. Dundee broke into a run. Jonathan heard him coming and stopped. Dundee reached his side.

"Massa, suh, fin's Tubal, I does."

"Wheah?" Jonathan asked quickly.

"He in my stable, suh. Comes theah an' tells me he goin' to hide theah or he kills me. He comes up the laddah, suh, an' when he haid come ovah the edge, I kicked him, suh, an' he falls off the laddah an' he busts he neck, suh. He daid."

"Show me," Jonathan ordered.

They returned to the stable. Jonathan saw the wryly twisted neck of the dead slave. He looked up at Dundee.

"Busted neck all right. Mayhap it was weak from the hangin' an' busted easy like. Don' wants to think yo' killed him, Dundee. He was mine to kill."

"Jes' kicks him off the laddah, suh. He busts his own neck."

"Well, I'm not goin' to argue that point. He daid an' that's whut counts. Wants yo' to go get fo' slaves, carry this heah sonabitch fo' buryin' not far from wheah the pigs are kept."

"Yes suh, massa. I does it fast."

"While the slaves are diggin' the grave yo' goes an' fin's Alameda an' brings her to the whuppin' shed."

"Yes suh. Brings her."

"I'll be theah in a li'l while. Don' yo' lets her get away."

"She be waitin', suh."

Jonathan walked back to the mansion. Elegant met him with a tray of sandwiches. He ate, tasting nothing, but satisfying the rumbling in his stomach and the gnawing of a vague feeling he'd not yet recognized as hunger.

Jonathan went upstairs. Dr. Latimer was lying fully dressed on the bed, trying to get some rest. He sat up as Jonathan came into the room. Daisy was exactly as Jonathan had left her, her face now softly illuminated by one of the smaller lamps.

"She jes' the same?" he asked.

"There'll be no change," the doctor assured him. "Not for a long time."

"If evah?" Jonathan asked.

"Yes . . . yes, Jonathan. Without a miracle there will be no change within any time limit I can put on it."

"Whut 'bout the baby she carryin'?"

"I can't say. But from all my studies, and my common sense, I would say that what happened to Daisy will have no effect on the baby. It will grow normally. Daisy is alive, everything functions except her brain. So the baby likely won't be harmed."

"Yo' sho' 'bout that?"

"Of course not. I'm only giving you my opinion, which may not be worth much. However, there is one thing in favor of the baby; Daisy will be in a hospital, where every care will be provided to see that she doesn't lose the child. And, when it's born, that same extra care will be right with her."

"Yo' sees to that?"

"I give you my word."

"Unnerstan', suh, don't care how much it costs. Daisy goin' to get well an' she goin' to have this heah baby to love. Yo' sees to that. Yo' an' the hospital."

"Of course, Jonathan."

"Fin's the bastahd, Doctah. He daid."

"He deserved it."

"Sho' did. Wishes I coulda killed him, but makes no diff'rence, reckon, so long he daid."

"This is going to be quite a shock to Benay and your father."

"Cain't get word to 'em. They's on a ship sailin' to Norfolk. They due in anothah week. So I cain't meet 'em an' I cain't even go with yo' an' Daisy to the hospital. Don' know how much Tubal been talkin' to slaves. Might be trouble an' it happens I gots to be heah. Trust yo' to take good care o' Daisy."

"The very best, Jonathan. Soon as your father gets back, you can come see her."

"I be theah sho'," Jonathan said. "Got some impohtant business to 'tend now. Comes back latah an' sits with Daisy rest o' the night so yo' kin get some sleep."

He made his way to an outlying area where pigs were raised. He saw four slaves digging the grave. Tubal's body lay alongside. The slaves stopped work at Jonathan's arrival.

He inspected the grave. "Digs it deeper," he ordered. "Don' put him in it till I gets heah."

"Yes suh, massa, suh," one slave said.

Another raised his head. "Kin I talk, massa, suh?"

"Talk," Jonathan said.

"We bows our haids in shame, massa, fo' whut happens."

"I should think yo' would," Jonathan said.

"Tubal, he comes heah an' he talks. Nevah seen him befo'. He say he a free nigger an' he

tells us how we kin be free. Massa, suh, we don'
listen. We think he crazy."

"All right. But nex' time a strange nigger
comes onto this plantation, bring him to me."

"Yes suh, we brings him."

"Get to wuk. I'll be back soon."

He went directly to the dimly lighted whipping shed. Dundee was there, and so was Alameda. Jonathan stepped up to her.

"Shuck down," he said, "an' put yo' arms
'roun' the whuppin' post."

"Massa, suh, don' whup me. I a good wench,
suh. Tubal, he say he kills me I don' he'p him."

"Do whut I says or I'll cut yo' rotten throat."

Dundee sprang forward, seized Alameda,
shoved her against the first post, yanked her arms
around the post, and handcuffed them. He then
walked around behind the girl, secured a grip on
the neck of her dress, and with one savage yank
pulled it off her. She stood there naked, wailing
her innocence, writhing in fear of the lash.

Jonathan took it down. Dundee reached for
it, but Jonathan shook his head. He stepped back
and began to count. It went to thirty before he
stopped, sickened. Alameda's back had been laid
open. Blood ran down her legs to form a pool on
the dirt floor. She was still alive, moaning softly.

"Yo' gets her free an' carries her," he told
Dundee. "Shows yo' wheah."

Dundee already knew where. He carried her
to the spot where Tubal's grave had been dug.
There, at Jonathan's command, he placed the girl
beside the dead slave. The grave diggers withdrew to stand by, wondering what was going to
happen next. They knew Alameda was still alive,

for she was moaning loudly now and moving about.

Jonathan bent, gripped her arms, and yanked her to her feet. He had to support her, for she was unable to stand unassisted.

"Yo' loves Tubal," he said. "He say whut yo' to do an' yo' does it 'cause yo' loves him."

"Yes suh," Alameda managed to say weakly. "Loves him, I do, suh."

Still holding her, Jonathan began to kick Tubal's body into the grave. It was difficult to budge the huge dead weight. Dundee came forward, seized Tubal's legs, and laid them over the side of the grave, then stepped back so Jonathan could shove the body over the edge.

Alameda began to wail. Jonathan said, "Yo' loves him, yo' sen's him to rape my wife. Loves her, I do, so I knows whut love is. Now yo' kin be with Tubal fo'evah."

He thrust her violently into the grave. She began screaming. Jonathan beckoned the grave-diggers.

"Cover 'em up," he said. "Yo' gets done, plants sod heah an' stomps it down till they ain't no sign o' this heah grave."

Dundee stepped back, gestured imperiously. The four slaves began to ply their shovels. No more moans or screams came from Alameda, for she had mercifully fainted. Jonathan stood by until the grave was filled in and two of the slaves went for sod. Four lanterns had illuminated the grim scene. Jonathan picked up one of them. It swung in his hand as he walked slowly back to the big house and the tragedy that awaited him there.

[20]

For the rest of the night, Jonathan sat on the floor beside Daisy's bed. Dr. Latimer had gone to another room to rest. All Jonathan could do was sit in silence and watch Daisy's lovely face in the soft glow of the lamplight. She had never seemed more beautiful.

"Hopes yo' kin heah me, Daisy. Mayhap yo' cain't, but I says it anyways. Loves yo' now an' it makes no diff'rence how long it take fo' yo' to get well agin. Takes yeahs, I still waitin'. Yo' goin' to be cared fo' by the bes' doctahs in the worl'. They goin' to make yo' well agin. Sweahs it."

He would stop and rest, then talk more. In the morning he was still seated on the floor with his head against the side of the bed, completely exhausted.

Dr. Latimer awakened him. Jonathan arose and looked sheepishly at the doctor. "Reckon I say I stays awake all night, but jes' couldn't. Tired, reckon."

"It's all right, Jonathan. I've sent for Domingo. We'll dress Daisy and as soon as the stagecoach is ready, we'll begin our trip. We'll reach my house if we start early and stop there. My wife will go with us the rest of the way to the hospital. Soon as I get back home, I'll send you word how Daisy is."

"I thanks yo'," Jonathan said.

Watching his desolate face, the doctor said softly, "All we can do is wait until she comes out of this. I promise she'll be cared for with just as much love as you would give her."

"Sees yo' nevah sorry fo' whut yo' done, an' I takes good care o' the hospital too."

"Fine. Now go about your work as usual. Try to think of Daisy as someone who is on a vacation and one day she'll come home again, whole and well. She will, Jonathan; she is young and strong."

"Yo' watches so the baby is all right?"

"Depend on it. Now get out of here so we can get to work."

Jonathan went down to breakfast. As he sat at the long table, he suddenly realized how alone he was. He ate because he was hungry, but he didn't know what he ate. Elegant waddled about the table trying to help. He wished she'd go away, but he didn't have the heart to order her to the kitchen.

Before long he heard them coming down the

stairs. The stage was already waiting with two of the plantation's best drivers. Jonathan went to the reception hall and stood there, feeling helpless, while they carried Daisy down the stairs. At the bottom she was able to walk, like a mechanical doll.

Jonathan stepped up to her and kissed her gently. She didn't respond. Her eyes were as unseeing as they had been when he first saw her on his return.

"Taking Domingo with me," Dr. Latimer explained. "When we get to my home, I'll have someone drive her back."

"We takes fine care o' mist'ess," Domingo said. Her eyes were reddened from crying. "She goin' to be jes' fine, massa, suh. Knows it."

He stood on the veranda to watch them put Daisy in the coach. Then it began to move and Jonathan turned away. He went directly to the library and began his day's work. His first order of business was to prepare a letter to his bank and make certain they collected fifty-five thousand dollars from Major Apperson.

Jonathan's feeling for the man, until now, had been one of amused disdain, but that had changed. If Apperson had not tried to cheat Jonathan out of all that money, Daisy might now be with him, full of life and love. There were moments when Jonathan thought he heard her coming down the stairs. He was sure he heard her voice, but he knew it was all in his imagination.

He fought the urge to give in to his sorrow. Instead, he left the house, visited the stable to make certain the mare was all right and that the

[429]

stallion had not died from the loco weed. Thanks to the veterinarian, the stallion had fully recovered.

Dundee stood by deferentially as Jonathan inspected the mare, then turned to him.

"Evah see a mare run like she did, Dundee? Price of Wyndward hosses goin' sky high now. Goin' to mate her with the bes' stud we got an' we gets 'nuff good racehosses from her to win ev'ythin' they puts on in Richmond or Norfolk or Lynchburg."

Jonathan had Dundee saddle a horse, and he rode over to the fields, where Hong Kong was watching the slaves at work. Jonathan pulled alongside him.

"Ev'ythin' goin' fine?" he asked.

"Yes suh. No bettah crop than this yeah, suh. It comin' real good."

Jonathan then rode to the little cemetery, dismounted, and stood at the foot of his grandfather's grave.

"Times changin', suh. Feels it comin'. Yo' knows whut happened. I was winnin' a race 'gainst Major Apperson. Reckon I feels so bad cain't talk 'bout it much. Tryin' to staht ovah agin, like Daisy on'y away fo' a time. Don' know wheah yo' an' Grandma are, or if yo' kin pray, but if yo' kin, yo' pray fo' her, please, suh. Both o' yo'."

He moved over to Nina's grave. "Gots to tell yo' that boy o' yours doin' good, Nina. He bettah with the hosses than Themba was. Gettin' hisse'f educated, too. Daisy he'ps him, till she goes away. Now I he'ps him an' befo' long, I asks papa to manumit him. Yo' kin be proud o' him, Nina."

Jonathan led his horse back to the stables and turned him over to Dundee. "Yo' comes to the big house soon's suppah ovah. I shows yo' how to do 'rithmetic. Used to hate it myse'f an' yo' goin' to hate it too, but yo' gots to learn it or yo' stays dumber'n a post."

"Yes suh," Dundee said joyfully. He'd been afraid with Daisy gone, there'd be no one to teach him. "Thanks yo', I does, suh."

"My wife would want me to do this, Dundee. We makes yo' the bes'-educated nigger in Virginia."

Dundee smiled and nodded. He took the horse from Jonathan and watched the man walk slowly back to the empty house. Dundee wished he hadn't killed Tubal so fast.

There was a great deal of desk work and Jonathan set about doing it. When his father and mother returned, he didn't want any unfinished business at hand. The plantation had weathered all this trouble very well. Tubal had been unable to make any progress in luring slaves away. In the birthing house, new children were born every day. The slave population was nearing the point when some would have to be sold. The market was still very high, despite all the fuss being made in the North.

Fitz couldn't return to a better-run plantation, free of trouble and torment, though shadowed with the sickness that beset Daisy. Jonathan fought hard to take his mind off her, but it seemed impossible. Days he worked as he'd never worked before, and at night he drank himself to sleep. Things would be better, he told himself, when his parents and his sister returned. Within three days he'd grown gaunt and red-eyed.

On one of these lonely evenings, after Dundee had returned to the stables, Calcutta announced a carriage coming down the drive. Jonathan was eager to have anyone call and rushed out to the veranda to greet his guest. Then he groaned in dismay, for it was Clarissa who got out of the carriage and ordered the driver to take it to the stables.

She walked toward the veranda with a sway of her hips. They were getting a bit fat and the sway seemed more pronounced than usual. She came up the steps and kissed Jonathan on the lips, holding the kiss a long time and pushing her body against his.

"Oh, po' Jonathan. Heahs whut happened to Daisy. Busts my heart that happen an' I comes soon as I heahs 'bout it. Old frien's kin comfo't one anothah, don' yo' 'grees to that?"

"Sho' does," he said. It was already evident that sorrow for Daisy's illness was not the only thing that brought her. "Yo' craves a drink, Clarissa?"

"Sho' does. Makes me glad yo' ain't sorrowin' too much. Awful thing. Skeered I goin' to get raped too. Niggers look at me like they wants to rape me an' skeers the hell outen me, Jonathan."

"Ain't s'prised," Jonathan said. "Yo' a nice-lookin' woman, Clarissa. 'Co'se yo' lots older'n me, but yo' still looks fine."

"I'm glad to heah yo' say that. Now, Jonathan, I'm goin' to be very frank. Do yo' mind I says whut's on my tongue?"

"Reckon not, Clarissa."

[432]

"Knows yo' all alone heah. When's Fitz an' Benay gettin' back?"

"Three days, they ain't no bad storms."

"That's too long to be all by yo'se'f, 'specially at night. I comes to give yo' love. To keep yo' company. Daisy ain't comin' back fo' a long time, way I heahs it. Jonathan, man like yo' gots to be dreened. That's why I'm heah, to see yo' gots yo' a woman. Been achin' fo' yo' a long time. Thinks yo' mighty good in bed. Reckon I knows yo' must be. Way I figgers, that night in the seedlin' shed, it was yo' who raped me. Fitz mighty good, but yo' bettah."

"'Members the night," Jonathan admitted with a laugh.

"I fo'gives ev'ythin' yo' did to me. Ev'ythin', Jonathan. Wants to love yo' right now. Clarissa horny as hell."

"Well now, that real nice o' yo'," Jonathan said. "Reckon yo' pretty good in bed too. Reckon yo' been there 'nuff to be good as any whore. But firs' we gets us a drink. I goes to tell Calcutta to fetch some rum an' watah."

"Fine, Jonathan," Clarissa said eagerly. "Some rum makes it all the bettah we in bed."

Jonathan found Calcutta on the back steps. "Now yo' listens real good. Yo' makes a mistake an' yo' gets yo' ass whupped raw. Firs', yo' brings rum an' watah. I sends yo' fo' mo', yo' firs' goes to the whuppin' shed an' fetches the cowhide. Not the snake, the cowhide. Knows whut it is?"

Having endured a lick or two with that heavy wide strap, Calcutta knew very well what it was. He shivered slightly.

"Massa, suh, ain't done nuthin' I gits whupped."

"Yo' won't be, less yo' makes a mistake. Yo' brings the cowhide an' yo' puts it under my bed. Unnerstan' that?"

"Gets the whup an' puts undah yo' bed. Yes suh, massa, suh."

"Then yo' fetches mo' drinks."

"I does it, massa, suh. I runs."

"Yo do this right, yo' kin have a good drink o' rum yo'se'f. Yo' sloths or yo' makes a mistake, yo' gets the cowhide. Now get!"

Jonathan returned to the drawing room and sat down on a sofa. He patted the seat beside him and Clarissa came over promptly. After the drinks were delivered, he casually let his hand rest on her knee. Clarissa spread her legs, wiggled, and leaned over to kiss him, her hands snatching her skirts above her knees.

He was exploring the ample depth of her bosom when Calcutta came back with a second drink and a quick nod of his head that the mission was complete.

"Reckon we takes our drinks an' goes upstairs," Jonathan said.

"Oh yes, Jonathan. I cain't wait. I'll pleasure yo' so yo'll fo'get Daisy. Been aimin' fo' yeahs to get yo' in bed. Kin I stay till yo' papa comes back?"

"Sho', yo' wants to." He drew an arm around her waist and walked her upstairs, down the corridor toward his room. Clarissa, breathing hard, broke free of him and with a little giggle and a clumsy pirouette she ran toward the bedroom. The bodice of her dress was already open and her breasts bounced with each step she took.

"Yo' comes in, yo' don' look. I be ready soon's I kin. Cain't wait long nohow. Yo' horny, Jonathan?"

"I mighty ready fo' whut's comin'," he replied wryly.

"Makes yo' happy, I will." She disappeared into the room.

He hurried downstairs, but he couldn't find Calcutta, who was likely drunk by now. So he sent one of the kitchen sluts to the stable with orders that Clarissa's carriage and driver be at the door in ten minutes. Then he went back upstairs.

When he opened the door, Clarissa stood in the center of the room, stark naked. Jonathan approached her with a nod of approval.

"Yo' sho' is somethin', Clarissa. Sho' is. Get into bed. I gets ready."

She slowly lowered herself onto the bed, using every seductive movement she knew for his benefit. He knelt beside the bed and stroked her legs, spread wantonly, and stomach. With his other hand he reached under the bed, exploring for the cowhide Calcutta had put there. His fingers encountered it. He suddenly seized Clarissa and turned her on her stomach, while she squealed in delight. He stepped back, raised the cowhide, and brought it down in one tremendous blow on her flabby behind.

She screeched in surprise and pain. As he raised the whip for a second stroke, the first was already raising a great lump and the area around it had turned bright red. She howled with the second slap of the whip. Jonathan threw the whip on the floor and stalked toward the door.

"Yo' carriage is waitin' fo' yo'. Get the hell

outen this heah house an' don' yo' evah come back. Heah?"

She sat up, though the pain caused by her weight against the bed was not easy to bear.

"Jonathan," she whimpered.

He looked back. "Don' wants to heah 'nothah word outa yo'. Comes back in ten minutes. Yo' ain't gone, yo' gets five lashes. Whut in hell makes yo' think yo' as good as Daisy? Whut in hell make yo' think I kin turn to some fancy whore like yo' as soon as my woman I really loves has to go away? Feels like givin' yo' five mo' lashes right now."

"I gots one thing to say to yo', Jonathan Turner."

"Say it, then, an' get the hell out."

"I hopes yo' dies with a hahd-on!"

He was still doubled up with laughter as he heard her hurried departure. He finished the drink he'd left in the drawing room and kept on laughing until he was back in the bedroom. Then the laughter ceased and he was again filled with loneliness.

He undressed and got into bed. He lay there a long time. He tried to persuade himself that Daisy would soon be well again. But the lonelineww grew more intense. He lay on his back, staring at the ceiling.

He heard the door open and close very quietly. He heaved a great sigh.

"No need to sleep on the flo', Domingo. Yo' gets in bed with me."

She came to him. She slid under the bedcovers he raised for her and she moved her body tight against his and that was how they both fell asleep.

[21]

MOMENTS AFTER THE SHIP DOCKED AT NORFOLK
Fitz received Jonathan's letter. He read it and
silently handed it to Benay.

"What's happened?" Melanie asked. "Mama,
you look so pale."

Benay was so overcome with weakness she
sat down, fearful she might faint. She covered
her face with her hands.

"Been trouble," Fitz told his daughter. "It's
Daisy. Sonabitch nigger raped her while Jonathan
was away."

Melanie cried out in horror. "Papa, is she
dead?"

"Jonathan say she got taken to the hospital
in Richmond. Wants us to see her on the way
home. Reckon least we kin do."

"Papa . . . does this happen very often?" Melanie asked.

"No. When it does, we hangs 'em quick aftah we hides 'em good. Bastahd who done the rapin', we strung up once fo' riotin', but he gets cut down by yo' mama's slave Alameda. She hid him, an' when Jonathan goes 'way, mayhap she gets this heah buck to rape Daisy."

"Why would she do such a thing?"

"Gave her to Daisy 'cause I thinks she mighty good," Benay explained, "but she steals from Daisy an' sasses her so she gets herse'f whupped an' sent to the fields. Reckon that made her so mad she gets this buck to rape po' Daisy out o' revenge."

"Is she still on the plantation?" Melanie asked.

"Jonathan say anothah slave killed the buck an' Jonathan whupped Alameda an' . . . buried her in the same grave with the buck."

"Buried her? She was whipped to *death?*" Melanie asked in fresh horror.

"Jonathan don' say. Happened once befo' on Wyndward. Slave gets my mama on a frisky hoss an' she goes ridin' with Nina. Hoss throws Mama so she lands in two o' three inches o' watah an' mud an' she drowns theah, bein' knocked out by the fall. The slave coulda saved her easy, but he too goddamn busy rapin' Nina. Papa has a deep hole dug straight down maybe twelve feet. He whups the slave an' then has him lowered into the hole head firs' so he kin eat dirt same as mama, while he dies."

"How awful!" Melanie said. "I never heard that before."

Fitz shrugged. "That was long time befo' yo' was born. Times kinda hard them days, reckon', an' slaves whupped wuss than now."

"But Jonathan did the same thing to this other man. And then he buried the woman too, perhaps alive. I didn't think my brother was capable of such terrible things."

"Melanie, honey," Fitz said, "ain't on'y one way to keep the niggers down. Yo' lets 'em get away with nothin'."

"Melanie," Benay said, "if Jonathan punished those two people, they deserved it. Yo' brother ain't a cruel man, he treats our slaves bettah'n mos'. But yo' jes' stop an' think whut it was like when he fin's Daisy been raped an' she so outa her min', she got to be taken to a hospital."

"Will she get better?" Melanie asked.

"Don' know," Fitz replied. "Jonathan say the doctah thinks mayhap she gets bettah, but takes long time. Mayhap yeahs."

"And I so looked forward to meeting her and having fun with her," Melanie said dolefully. "You told me she is young. I'm sure she'll get better more quickly than they think."

"We hopes so," Benay said. "Mayhap we fin's out, we gets to the hospital."

After the easy and pleasant sea voyage from Boston the journey to Richmond was arduous and tiring, first in the smoky, cinder-filled train for a few miles on a newly built railroad and from that point by stage, to cover the one-hundred-odd miles.

The hospital was a red brick building four stories in height, erected on the outskirts of Richmond, where it was quiet and beneficial to the patients. Fitz introduced himself and his wife and daughter to the head doctor.

"I am Dr. Wendell," the doctor said, "in charge of this hospital. Yes, we have your daughter-in-law here, Mr. Turner. Do you wish to see her?"

"That's why we came, Doctah," Benay said quickly. "Cain't she have visitors?"

"Yes, of course, but I warn you, she will not recognize you or even be aware of your presence."

"Oh, God," Benay exclaimed in dismay. "She that bad?"

"She suffered a severe shock and it did something to her brain. We still don't know much about these things, and we can't predict how long she will remain in this condition."

"She in pain?" Fitz asked.

"No. In fact, she feels nothing, and gives no response. Many such cases recover all of a sudden, but don't count on it with Mrs. Turner. It does not happen, far more than it does."

"We will see her," Benay said. "Mayhap she sees us."

"Very well," the doctor said. "I'll take you to her." He glanced at Melanie. "Do you wish to come along, miss?"

"Of course," Melanie said. "Is there any reason why I shouldn't?"

The doctor studied Melanie more carefully. He appeared dubious. "Well . . . you are very young, and sometimes . . . Come along. You want to, so perhaps you can endure it."

The doctor unlocked three doors before they reached Daisy's room. There too he used a key to enter. It was a drab room, painted gray. There was one window, a bed, one hard chair, and a bureau, the surfaces clear of all objects. Daisy occupied a chair beside the window, but she wasn't looking out. She sat rigid, her lovely face looking straight at the blank wall opposite. She gave no indication that she was aware of her visitors. Her breathing was slow, but strong and steady. She was dressed in a white uniformlike gown. Her hair was well arranged and she seemed perfectly normal except that she gave no response.

Fitz said, "God damn!"

Benay approached Daisy and held one of her limp hands. She knelt and looked up at her. "Daisy, honey, it's Benay come to see yo'. An' Fitz an' Melanie. Please heah whut I sayin', honey. We comes to see yo'."

There was absolutely no reaction. When Benay let go of Daisy's hand, her arm fell limply onto her lap. Benay got up and turned away to weep.

"Mama!" Melanie clutched at her elbow. "I want to get out of here. Take me away. I can't stand this."

Fitz drew an arm around his daughter. "Yo' mama feels bad 'nuff 'thout yo' pullin' at her. Yo' wants to go, I takes yo'. Comin', Benay?"

"I want to stay a few minutes," Benay said. "I jes' . . . cain't believe whut I sees."

Fitz led his daughter downstairs and sent her out to the waiting carriage. Then he returned and talked to Dr. Wendell.

"Suh, reckon this heah goin' to be long an' expensive. Wants yo' to know I got plenty o' money an' don' give a damn I spends ev'y cent o' it takin' care o' this gal. Yo' sees she gets the bes' o' ev'ythin', an' the bes' doctahs, if yo' has to send to Europe fo' them."

"Everything will be done, Mr. Turner. Your son told us the same thing. But you must understand that your daughter-in-law may never get better. This has been a terrible experience for her. Her mind won't let her think about it or remember it."

"Reckon I knows that now. I thanks yo' fo' whut yo' done an' whut yo' will do. Send us word she begins to come out o' it."

"Of course. I'm very sorry about this. She's such a beautiful woman, and so young. By the way, did you know she's going to have a baby?"

"Whut in hell? This heah buck—he knocks her up?"

"No, no! Not that. She was pregnant before this happened."

"She kin be like that an' have a chile?"

"She's physically sound. Her only trouble is in her brain. We trust she will give birth to a normal, healthy baby."

"My son knows this?"

"Oh yes. He was told right away."

"Wants a gran'chile real bad, doctah, but don' wants it this way. Po' Daisy."

Benay was escorted downstairs. Fitz shook hands with the doctor and led Benay out to the carriage where Melanie waited. After the carriage began its journey, Fitz told them about Daisy being pregnant.

"Oh, my God!" Benay exclaimed. "How is it possible she kin bear a chile in that condition?"

"Doctah say she have a good baby. Whut happens to her got nothin' to do with birthin' a chile. An' it Jonathan's baby. Daisy was knocked up befo' bein' raped."

"How awful!" Melanie exclaimed. "Do things like that happen all the time?"

"Whut in hell makes yo' think that?" Fitz asked.

"Well . . . you just seem to accept it. . . ."

"I accepts it 'cause they ain't a goddamn thing I kin do to change it. Would if I could. Cost me my own life I gives that, but when they ain't nothin', yo' accepts things, Melanie. Time yo' learned that. Whut in hell they teaches yo' in that fancy school, anyhow?"

"Please," Benay said. "Don' argue. Things bad 'nuff now. But I will say it gives me pure pleasure Daisy goin' to have a chile. Somethin' came o' that marriage anyhow, an' yo' don' throw 'way a blessin' like that."

By the time they reached home, they were exhausted.

Jonathan, grim-faced, met them. Backing him were all the house servants, led by Elegant, who enveloped Melanie in a hug that virtually made her disappear.

Benay put her arms around her son. "We sees Daisy an' she all right, Jonathan. She as beautiful as evah."

"She know yo'?" Jonathan asked.

"No, son. She don' know anybody."

"Reckon she knows it, she happy she goin' to have yo' baby," Fitz said.

"If she knows it, Papa. Way I sees it, she

nevah knows she has a baby. She goin' to live the rest o' her life in that place. She dies theah."

"Hold on now, the head doctah says they's a chance. Long as they is yo' don' give up hope," Fitz said. "Yo' does an' yo' sho' don' love that gal very much."

"I got no faith in whut the doctah says. Don' wants to talk 'bout it. Melanie, glad yo' home again. Yo' sho' growed up an' yo' sho' a mighty pretty gal."

Melanie hugged and kissed him. "Thank you, Jonathan. I only wish I could come home to a happier time. Don't give up with Daisy. Please don't."

Jonathan nodded. "Reckon I talks through my hat when I thinks 'bout her. Elegant gots ev'ythin' ready fo' a big dinnah. Calcutta sweahs yo' wants rum an' watah, he runs."

"Kicks his black ass he don'," Fitz said with a grin.

"Papa," Melanie protested, "do you always have to talk like that?"

"Like whut?" Fitz asked in a puzzled voice.

"Never mind," Melanie said. She looked about. "It's good to be back. I'd almost forgotten what the place looked like. It seems ten times as big, though."

"Reckon it bigger," Jonathan said. "Got two thousand slaves heah now."

"Don't be proud of that, brother Jonathan," Melanie said.

Fitz eyed her with a frown, but he said nothing. Benay put an arm around her daughter and led her away.

"Whut's wrong with Melanie?" Jonathan asked.

"She changed," Fitz said. "Whut else goin' on heah?"

"Soon's yo' leaves, Major Apperson comes an' says he got a hoss kin beat our mare an' wants to bet fifty thousand."

"Yo' took him up, I hope."

"Took him up an' gets Dundee to he'p."

"Dundee? Whut he got to do with it?"

"Dundee takes the mare to Norfolk an' I takes a stallion same size an' mos' same color 'cept fo' white stockin's. Dundee, he paints them on. Major Apperson he on the board of directors at the track an' he kin'ly gets us a fine stall. I takes the ringer an' puts him in the stall. On'y somebody throws some loco weed in theah. The stallion eats it an' gets sick. The mare woulda got that loco weed, wasn't fo' Dundee an' me."

"Yo' races the mare?"

"She wins by fo' or five lengths. Near busted the track record, she did. Bets on her so 'sides whut we won from the Major, reckon I banked mayhap seventy thousand."

"Mighty fine wuk," Fitz lauded his efforts. "Mighty fine, 'specially yo' fools that sonabitch. Reckon by now all he doin' is figgerin' how he gets back at us."

"Waitin' fo' it," Jonathan agreed. "But winnin' don' mean much. If I hadn' gone, Daisy be fine now. I been blamin' myse'f evah since."

"Whyn't yo' take her with yo'?"

"Meant to, but she feels sick an' wants to stay home. Reckon it be the sickness comes when

[445]

she gets the baby stahted. She comes back, I nevah leaves her agin, Papa. Been livin' a life o' hell evah since."

"Yo' cain't do that fo'evah, son. Whut happened is ovah an' now we waits fo' Daisy to get well agin, but it mayhap takes yeahs. Yo' cain't jes' sit an' feel sorry fo' yo'se'f."

Jonathan nodded. "Knows that. One thing mo' yo' gots to know, an' mayhap yo' hides me fo' doin' it. Caught Dundee readin' an' writin'."

"Yo' whups him good?"

"Don' whup him at all, Papa."

"No slave kin read an' write on this heah plantation! Or any othah."

"Hold on now, befo' yo' busts something. Way I sees it, Hong Kong gettin' old. Befo' long yo' has to retire him an' then we needs somebody to take his place. Dundee the smahtest slave we got an' he faithful as a man kin be. We goin' to need him an' when we do, it best he kin read an' write. That'll make him a bettah head driver than Hong Kong."

Fitz shook his head. "Fo' now, I goes 'long with it, but that boy slips, it's all goin' to change. Don' like the idee he kin read. Too much being printed 'bout slavery in the No'th. Them papers gets down heah an' he reads 'em an' gets idees he ain't s'posed to get."

"Kin trust him. He like yo' said Nina was."

"He half as good, we lucky," Fitz said. "Now let's go in an' talk 'bout crops an' money."

Life settled down after Fitz's return, though there wasn't a moment that Jonathan didn't think of Daisy. Reports came twice a week, always the

[446]

same. There'd been no change and she was not responding to treatment.

It was Melanie who gave them trouble they didn't expect. She had grown sharply critical of the way slaves were handled. Benay learned that one Monday morning during her customary routine of handing out the week's rations. Benay led the way to the supply house, unlocked all the doors, and the slaves came for their rations. They were given four pounds of bacon for each person, a peck of meal, and a quart of molasses. Occasionally dried fish was added.

That chore done, Benay called in the cooks and dispensed rations of flour, sugar, and meat. Benay supervised the distribution while Melanie watched it all.

"Mama, that's not enough for the slaves. Not enough, and there should be different things like ham and a chicken or two."

"Yo' thinks we got 'nuff chickens we gives one to each slave? We got two thousand slaves. They gets along fine on whut we gives 'em. Needs all that to wuk hahd an' sho'ly we got no reason to starve 'em. A hungry slave don' wuk good."

"I still say it's inhuman. And the way they have to line up. For such a long time."

"Yo' knows 'nothah way to feed 'em so ev'ybody gets his share?"

"There must be a better way."

"Tried 'em all. This wuks an' nuthin' else does. Why yo' actin' this way, Melanie? Thinks yo' been up No'th too long."

"Long enough for me to realize that you and Papa are living in a dream world if you think you

[447]

can keep Negroes enslaved forever. There are going to be changes, Mama, and they won't be long in coming. Alan says it will happen sooner than anyone thinks."

"Alan say. Reckon now I know it him talkin' an' not yo'. Befo' yo' goes No'th, nuthin' like this come into yo' haid. Things ain't changin'. Yo' are."

"Mama, I don't want to stay here."

"Been feelin' yo' were thinkin' like that."

"Look what happened to Daisy! I'm frightened all the time. Mama, if that happened to me, I'd die."

"Skeered, are yo'? Yo' listen to me. We all skeered some. That's why we keeps the slaves down an' we don' let 'em learn anythin' or talk to folks who came preachin' abolition."

"Mama, I wrote Alan and told him how I felt."

"Yo' aimin' to marry him, Melanie?"

"He asked me before we left and I said I would after . . . after we're a little older, but Mama, I can't stay here. I don't care if we are very young. Alan has a bright future. His people have money, they have been very nice to me."

"They got three million, honey?"

"Three million? I don't know."

"That's whut we got, yo' papa an' me. Three million an' mo' than that, I reckon. So don' get talkin' 'bout money to me."

"It's not the money anyway, Mama. I love him. I miss him so."

"Reckon he comin' down heah?"

"I . . . asked him to." Melanie lowered her head to stare at her feet. "I didn't want to do anything behind your back, but I didn't think you'd approve, and Papa will be angry. I'm sorry. I'm selfish, Mama. They taught me that in Boston."

"Knows that a long time, Melanie. An' no need fo' yo' to be skeered o' yo' papa. We both wants to see yo' happy mo' than anythin' else. Yo' wants to marry this boy, we sho' goin' to look happy 'bout it, even if we ain't. Let me talk to yo' papa 'bout this. Bets he comes to yo' an' says whut I did—wants to make yo' happy."

"I . . . want to go back North, Mama."

Benay nodded. "Reckon' yo' marries this heah Boston boy yo' gots to go wheah he is. Wheah he goin' to wuk. Missed yo' all this time yo' gone. Misses yo' agin, yo' goes away, but yo' gots yo' own life to live."

"You won't stand in my way?"

"I won't. Thinks yo' papa won't either."

Melanie hugged her mother and tearfully proclaimed her love for the best parents in the world. Benay knew she meant it, in her own way.

That night Benay told Fitz about it. "Ain't s'prised none," Fitz said. "Been a month she gets back an' she ain't gone outside the house 'nuff to get rid o' all that no'thern whiteness."

"She skeered o' the slaves. Seein' whut happened to Daisy has made her skeered to go out."

"She cain't go on like that," Fitz said. "Whut yo' thinks o' this boy from Boston?"

"Don' know him 'nuff to answah that, Fitz. Whut I sees o' him he fine, an' he talks good. Knows his people are the bes' any boy kin have. But Melanie ain't much mo' than a chile."

"She mo' than that, Benay. Kinda spunky too. When I tells her to get the hell outen the house, she say she goes out when she wants to an' she don' take orders from me. Near fell ovah she say that, but—like I say—she gettin' older an' she mighty independent. Comes from livin' in Boston. Knows all 'bout that."

"Fitz, I still 'members the speech yo' made. Mighty proud o' whut yo' said, an' nobody stood up to say yo' wrong."

"Seein' I'm not wrong, whut they got to stan' up fo'? But when Melanie say things changin', she right 'bout that. Mayhap things ain't changin' fas', but they changin'."

"Wheah we headed then?"

"Cain't say. Big trouble, reckon. Yo' thinks we let Melanie go?"

"Cain't stop her 'thout hurtin' the gal. Don' wants to do that. She say she in love. Knows whut that is, an' bein' young don' make any diff'rence. An' leavin' yo' folks don't make any diff'rence. It ain't bein' selfish, Fitz. It's on'y love, an' that stronger'n yo' an' me an' anything else."

"Reckon. One thing I gots to talk to her 'bout. She goes ridin' with Dundee, an' don' like no white gal ridin' with a nigger. Not even Dundee. Happen on'y once, but that too much."

"Whan't no harm in it, Fitz. Dundee sho' ain't no ordinary slave. He learnin' to read an' write so fas' reckon befo' long he talks better'n yo' an' me. No—that ain't true. When yo' turns yo'se'f back to bein' a No'therner, yo' talks mighty good."

"It like two diff'rent languages," Fitz said. "Gets mixed up sometimes. But my papa says I gets to speak like a southern gen'mun I wants to live heah an' run a big plantation. I don' do it, eve'ybody thinks I cain't be trusted an' I ought to go back No'th. Reckon both No'th an' South too damn set in they ways. Bein' 'tween 'em ain't funny. Cain't be on two sides, but gots to jes' the same. One thing do my heart good. Jonathan quite a boy. Gots plenty o' nerve an' ain't skeered o' nuthin'."

"Knows whut he done to Major Apperson. Worries me some. We been makin' a fool outen him fo' a long time. One o' these days he goin' to fin' a way to get back at us an' nex' time mayhap he wins 'stead o' us."

"Watches him, Benay. Knows he lookin' fo' a way, but we knows whut he up to, we skins him again. Likes to skin him fo' all the money he got."

"Thinks he a dangerous man, Fitz."

"Knows that too. Don' worry me much. Got frien's in Richmond an' they tells me he up to somethin'."

"Let's hope they warns yo' in time. Wants me to tell Melanie she craves to get married an' go No'th it all right?"

Fitz spread his arms in a gesture of defeat. "Whut else we do? We say no, she go anyhow. Knows her well 'nuff to be sho' she runs we don' lets her go."

"I'll tell her. Reckon that boy comes down. Gets her lettah a week ago. 'Spects him any day. I sees Melanie jumpin' ev'y time she heahs a carriage comin' down the drive."

"We made our own lives, Benay. Cain't say she too young 'cause we young once ... a hell of a long time ago."

Benay laughed softly. "In a way goin' to miss her, but in 'nother way, kinda happy she goes. She unhappy an' skeered, make me feel wuss than she leaves us. Boun' to go off some day. Might as well be now she gots the right boy."

"Reckon he comes down an' we talk, I fin's out. Jonathan heahs anythin' 'bout this?"

"Reckon he knows. Reckon Melanie tells him. They close—glad o' that." She hesitated, then said, "Jonathan pesterin' Domingo, yo' knows that? She sleeps in his room."

"Cain't blame him fo' that. Domingo mighty fine pesterin'."

"How yo' knows that?" Benay demanded.

"Knows it, that's all."

"How? Yo' tells me now."

"Well, hell, Benay, I ain't known yo' all my life an' befo' I meets yo', I done some pesterin' myse'f. Some o' these heah gals ain't musky an' they's good to sleep with. Keeps a man wahm in winter."

"This heah ain't winter."

Fitz began to laugh. "Nights ain't so wahm."

"Yo' evah pesters Domingo?"

"Benay, I so old all I kin get is a whore some-wheah to pleasure me."

"Reckon nex' time yo' goes to Richmond I goes with yo'."

"Now that'll be fine. Yo' comes, I don' need any whores. Oh, Benay, there ain't nobody in this worl' I loves like I loves yo'."

She went to him then and kissed him. "Fo'-gives whut yo' done pesterin' wenches fo' yo' meets me. Aftah that, I gets mad. Wants yo' to myse'f an' I don' give a damn who knows it. On'y gal I nevah jealous of was Nina."

"Worries some 'bout Jonathan. Sho' he loves

Daisy, but time goes by, he goin' to need dreenin'. Bettah he has Domingo."

"Bettah yo' don' have nobody but me."

"Sho'—bettah," he agreed. "Let's go to bed. Talkin' 'bout dreenin' gets me horny."

"Fitz, it gettin' late an' I kinda tired."

"Yo' thinks o' this. Got me mos' neah a thousan' wenches on this heah plantation an' I kin pester any one o' them, or all."

Benay said, "We goes to bed."

[22]

ONE DAY MELANIE AWOKE CERTAIN THAT ALAN would be at Wyndward within hours. She dressed carefully, choosing a pale blue muslin dress with skirt flounces heavily embroidered with pink roses. Narrow borders, embroidered with miniature roses, trimmed the bodice. The large pagoda sleeves were of the same blue fabric, but the sleeve beneath was pink, with blue roses embroidered around the narrow wrist.

The design was different and attention-getting, exactly what Melanie wanted. She looked breathtakingly beautiful and was completely aware of it. She was secretly ashamed of the way her family spoke, ashamed of their plantation way of life. She knew she would never be happy here and admitted privately she hated it. Above all, she feared that Alan would change his mind about marrying her.

That was why she had taken such pains with her toilette. After her bath she had stood before a mirror and admired her slender figure and full breasts.

She had allowed Alan the privilege of fondling them, but that was as far as she would go. It was as far as she had needed to. They drove him to distraction and so did she, for she had practiced feminine wiles before her mirror. Even postures which, though seeming quite innocent, could make a man horny. She caught herself up as that word came to mind. It was one used in her home. She tried to think of a more elegant way of putting it—"arouse his passions" was better, she decided.

She was seated on the veranda in one of the cushioned wicker rocking chairs, her eyes trained on the driveway, her ears attuned to the sound of hoofbeats. Her heartbeat quickened when she finally detected their distant thump.

She held tightly on to the arms of the chair to keep from jumping up and running off the porch and down the drive. When Alan's carriage finally did roll up, Melanie waited until he was out of it and then she arose, her smile serene, in full control of her emotions until she reached the edge of the porch. No longer able to contain her excitement, she ran down the steps, straight into his outstretched arms. She cried out in delight as he covered her face with kisses, murmuring her name over and over, telling her how beautiful she was and how terribly he had missed her.

Benay, watching from behind a curtained

window, felt her eyes film over, but she quickly dried her tears as Melanie and Alan ascended the steps to the porch. She opened the door wide for them to enter. Before she could speak, Alan embraced her and planted a kiss on her cheek. Benay knew then that Melanie had already written him of her parents' permission for them to marry.

"Welcome," Benay said when Alan released her. "We mighty glad to see yo'. Firs' thing yo' does it wash up. Took that damn ride myse'f an' never got so dirty. Fitz out in the fields an' Jonathan down at the stables. Reckon they sees yo' carriage an' comes."

"I rented the carriage," Alan said. "I'll put it away."

"Yo' ruins ouah reputation yo' does that. We got two thousand slaves to do it. Melanie, don' stan' theah like yo' struck dumb. Show Alan wheah he kin wash up. Knows it early in the day, but yo' craves a drink, Alan?"

"I'd love one. My throat is as dry as cinders. I must have swallowed a peck of them on that train."

"Calcutta!" Benay shouted.

Calcutta, never far off when visitors arrived, hurried into the room.

"This heah is ouah houseboy," Benay explained. "Laziest nigger on this heah plantation an' he drinkin' hisse'f to death, but he fixes a good bourbon an' watah. Calcutta, runs an' gets fo' drinks befo' Mastah Fitz gets heah or he shore kicks yo' black ass."

Melanie winced, but if Alan was shocked, he didn't show it.

"Yo' goin' to stay heah awhile might's well gets used to it, Alan," Benay remarked.

"I want to learn all I can about a southern plantation," he said. "I feel we in the North should understand your problems better."

"Alan is going to go into politics as soon as he gets out of school," Melanie explained.

"That's fine. But yo' sho' ain't goin' to favor us with our slaves, Alan. That's yo' right, but yo' minds we got rights too an' we jes' as proud folks as yo' in Boston."

Alan nodded. "The speech your husband made at the school still rings in the ears of those who heard him. They don't want to admit it, but they know he had many points in his favor. I was impressed."

"Someday," Melanie said, "Alan is going to make a great speech too. You'll see."

Jonathan arrived at that moment, sweaty and in old clothes, for he'd been timing horses. The two young men eyed one another, and grinned and shook hands.

"Begs yo' pardon, fo' the way I looks," Jonathan said. "Reckon I kinda sweaty."

"No more than I," Alan said. "I spent nights on that damn train and it belched so much smoke and cinders you could probably lay a mile of track with them."

"Get cleaned up, both o' yo', an' don't sloth," Benay ordered. "Fitz gets heah mighty soon now an' drinks comin', Calcutta don' fall asleep on the way."

None of them were inclined to dally with the important business at hand. In the drawing room, fortified with several drinks served by an increasingly drunken Calcutta, it was quickly agreed that Alan and Melanie should be married soon.

"Bes' it be done in Boston," Fitz said. "Melanie goin' to live theah, bettah yo' friends be theah than us."

"Papa, won't you come to my wedding?" cried Melanie.

"Wouldn't take that train ride fo' anythin', darlin' Melanie. Not even fo' yo' weddin'," Benay drawled.

"Firs' time I hears that," Fitz said. "But reckon got to be that way. Gettin' worried some. Been too much goin' on 'roun' this heah plantation. Don' say any o' our slaves ready to run or rebel, but othah plantations gettin' mo' an' mo' worried. Reckon yo' folks up No'th to blame fo' that."

"How in the world can you blame us?" Alan asked.

"Too much talkin' 'bout slaves bein' set free. Means to ask yo', ruther me an' Jonathan talk Boston? 'Co'se Benay cain't. She be too southern."

"I'd rather you talked just as you do, both of you," Alan said. "It would be strange to sit here in Virginia, surrounded by two thousand slaves, and hear their masters talking Boston. Do you mind if I offer an opinion?"

"Wants all the advice an' opinions we kin get," Jonathan said amiably.

"Mind now, I get around in Boston, New York, Philadelphia, and Washington. I have relatives deep in and high in politics, so I know what's going on. You're right, Fitz, in saying we stir up trouble. We're bound to, because we don't believe in slavery. Now you do, and that's your right, but the issue here is of great importance. It's even dangerous."

"What makes it dangerous, Alan?" Fitz asked.

"We maintain that you cannot keep two or three million black people in chains. All right—it will mean you'll have to pay them to do the work they do now for nothing."

"Hold on," Benay interrupted. "Yo' wants we shows yo' whut it costs to feed an' house an' clothe two thousand people? Slaves expensive. Yo' sells one yo' gets a good amount. Sometimes much as two thousan' fo' a likely buck, or a wench looks like she births a sucker ev'y ten months."

"I believe you," Alan said.

"An' yo' keeps in mind that we sittin' heah like we surrounded by half the gunpowdah in the worl'," Jonathan added. "We gets rebellion an' all them powdahkegs goes off at once. Reckon Melanie tells yo' whut happened to Daisy."

"Yes, she wrote me about it. I was terribly sorry to hear it. I suppose you know, Jonathan, doctors are beginning to get results in such conditions. You have every reason to keep hoping."

"Nevah stopped," Jonathan said. "Nevah will."

"To get on with this," Alan said, "I don't want to offend you in any way. What I say is in all candor and without the slightest enmity. You are some of the finest people I've ever met and I thank you for giving your consent to our marriage. I love Melanie dearly. My main purpose in life will be to make her happy."

"Yo' don'," Jonathan said cheerfully, "yo'll hear from us."

Alan smiled good-naturedly, then sobered. "What I'm getting at is this. So far, antislavery sentiments haven't been a very important factor up North. We talk about it, decry it, and we depend on it, for we get your products far cheaper than if you didn't have slaves. However, antislavery is now beginning to leave the realm of idle talk and enter politics."

"Hears that," Fitz said. "Goin' to make trouble."

"You're right, it is. Politicians are now beginning to campaign by saying how wrong and cruel slavery is. That's to people in states that have no slavery, never did have, and never will. It doesn't mean a thing to them, but newspapers print all these speeches."

"Knows whut yo' means," Benay said. "Word gettin' 'roun' too fas'."

"And too inaccurately."

Melanie said, "Isn't he clever, Papa?"

"Reckon he gets 'roun' an' heahs the truth 'bout how they feels in the No'th," Fitz said. "Don' like to heah 'bout it, but gots to."

"Soon," Alan went on, "it will enter national politics. Politicians running for federal office will begin taking it up, because it's going to be a popular issue."

"We got some pow'ful talkers heah too an' they goin' to get mad with that kin' speechmakin'," Fitz said.

"That's the point I'm trying to make, Fitz. They begin arguing, debating, running tickets of antislavery or proslavery, and those two tickets can never be compromised. Each politician believes in his side and is dead against the other."

[461]

"Whut's goin' to happen, then?" Jonathan asked.

"I don't know. I confess I do not know, but it's bound to be anything but good for the country."

"Yo' goin' into politics soon's yo' gets outa school, whut side yo' takin', Alan?" Fitz asked.

"I'm against slavery, sir. I can't help it, but I am one of those who believes slavery cannot last in this modern world."

"Whut if we says we agrees with yo'?" Jonathan said.

"Do you, Jonathan?" Melanie asked. "I never thought I'd hear those words spoken in this house."

"Of course you agree. There is no alternative," Alan said.

" 'Cept when we sets slaves free, it be in ouah own good time, Alan. We sets 'em all free now an' we got the goddamnedest mess yo' evah saw. Wheah they goin'? They free they thinks they don' have to wuk no mo'. They thinks they go wheaheveh they likes an' does whut they likes. Millions o' them, Alan. Millions! They gets the chance now they sloths, knowin' they gets whupped they caught. How do yo' think they be when they ain't skeered o' the whup no mo'?"

"It's a problem, but it's got to be faced, Jonathan."

"In our time," Fitz said. "It must be in our time. Gradually, gettin' some o' them into a society they don' know one damn thing 'bout. 'Cept fo' mighty few like carpenters an' blacksmiths, coopers an' the like, they ain't got 'nuff brains to do anythin' they ain't told to do. When

[462]

yo' talks 'bout settin' 'em free, yo' thinks hahd on how it goin' to affect the Negroes."

Alan said, "Talking that way up North would get you into a hot argument. I'm trying to understand because I'm going to marry a southern girl with fine southern parents."

"Alan, after you and I marry, I don't want you to tell anyone I'm from the South and that my father owns a plantation with two thousand slaves."

"Melanie!" Benay cried out in dismay. "We yo' parents. Don' yo' fo'get that."

"Alan, I want you to take me away from here tomorrow. As early as you can. I hate it here. I'm afraid of the slaves. I don't like the way they look at me."

"Whut the hell yo' sayin', sistah Melanie?" Jonathan exclaimed. "Yo' ain't been outside this heah house long 'nuff fo' a slave to look at yo'. 'Cept fo' Dundee, an' he knows good how he looks at a gal. A white gal."

"Dundee is a fine young man and I'm proud of the way you treat him and let him learn," Melanie said. "But all the rest of it, I can't stand. I've been away too long. I never liked black people anyway. None of them. If I stay here, I'll go mad."

"Yo' grew up heah," Benay reminded her. "We has a hahd time keepin' yo' from playin' with piccaninnies. Yo' 'members that?"

"I remember all right. Those children I played with are field hands now. If they're still here. Maybe you've sold some of them by now. I feel sorry for every Negro back there in those—those shacks you give them. I hate everything about this business. If I stay here, I'll hate you, and Papa and my brother. I don't want to hate any of you, but I won't be able to help myself."

Fitz said, "Reckon we lets Melanie go to her room now an' staht to pack. Breaks my heart to heah her talk this way, but knows she cain't he'p it. 'Members my mama. She comes heah an' she hates it. She ain't killed like she was, don' think she'd of stayed long. Loved my papa she did, but cain't nevah get used to our ways."

"Do you give me permission to go, Mama?" Melanie asked.

"The soonah the bettah," Benay said quietly.

"What about you, Jonathan?"

"Whut I gots to say is mighty simple. Yo' kin go to hell fo' all I cares."

Jonathan arose abruptly and walked out of the house. Benay shook her head. "He kinda touchy these days. Worries 'bout Daisy too much."

"I know. I certainly can't hold it against him," Alan said. "But you're right, Benay. We'd best leave soon, before we get into an argument that will make enemies of us. I don't want that. I want your respect and, in time, your love, because that's what I'm going to give Melanie. Most of all, I'll give her love. You will never have any reason to doubt that. Or ever need to worry about her."

Fitz nodded slowly. "Reckon ev'ythin' been said then. Knows yo' an' Melanie been 'way from one 'nother a long time. Mayhap yo' two goes fo' a walk. They's a nice moon."

"I wouldn't go out there," Melanie said. "Not among all those . . . people."

"Fo' a gal wants to set 'em free, yo' sho' loves 'em," Benay said sardonically. "Fitz, yo' an' me, we takes the walk. Ain't skeered o' any slaves. Don' hate 'em either. Gets yo' packin' done, Melanie. Like yo' papa say. Alan kin he'p yo'."

Out in the pleasant, moonlit night, Fitz lost some of his hostility. "Reckon we got to see Melanie's side. 'Members when my papa took me aboard his ship an' sailed to Africa. Now Papa never told Mama he was buyin' slaves an' he didn' bother to tell me. When I foun' out whut he was doin', my Boston blood began to get hot, like Melanie's is now. But Papa was no man to let an eighteen-year-old boy tell him whut he could or couldn't do. I didn' like it, I could jump ovahboard. But he tol' me whut it was about an' I comes to see his side too. Mayhap aftah all these yeahs, I gone too far on his side now. Gots to admit Melanie made me mad tonight."

"She our daughtah," Benay said mildly. "I don' agree with whut she doin', but it her life. Reckon won't be a bad one. Alan seem like a pow'ful nice boy, an' knows his papa an' mama impohtant people. Rich too. Alan got fine chances o' goin' far an' Melanie go with him, so— we jes' steps aside."

"Worries me some 'bout that boy, but he says one thing makes lots o' sense. Slavery should nevah be an issue in politics."

"Fitz, yo' knows I ain't too smaht in such things. Politics mean nuthin' to me. Depends on yo' to tell me whut it about."

"Ain't hard, Benay. In politics, the politicians begins to debate an' argue. It divides them. Makes two badly separated sections in Congress. One side be fo' the No'th, the othah fo' the South, an' slavery stan's right theah smack 'tween 'em. One side say it gots to go. The othah say it cain't be done, else the whole damn country goes bust. Somethin' to both sides. That's whut makes it so dangerous. Neither one is goin' to give in."

"Whut then? Seems like they ain't much givin' in now."

"Cain't say, but I hears some crazy talk that one o' the Carolinas talkin' kinda low, they thinks 'bout secession."

"That means they wants to leave the United States an' be a country by theyse'ves? Fitz, that's pure crazy talk!"

"Sho' is, but that's the talk. Don' like it, but cain't do nuthin' 'bout it. Ain't none o' us Southerners goin' to free the slaves. Fo' our own good an' theirs. Slaves got no trainin', no education. They free they got nowheah to go, nobody to go to. We keeps 'em an' pays 'em, whut's the diff'-rence? Sho' cain't pay 'em much. We do, we has to sell fo' mo' money an' No'therners ain't likely to pay it. Englan' an' France an' othah countries ain't got money 'nuff to pay high prices we gots to charge. So we cain't pay the blacks, we has to fire half o' them. I tell yo', Benay, ain't no man alive got 'nuff brains to figger this one out."

"Fitz," Benay asked, "if someone did come 'long an' tell yo' how to manumit all our slaves an' pay 'em to do the same wuk 'thout makin' us go bankrupt, would yo' set 'em free?"

"Now yo' got me so I cain't answer yo' eith-er. We don' know, we sets 'em free, they wuks fo' us o' walks off. Plenty of 'em runs even now knowin' they gets whupped they caught. They be free an' there be no whuppin', wondah how many would stay. They's an economy in this country an' 'specially in the South it's kinda delicate. Don' take much to swing it one way or 'nother. Freein' slaves sho' goin' to swing it, but nobody knows how much or in whut direction."

"If they were set free, I'd be 'fraid of them, Fitz."

"Reckon they be some who ain't got any likin' fo' us, but don' think they's many. How they feels ain't ouah fault, but the fault o' plantation owners who don' know how to treat 'em."

"Yo' thinks someday they be free, no mattah whut?"

Fitz nodded. "Reckon so."

Benay linked her hand under his arm. "Right now, Fitz, it don' mattah to us whut's goin' on 'cause I'm in love with yo', an' far as I go, nothin' is as impohtant as that. Not slavery, not Melanie, not whut happened to po' Daisy. Nuthin' 'cept we two people in love. They takes 'way Wyndward an' we po' an' not knowin' wheah our nex' meal comin' from, we togethah an' ev'ythin' else kin go to hell."

"Feels the same way," Fitz said. He brought her to a stop, took her in his arms, and kissed her soundly. "Don' know whut I do 'thout yo', Benay. Things go bad, like whut happens to Daisy, Melanie leavin' us aftah way we looked to her comin' home. Bad things happen an' I turns to yo' an' nuthin' bad any mo'. That's how yo' affects me."

She hugged him. They resumed their walk, and by the time they were back at the big house their spirits were healed.

In the morning, Jonathan brought around the stage, provided with two fine drivers. He walked up to the porch and sat down. Inside, Melanie was saying a tearful good-by to Benay, while Fitz and Alan stood aside in silent contemplation of what all this would eventually mean.

Fitz said, "Alan, you take fine care of this daughter of ours. She's inclined to be a bit rebellious, I'm afraid, but she has some reason to be. I don't agree with her philosophy, but I do agree with her decision to marry you. That's about all I can agree with as far as you are concerned. We live in two different worlds, it appears. You have a reason to like yours, as I have to like mine."

"Thank you," Alan said. "For speaking Boston language too. We have that in common, when you wish to use it."

Fitz chuckled. "Two different worlds is right. Now keep in mind the fact that Melanie is our daughter and we love her very much, despite our differences. If ever there is anything she needs— or you, for that matter—we can furnish it. I'm too goddamn rich as it is."

"Thank you, sir."

Melanie approached her father hesitantly and then, with a rush, she was in his arms. She kissed him, never uttering a word, then fled to the veranda. There she hesitated, saw Jonathan seated in one of the wicker chairs. She returned, bent and kissed him on the cheek. He made no attempt to respond. He didn't even acknowledge her presence, or Alan's. The servants filled the stage with luggage, Alan helped Melanie aboard and the stage set out, losing no further time in beginning the long journey to the depot.

Benay shook her head sorrowfully as she and Fitz stood at the top of the veranda stairs.

"Ain't no diff'rent now than befo' she comes home," Fitz said. "She wasn't heah long 'nuff we goin' to miss her much. Jonathan, get yo' ass outa that chair an' come into the library. We gots wuk to do."

Benay said, "Fitz, look theah! Ridah comin' an' sho' wastin' no time 'bout it."

"Oh, hell," Fitz said. "Ridah comin' like that mean nuthin' but mo' trouble. Sit down, Jonathan. We waits to fin' out whut's busted loose now."

It was a man sent from the telegraph office in the town. The message was addressed to Jonathan and he opened the envelope with fingers that shook.

"From the hospital." He looked up with wonder on his face. "Says Daisy talkin' a li'l an' walkin' 'roun'. Mama, she gettin' bettah!" He raised his voice to a shout. "Calcutta! Calcutta, get heah fas'."

Calcutta did move fast this time. Jonathan said, "Yo' runs to the stable an' tells Dundee to get a saddle on the bes' ridin' hoss we got. Get that hoss heah in ten minutes, an' no slothin'!"

Calcutta ran down to the stables. Jonathan hurried upstairs, changed into clothes suitable for the city, and packed a small case. Elegant swiftly prepared a package of food when she heard the news.

"Yo' lets us know, soon's yo' sees her," Fitz said.

"We'll have yo' room ready," Benay told him. "Gives Daisy ouah love. We so happy she gettin' bettah."

"Watch out fo' Colonel Coldwell's wife," Fitz cautioned happily.

"Papa, I rides by the Colonel's place so fas' she ain't even goin' to get wahm. Been prayin' fo' this. Now it happens. Comes home quick as we kin."

Jonathan rode the horse half to death before he reached the city. There were pauses only long enough to feed and water the horse and let it rest an hour at the most, before he was off again.

Jonathan had been to the city many times, but he'd never covered the distance quite as fast as he did this time. He was weary, covered with dust, aching in every muscle, but he went up the hospital stairs as if he hadn't expended an ounce of energy in days.

When he entered the doctor's office, he came to an abrupt stop. The doctor, who should have been as joyful as he, only rose to shake his hand and tell him to sit down.

"Yo' sends me the news she gettin' bettah," he said. "Now yo' looks like mayhap she daid. Whut happened?"

"She's not dead, Jonathan. She was coming along. She responded and she began to talk a little. Not much, and most times it didn't make sense, but she was aware we were around her. We even found her combing her hair one night. We had the greatest hope for her."

"I asks yo' whut happened?"

"By mistake, an employee of ours walked into her room. He thought he was entering someone else's room. When your wife saw him coming toward her, she screamed and fainted. Now—she's like before. Maybe worse."

"Man walks into her room an' she goes outa her haid again?"

"Jonathan, the man was a Negro."

Jonathan leaned back, his fingers turned into tight fists. His neck muscles bulged and his eyes grew fiery. Then, as if proper thinking returned to him, he relaxed.

"I sees her," he said.

"It won't be any different than before."

"Sees her anyway."

"I'm sorry, Jonathan. These things will happen no matter what precautions you take. The Negro is a free man, studying here to try and help his own people. He meant no harm. He just didn't know. It was a simple mistake."

"Don' hold yo' o' the man to blame. Got mo' sense than to do that. But I sees her, doctah."

"Come along then."

Daisy sat beside the window, in the same chair, in the same attitude. Jonathan dropped to his knees before her and once again took an unresisting, unfeeling hand between his.

"Daisy, if yo' kin heah me, wants yo' to know I loves yo' an' there nevah be anyone else. I waits rest o' my life. But yo' gets a li'l bettah an' mayhap yo' gets bettah agin. They's nuthin' to be skeered o' nevah agin."

Her listless face was as unmoving as if he hadn't spoken. Dropping her hand, he stood up and stared at her for a long moment. "Come back to me," he whispered. Then he accompanied the doctor downstairs and kept going, to leave the building, untie his horse, mount, and ride to the city.

He put up the weary animal in one of the

[471]

livery stables, carried his small piece of luggage, and checked into the first hotel he came to. It didn't matter which one. He fell onto the bed without undressing and with a cry of utter helplessness he turned his face into the pillow and sobbed.

When he awoke, it was dark. He'd slept for seven hours. Rising, he got out of his clothes, bathed, shaved, put on the one spare suit he'd brought, and went down to the bar. He had several drinks by himself, speaking to no one, never looking in the mirror he faced. He felt his head beginning to spin and realized he needed something to eat to offset all the bourbon.

He paid the bar bill and started through the fairly crowded room to seek the dining room when he was stopped by a tall, rangy man in a wrinkled white suit.

"Yo' be Jonathan Turner, suh?"

Jonathan nodded. "I be. Get outa my way."

"I'm a frien' o' Major Apperson, suh, an' I says yo' a cheatin' bastahd o' a bastahd father."

Jonathan swung one punch. It missed, and Jonathan suddenly found himself being hurtled across the room to land up against the footrail. He sat there, too stunned to get up right away. Then he saw two long, white trouser-clad legs standing over him. He struggled to get up. One leg went back to deliver a kick. Jonathan wrapped his arms around the other leg, tugged hard, and brought the man down. He scrambled to his feet, waited until his opponent was halfway up, and brought up his right knee against his chin. The man went down again. Jonathan waited this time until he was on his feet and then he launched an attack in which all of his disappointment, bitterness, and hatred inspired his blows. He drove the man back, never giving him a chance.

Someone pulled him away, hands restrained him. Half drunk, still raging, he fought those hands too, but finally he was forced into a chair.

"Mistah Turner, suh," someone said. "Don' wants yo' arrested fo' murder."

Jonathan cleared his head by shaking it violently. The restraining hands let go. He looked up, still half dazed. Two bar patrons were carrying the white-suited man outside.

"Reckon I be kinda crazy," he said. "Las' I knows I was on the flo' an' don' know how I got theah."

"Not yo' fault. Yo' was punched real hahd by that man in the white suit."

"Who he?" Jonathan asked. "Nevah saw him befo'."

"One o' Major Apperson's overseers. Mad 'cause yo' outfoxes the Major las' time yo' races. This heah overseer bets his shirt on the Major's hoss an' loses it."

Jonathan nodded. "Reckon he had a right to take one punch. Feelin' kinda sick. Needs some food. If yo' gen'mun excuses me . . ."

They helped him into the dining room, where he ate a large bowl of soup, followed by a thick steak and potatoes. This down, he began to recover his wits and the realization that he ached, both from the fatigue of the long ride and the blow which had floored him.

Into the lobby he saw a handsomely dressed woman of about thirty, her gown cut low to expose ample bosom. Jonathan approached her.

"Yo' busy tonight, honey?"

"Not too busy fo' yo', Mistah Turner, suh. Been paradin' heah waitin' fo' yo' to come out. Knows yo' papa real good, I does. Reckon I gets to know yo' too, suh, yo' wants it."

"Come on," Jonathan said. "Needs dreenin' like I nevah needs it befo'."

She began to take off her clothes a moment after Jonathan closed the door of her room. She lowered herself onto the bed and looked up at him appealingly. Jonathan had his shirt half unbuttoned.

"Now whut in hell I want yo' fo'?" He was talking to himself more than to the woman.

"Ain't I built right fo' yo', Mistah Turner, suh? Ain't been eatin' onions or nuthin' make me stink. Waitin' fo' yo' an' horny 'nuff to rise up an' pull yo' down."

Jonathan took money from his pocket, peeled off twenty dollars, and placed it between the woman's breasts.

"Yo' built fine, an' yo' sho' don' stink. But I ain't feelin' like I wants dreenin' tonight."

She sat up to curse him, changed her mind and folded the money instead. Jonathan was gathering up his things.

"Thanks yo', Mistah Turner, suh," she said. "Nex' time it fo' free. Feelin' kinda tired myse'f, suh."

By the time he turned out the light and closed the door, she was sound asleep.

$[$ **23** $]$

MELANIE AND ALAN WERE MARRIED IN AUGUST IN
Trinity Church in Boston, amidst wonderful splen-
dor, flowers, bridesmaids and ushers in formal
clothes. Her wedding gown was covered with
pearls. Her veil was so long, her flower girls
walked behind her, holding it up. Alan beamed
with pride, his eyes glowed with love.

Afterwards, a lavish banquet was given in
their honor by the bridegroom's wealthy and in-
fluential parents. Artists from the newspaper society columns were there in profusion, sketching
the bride, for she was breathtakingly beautiful in
her wedding gown and, as usual, completely
aware of it. Mostly though, she was aware of her
happiness. She was married, she was in Boston,
she was free of Wyndward and her parents.

The wedding banquet, which was given in the garden and the mansion, was served by Negroes in spotless uniforms. They were paid something like five dollars a month and what little they could tote. But they were free men and women—free to go home to quarters more squalid than anything Wyndward Plantation had to offer.

If anyone, including Melanie, noticed this, they made no mention of it.

On Wyndward things were going on as usual. There was a great deal of work. Tobacco crops came in better than ever. Fitz sold a hundred thoroughbreds for fancy prices, and three hundred more for breeding purposes. He didn't sell any slaves. He needed them all, he informed Benay, though she didn't quite believe him. She'd been particularly upset a year before when she saw him separate families. Benay pondered this attitude on her part, for she'd never before paid much attention to the sale of slaves. They were merely chattel from which a profit was to be expected. Fitz had never spoken to her about this, but he made it abundantly clear that he didn't care to break up the families any more. Now and then, he sold some bachelor who seemed discontent, but he hadn't formed a coffle in a year now. As Jonathan said, things were changing.

Jonathan made two trips to the hospital, returning both times with sadness and despair written on his face. Benay hoped he'd stop going. He could do nothing for Daisy—she wasn't even aware that he had come to see her.

On the first of these journeys Jonathan found

a supply of newspapers from Boston and scanned the society and wedding columns. He found those concerned with his sister's wedding, and wondered if he should destroy them rather than let his mother see how empty they were of anything concerning the bride's parents.

He took them home. Benay used a few words she hadn't used in some time. Fitz did a little thinking and one day handed Benay a draft drawn on his Boston bank. It was made out to Mrs. Alan Hayes in a sum that made Benay blink.

"Half a million dollahs! Fitz, yo' gone outen yo' haid?"

"Goin' to send this to Melanie. Goin' to see the newspapers heahs o' this too, an' then let's see whut they thinks o' us."

"Don't do it, Fitz. It's too much money. The whole thing ain't wuth any part o' this money."

"Goin' to send it anyways jes' to see whut happens. Knows these Boston folks like Alan's papa an' mama. They so goddam wrapped up in the sanctity o' they family, an' so impohtant 'cause they gots mo' than the nex' man, takes somethin' like this to make 'em know they ain't the on'y rich folks in this world."

"Half a million dollahs!" Jonathan declared with a gasp. "Papa, that a fortune!"

"Knows it. But don' yo' go thinkin' it money spent. Not yit."

During the following month they studied all the Boston papers. There was not the slightest mention of the wedding gift from the bride's family. One day, with the rest of the mail came an envelope bearing the return address of Mr. and

Mrs. Alan Hayes. It contained the draft, torn in half.

"Oh, Fitz," Benay said in dismay. "How could she do this?"

"'Members whut I told yo' I sends this? I says don't think it spent money yit. Knows it would come back. They took this, they standin' would go down a few notches."

"We looks at it this way," Benay said. "Melanie is happy, we 'spects. Reckon she goin' to stay happy. Cain't fo'get she got plenty Boston blood in her veins. It showin' up now. Wrote her one lettah an' she don' answer. Writes no mo' till I heahs from her. That be nevah, that's how it be."

"Reckon that boy goin' far," Fitz said. "Reckon Melanie goes with him. She likes it up theah. She likes all them snooty folks 'roun' her, that her business. I've known both an' I says I likes the southern way bes'."

"Damn the both o' them," Jonathan said. "Got somethin' mo' impohtant on my mind."

"Whut's so impohtant?" Fitz asked, lazily sipping his rum and water.

"'Members I gets into a fight with the Major's overseer? Befo' he hauls off an' puts me on the flo', he say Major Apperson goin' to get us yit. Soun's like the Major been talkin' 'bout it, an' ain't no way he kin back off, he been talkin' that way."

"Ready fo' him, whutevah he wants to do," Fitz said. "Right now ev'ythin' goin' too well fo' me to worry 'bout anythin'."

Another month went by, quietly, with no word from Melanie and no change in Daisy. She would soon bear Jonathan's child. Jonathan had been growing more and more nervous about it, but the doctors in Richmond assured him that while Daisy's condition never changed, the baby appeared to be coming along in a perfectly normal manner.

It was Seawitch who first came to Benay with the news. "Missy-ma'am, gots a chile awful sick. Cain't mind whut she gots, but it sho' bad. Reckon yo' kin come an' see? Yo' know mo' 'bout it."

"I'll come at once," Benay said. "Is the child feverish?"

"Burnin' up, ma'am. Sho' is."

The child, a little girl of about four, was in high fever, no doubt very ill.

"Seawitch," Benay ordered, "get watah from the cold spring. Have Calcutta fetch a bowl ev'y fifteen minutes. Brings me towels, anythin' we kin use to put on this chile's fo'haid to bring down the fevah."

The cold cloths quieted the child's whimpering, but it did not bring down the fever. Then word came that a fourteen-year-old girl was very ill. Benay went to her cabin and found her in the same condition—a high fever that refused to be controlled, with great restlessness on the part of the patient.

Late in the afternoon two more children came down with it and Benay sent for Fitz. He examined the patients clumsily, with an utter lack of medical skill. His common sense told him this was no ordinary ailment, and it seemed to be spreading.

"Send Dundee fo' the doctah," he said.

"Fitz, Doctah Boswick a good vet. Don' know nuthin' 'bout a sickness like this heah. I skeered two o' them sick ones goin' to die."

"Send fo' Dr. Latimer," Fitz said. "He ain't no vet."

"Will he come an' treat a slave?"

"He comes. He balks an' I offers him 'nuff to make him rich. He comes, Benay, I has to fetch him with a gun in my hand. Latimer a fine man an' a good doctah. I calls him he comes."

Dundee was dispatched but a doctor wouldn't arrive until next day. Even hard riding wouldn't get him there until midday at the earliest.

By nightfall, five more slaves reported in sick. These were adults, and they were very ill. Benay turned the care of others over to slaves she regarded as capable enough and she devoted all of her attention to the little girl who had first contracted this strange ailment.

The child was growing progressively worse and had now lapsed into what Benay believed to be a state of coma. Benay kept bathing her face, but there were no obvious results. The mother had been banished from the cabin and Benay sat beside the girl, her eyelids drooping with fatigue.

The girl was bathed in sweat again. Benay pulled down the covers and peeled off the girl's flimsy nightgown, then reeled back in horror. But she summoned all her courage and bent over the girl again. She covered her up and went out shouting for Seawitch, whose cabin was only three doors away.

"Seawitch, yo' stan's by that gal's do' an' nobody goes in. Nobody! Even the devil hisse'f comes, which is likely. Don' go in yo'se'f. Do like I say, but don' let anybody know whut goin' on. Be back quick."

She went running for the big house. Fitz was at the dining-room table with Jonathan.

"Wheah yo' been?" he asked. "Benay, yo' goin' to drop in yo' tracks."

"Papa, she lookin' bad." Jonathan got up quickly and caught his mother before she collapsed. He eased her into a chair and gave her a glass of water to drink.

"I'm all right," she said. "I'm jes' tired. An' I nevah been so skeered in my whole life."

"Whut the hell is wrong?" Fitz asked.

"That li'l gal I been taken care o', Fitz—she got smallpox."

"Yo' sho'?"

"Cain't be nuthin' else. She breakin' out."

"Mayhap she got measles?"

"Mayhap, less the others break out too. I comes heah fo' yo' 'cause I too skeered to go an' fin' out."

Fitz said, "Jonathan, come on. Quick now. Benay, yo' bes' gets to bed till yo' feels bettah."

He and Jonathan raced down to the slave row. Fitz found Seawitch at the door.

"Yo' been inside?" he asked.

"No suh. Mist'ess she say I cain't go in."

"Stay out," he ordered. "But don' go 'way."

Fitz moved one of the two candles closer to the little girl. She was breathing, but not much more. Fitz had never seen a case of smallpox in his life, but he'd heard enough about this dread

...e and its uncanny ability to spread like ...ildfire. He saw the lesions and he no longer had any doubts.

He left the girl and accosted Seawitch. "Yo' brings Hong Kong fas' as yo' kin. Aftah that, yo' fin's young an' strong gals who kin care fo' sick people an' yo' rounds 'em up. Othahs sick 'roun' heah too. Don' let anybody go neah them, Seawitch. An' yo' keeps this to yo'se'f. Thinks that gal in theah dyin' o' smallpox, an' it spread already."

Seawitch nodded and without a word hurried to obey her orders. Hong Kong arrived within five minutes and Fitz explained the situation to him.

"Feels sho' it smallpox. Yo' evah sees a case o' that damn disease?"

"No suh, but reckon it ain't hahd to tell."

"That's how I feel. Wants this done fas' as yo' kin do it. Gets one o' the overseers an' tells him to roun' up all of 'em an' they repohts to me in front o' the big house. Then yo' sounds the conch horn an' gets ev'y slave on this heah plantation who kin walk to gather outside the big bachelor quartahs. Nobody goes inside. Anybody sick, don' go near 'em, not even if they's dyin'. Keeps ev'y man, woman, an' chile in the open an' kinda spread out, yo' kin arrange that. Aftah that, yo' picks one slave who got 'nuff brains to do it, an' have him go to ev'y cabin, look inside, an' count ev'yone he fin's who is sick."

"Yes suh. Goes quick."

"But don' say a word 'bout this bein' smallpox."

"No suh, I says nuthin'."

Fitz went back into the cabin. The little girl wasn't dead, but very close to it, and he damned his ignorance which prevented him from helping her.

Jonathan called to him from outside the cabin and Fitz joined him.

"Papa, thinks this be smallpox."

"Yo' sees othahs breakin' out?"

"Yes. Two men. Grown men. They pow'ful sick, Papa, an' got them blisters all ovah they bodies."

"Dr. Latimer comin' tomorruh an' he makes sho' whut this is. But reckon we be crazy we don' do somethin' now 'stead o' waitin'."

"Reckon we bettah."

"All right. This goin' to be hahd to 'splain to the slaves, an' mayhap they gets unruly, but we gots to do this. Yo' takes all the overseers yo' needs, makes up burnin' brands, an' burn ev'y cabin an' shed on this heah plantation."

"Papa, 'thout waitin'?"

"Goin' to be done anyways an' might's well be now. Wants no mo' folks comin' down with this. Worries some 'bout Benay. Bes' I goes back an' makes sho' she all right. Yo' take care o' things. An' Jonathan, don' spread the word, yo' kin he'p it. An' yo' tells all the carpenters an' coopers to get they tools quick. 'Members all that?"

"Yo' sees to Mama," Jonathan urged.

Fitz hurried back to the big house. The overseers were gathered there in various forms of undress, mystified at what was happening.

Fitz said, "Yo' waits heah fo' a few minutes. Don' leave, any o' yo'. They's somethin' bad goin' on."

He found Benay asleep, but not feverish. He pulled down the covers. She mumbled something, but didn't wake up when he raised her nightgown and examined her. There were no red splotches, no postules. He decided she was simply exhausted. He covered her again, kissed her, and stilled her mumblings, for she seemed unable to fully wake up.

Downstairs again, he addressed the overseers. "Whut we got heah—an' I be pretty sho' o' it—we got us an epidemic o' smallpox."

"Jesus!" one man shouted. "My wife an' family!"

"Min' now," Fitz said, "so far we knows, this on'y in the slave quartahs. Firs' thing all o' yo' does is get all the wagons, load yo' families on 'em. Lets yo' womenfolk drive an' sends 'em to the village. They stays theah an' I pays all expenses. Don' tell them why. Don' want word o' this spread. Bad 'nuff now. Yo' gets through with that, all o' yo' goes down to wheah Jonathan got the carpenters an' coopers waitin'. Yo' tells 'em they uses all the spare lumber we got—they's plenty, 'cause we goin' to build two new curin' sheds an' nevah got 'roun' to it. Yo' picks places far from the old slave row an' has them build big barracks. An' some cabins. 'Nuff to take keer o' as many as possible. They's to put 'em up fas'. Wuk all night they has to, an' all day. Don't keer they be the bes' cabins built, jes' get somethin' wheah the gals kin live an' keep they suckers with 'em."

"Won't take long to do that," one man said. "Whut else yo' gots in mind, Mistah Turner? As if I didn' know."

"Yo' knows all right. All o' yo' knows. Jona-

[484]

than got torches waitin'. Light 'em an' burns ev'y goddamn cabin, barracks, an' shed on the place, 'cept the big house—an' the outhouses. Needs 'em. Goin' to be a hell o' a lot o' pissin' goin' on fo' this is ovah. Now yo' runs!"

Fitz returned to Benay's room. He sat at her bedside until she began to stir. He sat through the loud wails and moans of the slaves watching their cabins and possessions burn. The window was alight with the crimson glow of the fiery hell outside.

Fitz remained calm. His greatest worry had been about Benay and she appeared to be all right. Certain her breathing and temperature remained normal, Fitz left her to go out and look at the destruction. The work and planning of years was gone. Apparently Jonathan had issued some orders contrary to Fitz's sweeping decisions, for the commissary was intact, tool sheds had not been destroyed. The infirmary and the stable area were also intact, but everything else was gone, reduced to smoking ashes. The pall hung over the area still.

Slaves were controlled by the overseers and confined to a limited area of open space. They were not hard to handle, for all of them knew the cause and they feared the dread disease as much as Fitz. Already more than a hundred were crowded into the infirmary, and many of these would die. A dozen had already succumbed, and again it was Jonathan who took command of the procedure that followed. A sufficient number of strong men were assigned to grave-digging duties. When there was a death, the body was quickly buried, allowing no kind of service nor the presence of relatives. Those who were not ill had to be isolated and allowed no freedom that would bring them into contact with any carrier of the disease.

The slaves who had been in the same cabins with those who were ill were kept in a group far from the other slaves, and were constantly watched to see if any came down with the sickness.

Fitz ate a scant breakfast, then went back upstairs and made certain Benay was still showing no symptoms. He found Domingo seated at her bedside.

"Yo' knows my wife been with the sick slaves an' mayhap she goin' to get sick too?" he asked.

"Knows it, massa, suh," Domingo said quietly.

"Knows she gets sick, mayhap yo' gets it too?"

"Yes suh, massa, suh. Knows it."

"Yo' ain't skeered?"

"Mighty skeered, massa, suh, but stays anyways. Missy cain't be lef' alone, so I stays."

Fitz nodded, unable to express the thanks he felt. He went outside again to find a bleary-eyed Jonathan trying to make order out of the chaos, and apparently succeeding quite well.

"Yo' gets yo'se'f some sleep," Fitz said. "I handles ev'ythin' fo' now."

"How Mama?"

"So far she all right."

"Folks who took care o' the sick ones comin' down. Gots to watch Mama. When the hell the doctah goin' to get heah?"

"This mornin' fo' sho', Jonathan. Yo' sees any signs the slaves wantin' to run?"

"No. They's skeered to do anythin'—not thinkin' o' runnin'. We got fifteen daid an' buried. Mighty close to a hundred mo' come down sick as hell. Thinks we goin' to lose 'em all?"

"No way o' savin' 'em I heered of. Maybe Dr. Latimer knows somethin', but doubts it. Whut worries me is how it got heah. Wyndward not close to any othah fahm or town. Ain't no strangers come heah. Ain't bought no slaves. Somethin' brought this pestilence heah. Don' come by itse'f."

"Don' know 'nuff 'bout it to have any answers, Papa. Got to get some rest. Mayhap yo' goes an' talks to the slaves, yo' kin keep 'em quiet. So far they been fine, but cain't tell, they gets skeered mo' than now."

"Talks to 'em," Fitz said. "Look in on Benay. Domingo theah takin' care o' her."

Jonathan nodded and turned toward the big house, moving with slow steps. He was almost there when Dundee came running from the stables. Jonathan held up a hand.

"Stops wheah yo' are, Dundee. Don' come any closer. I been 'roun' the sick slaves. Yo' goes back to the stables an' stay theah. Don' go neah any buildin's lef' o' any o' the slaves. This sickness gets 'bout by goin' from one person to 'nother. Yo' stays away from ev'ybody, heah?"

"Thinks mayhap I kin he'p, massa, suh."

"Nuthin' yo' kin do. Don' try. 'Nuff dyin' now."

Dundee nodded and turned away. He had been about to ask permission to visit Hong Kong and Seawitch, but knew his request would be denied. He returned to his stables and, with nothing much to do, went to the loft and began studying.

In the midst of all this dreadful sickness, he didn't know what to do. He was unable to help, unable to even understand what caused this awful destruction of life. All he knew was that he must study even harder, for there were still so many things he didn't comprehend.

Jonathan made certain Benay was still peacefully sleeping, with Domingo seated on the floor beside the bed. Then he went to bed himself. He was hungry, but exhaustion took precedence over hunger. He did take time to wash up meticulously. He had heard that in fighting this disease, cleanliness was of vital importance.

More slaves died before noon. Fitz had them buried promptly. He kept looking up the driveway to the road for the first signs of dust from Dr. Latimer's carriage. It was midafternoon when he arrived, and Fitz hurried to meet him.

"Got mo' than twenny daid a'ready," he said, without any preliminaries of welcome. "Mayhap a hundred mo' sick. Burned eve'y damn cabin an' all they clothes not on they backs. Nuthin' lef', but still mo' gettin' sick ev'y hour."

"At least you did your best," Dr. Latimer said. "Now I'll do whatever I can, but I warn you, it won't be much. First of all, I'll need a number of young girls to act as nurses. Can you get these slaves to help me, or are they too scared to go near a sick person?"

"Doctah, they's skeered, like I am, an' ev'ybody else, but they been askin' kin they care fo' the sick ones. So far I says no. Don' know whut in hell to do."

"All right, Fitz. Now you get me some help. How many in the infirmary?"

"Reckon 'bout a hundred. They dyin' so fas' cain't keep count."

Dr. Latimer had brought along what medical supplies he needed, though he knew there was little he could do for those who had become ill. Some lived, most died. Good care sometimes spelled the difference and Fitz enlisted the service of thirty young slaves, mostly girls.

Fitz addressed a crowd of frightened, silent slaves. "Doctah heah now an' needs young gals to he'p. Wants any gals who ain't skeered to come fo'ward an' be counted. Needs 'bout thirty now. Maybe mo' latah. Minds now, it ain't kin' o' wuk I wants to send anybody to, but the sick slaves gots to be cared fo'. How many willin' to do this wuk?"

About a hundred stepped out. Fitz shook his head. "Reckon all o' yo' goin' to be needed soon, but now I picks thirty."

He went along the line to select the sturdiest-looking girls, and he also picked a dozen young bucks. They were all serious, knowing what they faced, but if there were any shirkers, they were well hidden in the vast crowd of slaves.

"I makes no promises whut I does to reward yo' who are willin' to he'p, but there sho' be some-thin'. Now yo' all repohts to the doctah at the infirmary. All othahs jes' wait. No field wuk till this damn epidemic ovah with. Cooks goin' to fix good meals, like it Christmas. Eats all yo' kin. May-hap this disease lookin' fo' folks who ain't got they bellies full."

He turned away and went back to the house. In the silence of the library he sat alone, feeling more helpless than he ever had in his life. He knew Wyndward would lose a large number of slaves. Perhaps those who survived wouldn't be fit for hard work, and must be accommodated. His first thought was to proceed to Richmond as soon as the danger was over and buy enough slaves on the market to replace those he lost. On second thought, he decided he'd wait to see if he had sufficient slaves. Nearly two thousand was an unwieldy number. He'd bought some of them purely on whim. Some of the older ones had been bought by his father, also on whim, with the idea the more slaves the better.

Jonathan joined him at the early supper and, to Fitz's complete delight, so did Benay. He hugged and kissed her as if she were a bride.

"Been worried," he admitted. "Yo' sleepin' like a baby. Yo' didn' even know when I pulled down the covers an' lifted yo' nightdress to see yo' had any o' them damned blisters."

"If yo' had me nude," Benay said, "I sho' must've been sleepin' sound. How many daid so far?"

"Ain't done no countin'. Doctah heah an' he in charge. Cain't do nuthin' myse'f so I keeps my nose outen the doctah's way. Yo' sho' yo' feelin' fine, Benay?"

"I was so tired I couldn't even think," she said. "I know yo' burned ev'ythin'. Smelled the smoke. Fitz, it needful, yo' burns this heah house too."

"Ain't needful so far," Fitz said.

"Yo' burns this house on'y if yo' gots me lyin' 'side Grandpa an' Grandma," Jonathan said hotly. "Figgers to spend the rest o' my life in this heah house, so don' yo' go settin' it on fire."

"Las' thing we'll burn," Fitz said. "But this spreads an' we comes down with it, or the house servants ketches it, the house gets burned yo' likes it or not."

"Fights me firs'," Jonathan said.

"Mayhap do that too."

"Stop yo' silly talk," Benay said. "Soon's I eat I'm goin' back to he'p the doctah."

"Benay, yo' done 'nuff. They plenty wenches he'pin' him now."

"Slaves ain't 'nuff," Benay said. She arose from the table, leaving her plate half full of uneaten food. "Gots to get down theah quick as I kin. Jonathan, yo' stay 'way from the slaves, heah me?"

"Thinks I got 'bout as much courage as Melanie," Jonathan grumbled. "Whut the hell she thinks I do, sit on my ass while slaves are dyin'?"

"Ain't much yo' kin do," Fitz said. "We kin handle slaves runnin' or rapin', an' we kin get them to wuk hahd, an' we kin cheat Major Apperson, but when it comes to takin' care o' people sick with this goddamn disease, we's wuthless, an' don' I know it."

"How long yo' thinks this is goin' to last?"

"Who knows? Mayhap we lose three-fo' hundred slaves. Been bad epidemics befo', an' no reason to think this ain't goin' to be bad as the othahs. Been thinkin' 'bout whut we do this is ovah an' we short so many niggers. Yo' think we should go buy mo'?"

"Papa, we got plenty heah. We ain't sent a coffle to market in a long time. Birthin' house full o' suckers. They grows up quick 'nuff. Reckon we don' need no mo' slaves."

"Whut I was thinkin'. Hell, we got 'nuff money anyways."

"Been thinkin' o' spendin' mo' time in Richmond, Papa. Kin see Daisy mo' often."

"Fo' whut? To sit an' look at her? She don' even know yo' theah. Bust yo' own heart yo' does that. It he'ps her, then yo' goes an' stays all the time, but yo' does her no good an' makes yo' own life barely wuth livin'. Yo' stay heah an' he'ps me put this place back on its feet. So when Daisy come home someday, she comes home to somethin' good."

"Yo thinks she goin' to come back?"

"Cain't think no diff'rent, son. Ain't no time to give up hope."

"I feelin' kinda sorry fo' myse'f," Jonathan admitted.

"Bettah yo' feels sorry fo' Wyndward. Yo' go down to wheah they buildin' the new cabins an' barracks an' see how thing's comin'. See if yo' kin figger out how many mo' cabins we needin'. Then yo' sends to Norfolk fo' mo' lumber an' tools. We got 'nuff food fo' a few mo' days an' we got 'nuff slave clothes an' shoes. Lucky it be wahm this time o' yeah. It cold like wintah an' I sho' don' know whut we does with near two thousand slaves. They sleeps on the groun' now, but they used to that."

"Reckon I keeps myse'f busy," Jonathan said.

There was far more to be done than Fitz had estimated, and during the next four days they had barely enough time to sleep. Benay, working hand in hand with the harassed and exhausted doctor, overworked herself too.

So far a hundred and ten slaves had died,

and there were more than two hundred others down with the disease. Everything possible had been done, even to burning sulphur candles in the big house and the warehouse. So far, anyone working at the stables seemed to remain immune. Fitz issued strict orders there would be no contact between the slaves there and those now dispossessed and camping out. Dundee was placed in charge of this measure and he enforced it.

Work in building new quarters progressed well, though much time was lost in getting lumber to the plantation because it had to come from so far away. The teamsters who brought it refused to go all the way to the plantation, dumping their lumber alongside the road half a mile away.

In a way, Fitz was glad that the outsiders were that fearful. Bringing the lumber to the building sites kept many of the slaves busy. Too much idleness was beginning to make the slaves restless, and more frightened with each burial.

Fitz finally decided to set them to work in the fields again, where the tobacco plants were in serious need of attention. Ten days after the outbreak, the plantation was running again, after a fashion. The numbers of new patients began to dwindle and Dr. Latimer thought he saw a ray of hope that the epidemic was slowing down.

Benay was exhausted, growing thinner by the day, for she neglected to eat properly and to get sufficient sleep. In his bones, Fitz had felt all along it was going to happen and dreaded the moment, praying it would not come.

On the eleventh day, Benay didn't come down for breakfast. Instead, it was Domingo who entered the dining room. "Massa, suh, thinks mist'ess sick, suh."

Fitz went upstairs as fast as he could get there. Benay was feverish, no doubt of that. He turned to Jonathan, who'd been at his heels.

"Go fetch the doctah—run!"

Jonathan went off at top speed. Fitz dragged a chair over beside the bed. "Benay, yo' heahs me? Benay . . . open yo' eyes."

She murmured something in a weak voice, but her eyelids remained closed. Fitz arose, paced the room. Domingo had brought cold water and towels. She tried to bring down the burning fever, which by now had turned Benay's cheeks a bright pink.

Jonathan returned with Dr. Latimer. He made a quick examination. "I'm sorry, Fitz. She's got it. No question of that. She must be moved."

"She stays heah," Fitz said. "If we has to burn the goddamn house latah on, we burns it, but nobody is movin' Benay. Jes' make her come through this, Doctah. Don' let her die."

Dr. Latimer made no reply. He took over trying to bring down the fever. Finally, exasperated at Fitz's pacing, he ordered him out of the room. Fitz went downstairs and began drinking until Jonathan warned him off it.

"Cain't tell Mama goin' to need us," he said. "Yo' drunk, whut good kin yo' be?"

Fitz set aside the bottle. "Co'se yo' is right. She dies, whut I goin' to do 'thout her?"

"Papa, she ain't daid an' mayhap she won't die. Worryin' 'bout it no bettah than me sittin in Daisy's room waitin' yeah by yeah fo' her to get bettah. Cain't be done."

"Thinks we go fo' a walk. Comin'?"

"Might's well, ain't nothin' else to do. We goes down an' sees how the hosses comin'. Dundee doin' a good job, Papa. Bes' hoss handler I evah sees."

They found everything at the stables and in the lush fields where the horses grazed in fine order. Dundee accompanied them on their rounds. Once he dared ask a question.

"Heahs mist'ess sick. How she, massa, suh? Yo' lets me ask."

"Don' know," Fitz said. "Not yit."

"I'se sorry, massa, suh."

"Knows that," Fitz said. "Now get back to yo' wuk."

Dundee hurried away and Fitz and Jonathan continued on to the house. They found Hong Kong in the kitchen with Elegant. He asked permission to speak.

"Hong Kong, yo' kin speak anytime yo' likes. Yo' ain't a slave no mo'," Fitz reminded him.

"Sometimes cain't remembah," Hong Kong said. "Gots me a slave don' know whut to do 'bout."

"He runnin' or talkin' rebellion?"

"No suh," Hong Kong replied vehemently. "Not this one, suh. He dyin'."

"Whut 'bout him then?"

"Nevah sees him befo'. Don' know wheah he comes from."

"They's mo' than that," Fitz said.

"Yas suh. Mo' than that. Asks 'bout him an' nobody knows who he is. But . . . he the firs' slave to drop in he tracks this smallpox comes."

"Well, whut——?" Fitz began.

[495]

Jonathan said, "Papa, see whut he means? He the firs' one to come down, nobody knows who he is or wheah he comes from. He mus' be the one brings the disease heah. Gots to be the one."

"Hong Kong," Fitz said, "yo' takes us to him fas' as yo' kin."

Dr. Latimer came down the stairs, wiping his face and moving very slowly.

"How Benay?" Fitz asked.

"Sleeping. The fever hasn't broken yet. The postules have formed. Fitz, I'm not sure what will happen. You understand I'm doing all I can."

"Knows that. Doctah, we jes' fin's out they's a slave heah dyin' now. He a stranger, but he the firs' one to gets sick. Thinks he kin have brought the sickness heah?"

"It's not only likely, it's probably true. He must have wandered away from his own master and just drifted here."

"Fin's out real quick," Fitz said. "Come 'long, Jonathan. We gots to talk to this heah slave fo' he dies."

Hong Kong led them to a cabin, not burned, but turned into part of the infirmary. It contained only this one slave, a man of about thirty, lying on a sweat-soaked blanket. His eyes were already half glazed. His face was covered with the ugly postules. It was evident that he was not going to get better and would probably die soon.

Fitz said, "Jonathan, get the hell outa heah. Wait outside."

"I stays," Jonathan said curtly.

"Ain't no sense we both comes down from seein' this nigger."

"I stays," Jonathan reiterated. "Asks him, he kin talk, how he gets heah, Papa."

"Now whut diff'rence that makes?"

"He comin' down with smallpox, Papa, he ain't walkin' all the miles 'tween Wyndward an' the nearest plantation or village. Reckon he brought heah."

"Jonathan . . . yo' thinkin' . . . ?"

"I thinkin'. Ask him fo' he dies."

Fitz raised the man's head, saw his dry, cracked lips and gave him a drink of water. He eased him back, propping him up slightly by bunching the blanket behind his head.

"Yo' mighty sick," Fitz said. "Wants to know wheah yo' comes from. Yo' gots a woman we sends fo' her."

"Got me . . . woman. . . ."

"Yes—wheah she?"

"Goin' to die I is. Goin' to die."

"Mayhap yo' don' we gets yo' woman heah to comfort yo'. Wheah she?"

"Tells me come heah . . . tells me I gets whupped, I don' come to Wyndward. . . ."

"Who tells yo'?" Fitz said softly. "Wants to he'p yo', but cain't yo' don' tells us wheah yo' comes from."

"Majah . . . suh . . . Majah suh . . . tells me."

Fitz said, in a voice now gone cold, "Yo' speaks o' Major Apperson?"

"Majah . . . Apperson. Tells me I comes heah. I says I too sick. He brings me—say he sells me to Wyndward an' I goes to the othah slaves. Don' know whut he means. I so sick don' know whut I doin', massa, suh."

Fitz rose. "I cain't believe it true. Cain't believe even the Major would stoop to this. Killin' folks jes' because he mad at us."

"Papa, he gone crazy. Seems like he finds this slave, sees him comin' down with smallpox an' brings him to Wyndward so our slaves gets sick an' dies. Ain't s'prised he hopes we gets it too."

"Ain't nuthin' we kin do fo' this nigger," Fitz said. "Bes' we goes back an' talks to the doctah 'bout this. Wants to be sho' we knows whut we talkin' 'bout we calls on Major Apperson."

They returned to the house, where Fitz first washed up thoroughly, on the advice of Dr. Latimer. Jonathan called the doctor down from the sickroom.

"Doctah," Fitz said, "we fin's a slave dyin' back in one o' the cabins saved from burnin'. He say he comes heah from Major Apperson's place. He gots smallpox, kin he walk all that way?"

"Not likely," Dr. Latimer said. Then his face grew rigid with horror. "Do you mean the Major sent this sick man here to spread the disease?"

"Cain't think nothin' else. Talks to the slave an' he say Major sends him. Major musta brought him, I thinks, he got the nerve to ride with a sick man."

"If this is true, Major Apperson is guilty of murder many times over."

"Reckon he is," Jonathan agreed.

"What do you intend to do about it?"

"Kill him," Fitz said quietly. "It kin wait. How Benay?"

"Not good." The doctor shook his head. "The fever should have broken by now and it has not.

In fact, it seems a little worse. Fitz, we have no medicine to conquer this illness. We don't know much about it except that it spreads like fire gone wild. And . . . not many recover."

"Benay goin' to die?" Fitz asked.

"I'm . . . afraid so, Fitz. I'm doing all I can."

"Jonathan," Fitz said, "yo' takes ovah an' runs things. I be sittin' by Benay."

"Yes, Papa."

"Yo' goes aftah Major Apperson 'thout me, I kills yo' too."

"I waits fo' yo', Papa."

Fitz nodded and followed the doctor up the stairs. He moved much as Daisy had moved during the brief interim when she seemed to be recovering. His steps were wooden, his face masklike. His heart was heavy and his hope all gone.

{ 24 }

THE DEATHS KEPT ON WITH A DREADFUL MONO-
tony. Precious few were pulling through. Jonathan supervised things as best he could, though
there was little to be done. The work on the plantation was slipshod, almost nonproductive. Even
the overseers let slothing go by—nobody was
whipped, nor was there the slightest thought of
it. Slaves were kept busy, because it kept them
from congregating and growing even more terrified than they were.

Jonathan, tired. but at least now hopeful the
worst was over, returned to the big house for the
first time in almost twenty hours. Fitz was coming down the steps. He didn't glance at Jonathan,
but went slowly and resolutely to the library.
Jonathan, certain something was amiss, followed

him and saw his father open a gun case and re-move a heavy revolver, which he proceeded to load. He thrust it under his belt.

"Papa, is Mama daid?"

"Died half an hour ago. Nevah woke up. Nev-ah heerd me talkin'. We waits till I gets back befo' we buries her."

"Goin' with yo'," Jonathan said.

"Yo' stays."

"Goin' with yo', less yo' uses that pistol on me. Major Apperson goin' to die, I he'ps. Don' fo'get, my mama daid."

"Doctah in charge," Fitz said. "Go get hosses saddled, I gets grub from Elegant. We don' stop till we gets to the Apperson fahm."

Jonathan nodded and hurried off. Elegant, already apprised of her mistress's death, dried her tears, but never stopped her moaning while she prepared enough food, which Fitz slipped into the saddlebags when Jonathan returned with the horses.

They rode all day and night, stopping only to let the horses rest briefly and to eat. They spoke little. There wasn't anything to say. The grim pur-pose of their ride occupied their thoughts. There was no reason it must be discussed. Fitz went into the deeper woods twice during the journey, to return after the horses were rested, eyes red from weeping.

They reached the Apperson plantation early in the morning. They rode straight up to the big house, dismounted, and walked side by side up the stairs to the veranda. The front door was partly open.

Fitz signaled Jonathan to be careful. He drew

the heavy revolver, approached the door warily, and kicked it open. Nothing happened. He went inside, with Jonathan following him.

"Major!" Fitz shouted. "Ain't no place yo' kin hide I don' find yo'."

Jonathan said, "Nobody heah, Papa. Not even slaves."

"We makes mighty sho' o' that. Keep yo' eyes open. Don' trust this bastahd nohow."

They searched the big house, room by room. They found enough evidence to show that the Major must have learned that his trick had been discovered and Fitz was bound to come for him. The Major had apparently fled.

The two men walked down to the overseers' quarters. All but one house was unoccupied and the elderly man there told them what they wanted to know.

"Major, suh, fires all us overseers yesterday an' say he closin' the plantation. But the slaves still heah. I stays to see they gets fed an' don' run. Whut's goin' on, suh?"

"Tells yo' this," Jonathan said, "the Major ain't comin' back. Don' know whut yo' kin do 'bout the slaves."

"Let's 'em run, yo' wants to," Fitz said. "How many he got?"

"Fo' hundred, suh."

"Mind this, yo' ain't nevah goin' to get paid by the Major. Yo' wants to wuk fo' me, yo' hired now."

"Yo' Fitz Turner, suh? Who owns Wyndward?"

"That's me an' this heah my son. Yo' willin' to take my orders?"

"Yes suh, mighty happy to take yo' orders, suh."

"Then get all the slaves outen they cabins an' ev'y buildin' heah. Herds 'em somewheah an' soon's yo' kin, takes 'em to Richmond fo' sellin' in my name. Gets them out in fifteen minutes, heah?"

"Yes suh, I'll get 'em out. Whut yo' aimin' to do, Mistah Turner, suh?"

"Major Apperson runs 'cause he knows I kills him he don'. Mayhap he thinks he comes back someday, but not to this plantation. I'm burnin' it to the ground an' ev'y goddamn buildin' on it. Don' wants nobody hurt. Yo' sees to that."

"Right away. My name's Lawrence. Tim Lawrence, suh."

"Good 'nuff," Fitz said. "Yo' comes by Wyndward, but not befo' three or fo' days."

Fitz and Jonathan returned to the big house. There they collected all the lamps and found the oil supply. They methodically treated every room before they backed out. Fitz lit the lamp he still held, turned the wick all the way up, then hurled it deep into the house.

Down at the cabins, they fashioned torches and went from cabin to cabin, setting the flimsy structures on fire. When they finished, the big house was one mighty mass of flame. Walls and roofs, caving in, added more fuel to the blaze.

They didn't wait to see it utterly destroyed. They mounted and rode away, never looking back. They could smell the smoke for the next half-hour.

When they reached Wyndward they discovered that Dr. Latimer had everything prepared. Benay lay in her casket, dressed in white. There could be no delays now. Fitz knelt before the coffin for five minutes, showing no tears, but only a grimness that kept everyone near him silent.

They left him alone for another few minutes. In the library, Dr. Latimer apprised Jonathan of the situation.

"The epidemic is almost over. You have lost almost two hundred slaves. Did you find Major Apperson?"

"No suh. Reckon he heerd whut was goin' on an' he an' Clarissa, an' likely her husband, they all runs. They didn't, Papa would have killed all of 'em fo' sho'."

"The Major deserves it, that's certain," the doctor said. "Now all is ready at the cemetery. We'd best get it over with as quickly as possible. Your father all right?"

"He kin stan' up to anythin', Doctah, even this. So kin I. I goes an' fetches him."

"The slaves asked to carry her," the doctor said. "I have overseers waiting in case you or your father want them to do it."

"She died carin' fo' slaves. Let 'em carry her," Jonathan said.

He went into the drawing room and touched his father on the shoulder. "Waitin' fo' us, Papa," he said.

Fitz nodded, rose from his knees, and slowly closed the coffin lid. He left the room. When he heard them nailing the lid down, he showed no emotion.

Four slaves raised the casket to their shoulders and carried Benay to the cemetery. They walked with measured steps, as if they were afraid of disturbing the burden they carried.

Outside, all the slaves had formed two lines and began chanting as the bearers appeared. The rows of chanting slaves fell in behind the coffin as the procession wended its way to the cemetery, where a grave had been dug beside that of Fitz's mother. It was over quickly. There was no clergyman. Dr. Latimer committed the body and signaled for the grave to be filled in. The slaves broke ranks and wandered off quietly. Fitz and Jonathan returned to the big house. Calcutta, red-eyed, had drinks ready. The two men sat down on the veranda and sipped their drinks.

Fitz said, "My papa had no luck with his wife, seems like I had none with mine, an' yo' didn' do so good yo'se'f, Jonathan. Whut's the mattah with us?"

"Yo' askin' the wrong man, Papa."

"Hell of a thing."

"Hell of a thing," Jonathan agreed.

"Ain't even got my daughter lef', she gone off to the No'th. Don' gives a damn 'bout us."

"I writes an' tells her mama daid," Jonathan said. "Sometime I writes."

"No hurry fo' sho'. Whut we goin' to do now?"

"Knows whut my mama likes us to do."

"I'm listenin'."

"We makes Wyndward Plantation bigger'n it is now. We makes it the bes' goddamn plan'ation in Virginia. In the whole South. We buys mo' lan' an' mo' slaves. Benay mighty proud o' Wyndward. Thinks she likes it we don' jes' give up."

"Who said anythin' 'bout givin' up?"

"Knows yo' wouldn't. We got troubles behind us, Papa, we gots to fo'get them bes' we kin."

"Won't be easy."

"Knows that. But mo' trouble comin'. Feels it."

Fitz nodded. "Reckon so. Bes' we be as ready as we kin."

"Be kinda lonesome. Got to face it."

"Time we done some figgerin', son. Place to do that in the library. Calcutta!"

He appeared as if by magic. "Brings rum an' watah to the library an' yo' keeps on bringin' it till I says yo' stops."

"Yes suh, massa, suh. I brings it. I runs."

"Po' sonabitch," Fitz said, "all he knows. To run fo' drinks."

They were arguing the merits of acquiring new fields or new slaves first when Dr. Latimer came in. He held a telegram in his hand.

Jonathan said, "Oh no! Doctah—no!"

"I haven't read it," the doctor said, "but the messenger did. It's a fitting end to all that's happened here. All the worry and care. All that you will have to remember. This will help."

Jonathan removed the telegram, read it, laid it down on his lap.

"I be goddamned," he said.

"Yo' be double goddamn somebody don' tell me whut's goin' on," Fitz said.

"Papa, Daisy—her chile born."

Fitz sagged in the big chair. "Got a grandson?" he said, in a voice full of wonder.

"Got two," Jonathan said.

"Whut in hell yo' talkin' 'bout?"

"Yo' got two grandsons. Daisy had twins. Telegram say she fine, but no change. Nevah knew she has two babies."

Fitz rose and embraced his son. "Soon's they old enough to travel, we fetches 'em home. Gets 'em a wet nurse. We raises those boys ou'selves, till Daisy bettah."

He turned back to his desk. "Got to make Wyndward bigger'n we been plannin'. Mo' lan', mo' slaves. Whut yo' sittin' theah fo', Jonathan? We gots wuk to do."

PULSE-RACING, PASSIONATE HISTORICAL FICTION

CARESS AND CONQUER by Donna Comeaux Zide (82-949, $2.25)
Was she a woman capable of deep love — or only high adventure? She was Cat Devlan, a violet-eyed, copper-haired beauty bent on vengeance, raging against the man who dared to take her body against her will — and then dared to demand her heart as well. By the author of the bestselling SAVAGE IN SILK.

PASSION AND PROUD HEARTS by Lydia Lancaster (82-548, $2.25)
The bestseller that brought Lydia Lancaster to national fame, this is the epic historical romance of the remarkable Beddoes family, joined by love and promise, divided by hate and pride, played out against and paralleling the historic sweep of the decades surrounding the Civil War.

DESIRE AND DREAMS OF GLORY by Lydia Lancaster (81-549, $2.50)
In this magnificent sequel to Lydia Lancaster's PASSION AND PROUD HEARTS, we follow a new generation of the Beddoes family as the headstrong Andrea comes of age in 1906 and finds herself caught between the old, fine ways of the genteel South and the exciting changes of a new era.

GARNET by Petra Leigh (82-788, $2.25)
For the love of a man, she sheared her long hair and bound her curving body into the uniform of a British ensign. No war would keep Garnet Mallory from the man she wanted. Disguised, she searched for him across Europe, only to discover that hers was not the only charade; that love itself often wears a mask.

A LOVE SO BOLD by Annelise Kamada (81-638, $2.50)
Gillian was the wife of a brutal, sadistic noble — who was an intimate of the King. And James was bound by memories and guilt to another woman. In 14th Century England, such a love was doomed, but this was a love that would not surrender, a love so bold it obeyed no law but its own.

THE BEST OF THE BESTSELLERS
FROM WARNER BOOKS

THE WOMAN'S DRESS FOR SUCCESS BOOK by John T. Molloy (87-672, $3.95)

America's foremost wardrobe engineer gives you a set of rules to make your clothing and accessories work for you — not against you. Based on years of wardrobe research, this book tells you how to dress for a successful business career by projecting an image of authority, leadership and power.

GAMES MOTHER NEVER TAUGHT YOU by Betty Lehan Harragan (81-563, $2.50)

What every woman who works should know about breaking through the male monopoly on success to make it to the top in business and stay there. Here are the specific, unwritten rules for playing, judging and winning the corporate power game.

MOTHER'S DAY IS OVER by Shirley L. Radl (89-673, $1.95)

Until now, millions of women have secretly shared and silently endured a profound guilt: They love their children, but they do not love being mothers. This book will end their solitude, eliminate their guilt and make them more self-confident human beings.

SEXUAL HONEST: BY WOMEN FOR WOMEN compiled and edited by Shere Hite (89-464, $1.95)

In response to a nationwide questionnaire on their sexuality, more than 2,000 women between the ages of 14 and 64 wrote down the truth about their bodies, their lovers, and their attitudes on sex. Read their replies for an eye-opening look at women's sexuality.

THE WONDERFUL CRISIS OF MIDDLE AGE by Eda LeShan (82-551, $2.25)

". . . An antidote to those books that suggest spending middle age searching for the perfect orgasm. LeShan talks sensibly about the pressures on the family, Women's Lib, kids, love and the special problems of the middle-aged man." — *Chicago Tribune*